CASTLE MAGIC

Hannah Howell

Judith E. French

Colleen Faulkner

Zebra Books
Kensington Publishing Corp.

http://www.zebrabooks.com

ZEBRA BOOKS are published by

Kensington Publishing Corp.
850 Third Avenue
New York, NY 10022

First Printing: August, 1999
10 9 8 7 6 5 4 3 2 1

Printed in the United States of America

HIGHLAND KISS

Tatha sank down to sit on the soft grass. When she lifted a large, stoppered jug from her bag, David frowned slightly. "What is that?"

" 'Tis what I carry water from the well in. I use only this water in my medicines and teas. I felt 'twas the wisest use of its healing powers."

Her eyes widened when he dropped down beside her and grasped her by the shoulders. " 'Tis just water. Clear, fresh, and sweet of taste, aye, but 'tis just water."

Tatha's expression slowly grew mutinous. Instead of her obstinacy adding to his anger, however, David found his increasingly errant lust creeping to the fore. The frown on her sweet face made him want to kiss the hard line of her lips into softness again. He cursed softly and pulled her into his arms.

"Sir David," she began to protest, but felt her breath stolen away by the feel of his hard body pressed so close to hers.

"Hush. Ye can scold me later." He brushed his lips over hers. "I have been thinking of this all week."

That one squeaked call of his name was all the protest Tatha intended to make. It was flattering beyond words that he had been considering kissing her all week. She had been thinking the same with an increasing and embarrassing regularity. What lass would not want such a beautiful man to kiss her at least once? Her curiosity demanded satisfaction. How much could one brief stolen kiss hurt?

When she parted her lips in response, Tatha became acutely aware of the danger of even one kiss. Everything inside of her was responding with a dizzying strength. Her heart pounded, her skin felt warm, and there was an exciting, heated sense of fullness between her thighs. This was lust in all its heady, fierce glory. What frightened her was that instinct told her it was also a great deal more. . . .

—from "Tatha" by Hannah Howell

CONTENTS

TATHA

Hannah Howell

Chapter One

Scotland, 1385

"Weel, there be another of the wretched lasses set-tled."

Tatha Preston halted as she reached for the latch on her father's chamber door. His deep voice penetrated even the thick oak of the door, but she did not fully comprehend what he was saying. The way he referred to her and her sisters as "wretched lasses" stung. It always did. Malcolm Preston, the laird of Preston-moor, was always complaining about the fact that thirteen of his fifteen children were female. The way he said *settled* sounded ominous to her, and she pressed her small, slender body closer to the door, eager yet frightened to hear more.

"Are ye certain they will offer no complaint?" asked an even deeper, rougher voice Tatha recognized as that of her eldest brother, Iain. "All the lasses arenae as meek as Margaret and Elizabeth."

"Those two were settled at cradleside, as is natural," replied Malcolm. "It isnae that hard to settle one or two daughters. 'Tis nigh on impossible to manage when ye are cursed with thirteen of them."

Married? Tatha thought, and felt a cold knot of fear twist tightly in her stomach.

Marriage was something Tatha had given little thought to, despite being nineteen. From a young age she and most of her sisters had understood that there were no dowries for them, that the two eldest sisters had used up what little coin and land there had been for such things. Unlike her sisters Bega and Isabel, who, at three and twenty and one and twenty, were unhappy spinsters, Tatha had seen it as a good thing. Without the usual lands, alliances, and coin tainting a betrothal, she had thought she would have the luxury of choice, might even experience the miracle of marrying for love. It sounded very much as if her father intended to steal all that away.

"I just dinnae feel right about selling them," muttered her other brother, Douglas. "What sort of mon needs to buy himself a wife anyway?"

"I am sorry if this offends your delicate sensibilities, laddie," Malcolm said with a sneer. "God's bones, it isnae all that different from the way such matters are usually handled. Money and land exchanged hands when your first two sisters were wedded off. Aye, and most of it left our hands. Now at least we can get some benefit from the arrangement. And dinnae think the mon putting up the bride price goes away unhappy. He may get no dower, but he gets a healthy young lass of good blood to warm his bed, tend his hearth, and bear his bairns. 'Struth, I think the way I am doing this is by far the fairer way."

"And it certainly helps to fill our empty pockets," drawled Iain.

"Weel, aye, there is that sad truth," agreed Douglas. "I just wish the men werenae such sad specimens. It would seem that the lasses deserve better."

"They have naught now and no promise of anything," snapped Malcolm.

"Just dinnae expect them all to smile and thank ye. Bega and Isabel may not say too much, as they seem to be verra concerned about being spinsters, but Tatha willnae accept all of this so verra sweetly. Nay, not when she discovers the aging rogue who has bought her."

"Sir Ranald MacLean is wealthy, with some verra fine lands to the north."

A shudder went through Tatha. She knew Sir Ranald. He had been lurking about quite frequently of late. She still had bruises on her backside from his last visit, when she had been a little too slow to completely avoid his pinching fingers. The man had to be fifty if he was a day, had a sickly complexion, was lecherous, and was soft, like some pampered, overfed woman. He had also buried three wives with only one spindly legged, sneering son to show for their sacrifice. Marriage to him would be pure hell and nothing less.

Creeping away from the door, Tatha maintained her stealth until she felt she was far enough away not to be heard, then raced up the stairs to the weaving room where her sisters were gathered. She had to warn them of the plans being made for them. When she burst into the room she saw the way her sisters looked at her in surprise and then dismay, touched with a hint of disgust. Tatha was suddenly not sure they would see anything wrong with what their father was doing, and it saddened her. Although there was still hope that the six youngest girls, ages fifteen to nine, would display some pride and backbone, the others seemed to have accepted their father's oft-repeated opinion that they were little more than a burden upon him. Nevertheless, it was her duty to warn all of them.

"Ye really must learn some manners, Tatha," said Isabel, her voice heavy with disapproval.

For a moment, Tatha considered letting Isabel remain blissfully ignorant of her fate; then she shook aside her annoyance with her prim, self-righteous sister. "Father is selling us," she announced.

"What nonsense is this?"

"Ye are aware that there are no dowers for any of us?" Her sisters nodded, the older ones looking far more downcast by their circumstances than the younger ones. "Father has found an answer to that problem."

"He has found the means to dower us?"

"Nay, Isabel, he is allowing men to pay him to take us for their wives. He is selling us off to the highest bidders."

"And there are men who are ready to concede to this arrangement?"

Isabel actually looked delighted, and Tatha wondered if her sister truly understood all of the implications. "Our father is selling us off like cattle, Isabel."

"He is getting us husbands."

Tatha glanced at her other sisters and realized that they were going to allow Isabel to speak for all of them. "And what sort of mon needs to buy himself a wife? Have ye thought verra much on that?" She noticed a fleeting look of consternation on Bega's round face but, before her hopes could be raised too high over this hint of rebellion, it was gone.

"They will be husbands, something we have little or no hope of obtaining now," Isabel said firmly.

"Oh, aye, husbands. Useless, disgusting men like Sir Ranald MacLean. That is the gift my father gained for me." Only her younger sisters showed any sign of sympathy for her. The ones of marriageable age revealed only relief that they were not going to be given to such a man. "Doesnae that make ye begin to worry o'er who may be buying you?"

"Nay," Isabel replied before anyone else could speak. "We are spinsters. Our fate, until now, was to grow old and barren in our father's house. Even a bad husband will be better than that. At least we will have our own households to lead and, God willing, bairns."

"Weel, I dinnae see it that way."

"Mayhap ye should. Ye too are a spinster, or near to. Aye, and ye are a too-thin lass with flame-colored hair. Red-haired and left-handed. Two curses in one wee lass. Ye also hold some verra odd ideas. Nearly blasphemous. Some have e'en whispered that ye are a witch, just as Aunt Mairi was. Aye, ye do have a verra fine pair of blue eyes, but they arenae so fine as to outshine all of your faults. If I were you, I should shut my mouth, bite down hard on my sharp tongue, and take what ye can get and be thanking God for it."

"Nay, I think not." Tatha fought down the pain caused by her sister's harsh words.

"And just what do ye think ye can do?"

" 'Tis none of your concern."

Tatha walked away, deeply saddened by this further proof of how different she was from her sisters. She had been her Aunt Mairi's favorite, spending most of her time in the old woman's tiny cottage. It was not only that Aunt Mairi had had nearly all of the raising of her that had separated her from her sisters, but the things Aunt Mairi had taught her. The woman had intended that Tatha would take her place as the healer for the clan. She had taught her niece all about herbs, medicines, and the arts of healing. She had also filled Tatha's greedy young mind with a myriad of old beliefs, beliefs the Church frowned upon. Such beliefs had been what had marked Mairi as a witch and threatened to mark Tatha with the same brand. In the year since Mairi had died, many people had sought Tatha out to make use of her indisputable skills at healing. Some people, however, also made the sign of the cross whenever they saw her.

As she slipped into the room she shared with her sisters Elspeth and Jean, Tatha wondered if her skill in the art of healing was one of the things Sir Ranald wanted her for. The man did not look very well at all, and Tatha now recalled Sir Ranald's deep interest in her knowledge of herbs. She dragged her saddlepacks out from beneath her tiny bed and started to fill the panniers with her meager belongings even as she wondered if Sir Ranald suffered from some specifically male difficulty, for the herbs and medicines he had been the most interested in had been the ones pertaining to lust and one's performance in the marriage act. As she packed her herbs and small collection of stones, she decided that the man was probably just twisted in some sick, carnal way.

Elspeth entered their chamber just as Tatha finished packing. "Where are ye going?"

"To collect herbs," Tatha replied, hating to lie to her sister but feeling that it was best if no one knew of her plans.

"And ye need all ye own to do that, do ye?"

"Dinnae press me, Elspeth. 'Tis best if ye dinnae ken anything about this."

"Aye, probably. I am a verra poor liar, and eventually ye will be missed. Did ye happen to hear who may have bought me?"

"Nay. I panicked when I heard who I had been sold off to. No one may have bid on you yet."

"Ye should be more understanding of the others, Tatha," Elspeth said quietly. "We are nay all as brave as ye. And how is this so verra different from what was done with our eldest sisters?"

"Nay so much, I suppose. I had accepted that, without a dower, I would have no match arranged for me. Aye, in truth, I liked it that way. It meant that I might actually have some choice in the matter, might e'en have been able to marry a mon I loved. That has all been stolen away from me now."

"No lass has such a thing. Ye simply fooled yourself into thinking that ye did."

"Mayhap. And, aye, now that I think on it, this *is* different from what our sisters had arranged for them. This is nay the custom. At least when there is a dowry some care is taken in the choice of a husband, even if 'tis only an eye to alliances made and the land involved. There is no care at all taken in this. Our father may as weel stand us in the market square and let all and anyone toss out a bid on us."

" 'Tis nay that horrible. I am sure Father is choosing carefully."

"Aye? Ye think that drooling old lecher Sir Ranald shows careful choosing, do ye?" She nodded and picked up her saddlepacks when Elspeth flushed and made no reply. "The mon has set three wives in the ground. I dinnae intend to be the fourth."

"Our father has made a bargain."

"I didnae agree to it, didnae put my mark on anything."

"Where will ye go?"

Remembering that she could not tell Elspeth the whole truth, Tatha murmured, "To the forests, as I always do."

Elspeth gave Tatha a brief hug and a kiss on the cheek. "Take care. The forest holds many a danger a wee sheltered lass doesnae ken much about and cannae defend herself against."

Tatha touched the cord with nine knots that was loosely tied around her waist. "I have protection."

A grimace briefly touched Elspeth's pretty face when she glanced at the rope. "Some of Aunt Mairi's witchery."

"She wasnae a witch. Aunt Mairi simply kenned a lot about the old ways. I dinnae believe they go against God and all His teachings, so I can see no harm in them."

"Then let us hope such charms work."

No one could hope that any more than Tatha herself as she went to the stables and saddled her stout Highland pony. As she rode away from her father's keep, no one tried to stop her. She often wandered away on her own, either to tend to someone's illness or injury, or to gather some herbs and wild plants.

What had Tatha's heart beating so fiercely it hurt was the knowledge that this time she could not return, might never be able to come home, at least not as long as the marriage to Sir Ranald was planned for her. Her family was not a very close or loving one, but it was all she had ever known, and it hurt to turn her back on them all.

And what lay ahead? she mused, as she rode through the forest, impulsively stopping now and again to collect some herb or other useful plant. She could probably survive by practicing her healing art, she decided. If nothing else, that skill would probably gain her a meal and a bed as she needed them. She would have to be careful about whom she met or spoke to, or she could quickly find herself returned to her father and Sir Ranald. Although some people might share her disgust for what her father was doing, she was her father's chattel, and now probably Sir Ranald's as well. If she met with anyone who knew of either man and had heard of her escape, that person could well feel it was his duty to take her back home.

By the time Tatha stopped to make camp for the night, she was exhausted and afraid. The only thing that stopped her from racing back to the safety and comfort of her home was the knowledge that Sir Ranald would be waiting for her. The fear gnawing at her while she sat alone before a small fire was a tiny one compared to that which was stirred by the thought of becoming Sir Ranald's wife. She prayed that her father would soon see the error of his ways when he realized that she had run away, but she did not really hold much hope of that happening. Sir Malcolm was a very stubborn man. He was about to discover, however, that his seventh-born child could be just as stubborn.

The dawn mists woke her with their chill. Tatha winced as she stood up and discovered that sleeping on the cold, damp ground made a person very stiff. It was not until she had seen to her personal needs, washed up, and dined on cold oatcakes that her stiffness had eased enough for her to saddle and mount her pony. She hoped she did not have to spend too many nights outside, especially not with summer rapidly coming to an end.

"Ah, me, Stoutheart," she murmured to her little pony after several hours of riding. "Is this madness?"

Her little pony snorted, and she smiled faintly. As she glanced around she saw little save the occasional crofter's hut and cattle. It appeared as if she had inadvertently picked a very isolated trail. It was going to be very hard to make a living if she never saw a village or a keep. Tatha decided that she would give it one more day, and then she would turn east. If she rode in a straight line she would eventually reach the coast, and there would be more than enough people there, from small fishing villages to larger port cities.

It was just as she was thinking that she should find someplace to camp for the night that Tatha saw the keep. For hours she had been feeling an increased reluctance to turn east as had been her plan, even though it was a good one. Despite the emptiness of the land, her heart urged her onward, north toward the Highlands. Now, suddenly, as she looked at the dark hilltop fortress ahead, that urge made sense, yet she would be hard-pressed to explain why.

As her pony cautiously picked its way through the bogs and the marshes that protected the approach to the keep, she noticed the river that bordered it on the north side. An admirable protection against raiders, she mused. In fact, everything about the keep promised one safety from the dangers of the world. And yet, she thought, frowning, that did not fully explain why she continued to ride toward its high, iron-studded gates.

Tatha suddenly smiled as she realized what pulled her ever forward. It was the call of the old ways, as Mairi had loved to refer to it. There was something or someone at that dark tower house, behind that high, dark curtain wall, that called to her knowledge, to her understanding of the old ways. Nudging her pony forward and keeping a close watch for the dangers all marshes held, Tatha prayed the holder of the tower house would allow her the chance to answer that call.

Chapter Two

Sir David Ruthven scowled down at the small figure riding toward his keep. He did not really have to see the long flame red hair swirling around the tiny rider to know that a female trotted toward his gates. In the five years since his mother's death it had become a somewhat common sight. If he had known how many women would seek refuge at Cnocanduin, he would never have made the vow he had to his dying mother. The last thing he wished to do right now was give refuge to another troubled woman, but, he thought with a sigh as he moved down off his walls, he knew he would yet again accede to his mother's wishes. He wondered crossly if some herald had been sent out to tell the world about the vow he had made.

"There is a—" began the tall, lanky young man who met David at the base of the curtain wall.

"I ken it, Leith. I saw the lass," David replied as he

strode toward the tall gates, his cousin Leith quickly falling into step behind him.

"Mayhap this one isnae fleeing a husband."

Wincing as he recalled the trouble caused by the last woman to seek refuge at Cnocanduin, her evil-tempered husband hot on her heels, David nodded. "I cannae believe my mother intended Cnocanduin to become a refuge for wayward wives."

"Weel, mayhap ye ought to just ask the lass if she has a husband first, ere she even asks for refuge and ye are forced by your vow to bid her welcome."

"Aye, mayhap. 'Twould save us a lot of grief, but I would probably suffer a bellyful of guilt o'er it."

Although he felt the first pinch of guilt even as he stood blocking the way through the gates with his body, David decided to try Leith's suggestion. The last woman had nearly set him in the middle of a bloody clan war. He simply could not believe that had been his mother's intention when she had wrested that vow from him. Then again, he would have sworn to almost anything she had asked as he had stood by her deathbed, watching her life's blood slowly flow out of her broken and battered body.

The woman reined her pony in but a foot from him and, to his astonishment, frowned at him. There was no fear or sadness on her small heart-shaped face, no look of helplessness in her beautiful blue eyes. David wondered if she was simply a traveler who sought no more than food and shelter, or even was simply lost. If she was not running from something, it seemed odd that such a slight, delicately built lass would be riding over the dangerous countryside unescorted. What was puzzling at the moment, however, was the way she was looking at him as if he annoyed her. He had not even spoken to her yet.

Tatha started to order the man to get out of her way, but a flicker of good sense kept the words back. The closer she had drawn to the keep, the stronger the pull of the place had grown. Once past the danger of the bogs she had urged her little pony into a faster gait. If the man had not suddenly appeared directly in her path, she suspected she would have heedlessly galloped right through the huge, imposing gates. Tatha forced herself to calm down. She could move with a little more caution and still find out what was drawing her to this place.

She studied the man blocking her path and wondered if it was him. He was certainly handsome enough in a dark, somber way. Thick black hair fell to just below his broad shoulders. He was tall and leanly muscular. Rough deer-hide boots were laced around a pair of well-shaped calves. The plaid he wore swirled gently in the breeze, giving her brief glimpses of smooth, muscular thighs. His white shirt was unlaced, revealing a broad, dark chest. His form was fine enough to cause her heart to beat a little faster, but it was his face that truly held her fascinated when she finally took a good look at it. It was a beautiful face. The lines sharp but not too sharp, lean but not too lean. High cheekbones, a long, straight nose, a firm jaw, and a nicely shaped mouth, the lips holding just a hint of fullness. His eyes, set beneath faintly arched brows, were dark, appearing almost black, and were thickly lashed. One of those dark brows was suddenly quirked upward, telling Tatha that she had been staring at the man for just a little too long.

"I am—" she began.

"Are ye wed?" he demanded.

Slowly, Tatha blinked, confused by his abrupt question and somewhat bemused by his deep, rich voice. She started to wonder why he should wish to know that, then quickly stopped herself. There were simply too many possibilities.

"Nay," she replied cautiously. "Ye dinnae wish wedded lasses behind your walls?"

"I dinnae wish the trouble wedded lasses fleeing their lawful husbands bring along behind them."

Tatha wondered if that would include lasses fleeing a betrothal. Although she felt a pinch of guilt, she decided that, since he had not asked, she did not need to tell him. She dismounted, marched up to him, and held out her hand, trying to ignore the fact that she reached only to his chest.

"I am Tatha Preston. I was wondering if I might seek refuge here for a wee while."

David stared down at her small, long-fingered hand, sighed with resignation, and shook it. "Aye, come along." As she grabbed hold of her pony's reins and followed him through the gates, he said, "I am Sir David Ruthven, laird of Cnocanduin. As long as ye feel a need to, ye may shelter here."

"That is verra kind of you."

"I promised my mother on her deathbed to always shelter troubled lasses."

The tone of his voice told Tatha that it was a promise he was beginning to heartily regret. "I shall say a prayer for her."

"That would be kind. Aye, and needed. There were some dark lies muttered about her ere she died."

"I am sorry. I shall say several prayers."

He waved a stablehand over to take her pony. "Your mount's name?"

"Stoutheart." She shrugged when he looked at the pony, then at her, amusement lightening his dark eyes. "He got me through the bogs," she said as she took her bags off the pony's back.

"True. Ye are from the north?" he asked as he took her by the arm and led her to the tower house.

"Nay, from south of here. The pony was a gift from an uncle when I was just a lass." When Tatha caught him looking down at her, the hint of a smile on his lips, she briefly thought about trying to stand taller, then inwardly shrugged. The only way to do that would be to stand on tiptoe, and that would look silly. "Six years ago, when I was but three and ten." She tried not to feel insulted when his beautiful eyes widened briefly with surprise, indicating that he found her not so great age of nineteen a shock.

"Jennet will show ye to a bedchamber," he said as he stopped near the foot of a steep, narrow flight of stone steps and waved over a young, dark-haired maid. "She can get ye all ye may need. We will be gathering in the great hall for a meal in but two hours."

David watched the woman follow Jennet up the stairs. Tatha Preston was a tiny, delicate woman. She was almost too slender, but, recalling how her small, high breasts shaped the front of her deep green gown, and watching the feminine sway of her slim hips as she climbed the stairs, he decided she had curves enough to tempt a man. With each step she took, her thick, flame red hair brushed against her hips, and David found himself wondering how it would feel in his hands or how it would look spread out beneath her body. That taste of lust struck him as odd, for she could not really be called beautiful. Her wide, bright blue eyes, heavily trimmed with long brown lashes and set beneath delicately arched brows, were her best feature, were in truth incomparable. Her nose was small and straight with a faint smattering of freckles, and it pointed to a slightly wide, full-lipped mouth that was very tempting indeed. There was a lot of stubbornness in her gently pointed chin. Her skin was a soft white with the blush of good health, and, David had to admit, it begged to be touched.

"She is a bonny wee lass," murmured Leith.

Startled, for he had not realized that his cousin had followed them inside, David turned to look at Leith. "I was just thinking that, and yet, at first glance, I would ne'er have said so."

"Aye, she takes looking at, but 'tis often those lasses who wear weel. At least she isnae a wedded lass."

"Nay, and yet I think she may be trouble."

"What kind of trouble?"

"I dinnae ken, Leith. I just dinnae ken. 'Tis nay more than a feeling in my innards. If naught else, one must wonder what such a bonny wee lass is doing riding o'er the countryside all alone, and I dinnae think the answer to that question is one that will please us."

Tatha watched the door shut behind the little maid, then flopped down on the huge bed with a heavy sigh of relief. She was inside the walls of Cnocanduin and, by what the laird had said, she could be staying until she chose to leave. Sir David had, in many ways, offered her sanctuary. The deathbed oath to his mother was a vow he would be loath to break.

She felt a twinge of guilt. He had asked her if she was married and she had been able to reply with a truthful no. But it was not the whole truth, and she knew it. Her father had sold her into a betrothal, promised her hand in marriage to Sir Ranald, and most people would consider that as binding as a marriage. Tatha doubted she would have an easy time finding someone to agree with her opinion that her consent was needed, or even that she should at least have been consulted.

Suddenly aware of how dusty she was and the strong smell of horse on her clothes, Tatha scrambled off the bed and began to undress. Even as she stood in her shift and started to unpack her bags, Jennet arrived with fresh, heated water and a tub, other maids quickly following with enough water to fill it. Tatha was barely able to wait until they had all left the room before she flung off her shift and climbed into the tub. With a sigh of pure enjoyment she sank down into the warm water, took a deep breath of the lavender-scented soap, and began to scrub away the scent of travel.

It was as she slipped on her clean shift and began to brush her hair dry that her guilt returned. She was accepting all of this grand hospitality under false pretenses. Tatha tried to soothe her unease by promising to tell Sir David the whole truth if he asked, but that helped only a little. Finally, she vowed that, if there was any sign of trouble due to her fleeing a marriage to Sir Ranald, she would leave Cnocanduin immediately. That restored her confidence, and she began to dress for the meal in the great hall in a much improved mood.

Her newly restored confidence wavered a little when she stepped through the heavy doors leading to the great hall. It struck her quite forcibly that she did not know any of the people now looking at her. She knew only the name of the laird.

To her relief, Sir David stood up and waved her to a seat on his left. As she smiled her gratitude and sat down on the bench, she promised herself she would spend the next day getting to know some of the people of Cnocanduin. For that reason, she smiled brightly when he introduced her to his cousin Leith, who sat on his right, and hoped that the dark young man's very brief smile in return did not mean her welcome was already wearing thin. She needed to find a few companions aside from the laird. Sir David undoubtedly had better things to do than to become her sole source of entertainment and conversation.

Although, she mused, as he placed some tender roast beef on her trencher, he was welcome to spend as much time with her as he pleased. Tatha surprised herself a little with that thought, for, until now, she had found little about men to interest her. His beauty of face and form was unquestionable, but she did not know the man at all. Thus far, he had offered her little to really hold her interest, yet she felt herself wishing that he would try, and even worrying that she would never be able to hold his.

"I find it curious that ye are riding o'er such danger-ous country all alone, m'lady," David murmured, glancing at her and deciding that Leith was right, that Tatha Preston was a lass who wore very well on the eyes.

"Do ye? Why?" Tatha decided there was nothing to gain in questioning his form of address. Although her father was a laird, she was not sure titles of any sort should be used for the seventh of fifteen children.

"Ye are weelborn, are ye not?"

"Weel enough."

"And yet your kinsmen allow ye to trot about Scotland unguarded?" David frowned, the flicker of unease he had felt upon her arrival returning and growing stronger. "Ye have run away from something, havenae ye?"

Tatha sighed and took a deep drink of wine from her wooden goblet to steady herself. "I am neither a murderer nor a thief, so what does it matter?"

"It matters because whatever or whomever ye have run from could weel come pounding upon my gates."

"I dinnae believe anyone will come looking for me. Howbeit, if someone does, I shall leave. Is that nay fair?"

"Aye, fair enough, but why dinnae ye just tell me what it is ye are running from?"

Her reprieve had been a very short one, she mused, and sighed. "My father, Sir Malcolm, laird of Prestonmoor, has fifteen children," she began, her reluctance to explain clear in her voice.

"The mon is blessed. Your mother?"

"Dead. She was the second of his wives. He has just wed his fourth wife who, thank God, appears to be barren." She winced. "Nay, that was most unkind. She may weel wish for a bairn of her own. 'Tis nay her fault that her kin wed her to a mon who needs no more."

"Why so many?" asked Leith. "Does the mon plan to breed his own army?"

"If so, he had best work harder, for, much to his oft-announced dismay, thirteen of those fifteen children are females." She smiled faintly at the brief looks of horror the men could not hide. "My two eldest sisters were easily settled, betrothed at cradleside, if nay whilst they were still in the womb. Howbeit, that took all the dower money and dower land. There are nay so many men who are eager to bind their family with ours when there is no dowry to be had with the bride. So, depleted of dowries and unable to gain any more, my father realized that he was still burdened with eleven daughters. He has thought up what he believes to be the perfect solution—he is selling us."

"Selling you?" David was relieved that she had not lied about being unwed, but it was beginning to look as if she was not exactly free either.

"Aye. If there is a mon who feels in need of a wife, he can buy cne from my father. I was being sold to a Sir Ranald MacLean." She was pleased to see the grimace of distaste on David's and Leith's faces, although disappointed when they quickly recovered their composure. Their swift attempt to hide their sympathy indicated that they did not want to give in to it. "I warned my sisters, but the two who are older than me are verra worried about becoming spinsters. They didnae care how a husband for them was found. They also held sway o'er the others, although only Elspeth, who is eighteen, and Jean, who is sixteen, are in any immediate peril."

"And, so, because ye didnae approve of your father's choice, ye left," David said, trying to sound disgusted even though he fully understood why a woman would flee Sir Ranald.

"I did and, unless my father changes his mind on this matter, I willnae return to Prestonmoor."

Tatha could tell he was displeased, but he said nothing more. It was courtesy alone that made him offer to walk her around his keep and the inner bailey. She knew it but she accepted anyway. Perhaps, if he came to know her better, Sir David would cease trying to smother the sympathy she knew he felt for her. Tatha also admitted, with a mixture of sadness and alarm, that she was strongly tempted to spend some time with him. That attraction was most unwise. Even if she were not toting a lot of trouble along with her, Sir David Ruthven was not a man who would look favorably upon a skinny, left-handed redhead.

An instant later all thoughts of Sir David were pushed from her mind as he pointed out the well where his people drew their water. It was in a sad condition, tempting complete ruin if it was not seen to soon, but Tatha saw its beauty through the dirt, rubble, and tangled undergrowth that nearly obstructed all paths to it. She tried to go to it, but Sir David impatiently pulled her along as if he was anxious to leave the place. She allowed him to lead her away, but swore that she would return at first light. Suddenly she knew exactly why she had been drawn to Cnocanduin. It was not the promise of refuge. It was not a tall, dark-eyed man who made her blood flow warm. It was a neglected well that called to her, and Tatha was determined to find out why.

Chapter Three

"Where is she?" muttered Sir David as he finished his morning meal and realized his new guest had yet to appear in the great hall.

"I dinnae ken," replied Leith before having a deep swallow of sweet cider. "Mayhap she went on her way."

"We have ne'er been so lucky," Sir David grumbled, annoyed when he realized he did not wholly mean his cross words. He spotted the maid he had assigned to their guest over by the buttery. "Jennet, have ye seen the lady Tatha this morning?"

"Nay," Jennet replied, blushing upon being noticed by her laird. "She was already up and away when I rapped on her door to tell her 'twas near time to break her fast."

"Do ye think she has left Cnocanduin, continued on her journey?"

"Nay. All of her things are still within the bed-chamber."

"I saw her by the well o'er an hour ago," called out one of the serving maids.

"She was fetching her own water?" David was certain the woman had been telling the truth when she had said that her father was a laird, yet tending to herself was an odd thing for a wellborn woman to do.

"Nay, though she was drawing water," said the plump serving maid. "It looked as if she had been clearing away the rubble when I saw her."

David frowned and sipped at his cider. He suddenly recalled his guest's intense interest in the well. She had tried to make him stop by it, then plagued him with questions until she realized he would not answer them. His mother and his grandmother had both cherished that well, had felt that it was a place of magic. The spring that fed it was the reason Cnocanduin had been built. Although he kept it in enough repair to continue to supply the tower house with water, he had otherwise let it sink into ruin. He was sure that it was his mother's talk of the well's magic, her deep belief in its powers, that had led to her violent death. David began to feel uneasy, suddenly certain he had seen that same gleam in Tatha's rich blue eyes.

"I believe I will go and see what mischief our guest has gotten herself into," he mumbled as he rose and strode out of the great hall. If Tatha was another who spoke of magic and the old ways, he would soon put a stop to it.

* * *

Tatha felt a rising excitement as she pulled the last of the rubble and overgrowth away from the side of the well. She dampened a rag in the water and rubbed away at an area that appeared to have some carving on it. Once she had the whole area cleaned off, she sat back on her heels and studied the inscription. It was in the old script, and, although her aunt had taught her the words, she had not been the best of students.

Again and again she struggled with the words. Slowly, word by word, she sorted out its meaning. Leaning forward, she traced each letter with an unsteady finger. Her voice softened with awe, she read aloud: " 'Any woman of pure heart who drinks from the well of Cnocanduin will find protection, strength, and happiness as long as it holds water.' "

Although she thought it might be vain to think of herself as a woman with a pure heart, Tatha stood up. She drew some fresh water from the well, took the battered dipper from the hook on the side, and drank deeply. Frowning slightly, she stared into the dipper, then peered into the well. Tatha was sure she would not experience any sudden overwhelming change in herself, yet she thought she ought to feel more than a simple easing of her thirst.

"Ye have been neglected for a long time, havenae ye?" she murmured and patted the cool stone, its whiteness dimmed by years of dirt.

She turned to the small bag she had brought with her. Pulling out a thick cord, she visualized a shield and, softly repeating the promise carved into the side

of the well, tied nine knots in it. Tatha then attached
this protective binding to the bottom of the bucket.
She repeated the simple spell and hung the second
cord from the rowan tree that grew next to the well.

Next she took out one of her holed stones, painstak-
ingly gathered from the sea. She rubbed it between
her hands as she murmured, "Stone, evil ye will deny.
Send it to the earth and sky. Send it to the flame and
sea. Stone of power protect Cnocanduin and all who
dwell within its walls."

Then, with a pinch of regret over giving up one of
her precious stones, she dropped it into the well. It
was a worthy sacrifice, for not only would it enhance
the protection the well promised, but it would
strengthen the healing power of the water. Aunt Mairi
would approve, she mused, as she lowered the bucket
and drew up some more water to take another drink.

"What are ye doing?"

That deep voice sounding so close behind her made
Tatha start and gasp in surprise. Since she was taking
a deep drink of water at the time, she began to choke,
some of the water going the wrong way down her
throat. The rest, what was in her mouth and in the
dipper, soaked the front of her gown. Sir David began
to slap her on the back with such force that she
stumbled against the well and had to grip the edge
to steady herself. As soon as she got herself under
control, she wiped the tears from her cheeks, and
turned to glare at the man.

David glared right back. He had watched her for
several minutes before speaking and did not like what
he had seen. She was doing the same sort of things
that had led to his mother being feared, then murdered. That alone was enough to infuriate him, lash-

ing him with dark, painful memories. What troubled him was the fear he felt. It was not a fear of what she did, but of what such beliefs could cost her. He did not even know this tiny, flame-haired woman, yet his blood ran cold at the thought that she could soon suffer as his mother had. His fear was for her, and that made no sense. Unless it directly affected his people, what happened to a stranger should not matter much to him, but it did, and that only made him angrier.

"Ye scared several years out of me," Tatha complained as she tried to dab the water from the front of her deep blue gown with a scrap of clean linen. "Do ye always creep up behind people?"

"Only when they are behaving in a strange manner," he snapped.

"Strange? I wasnae doing anything strange."

"Nay?" He stepped closer to the rowan tree and reached up toward the knotted cord she had draped in the branches. "And what is this then?"

Tatha quickly moved to his side and slapped his hand away. " 'Tis naught to concern you."

"Ye dinnae think people will wonder why there is a knotted cord in this tree?"

"Nay. I doubt anyone will e'en see the thing. Ye wouldnae have seen it put there if ye hadnae been tiptoeing about."

"I ken what that is. 'Tis some spell of protection."

Her eyes widening, Tatha looked at Sir David in surprise and a deepening interest. "The old ways are practiced here?"

"Nay, that nonsense isnae done here. I willnae allow it."

"Nonsense? Nay here?" Tatha stepped back to the

well and smoothed her hand over the stone. "Aye, that *nonsense* is here. I suspect that *nonsense* has been here since long before this keep was built. And ye ken what it is, for all ye call it *nonsense,* or ye wouldnae ken the meaning of that knotted cord. Someone has taught ye a thing or two."

"Aye," he said in a cold, flat voice, "my mother, who learned such foolishness from her mother, and 'tis just such blasphemous games that got the woman beaten to death five years ago."

Although she felt a surge of sympathy for the man, Tatha smothered the emotion, knowing that he neither wanted it, nor would he appreciate it. He was trying to frighten her. He succeeded to some extent, but fear of the dangers of superstition was an old one to her. Tatha had been taught at a very young age how to face it, accept it, and then push it aside.

"I am sorry. Ignorance and fear can be dangerous, deadly things," she said quietly. "My aunt Mairi was oftimes threatened and was the subject of many an evil whisper. 'Tis odd, for she did no one any harm. In truth, she was a great healer. She taught me all of her skills. I oft wonder if the skill to fix that which so afrightens people, sickness and injury, is what marks healers. We touch, study, and sometimes cure what others consider evil, terrifying. Mayhap, because they believe God inflicts diseases and such, they think that we go against His will when we try to cure such things. Odd, though, that they dinnae turn against physicians, isnae it? But mayhap that is because physicians, or leeches if ye prefer, are men."

David blinked, opened his mouth to reply, then clamped it shut. He needed to regain his calm and put some order into his thoughts. Her words stunned him with their truth. His mother had done little more than try to help people, to heal their ills and soothe their pains. Some people had come from far away to seek her aid, her fame as a healer having become quite widespread before she was killed. David had always assumed, though, that the danger had come from her talk of such things as the power of the water, the magic of the stones, and the occasional little charm, but he realized that he had never fully believed that. His mother had understood, though scorned, people's fears, and, on most occasions, had tried to be circumspect about her beliefs. He shook his head. He did not want to think that simply helping people had cost her her life.

"Those men dinnae speak of magic waters or babble blasphemous words over rocks," he snapped.

"Ye shouldnae have seen that," she muttered.

"Weel, I did."

"Only because ye crept up on me like some thief."

"One of the maids saw ye."

"Nay, all she saw was me drawing water from the well and trying to clear away this mess. I was most careful, for my aunt taught me about the fears so many people hold." She frowned at the well. "Your mother told people of the well's powers?"

"She told some. Aye. She was verra proud of the power she mistakenly believed it held."

Tatha decided she would gain little by trying to argue the truth of his mother's beliefs. " 'Tis odd then that the ones who killed her didnae attempt to destroy this well, too. When people cry such as we witches or worse, then try to kill us, they also try to destroy all they believe we gained our power from."

"She wasnae killed here," he said, pained by the

memories yet intrigued by what she said. "She had been called to a village a half day's ride from here, on Sir Ranald MacLean's lands." He noted the way her beautiful eyes widened and she paled, but did not remark upon it. "By the time we heard of the trouble it was too late to save her."

"Sir Ranald had her killed?"

"I did wonder if he was part of it, but there was no proof of that. 'Twas his men, however, who stirred the people into a fury, and his men who beat her. They will beat no more women," he added in a cold, flat voice.

"Why was she called to that particular village?"

"What can that matter?"

"It may matter a great deal to me. Sir Ranald kens what I am, yet paid a goodly sum to my father to take me as his wife. Aye, to take me to a place where one healing woman has already been murdered."

David frowned, suddenly wondering if there was more behind his mother's death than he had suspected. He had not been able to gain any proof that Sir Ranald had been involved in the murder in any way, and the man had allowed David to kill the men directly involved, had simply ignored the reckoning taken. Yet, despite the obvious temptation of Tatha's youth and beauty to a man like Sir Ranald, it did seem strange that he would seek a wife he knew his clansmen would hate and fear. Despite the man's age and unappealing nature, David was sure Sir Ranald could have looked elsewhere for a young wife if that was all he sought, one with a dowry.

"I will see what I can find out," he finally said. "It may not be easy. It has been five years and I had thought that the matter was settled. I buried my

mother, a reckoning was taken, and no feud ensued.
I believed that was the end of it all. Howbeit, ye have
stirred my curiosity anew, and ye are right to think
it could be of importance to you."

Tatha studied Sir David even as she reconsidered
all she knew about Sir Ranald. "Was your mother
bonny?"

"Aye," David replied cautiously. "I think so. She
was a small woman, much akin to ye in size, only . . .
weel, fuller of figure. Her coloring was akin to mine
save that she had green eyes. She was also only nine
and thirty when she died, yet looked verra much
younger."

"I see." Tatha began to think Lady Ruthven's healing gift and belief in the old ways had had very little
to do with her death. "Did ye seek me out for any
particular reason?" she asked, deciding there was
nothing to be gained in continuing to talk about Sir
David's mother, not until she had a few more facts.

Her abrupt change of subject confused David for
a moment; then he recalled what he had seen as he
had approached the well. "I had heard that ye were
here and, after remembering your interest in this well
last evening, decided I would come to see what game
ye were playing."

" 'Tis no game." She rubbed her hand along the
stone, eager to return to the work of cleaning it. "I
believe this is why I was drawn to this place."

"The well called ye, did it?"

She ignored his sarcasm. "Aye, it did."

David cursed and dragged his fingers through his
hair. "Ye willnae practice this foolishness."

"Are ye intending to forbid it?"

He opened his mouth to do just that, but the words

would not come. This young woman believed in all the things his mother and grandmother had believed in. Somehow it seemed disloyal to their memory to keep her from practicing her healing. He cursed.

"Nay." He glared at the knotted cord that was actually very well concealed in the branches of the tree and then at her. "Ye will nay flaunt it, though. I willnae have all that trouble stirred up again."

"I will be verra careful. I have always been," she assured him quietly, understanding the anger in his voice. "If I or my beliefs bring trouble to your gates, I will leave."

When David realized he was about to vehemently argue that plan, he cursed again, and strode away. She had been at Cnocanduin only one night, yet she had him so beset by conflicting emotions he could not think straight. If the well had drawn Tatha Preston to his keep, it was certainly not working in his favor, he thought crossly.

Tatha sighed as she watched him leave. It saddened her that her beliefs should anger him and push him away. She decided it might be for the best not to study too closely why that should be. There was far too much else she had to worry about.

As she returned to the work of restoring the well to its former beauty, she found herself puzzling over the chilling coincidence that the same man who tried to buy her for his wife was connected to Sir David's mother's brutal murder. Suddenly she knew she was at Cnocanduin to do more than restore the well, that perhaps fate or even the restless spirit of Lady Ruthven had dragged her here. The more she considered the matter, the more she was certain she had been led to Cnocanduin for several purposes. Sir

David needed to believe again, needed to yet again appreciate the heritage of the women in his family. The beauty and the power of the well needed to be renewed. And, most important, the truth behind Lady Ruthven's death had to be revealed. If she was right, it was a heavy burden fate had thrust upon her. Tatha prayed Sir Ranald and her father would leave her be until she could accomplish it all.

Chapter Four

"Where is she?"

Leith groaned and would have banged his head on the heavy oak table if his trencher of food was not in the way. "Ye have fretted o'er where the lass is nearly every morning of the mere week she has been here."

"I dinnae trust her," David muttered and savagely ate a chunk of bread.

That was not really the truth, and he accepted Leith's mildly disgusted look as well earned. He found that he did trust Tatha, trusted her in ways he had not trusted a woman for a very long time. Since he had known her only a week, he had to wonder why. What he was not sure of was whether she truly had the skill and the understanding to keep her beliefs hidden, to comprehend and guard against the danger such beliefs could plunge her into. David worried about her, a lot, and he did not want to.

"Weel, I think she is one of the best to yet arrive at our gates," Leith said.

"Oh, aye? She doesnae act much like a guest. She has fair usurped all running of the keep."

"She but tries to help. The lass is a skilled healer." Leith flushed and glanced warily at David. "I think she may be as good as, or better than, your mother ever was."

"High praise. What prompts it?"

"Ye ken that I have e'er suffered from rashes and the itch of them."

"Aye. Mother gave ye many a salve for them."

"And they truly helped ease my torment, but naught she did cured it."

"And this lass has cured you?" David frowned and studied his cousin, his eyes widening suddenly when he noticed that Leith's neck was no longer covered with red blotches.

"Aye, and 'twas nay with any magic or strange potions. I dinnae have some skin ailment. 'Tis the wool."

"The wool? What does wool have to do with your skin?"

"Weel, my skin cannae abide the touch of it. Aye, I thought it all madness too," he said when David stared at him in disbelief. "How can ye nay wear wool? Weel, she told me to just try nay letting it touch my skin for just a wee while and gave me a willow-herb ointment to soothe my rashes. It couldnae hurt, I thought. So I still wore my plaid but I put a linen shirt on, and . . ." He blushed, looked around to make sure no one was watching them, and lifted the skirt of his plaid to reveal that he also wore linen leggings. "It took only a day or two for me to see the change. Beneath all of this wrapping there isnae one red spot. For the first time in my life I am nay itching myself. I have asked the lasses if they can weave me a plaid that isnae of wool, for e'en touching it causes me a few troubles still. Aye, and 'twill cost me dear to have warm clothes made that arenae of wool, but e'en after only a few days of ease, I feel the cost will be worth it. If only for the ease in my nether regions."

"Weel. Who would have thought it."

"Seems the lass kens a lot about what can trouble your skin. Ye wouldnae believe how many questions she asked of me, and some put us both to the blush. I have noticed that she doesnae wear wool, either. And many of your people have already sought her out for help. Donald's wife Sorcha was one of the first, for she is with child again."

"I pray to God that she can carry this one to term." David scowled. "Tatha hasnae promised that, has she?"

"Nay. The lass says such things are in God's hands. But she also said that women must ken a few things to help God's work be accomplished. She told Sorcha to nay lift anything heavy, to rest with her feet raised several times a day, to avoid strong smells that can oftimes trouble one's belly, for the retching can be harmful. Then she gave her a verra long list of foods she cannae eat."

"Such as what?"

"Weel, all Donald and Sorcha could recall was thyme, parsley, and juniper berries, but there were many others. Sorcha says she will simply eat verra plain food, nay a spice or an herb. And the lass gave her a sage brew to drink, sparingly. If the bairn still rests in her belly come harvest time, Donald may be asking ye to let his wife stay out of the fields.''

"I shall tell him today that he need not fret on it. If 'twill give them a bairn, Sorcha can crawl abed now and stay there until the birth. It appears the lass has cured you and, if her advice gives Donald and Sorcha a live bairn, we may ne'er see the lass leave.'' He sighed. ''And I will confess that e'en in the short week she has been here, the keep is cleaner, e'en to the smell of it.''

"We didnae have a great problem with vermin such as fleas, but what few were here are now gone.'' Leith grinned. ''Donald complains that the stables smell like a fine lady's bath, but I notice he doesnae remove any of the herbs she has hung up in the place.'' His smile widened and held a hint of lechery. ''She may have e'en helped old Robert with his back trouble. Ye ken it has been a month or longer since he hurt it and it hadnae eased at all. He spoke to the lass and she told him all of the usual things, nay any heavy lifting, rest, and gave him a salve to ease the ache. Then she discovered that he has himself a bonny new wife and tried to tell him to leave her be until his back is better.''

"And Robert wasnae going to heed that advice, was he?'' David laughed softly.

"Nay, said so clear and loud. Then he said that, though the lass was blushing as red as her hair, she called him a randy old goat and since he wasnae going to be wise, then he could at least change his ways.''

"Change his ways?''

"Aye.'' Leith's voice was choked with laughter.

"She told him to let his wife ride." He collapsed into loud, helpless laughter at the look of utter shock on David's face.

David shook his head, then finally laughed. He was also relieved by what Leith had told him. Tatha was not dealing in charms and potions. In truth, her healing skills seemed to depend a great deal upon common sense and getting people to act with a bit more wisdom. That she spoke freely and often of God's will was also good. Although it caused him a pang, and he muttered a prayer for forgiveness for any unintentional hint of disrespect for his mother, David began to think Tatha revealed a bit more common sense than his mother ever had. At times his mother had shown little tolerance or understanding of people's fears. It was an arrogance she had learned from her mother, one she had not learned to temper completely, and one that had often made the women seem to spit in the eye of God and church. Tatha seemed blissfully free of that vanity.

"Ye still havenae said if ye ken where she is," David said when his cousin finally grew quiet.

"She could be working in your mother's herb room or she could be out looking for more herbs and plants. She said there was little time left to gather a goodly amount ere the fall comes."

Even as he stood up and started out of the hall, David wondered what he was doing. Ever since Tatha Preston had arrived at his gates he had been overly concerned about where she was and what she was doing. It was true that he worried about her, his mother's brutal death and the reasons for it ever clear in his mind. Ruefully, he admitted that he just liked to look at her, to talk to her.

It did not take him long to discover Tatha had ridden to the village, begged by a woman to come and look at her sick child. David had his horse saddled and set out after her. After all Leith had told him, David was intensely interested in seeing Tatha at work. He hoped it would ease some of his concern for her safety.

Softly praying that she had the skill needed to save the child, Tatha followed the plump woman into the tiny cottage attached to the blacksmith's shop. The one thing she had never been able to accept with ease, to wholeheartedly embrace as God's will, was the death of a child. One look at the feverish, thrashing boy on the tiny bed made her heart sink. He could be no more than five, and he looked dangerously ill.

All the while she looked over every inch of the little boy, Tatha questioned the mother. Finally, Tatha found what she felt was the cause of the child's dire condition. On one thin calf was a small wound. It was closed, had ceased to bleed, but the area around it was hot, red, and swollen.

"Where did he get this?" she asked the mother as she dampened a scrap of cloth in some heated water and gently washed the child's leg.

"That wee scratch?" The look in the woman's dark eyes clearly told Tatha that she could not see why such a meager injury would hold any interest. "He cut himself whilst playing with his father's tools. 'Tisnae bleeding. It closed up verra quickly."

"Aye, too quickly. It shut all the filth and bad humors inside. Ye are going to have to hold the wee lad steady so that I may reopen this wound." Tatha took her knife from its sheath at her side and washed off the blade.

"Open it? Why?"

"I will do it," said a deep voice that was already achingly familiar to Tatha. David curtly nodded to the flustered blacksmith's wife and stepped over to the child's bed. "What do I do?"

"Hold him as firmly as ye can so that I can make a neat, small cut." Tatha looked at the boy's mother. "I will need clean rags and verra hot water. Do ye have them at the ready?"

"Aye." The woman hurried away to get what Tatha needed.

After taking a deep breath to steady herself, and checking that David had the child held firmly, she quickly made a cross cut over the boy's wound, neatly reopening it. The child screamed, then lay still. Tatha wrinkled her nose in distaste at the odor of the muck that immediately began to seep out. She was only faintly aware of how David cursed and the child's mother gasped in horror. Quickly taking the bowl of steaming water and bundle of rags from the shocked woman before she dropped them, Tatha began the slow process of trying to drain all of the poison from the wound. Once she deemed the wound clean, she washed it once more with water from the well, put a poultice of woad leaves on it, and wrapped it in a strip of clean cloth.

As she straightened up, Tatha grimaced at the ache in her back and realized that she had been bent over the child for a long time. She forced some blackthorn bark tea down the child's throat to help reduce his fever, although he was already looking less flushed and troubled. If her instructions were followed she felt the child would survive.

"A wee scratch and it could have killed him," muttered the boy's mother as she sat down on the edge of the child's bed.

" 'Twas the dirt," said Tatha. "I dinnae ken the why of it, but clean wounds heal better than dirty ones. I have seen the truth of it too often to question it." She carefully set out some medicines on a stool next to the bed. "I will leave ye the leaves to make another poultice or two and some of the blackthorn bark to make a few more cups of tea to ease his fever. God willing ye will need no more than that. If ye dinnae see him growing better in a day or two, fetch me. I think I got all of the poison from his wound, but I cannae be sure. Aye, and keep him, his bedding, and his bandage verra clean."

"Ye didnae stitch it?"

"Nay, 'twas but a wee wound, e'en after I reopened it. And, because it had become poisoned, I think 'tis best left open. 'Twill leave but a wee scar. I could return and—"

"Nay," the woman said, impulsively hugging Tatha. " 'Twill nay trouble the laddie to have a wee scar."

Sir David escorted her out of the tiny cottage, and Tatha frowned up at him when he paused by his horse and stared at her. "Ye dinnae intend to tell me to cease helping people, do ye?"

"Nay." He mounted and held out his hand. "I will take ye back to the keep."

Tatha warily eyed the huge black gelding and slowly shook her head. "Nay, I dinnae think so."

David watched her cautiously back away from his horse then start walking back toward the keep. He considered the look he had seen in her eyes when he had offered to pull her up onto his saddle. Tatha did not ride her pony simply because it was a gift. It was probably the only horse she was not afraid of. He quickly dismounted, grasped his horse's reins, and hurried to catch up to her.

"So, ye are afraid of horses," he drawled, watching her closely, and grinning when she scowled at him.

"I am nay afraid of them," she said, trying to sound confident, even haughty. "Stoutheart is a horse, isnae he?"

"He is a wee, runty pony."

"He gets me where I need to go." She frowned at him. "Just why did ye search me out? Is someone ill or hurt?"

"Nay. I but wished to see how ye used your skills."

"I told ye I would be careful," she reassured him. "My aunt Mairi was most clear about the danger of raising people's fears or attracting the critical eye of some churchman. And I am no heretic or witch."

"I ken it. I begin to think your aunt was a verra wise woman, that she taught ye the good sense and caution my grandmother ne'er really taught my mother."

"And ye still think your mother was killed because she was too brazen about her beliefs? Hold," she ordered him in a quiet but firm voice as she moved toward some lichen growing at the base of a tree. "This makes a good poultice."

David leaned against the tree and watched as she carefully gathered the plant, wrapped it in linen, and placed it in her sack. "I will confess that your questions and observations have made me begin to wonder. I have many people trying to recall all they can of that time. And if 'tis shown that Sir Ranald had a hand in my mother's murder, would your father end the betrothal?''

Tatha sank down to sit on the soft grass and sighed. "I dinnae ken. Nay long ago I would have stoutly cried aye, but that was before he sold me to that drooling old fool, before I realized that he saw me as no more than a means to fill his pockets."

When she lifted a large, stoppered jug from her bag, he frowned slightly. "What is that?"

" 'Tis what I carry water from the well in. 'Twas that water I used to wash the lad's wound the first and last time, and I use only this water in my medicines and teas. I felt 'twas the wisest use of its healing powers.'' Her eyes widened when he dropped down beside her and grasped her by the shoulders.

" 'Tis just water. Clear, fresh, and sweet of taste, aye, but 'tis just water,'' he snapped.

Her expression slowly grew mutinous. Instead of her obstinacy adding to his anger, however, David found his increasingly errant lust creeping to the fore. The frown on her sweet face made him want to kiss the hard line of her lips into softness again. The way her small, firm breasts rose and fell as anger flooded through her had his blood running warm. He cursed softly and pulled her into his arms.

"Sir David," she began to protest, but felt her breath stolen away by the feel of his hard body pressed so close to hers.

"Hush. Ye can scold me later." He brushed his lips over hers. "I have been thinking of this all week."

That one squeaked call of his name was all the protest Tatha intended to make. It was flattering beyond words that he had been considering kissing her all week. She had been thinking the same with an increasing and embarrassing regularity. What lass would not want such a beautiful man to kiss her at least once? Her curiosity demanded satisfaction. How much could one brief stolen kiss hurt?

When she parted her lips in response to the prodding of his tongue and he began to stroke the inside of her mouth, Tatha became acutely aware of the danger of even one kiss. Everything inside of her was responding with a dizzying strength. Her heart pounded, her skin felt warm, the tips of her breasts hardened, and there was an exciting, heated sense of fullness between her thighs. Aunt Mairi had been a blunt, earthy woman who had believed that Tatha should know all about the ways of the flesh, so Tatha knew exactly what was happening to her. This was lust in all its heady, fierce glory. What frightened her was that instinct told her it was also a great deal more. The moment David paused, she scrambled away from him before he could tempt her with another kiss.

"We had best return to the keep," she said as she grabbed her bag, her voice so husky and unsteady she barely recognized it as her own.

David opened his mouth to protest but Tatha was already striding away. He quickly gathered his horse's reins and followed. He had felt the passion in her, seen it in her beautiful eyes. If she thought one brief kiss was the end of it, she was wrong. Tatha Preston definitely tasted like more.

Chapter Five

"Where is Sir David?" Tatha asked, intercepting Leith as he strode toward the stables and wondering why he looked as if he was fighting the urge to laugh.

"Out on a hunt," replied Leith, grinning widely. "I am about to ride out to join him. Do ye have a message for him?"

"Nay. Naught but a question or two about something we discussed earlier. It can wait."

Tatha cursed as she watched Leith disappear into the stables. She had wanted to ask Sir David if he had found out anything more concerning the day his mother had been murdered. Deep in her heart, however, she knew that was not the only reason she sought out the laird of Cnocanduin. It had been only two days since he had kissed her, but she had done little else but think about it. As she tossed and turned on her bed at night she struggled between a fear of

what could happen if she returned to his arms and
an eagerness to do just that. The knowledge her aunt
Mairi had given her about men and women filled her
thoughts with detailed images that made her sweat
with longing.

She fetched some water from the well and hurried
to the herb room she had restored to its former use-
fulness. Tatha already loved the place. At Prestonmoor she had never had such a wonderful place to
work in. As she began to prepare some of her salves,
she prayed she could lose herself in her work. She
was sure she would see Sir David at the evening meal,
and she did not want to meet him while her blood
was still heated from some sensual daydream.

David cursed as his arrow missed its mark again.
Robert stepped forward to neatly bring down the
deer. David had hoped that a day of hunting would
take his mind off a certain flame-haired woman, but
she refused to be shaken from his thoughts. Tatha
had sought shelter at his keep. He had offered her
safety. It would not be honorable to seduce her, but
the constant ache in his body was swiftly pushing aside
honor. He wanted her more than he had ever wanted
a woman before, and with her so constantly close at
hand, temptation was becoming very hard to resist.

He had also tried to distract himself with the puzzle
of his mother's death, but even that was not fully
successful. As little pieces of memory came together,
his own and those offered by others, he did begin to
think that Tatha was right to wonder. He had readily
accepted the tale that fear and superstition had
brought about her death, and now thought that was

because he had always anticipated such an end for his mother. It began to look as if that expectation had blinded him to the truth, had in fact been used against him to keep him from looking any closer. The men he had killed in retribution had deserved their deaths, but he began to think at least one other had his mother's blood on his hands.

"Nay need to look so fierce, laddie," said Robert as he rode up beside David. "There will be meat aplenty."

" 'Tis nay my failing aim I frown o'er," said David. "Of late I have been puzzling o'er my mother's murder."

Robert scratched his grey and brown beard and nodded. " 'Twas an odd thing, but ye took a fine reckoning."

"Aye, but I now wonder if I truly found all who were guilty."

"Sir Ranald did seem verra willing to let ye hunt down and kill three of his clansmen." Robert eyed David warily as he added, "Especially when they claimed they had done naught but kill a witch."

"I ken it. E'en the church would have praised them. Yet ye are right, Sir Ranald was verra amiable when I demanded my reckoning. Too amiable. One of the men was his own cousin."

"Wee Tatha may ken more about Sir Ranald than we do. I have heard a few rumors and I ken he has buried three wives, but I think the mon visited her father's keep from time to time. I think they may be allies or friends. She may have more fact than rumor. Ken the mon better and ye can more clearly judge what may have really happened that day."

" 'Twill certainly help me seek out the truth. Ah,

here comes Leith." He smiled faintly at his cousin, who took the departing Robert's place at his side. "Mayhap ye will bring me luck. My aim has consistently fallen short this day."

"Mayhap your mind is on other things." Leith tried and failed to bite back a smile. "She was asking after you."

For one brief moment David considered telling his cousin he was not interested and not to be such a smugly grinning fool, then decided not to bother. He was interested and suspected too many of his clansmen knew it. "Did she now?"

"Aye. Caught me as I was headed to the stable. She asked where ye were and, after ye asking me where she was nearly every morning since she arrived, I fear I nearly took to laughing. She probably thinks I am daft."

"Ye are. What did she say she wanted?"

"She said she just wished to ask ye a question or two about something ye had discussed earlier."

"Ah, my mother's murder."

"I suppose. She was blushing like fire though." He returned David's sudden grin. "Now, I willnae claim to ken much about the lasses, but it seems to me she wouldnae be so unsettled if that was truly the only reason she was looking for you."

"Nay, it seems that way to me too." David was unable to hide his satisfaction.

"Just what do ye plan to do with the lass?"

"Does it matter to you?"

"Aye, there is the odd thing, but it does."

"I have a suspicion it matters to others too." David shook his head. "Aside from wishing to see her sprawled naked on my bed, I am nay sure. Dinnae frown. She is a weelborn lass under my protection. I ken what honor demands of me. I ken I'd best be prepared to offer her more than a tumble in the heather if I let my passions rule."

"And ye dinnae ken if ye want to do that?"

David muttered a curse and dragged his fingers through his hair, deciding that, if he had to reveal his confusion to anyone, Leith was the safest choice. "She believes as my mother did, although she shows more common sense about it all, and doesnae wave the pennant of the old ways in everyone's face and demand acceptance. She is also betrothed. Although her father sold her like cattle to that swine Sir Ranald, and Tatha makes it clear she doesnae want the marriage, it doesnae change the fact that she has already been promised to a mon. Those two things alone create quite a hedgerow to leap."

"I think ye worry too much o'er her beliefs. She seems to mix the church's teachings with those of her aunt verra weel, yet only lets most people hear her speak of God's will. And aye, she has been weel taught to respect fear and superstition. As for the betrothal, weel, once ye prove Sir Ranald killed your mother, that will be at an end."

Staring at his cousin in surprise, David asked, "Do ye believe Sir Ranald was behind my mother's murder?"

"Aye, always have."

"Why?"

Leith blushed slightly, and there was a wary look in his dark grey eyes. " 'Tis nay something a mon should tell another mon about his mother. She didnae do anything to encourage the fool, ne'er think that, but Sir Ranald wanted her. Aye, wanted her bad and had for years. My mother told me about it, for I was oftimes the one sent to ride guard on your mother, and she wanted me to keep a watch out for the mon. Several times he appeared where your mother was called to go and 'twas clear that he had tried to arrange it. I didnae go with her on the day she was beaten, but I ken it was another ploy by Sir Ranald.''

"Ye ne'er told me of this."

"Your mother didnae want it told. It embarrassed her. I was made to swear myself to silence. Weel, she has been dead now for five long years and ye are finally questioning if ye have the whole truth, and''— he shrugged—"I think we are strong enough to fight the bastard now. We werenae then.''

For a moment David struggled with his anger over such secrets being held from him. Then he let reason rule. Leith, and probably everyone else who had known, had been sworn to secrecy by his mother. He had to respect the fact that such an oath was kept. And at the time, the cold truth was that a battle against Sir Ranald would have resulted only in the complete decimation of his people. They had been weak, the keep nearly in ruins due to battles with the English and raiders, and time had been needed to recover from several years of battle, hardship, and poor harvests. He had also been firm in his opinion that his mother's beliefs had led to her death.

"I am nay sure I would have heeded the truth anyway," he admitted quietly.

"Nay, ye had your own at the time and werenae to be swayed."

"And for that blindness my mother's killer has escaped justice for five years."

"Weel, aye, but ye did quickly seek a reckoning from the ones who actually did the deed. Sir Ranald's guilty of bringing it all about, I am fair sure of that, but he didnae actually bloody his hands."

"He didnae actually strike my mother, but he is guilty, as guilty as the ones who did, and I will now work to prove that."

A cry went up from the men who rode ahead of them. At first David thought it signaled the sighting of some game. The next cry, however, had him tense and drawing his sword. Even as he realized they were under attack, an arrow slammed into his shoulder, propelling him back off his horse. Leith was swiftly at his side, sword in hand and using both their mounts to help shelter him. Just as David gathered enough strength to reclaim his sword and stand up, he knew the brief, fierce attack had already come to an end. A groan of pain escaped him as he sat down on the hard ground.

Leith sheathed his sword and, breaking off the tip of the arrow that protruded out of David's back, yanked the shaft out of his body. Grimly, David clung to consciousness as Leith bathed and bound his wound. It was not only strange that they had been attacked, but that the battle would be so swiftly ended. He needed answers.

" 'Tisnae mortal," Robert said as he walked over and studied David, the rest of the Ruthven men gathered behind him. "The wee lass will soon mend it."

"Who was it?" demanded David, wondering which of the many treaties he had negotiated with the other clans had just been broken.

"Weel now, there is an odd thing. They obviously took pains to hide their clan identity. We killed two, but the wounded were taken away, so there is no one to question. Howbeit"—he held out an easily recognizable clan badge—"one of the dead clearly loved this sad bauble too much to leave it behind."

"MacLeans."

"Aye. Sir Ranald's men. Methinks your sudden interest in your mother's death isnae much appreciated."

"Was anyone hurt?"

"Only ye, and the moment ye flew out of your saddle, the MacLeans retreated. That speaks clear, doesnae it?"

David nodded as Leith helped him stand. "I was the target. Weel, we had best return to Cnocanduin. I need to get this wound seen to. The sooner I am healed, the sooner we can take a reckoning that I now believe has been long overdue."

Ignoring David's complaints, Leith mounted behind him and let someone else lead his horse home. It was not long before David was grateful for the support, the loss of blood weakening him. He smiled crookedly as they rode through the gates of his keep. Now he would see for himself if Tatha's growing reputation as a skilled healer was fully deserved.

Tatha stared down into the water of the well. With the sun high overhead it was one of the few times she could clearly see the water, even see her reflection in its cool depths. Aunt Mairi had once told her that gazing steadily into water could bring on visions, could show one the path one must take. She desperately needed some sign at the moment. The path she wished to run down led straight into Sir David

Ruthven's strong arms, but Tatha was not sure that was the right one.

She grasped the edge of the well. After staring into the water for nearly half an hour and forcing her mind clear of all thought, she was beginning to feel a little unsteady. She was determined to give this water-gazing trick her best try, however, for she desperately needed answers. Was it the well that had drawn her to Cnocanduin or the need to find the truth behind the brutal murder of a healer? Or had fate done its best to lead her to her true mate?

It was just as she began to think it was all foolishness, and the sun had moved enough to begin placing the water back into the shadows, that Tatha noticed something. She could still see her reflection, but it began to slowly change. Soon the newly forming image grew clearer, and Tatha gasped softly when she saw Sir David's handsome face. She continued to stare, deaf and blind to all around her, as if by the sheer force of her will she could make the well show her more.

Another gasp escaped her when, a few moments later, she saw Leith's narrow face off to the side of David's. It was as if he was peering over David's shoulder. Leith's mouth moved and she leaned closer. Suddenly, a hand tightly grasped her by the shoulder and yanked her back, away from the edge of the well. Tatha stared at a scowling Leith, who stood by her side, and felt a little foolish. The only thing that kept her from thinking it was all a dream was that there was no sign of David.

"It looked as if ye were about to fall in," Leith said, quickly taking his hand from her shoulder.

"Nay, I thought I saw something and was just trying

to get a closer look." She suddenly noticed how grim the usually amiable Leith's expression was. "Is something wrong?"

"David has been wounded," he replied, watching with intent interest how her eyes widened in alarm and she grew very pale.

"How?" she demanded as she quickly filled a bucket with water from the well.

"An attack whilst we were hunting." He hurried to keep pace with her as she strode off toward the keep.

Tatha belabored him with questions all the way to the keep. She dragged him into her herb room and ladened him with all the salves, brews, and bandages she thought she would need to treat David. When she burst into David's bedchamber everyone moved out of her way as she hurried to the side of their laird's huge bed. Tatha gave him one slightly frantic but thorough looking-over, then set to work. Her mind told her that he would be all right, that the wound need not be a severely troubling one if it was taken good care of, but her heart remained twisted with fear and concern. By the time she had him stripped, bathed, stitched, and bandaged, everyone had wandered away, feeling sure that their laird was in good hands.

After forcing a weak David to drink an herbal potion, Tatha sat in a chair Leith had set by the bed, and asked bluntly, "Who tried to kill you?"

"MacLean," he replied, smiling grimly when she paled. "Do ye think your betrothed kens that ye are hiding here?"

"Nay. And if he learned I was here, he would either

come and collect me, as is his right, or tell my father to do so."

"Aye, so I thought." Feeling too weak and sleepy to discuss the matter, he closed his eyes, using the last of his strength to issue a stern command. "Ye arenae to leave the keep, nay to step one wee foot outside these walls."

Even as she opened her mouth to argue, she realized it was useless. He had gone to sleep. She felt a little bit like some carrion bird as she sat there watching him sleep, waiting, hunting constantly for some sign of fever. The arrow could have been tainted, or just filthy. Tatha had cleaned the wound as best she could, but it had been over an hour between when the wound had been inflicted and when she had been able to tend to it. Fever was a possibility, and she wanted to be right there to fight it from the start.

Several hours later, Tatha felt herself falling asleep, her eyes stinging from staring at David for so long. She rose from her chair, stretched, and went to the washbowl to scrub her face. As she held a cloth against her eyes, trying to soothe them, she wondered if she should get someone else to sit with David for a while, then shook her head. Time would be lost while they decided whether he even had a fever and then as they came to get her. A fever was best fought from the very beginning, before it could get too high.

As she prepared to sit down again, she suddenly tensed and leaned over David. A soft curse hissed past her lips as she touched his face and felt the warmth on his skin. Her whispered prayers were to go unanswered. The fever was on him, and now the battle would truly begin.

Chapter Six

David winced as he opened his eyes. He felt weak; his thoughts were unclear. Partial memories of cool water against his burning flesh, of a sharp, scolding voice telling him to drink, and of the same husky voice, soft and coaxing, urging him to fight, crowded his mind. Slowly, he became aware of the fact that he was not alone in the bed. He wondered why, when he had been so ill, he would have taken some willing lass into his bed. Then he recalled that he never bedded the lasses at the keep, and at the moment, there was only one he was truly interested in.

Cautiously, he turned his head, fully aware now of the wound in his left shoulder and not wishing to move that arm much at all. His eyes widened when he saw Tatha curled up at his side. Only for a moment was he concerned that he had attacked her while delirious with fever. She was still dressed and lay on

top of the covers. There were dark smudges under
her eyes and her hair was a bright, tangled mass
around her face, but he found her beautiful. He also
knew exactly who had taken care of him during his
illness. As more memories rushed into his mind, he
faintly recalled that his fever had broken during the
night. Leith had been there helping Tatha wash him
down and change the bed linen.

Slowly, so as not to cause himself pain or wake
Tatha, he wriggled himself up into a partially seated
position. His mouth felt as if someone had stuffed a
dirty woolen rag into it and left it there for a few
days. Using some of the wine set at his bedside, he
rinsed out his mouth, gently rubbed his teeth clean
with a scrap of the linen rags piled neatly on the
heavy table, and then had a drink to ease the dryness
in his throat. Although he still felt a bath and a good
hair washing would be most welcome, and were decid-
edly needed, he felt more presentable.

As he made himself comfortable by Tatha's side,
she murmured and huddled closer. When she placed
her small, long-fingered hand on his bare chest, he
drew in a sharp breath. His body's response to that
light touch was startling. Despite the weakness left by
his illness, he grew hard and warm with desire. The
kiss they had shared had told him that he desired
her; he just had not allowed himself to consider how
much. Now there was no ignoring the fact that she
was a fever in his blood.

He gave in to the need to touch her and brushed his
lips over her forehead. Tatha murmured and shifted
closer to him. The feel of her soft breasts pressed
against his side had his heart pounding so hard and
fast he was surprised it did not wake her up. He

touched a light kiss to each of her eyes and felt her lids flutter beneath his lips. Watching her eyes open as he brushed his lips over her cheeks, his breath caught in his throat at the soft warmth visible in their rich blue depths.

"What are ye doing?" she whispered, trapped by the heat in his dark gaze.

"Kissing you." He touched his lips to hers. "Your fever has truly passed, I see."

"Has it? I am nay sure, for I am feeling verra heated." Her husky giggle made him tremble. He thanked God that the woman seemed blissfully unaware of the power she held over him.

"This isnae good for your wound."

"It feels verra good to me."

"I think ye are a rogue."

"Nay, lass. Although there is something about ye that makes me feel like one."

Before Tatha could say anything he kissed her. She hesitated only a moment before slipping her arm around his waist and pressing closer to his hard body, eagerly parting her lips to welcome the invasion of his tongue. The way his hand pressed against her lower back, moving in small circles, warmed her, urging her even closer, until she was almost sprawled on top of him. She trembled and heard herself groan softly in delight when he slid his hand over her bottom, moving her groin gently against his leg. Tatha found herself aching to rip away the covers between them, almost frantic to get as close to him as possible.

"Ye shouldnae," she mumbled in a weak protest as he began to kiss her throat. "Your wound."

"I am barely moving that arm." He slowly ran his tongue over the pulse point in her throat. "Ah, lass, ye taste so sweet. I fair ache to lick every soft, pale inch of ye.''

When she gasped softly in shock, he quickly kissed her again. His whole body trembled with the force of his need for her. The signs that she returned his passion, her rapid pulse, the soft noises she made, the faint tremor in her lithe body, all enhanced his own desire. He cursed his wound, his lingering weakness, and all else that kept him from fully possessing her now while she was warm, willing, and in his arms.

"Weel, 'tis glad I am to see that ye have recovered, cousin,'' drawled Leith.

That highly amused voice acted on Tatha like a dousing of icy cold water. She squeaked in dismay and pulled away from David so fast she tumbled off the bed. Tatha sprawled there on the sheepskin rug, almost afraid to move. She did not think she could add to the embarrassment she felt now, but she was not sure she wanted to risk it. Through her lashes she saw David leaning over the side of the bed to look at her and heard Leith walk to her side. She silently cursed, almost able to feel their amusement.

"Are ye all right, lass?'' asked David, his voice strained as he struggled against the urge to laugh.

"Aye,'' she replied. "I shall just keep my eyes shut for a wee while so that the two of you are allowed the privacy to laugh.''

"Oh, lass, ye need not do that.''

"Nay?'' She slowly opened her eyes to look at a widely grinning David.

"Nay, we dinnae mind having a good laugh right in front of ye.''

When he and Leith burst into hearty laughter, Tatha cursed and scrambled to her feet. Complaining loudly about men who had no respect for a lass's sensitive feelings, she grabbed her shoes and marched out of the room. Even when she slammed the door behind her they did not stop laughing. Tatha cursed again and strode off to her bedchamber.

By the time she had washed, changed her clothes, and flopped down on her bed to rest for a while, her embarrassment and sense of ill usage had passed. Tatha then began to wonder what to do about Sir David and the fierce, blinding desire he stirred inside of her. He was pure temptation from his thick black hair to his long, muscular legs, and she was tired of fighting that.

And why should she fight it? she suddenly asked herself. She was nineteen, a spinster by many people's reckoning. She was free of all bonds and vows. Her own father had sold her into a betrothal to a man she loathed, a man who might well have ordered the murder of David's mother. She dared not hope that some miracle would free her of the obligation her father had thrust upon her. There was still the chance that she would be found and forced to honor the agreement he had made with Sir Ranald. Tatha knew she would never allow David to put himself at risk by placing himself between her and her father.

"And why should I cling to my maidenhead for that disgusting old mon?" she asked herself. "Why should I hold to something my father bartered away without a thought?"

The answer to both those questions came swiftly. She should do as she pleased. There would be consequences if she found herself back in her father's hold, a maiden no longer yet still bound to Sir Ranald, but she could not make herself be concerned about those.

Marriage to Sir Ranald would be such hell, a little sinning now seemed perfectly acceptable.

And she loved, she thought with a sigh. There was no ignoring it, no denying it. Her heart and mind would no longer allow her the comfort of a lie. She loved Sir David. Tatha suspected she had probably started her ill-advised fall into love from the moment she had set eyes on him. The kiss they had shared had sealed her fate.

As she huddled beneath her blanket and tried to relax enough to sleep, she decided that seeing Sir David's face in the well had indeed been a sign. There were several reasons she had been drawn to Cnocanduin, but the well wanted her to see that one of those reasons was most assuredly to meet Sir David. There was also the fact that he could turn her brain to watery porridge with just one warm look from his sinfully dark eyes. As the urge to sleep crept over her, she decided that the next time Sir David took her into his arms she would do her best to stay there. The chance that she might have to leave still loomed like a black cloud overhead, and she was now determined to savor all the joy she could before that time came. And, she mused, a faint smile touching her lips, there was always the chance that Sir David's passion could grow into something deeper. Occasionally miracles did happen.

"She has been sold to Sir Ranald," Leith said quietly as he helped David sit up and put a tray of bread and cheese on his lap.

"I ken it." David slowly began to eat the plain

fare. "To even think of that mon touching her is an abomination."

"Aye, but ye needed to be reminded. 'Twas a bargain made by her father, and the mon may yet find her and demand she hold to it."

"By then I hope to have proven the bastard a murderer."

"It has been five years. That may not be possible."

David frowned at his cousin. "Are ye purposely trying to depress my spirit?"

Leith smiled as he sat on the edge of the bed. "Aye and nay. I but try to make ye see all of the truth, nay just what ye wish to see. Aye, no lass that young and sweet should be given o'er to a mon like Sir Ranald. Howbeit, she is her father's chattel, and unless ye can prove Sir Ranald had a hand in your mother's death, there is naught save war to stop her father from taking her back and handing her o'er to that mon. Aye, and fighting him o'er that right could cause ye more trouble than ye may realize. We dinnae ken how powerful her father is. If he has the king's ear, ye risk outlawry."

A soft curse escaped David and he chewed his bread rather savagely. "I cannae let Sir Ranald have her. Aye, proving he had a hand in my mother's murder may be impossible after five long years, but I now believe him guilty. That also makes me wonder why he wants another healer, and I do believe Tatha's healing skills are one reason the mon seeks her. Mayhap the only reason."

"Have ye learned much about the mon from Tatha?"

"Nay too much aside from the fact that she loathes him. I was seeking time to speak about him when I got wounded. I dinnae believe her aversion to the mon rests solely in his age and ill looks or e'en in simple reluctance to obey her father.''

"Nay, I think there had to be more than that to make her ride away from her home, alone, and with no place to go. She is a high-spirited lass but she isnae a stupid one.''

David considered that as he finished the meal of bread and cheese and drank the wine Leith poured for him. His cousin was right. There was a streak of stubbornness and defiance in Tatha, but that alone would not have driven her to leave her home and family, to travel alone over some very dangerous countryside. She would have stayed and argued the matter if it was simply a matter of not wanting an aging, unattractive husband. Even in the short time he had known her, David had seen how well Tatha could judge people, how easily she could see into their hearts. He strongly suspected she saw something in Sir Ranald that was terrifying enough to make her choose traveling alone, seeking a life elsewhere.

Then he worried that he might just be making excuses, trying to find some reason to hold her. She had said she would leave if her presence brought trouble to his gates, and he believed her. There was a chance his desire for her made him try to find reasons to convince her to stay no matter what happened, perhaps even to excuse his taking up arms to keep her.

After another moment's thought, he inwardly shook his head. Even if he could not get her in his bed, there was reason enough to defy her father's plans for her. In his heart he was sure Sir Ranald was a murderer. David knew he could never hand any lass over to the man.

"Ye are looking verra troubled, cousin," Leith said as he removed the tray and helped David lie down again.

"I but argued with myself. I wondered if lust clouded my reasoning."

"Weel, 'tis clear ye lust after the lass, but e'en if ye didnae, she doesnae deserve the hell of being wed to that bastard."

"True. I wish I had more proof. Then I would send word to her kinsmen. Her father may be a hard mon who thinks naught of selling his daughters like cattle, but I cannae believe he would sell them into a sure grave."

"One would hope not. Then again, I am nay sure how I would feel if I carried the weight of thirteen daughters."

David chuckled. "Aye, 'tis a mighty burden. I dinnae envy the mon. Howbeit, she seemed honestly hurt and e'en confused that he would do this to her, so one must assume that it all came as a surprise, that she ne'er saw him as cruel or completely unfeeling."

"True. And if ye do save her from Sir Ranald's clutches, what do ye mean to do with her?"

"Ah, weel, there is a puzzle. I am in a fever for the lass, a heat I have ne'er suffered from before."

"Then wed her."

"At the moment her father has betrothed her to another mon. The bride price may already have been paid. I could pull us all into the middle of a clan war. Or, as ye said, I could risk outlawry."

Leith cursed and ran a hand through his thick hair.

"Since the mon was willing to sell her to one mon, mayhap he would accept a higher bid."

" 'Tis a thought, but we dinnae ken what was paid for her. Sir Ranald is far richer than we are. E'en if we offered more than he has, he could simply top my bid. There is also the matter of a bargain made. 'Tis nay too honorable to break a bargain."

"I dinnae think it too honorable to sell your daughters off to the highest bidder."

"Most people would see nay real wrong in it. Nay, especially when 'tis discovered just how many daughters the poor mon has. Most would probably think he was mighty clever."

Leith stood up and idly fixed the blankets over David. "Then the only answer is to prove Sir Ranald is a killer or pray that he has given up on her because none can find her."

"Tatha is a skilled healer. Word has probably already begun to spread. It doesnae have to go verra far to reach Sir Ranald's ears." He curled his good hand into a fist and lightly pounded the mattress. " 'Tis a poor time for me to be trapped abed."

"Dinnae waste your strength fretting o'er that. I will work to find proof, at least enough to convince her kinsmen that they made a poor choice."

"Thank ye."

"I do it for her too."

"I ken it."

"And I still think ye would be wise to marry the lass."

David smiled sleepily. "Aye, ye may be right. I wasnae looking for a wife, but mayhap 'tis past time I took one. The fever she can put me in certainly makes her a good choice."

"And ye are no longer troubled by what she is?"

"Ye mean her beliefs? Her healing skills? Nay, not truly. She isnae as caught up in the old ways as my mother. As she says, she is no heathen. Aye, mayhap that is what I must do. Wed her." He closed his eyes. "It begins to look as if I will bed her if she gives me the chance, and honor will demand it anyway."

"If ye mention marriage to her, I think I would try to be a wee bit more romantic," Leith drawled as he started to leave.

David laughed softly, then sighed as he heard the door close behind Leith. The only thing he was sure of concerning Tatha Preston was that he wanted her in his bed, needed her there. If there was a romantic way to explain that, he was too weary to think of one.

He had known she was trouble the moment she had appeared at his gates. A part of him wished he had turned her away, but even if he had not been bound by his vow to his mother, he suspected he would never have done so. From the moment she had frowned at him he had been captivated. He had just tried very hard to fight it. Now he had to admit that he had lost the battle.

Sleep pulled at him and he let it. It was the surest way to regain his strength, and he knew he was going to need it. He had a little flame-haired woman to seduce and woo, a killer to capture, and a father to soothe.

Chapter Seven

"What are ye doing out of bed?" Tatha demanded as she entered David's bedchamber and saw him standing by the window.

"Walking," he answered, and grinned at her look of disgust.

Tatha set the tray of food she had brought on the table by his bed, then placed her hands on her hips and tried to look stern. "Ye had the stitches taken out only yesterday. Ye should be resting."

"I cannae rest any more," he said as he walked to the bed and sat on the edge, reaching for the flagon of ale she had brought him. "I have rested for almost a fortnight. There is too much I must do."

"Ye can tell others what ye need done. Ye need not do it all yourself," she complained as she sat down on the chair facing him.

She tried not to stare at him as he ate. Ever since

Leith had caught them kissing she had approached David cautiously or only when someone else was in the room. They were alone and he was looking very healthy. It made her nervous. Although she had decided not to fight her attraction for him anymore, the thought of letting her passion rule was a little frightening.

Then she frowned. Since that kiss he had not really tried to steal another. She might be ready to succumb to desire, but she suddenly wondered if his had faded. Tatha mused that it would be highly annoying if, now that she had decided to give up her innocence, David was no longer interested in taking it. It would also hurt, but she struggled not to think about how much.

"No need to look so cross, lass," he said. "I willnae do so much that I weaken myself. I ken the benefit of rest."

"Aye, I suppose ye do. Ye have been a verra good patient." She stood up and nervously smoothed down her skirts. "Weel, if ye promise nay to do too much, I will leave ye to your meal."

He caught her by the wrist as she started to move away. "Nay, lass, stay and keep me company." He smiled when she cautiously sat down again. "I have a few questions for ye and have put off the asking of them for far too long."

"What questions?" She clutched her hands together in her lap, afraid that he was about to try to convince her she should return to her father.

"About Sir Ranald."

"I willnae marry the mon."

"I cannae fault ye on that. Nay, I but realized that ye may have knowledge of the mon I dinnae have. He came often to your father's keep?"

"Often enough, although I did my best to avoid him."

"Why?"

"He is a pig. A lecherous dog. The last time he was at my father's keep, I didnae get out of his way fast enough and had bruises in far too many places. The mon feels a lass likes a hard pinch. He savaged a maid or two."

"And your father did naught?"

"They werenae virgins or weelborn lasses. If he kenned what happened, he didnae consider it important. Many a mon doesnae concern himself with what befalls a maid, especially one who is kenned to bed down with a mon or two as the fancy takes her. I am nay sure the lasses told my father what had been done. I had to treat the bruises and welts left, but I didnae say anything either. I dinnae ken why." She frowned. "Mayhap I thought they would or, in my heart, I didnae wish to hear my father actually admit that he didnae care what had happened to them."

"Mayhap if ye had told him, he wouldna have sold ye to the mon."

The way his long fingers almost idly caressed her wrist clouded her mind with desire. Tatha found it a little sad that she could be so deeply affected by a touch, yet he seemed completely at ease. It would have been fine indeed if he were as mindlessly affected by her as she was by him.

"I am nay sure it would have made a difference. My brothers have bedded those lasses, and I think my father has too. The ones Sir Ranald set upon are used by many a mon. I dinnae ken what I thought. I just mended them and tried to forget it all. Again, mayhap I feared it would make no difference. In truth, once I realized I had been sold to that mon, I thought of little else save getting away ere he could get me."

David nodded. "I think I can understand that. Did ye learn much aside from his lechery?"

"He was most interested in my knowledge of herbs." She grimaced. "E'en that interest was based in his lechery. He mostly asked about what I might have to enhance a mon's virility, if there was something I had that could make a mon a better lover. Such as that. I began to wonder if he had some, weel, some male difficulty. I probably should have asked the maids. Mayhap he didnae savage them whilst taking his pleasure, but because he couldnae gain any from them. I just didnae wish to ken much about the mon. Whene'er he was about, I just wished to hide."

Seeing her agitation, he took both her hands in his and kissed each palm. "Dinnae fret, dearling. Ye cannae be expected to have foreseen that it was knowledge ye may be in need of. 'Tis also understandable that ye should shy away from such truths. Then too, mayhap the lasses said naught for they ken such treatment is the cost of their whorish ways."

"No woman deserves such treatment, be she whore or nun."

"I ken, and none of my men would be allowed to behave so, but few would agree with us. Ye cannae change the world. Just your own wee corner of it. Ye also had your own fate to change. Did ye, weel, sense anything else about the mon?"

She tried to concentrate, but David was kissing her hands, her wrists, even the inside of her arms. Tatha knew she ought to yank her hands away and soundly reprimand him for being so bold, but she sat there and let him have his way. She wanted him so badly she could taste it, she thought with a sigh.

"I ne'er liked the mon and wondered why my father tolerated him. Sir Ranald is sly, sneaking, and I dinnae think he holds his honor too dear. I ne'er felt he could be trusted, but it appeared that my father trusted him, so I had to wonder if I was wrong in my judgment of the mon. Or mayhap my father didnae care what the character of the mon was because it didnae matter to what he sought to gain from him. I wish I could tell ye more, but I and my sisters were ne'er allowed to ken what games my father played. He felt it none of our concern who he sought as ally or friend and why."

David decided he had heard all she knew about Sir Ranald, and his thoughts quickly turned elsewhere. Her skin tasted sweet and warm against his mouth. Her eyes had darkened and her breath was uneven, occasionally catching in her throat. It was clear that, despite her attempt to avoid him since his fever broke, her desire for him was still easily stirred. Those hints of passion made his own needs leap to the fore. Cautiously, watching her closely for any hint of rejection, he tugged her out of her seat and into his arms.

There were many reasons why he should not do exactly what he was going to try to do. She was a wellborn lass, a virgin. Her father had betrothed her to another man. It was wrong to take advantage of her innocence and untutored passion. He brutally silenced all qualms as he cupped her face in his hands and gently kissed her. He might not know what he wanted of her or felt for her besides passion, but if he had to wed her to feed the hunger he felt, he would. At the moment it seemed a very small price to pay.

"I dinnae think this is particularly wise," Tatha managed to say as he fell back onto the bed, taking her with him.

"Nay, 'tis probably the greatest of follies. 'Tis madness, but a verra sweet one."

"Aye," she whispered in agreement, shuddering faintly when she saw the desire darkening his eyes.

"I have tried to argue myself out of this hunger time and time again," he said as he turned until she was sprawled beneath him. "It willnae go away."

" 'Tis a torment."

"Oh, aye, that it is."

"I should hit ye and push ye away."

"Aye, ye should." He began to unlace her gown.

Tatha sighed and eased her hands beneath the jupon he wore, shaking as her hands touched his skin. "Mayhap later."

"If ye are going to cry me nay, lass, do it now. I dinnae want ye coming to your senses later and berating me. If ye lie with me now, ken in your mind and heart that it is what ye truly wish to do."

It was the perfect chance to retreat. Tatha knew she should take it. Every rule she had been taught told her to do so. He still offered her only passion, not love or promises of marriage. But as she searched her heart and mind, the only answer she got was a resounding yes. She loved him, ached for him.

"If I suffer any guilt afterward, I promise to keep silent."

"Ah, Tatha, bonny Tatha, I mean to burn away all thought of guilt."

As he moved to take off her shoes and stockings,

his big hands caressing her legs, Tatha decided that was no idle promise. When modesty prompted her to object to the removal of her clothes, he kissed away her protests. She trembled beneath the almost casual touches of his hands as he stripped her. It was not just embarrassment that caused her to tremble, however, when she finally lay naked before him. The heated appreciation in his gaze made her passions soar, and she felt almost beautiful.

David crouched over her for a moment, studying her from her thick, bright hair to her delicate feet. He was breathing so hard, he almost felt dizzy. Her breasts were small, but high and firm, the tips a tempting rose. Her waist was slender, her belly taut, and her hips gently rounded. Her skin was a soft, gently blushed white, begging to be stroked. The light tangle of flame red curls that hid her womanhood promised a warmth his body ached to savor. Her long, slender legs shifted slightly, and he forced his gaze back to her face, smiling at the deep blush coloring her cheeks.

"Ah, lass, ye are bonny. All soft cream and a tempting hint of fire," he said as he rapidly shed his clothes.

"I am too thin."

"Ye are lithe."

"I am too red."

"Nay, ne'er that. I like the hint of fire. It promises me a heat I ache to bury myself in."

She found speech impossible when he shed the last of his clothes. He was big, big and achingly beautiful. Broad shoulders, a smooth, hard chest, a trim waist, and narrow hips all tempted her. A narrow line of black hair started just below his navel, blossomed around his manhood, and lightened to a faint cover over his long, muscular legs. The only thing that caused her to hesitate as he lowered himself into her arms was that fully aroused manhood. She had seen naked men before, some even aroused, unable to control themselves in the depths of their illness, but she had to wonder if Sir David had been blessed with a little more than most men.

"Ye frown," he murmured as he gently trailed kisses over her face. "Am I nay pleasing to your eye?"

"Verra pleasing. Headily so. I am just nay sure ye will fit."

He bit back a laugh. "Oh, aye, I will. 'Twill hurt the first time."

"I ken it. My aunt told me all about such matters." She gave in to the urge to run her hands over his broad, smooth back and felt the hint of a tremor beneath her touch. "She didnae believe maids should be keep ignorant, and also wished me to ken enough nay to be shocked by what I might see as I treated men for illnesses or wounds."

"Weel, 'tis just that ye have caused it to be at its fullest."

"I have seen that too." She smiled at his dark frown, sensing the hint of angry possessiveness behind the look and pleased by it. "I learned that it has a mind of its own and oftimes cannae discern between a touch meant to help and one meant to tease."

"They can be disobedient fellows."

She laughed, but her laughter caught in her throat when he covered her breasts with his big hands. Tatha cried out softly, wrapping her arms around his neck, when he touched a kiss to the hardened tip of each breast. Pure fire shot through her, and she arched into his kisses. When he drew the aching tip of her breast deep into his mouth and began to suckle, she feared her passion bordered on insanity, it grew so fierce.

An almost painful ache grew low in her belly. She felt compelled to rub against him, but it was not enough to ease the demand of her body. Touching him, running her hands all over his lean, hard body, made him less gentle, but it still did not satisfy her. When he slid his hand over her belly and tangled his fingers in the tight curls at the juncture of her thighs, shock was but a brief flare of resistance in her mind. He stroked her and she pressed herself into his hand.

David felt the damp warmth of welcome as he stroked her, watched her whole body shake, and knew he would soon have to possess her. Her passion fed his own, though it did not really need feeding; it was already glutted. He gently eased a finger inside of her, and feared he would spill his seed then and there. She was so hot, so tight. He took several deep breaths to try to calm himself. It was important to bring her pleasure. The more pleasure she was feeling when he did take her, the less pain there might be.

He kissed her as he stroked her, his body trembling as he fought to control his own raging need. The moment he felt her tense, then shudder with her impending release, he spread her legs wide and plunged into her. He met her maidenhead, gritted his teeth, and breached it.

Tatha cried out, but she was not sure if it was from the strength of the pleasure raging through her or the brief, sharp stab of pain that cut through it. She wrapped her limbs around him, but was it to steady herself or to pull him closer? Tatha felt confused by the feelings assaulting her.

"Lass, are ye all right?" he asked, as he held himself

still, sweating from the effort, allowing her body to adjust to his invasion.

"I think so." She wrapped her legs more securely around his hips and cautiously arched upward. " 'Tis wondrous strange."

That slight movement drove him deeper inside of her and he groaned, not sure he could put two coherent words together. "I was hoping it would be a wee bit better than strange."

"Oh, it is." She placed her hands on either side of his face and touched a kiss to his lips. " 'Tis beyond words. 'Tis worth every penance I might be forced to pay."

David laughed shakily, then began to move. When Tatha gave a soft cry of pure delight and immediately met his thrust, he lost all ability to go slowly. He gave a shout of triumph and deep joy when he felt her body tighten around him. Slipping his hand between their bodies, he searched out that spot that could stir her passion to new heights and stroked her toward a second release. The way her lithe body moved almost frantically around him as she reached passion's heights was enough to pull him into that abyss along with her.

It was a long time before sanity returned and David realized he had collapsed on top of her. He suspected he ought to move, but he felt too wrung out to make the effort. The way she idly stroked his back with her small, soft hands implied that she had no objection to his position, so he took another moment or two to try to recover.

Slowly he eased the intimacy of their embrace, propped himself up on his elbows, and looked at her. The passion they had shared had gone far beyond his heated imaginings. He had suspected there was a fire in her, but had never suspected it would burn so brightly for him. The way she had made him feel was startling, even a little frightening. He took some comfort in the fact that she seemed to feel the same blinding hunger.

He smiled at her, and to his delight she smiled back. "Weel, do ye think it was worth a penance or two?" he asked, hoping a light tone would hide the uncertainty he suddenly felt.

Tatha fought to hide her disappointment. It was foolish to think he would suddenly spout love words and declare undying devotion just because his lust had been satisfied. The only thing that eased her disappointment was the certainty that he had been as swept away as she had. Innocent she might be, but instinct told her he had shared the ferocity of the passion that had swept her.

"Oh, aye, one or two," she drawled.

"Impertinent wench."

He rose from the bed and, ignoring her blushes, cleaned them both off. As he returned to the bed, she started to get up, and he pulled her back into his arms. "Where are ye going?"

"To my bedchamber," she replied even as she let him tuck her up against his side.

"Nay, ye will stay here."

"Are ye sure that is wise?"

"Nay, but I dinnae care. I have ached to have ye right here since ye first stormed my gates. I have ye now and ye willnae leave."

She cuddled up to him and bit her tongue against the words she wanted to say. Although she had no real objection to sharing his bed, she was a little concerned about becoming his leman. There was also the matter of her father and Sir Ranald. Those troubles still lurked and could easily pull her from his arms. She closed her eyes and forced herself not to think at all. Ignoring the problems and doubts would not make them go away, but, for a little while, she was determined not to let them steal any of the joy she now felt.

Chapter Eight

Tatha gently tied the bandage around the warrior's now cleaned and stitched leg wound. She struggled to return his smile of gratitude as she put all of her things back into her small sack. This was the seventh man she had had to tend to in almost as many days. David might not wish to admit that he had been plunged into the midst of a war with Sir Ranald, but it was clear that was what had happened.

At the moment, no one had died. The war as yet consisted of small forays made by Sir Ranald's men that were quickly retaliated against by David and his men. In truth, Sir Ranald was faring far worse than Sir David, for his men were dying. That did not really make Tatha feel much better. It was simply a matter of time before David's men also began to die.

As she walked back to her herb room, she struggled to decide what was the best thing to do. Tatha did not think this was because of her. Even if Sir Ranald had guessed she was here, the fighting was because David was too interested in what had really happened to his mother. The fact that Sir Ranald would try to put an end to that curiosity rather proved his guilt. Nevertheless, she had been the one to stir David's curiosity, to make him want to take another look at his mother's murder. So whether Sir Ranald was after her or not, this was still her fault.

There was also the matter of what existed or did not exist between her and David. For a month now they had blithely indulged their passions despite the increasing turmoil around them. She had worried that the people of Cnocanduin would be disgusted by her, but they showed no sign of that at all. They actually seemed quite pleased that she was sharing their laird's bed. Tatha had the sinking feeling that they foresaw a marriage, believed that Sir David had finally chosen a lady to be his wife and bear him an heir. She wondered if she ought to remind them that she came from a family of thirteen daughters. Begetting a son off her might be nothing less than a miracle.

Cursing softly, she sat down on the stool next to her worktable. While it was true that the fighting, small as it was, was not because of her, she could not help but wonder if she could put an end to it. If nothing else she might be able to draw Sir Ranald away from Cnocanduin. She might even be able to distract the man long enough for David to get the proof he needed, proof that would allow him to come out against Sir Ranald in force. David would probably do that now, and be justified, if not for her. He was in danger of having his motives questioned as long as she was at Cnocanduin, and especially for as long as she shared his bed.

She moved to begin work on some salves, hoping that work would help her think more clearly. Instinct told her that her presence was tying David's hands, but she needed to be sure in her heart. There was always the chance that she was trying to find a reason to leave him. Although she loved him more than was wise and she found only pleasure and joy in his arms, her heart could not long endure being no more than his leman. Slowly but surely, his lack of love and promises of a future for them would steal away that pleasure and joy. However, if she walked away from him, she wanted it to be for a better reason than the fact that she was too much of a coward to stay and hope for more than passion from him.

"We should just attack the fool and wipe him off the face of the earth," snarled Leith as he sat down at the head table in the great hall.

David slouched in his chair, sharing Leith's frustration, but trying not to give in to it. "We cannae. I still hold Tatha here. If we attack and win, and that becomes known, all my reasons for fighting the mon become questionable."

"Why? He killed your mother. This sly war he fights with us is because ye went searching for the truth. It proves his guilt."

"I believe it does. Yet if I claim that as my reason, will I be believed when I have no hard proof, or will it be thought I but try to make excuses for why I keep his betrothed wife in my bed? And to claim that before all will only dredge up all the ill talk of my mother.

All the whispers of witches and heresy will be renewed. Aye, and once those fears are revived, how long will it be before they threaten Tatha?"

Leith cursed and dragged his hands through his hair. "Aye, I can see the danger of having people think of witches and Cnocanduin in the same breath whilst Tatha resides here." He frowned. "Ye dinnae think Sir Ranald kens she is here, do ye?"

"He may have guessed by now, but this battle was begun ere he could have e'en heard the first whispers about a new healer at Cnocanduin. If he has heard something, I wonder if he remains uncertain, for it would give him a perfect reason to attack us in force. Aye, he would be within his rights to have me killed and need not even do so honorably. No one would fault him, for I have given him a grave insult by bedding his bride."

"Since ye have already insulted him by bedding her, why have ye not wed her?"

"I must needs summon a priest for that, and if Sir Ranald is still in doubt, word of a marriage would quickly end it."

"So we must endure this constant harassment."

"For the moment." David frowned and sipped his ale. "I begin to think I should send word to Tatha's father, tell him of my suspicions of the mon."

"But then he will ken where she is, and if he doesnae care or doesnae believe you, he may weel join forces with Sir Ranald."

"I need not mention Tatha. If I send word of my suspicions to all who ken Sir Ranald, it will appear that I but try to get the truth out, to win my right to openly fight him."

"That may work."

"There is but one problem with that plan."

"What?"

"It will stir up the ill talk about my mother again unless I can give some reason, other than claims of witchcraft, for Sir Ranald wanting my mother dead."

"She refused his suit."

"Aye, that could be enough. Something Tatha said makes me think there was more, however. She thinks he may have some problem with his manhood." He quickly told Leith all Tatha had said about what potions and herbs Sir Ranald was most interested in and what the man had done to the maids. "I believe the mon may be impotent and somehow thinks a healer can cure him, either with her healing skills or even through the bedding of her."

"Aye, 'tis possible. Despite three wives, he has but the one son, and he was born of the first wife, shortly after the wedding. There were no other births, no other breedings. It may even explain how three of his wives died but nay in childbed, which is what steals the life of most wives."

"If that is the way of it, then one must wonder what would happen to Tatha if he gained hold of her and she couldnae cure him."

"Another dead wife."

David nodded, his hands clenching on his tankard so hard his knuckles whitened. He ached to simply kill Sir Ranald, but he had to think of more than the man's threat to Tatha. His people were now in danger as well. If he acted too rashly and brought condemnation upon himself, it could cost his people dearly, even to their lives. He could not allow himself to forget that Sir Ranald had more power than he did, a closer relationship to the king, more allies, and more coin. Sir Ranald was a man one had to have firm, incontrovertible proof against.

"'Tis a shame he is too much the coward to join his men in these attacks," murmured David. "All our problems would be solved if he met his death whilst raiding my lands."

"Aye, 'twould free Tatha and end this war that isnae a war," agreed Leith. "Ah, weel, winter fast approaches and mayhap that will give us some respite. Time to come up with proof or a plan."

"Aye, although 'tis irritating beyond words to pray that weather will be your ally."

"And if Tatha is freed? Do ye mean to wed her or has the fire that drew ye to her already begun to wane?"

"Oh, I will wed her, and nay just because all of ye seem to think I should. Nay, the fire hasnae waned and I begin to think it ne'er will."

"Do ye love the lass?"

David shrugged. "I dinnae ken. I am nay sure love is much more than a troubadour's song. I like the lass and she warms my bed. Why fret myself to see what, if anything, that means?"

"Weel, when ye do get around to telling her, be a wee bit softer in your speech. There are times when pretty words will gain ye more than the cold truth."

As David sprawled on his bed and watched Tatha brush her damp hair dry before the fire in his room, he thought about what Leith had said. Pretty words. He was not very skilled in flatteries and soft words, but he decided it was past time he gave it a try. When he was finally able to ask Tatha to be his wife, and he refused to believe that time would not come, he wanted her to show no hesitation in accepting. Some soft words now might well ease the way. It had been arrogant to think that, because she shared his bed, she would simply fall in with whatever plans he made for their future. Passion could have made her as heedless of the future as it had him.

It troubled him a little that she did not speak of love, did not tell him anything of what might be in her heart. Although he offered her only mumbled words of passion, he wanted more from her, unfair as that might be. He wanted her bound to him, tied in a way that would always keep her at his side. His sense of possessiveness was strong, and he made no attempt to understand why that should be, just accepted it.

When Tatha walked to the bed, shed her robe, and hastily slid under the covers, the color of a lingering modesty tinting her cheeks, he smiled and pulled her into his arms. He would make her love him. The passion she felt for him was easy to see, and he felt no doubt about its strength. He wanted more. Marriage would tie her to him by the laws of the Church and the king, but he wanted her heart to be his. Instinct told him that, if Tatha gave her heart, it would be forever. He wanted that depth of commitment.

"Lass, ye are the bonniest, softest woman I have e'er held in my arms," he murmured as he warmed her slender throat with soft kisses.

"I am nay sure ye ought to be mentioning those other women just now," she drawled.

David considered his words and inwardly grimaced, but since he could not claim to have lived the life of a monk, he decided to fumble on. "Not e'en to say that ye put them all in the shade? That ye make them such dim memories I cannae recall their names or faces?''

"Weel''—she slid her hand down his stomach and tentatively curled her fingers around his erection, enjoying the tremor that shook his body—''tis flattering in a way. 'Tis a pity, is it not, that I cannae repay the compliment in kind.'' She grinned at his brief look of disgust. ''I do think that ye may be the brawest laddie I have e'er seen.''

"Aye, I am.'' He laughed softly, then murmured his pleasure over the way her soft stroking made him feel. ''Ye are making me feel more braw by the moment.''

Tatha smiled against his skin as she kissed his chest. She had finally come to a decision. She would leave Cnocanduin. It would not solve all of David's troubles, but it would free his hands to act as he must to protect his people. It would rip her heart out to leave him, but it had to be done. Tonight, however, she intended to soak herself in the pleasure he gave her so freely. She planned to crowd her mind with so many memories it would be years before they began to dim, if ever.

Cautiously, alert for any sign of shock or disgust, she kissed her way down to his taut stomach. She had every intention of leaving her memory firmly planted in David's mind. Her free-speaking aunt had told her of the things men liked, and she decided it was time to put some of that knowledge to the test. She touched a kiss to the inside of each of his strong thighs, then slowly ran her tongue along the thick, hot length of him. The way he groaned the word *aye* and curled his fingers in her hair to hold her where she was told her clearly that he liked that. Tatha grew even bolder.

David clutched the sheets in his fists and struggled to cling to his control. He wanted to savor what she was doing to him for as long as he could. When the moist heat of her mouth enclosed him, he arched up off the bed and knew his control would not last much longer.

Finally, his endurance broke. With a harsh cry he pulled her up his body. When she straddled him, he slid his hand between her thighs and growled his pleasure when he found her already damp with welcome. He plunged into her and savored her gasp of pleasure. She quickly learned the art of riding her man and took them both to a shuddering climax.

After washing them both clean, he slipped back into bed and pulled her close. "Tatha, I mean no insult, but where did ye learn of that?"

"My aunt," she replied, idly smoothing her hand over his broad chest. She loved the feel of him, loved his scent and his taste. "She was an earthy woman and much enjoyed her time in her husband's bed, sadly short as it was. She was still a young woman when he died and, although she ne'er married again, I believe she took a lover or two."

"And she spoke freely of such things?"

"Aye. She ne'er saw the sense of keeping maidens so ignorant. Aunt Mairi felt knowledge protected a lass against seduction and would aid her in keeping her mon's bed warm."

"I seduced you," he said, feeling a pinch of guilt.

"We seduced each other."

He grinned and pushed her onto her back. "And did your aunt tell ye what a woman likes?"

"Some," she answered, blushing faintly. "I think she felt I would learn what I liked all by myself."

She shivered with pleasure as he trailed kisses over her breasts. Curling her fingers in his hair, she held him close as he lathed and suckled her breasts, restirring her passion. Tatha dared not even think about how much she was going to miss him.

"Ye like that," he murmured against her stomach.

"Oh, aye."

"Weel, let us see if ye like me tasting your secrets as much as ye seemed to like tasting mine."

It took but one stroke of his tongue to make Tatha cry out her pleasure over his intimate kiss. Modesty fled hand in hand with sanity. She offered herself freely to his mouth and let her passions rule. He took her to the heights of pleasure, then, barely allowing her to catch her breath, drove her close to the brink again. Even as she demanded he join her this time, he sat up, dragging her with him. He straddled her across his lap and plunged into her. Bending her back over his arm, he slowly drew the tip of her breast deep into his mouth. Tatha cried out as she lost all sense of where she was, knew only the pleasure raging through her. As her release shuddered through her, she was faintly aware of his cry signaling that she did not travel to that pinnacle alone.

Later, as she watched him sleep, she fought against the urge to weep. There would be time for tears, too much time. There were still several hours before dawn, and she decided she would let him rest for a short time, then draw him back into her arms for one last taste of the joy they could share. She would be exhausted come the dawn, but she could not bear to spend her last night with him only sleeping.

* * *

Dawn was but a hint of color on the horizon as Tatha led her pony out through the gates of Cnocanduin. Some of the men on the wall called to her, but seemed to accept her explanation that she was just going to collect some herbs. She thanked God that they were, perhaps, too sleepy to recall that David did not want her riding out alone. Leith would have remembered, but luck was with her and he was still abed.

She mounted her pony and rode toward the forest to the north. Although she felt as if she were slowly dying, she kept on riding. When she had first arrived she had sworn that, if her presence caused Sir David any trouble, she would leave, and it was time to hold to that vow. Her whole body ached with the excesses of the night, but she savored that discomfort. She had made some very warm memories, and she would force herself to be satisfied with that.

Chapter Nine

"Where is Tatha?" asked Leith as he answered David's sharp command to enter his bedchamber and looked around.

"I think she has fled," David replied as he buckled on his sword.

"Fled? What did ye do?"

"Naught, curse it."

He sighed and ran his hand through his hair. When he had awakened to find his bed empty he had not given it much thought, but a swift search through the keep and a few questions had revealed that Tatha had left at dawn. Loudly berating the guards who had let her ride away alone had not eased the sudden fury and fear that had seized him. He had returned to his bedchamber to arm himself, thinking to ride out after her, but now he wondered if that was wise.

After the passionate night they had spent he had

found it hard to believe she would leave him. Then he had begun to see that she had been saying good-bye. The question was, Why? The only thing that lay beyond the walls for Tatha was danger. What would make her wish to risk discovery by Sir Ranald? He simply could not believe it was something he had done or said. No woman could make love to a man as thoroughly and as often as she had if there was no longer some feeling for him. That left him with no answers, however.

"I dinnae ken why she has left. She told me naught, gave me no hint that she considered leaving," David said. "She simply crawled out of my bed and rode away."

"Were ye going after her?" Leith asked, glancing at David's sword.

"That was my first thought, but now I wonder if that would be wise. Sir Ranald is trying to kill me. Riding o'er the countryside searching for some fool lass is a sure way to give him an easy target."

Leith frowned as he followed David out of the room. "Do ye think she has decided to go back and face her father?"

"Nay," David answered as he entered the great hall, not really hungry but knowing he needed to eat something to keep up his strength. It could prove to be a very long and exhausting day. "The fools who let her ride out say she headed toward the forest to the north of us."

"Toward Sir Ranald's lands?" Leith sat down and began to fill his trencher with food. "Nay, there is no reason for her to go to him. He is why she ran away from her family."

"I dinnae think she goes to him. She just goes."

The food David ate tasted like ashes in his mouth, but he forced himself to keep eating.

"Mayhap she grew weary of being your leman with no hint that she would e'er be more than that."

David frowned as he considered that possibility for a moment, then shook his head. "Nay. I believe Tatha would have said something. She slipped away ere I woke because she intends to do something she did not think I would agree with. Yet I cannae believe she would willingly walk into Sir Ranald's grasp. She kens that her presence here isnae why he is tormenting us."

Leith stared at David for a moment, then said quietly, "Nay, but she may have wit enough to ken that she is the reason we dinnae strike back fast and hard."

After a moment of thought, David cursed, then took a deep drink of ale to soothe his agitation. "Aye, she has wit enough. That is it. She saw that she was tying our hands. God's beard, she may have e'en heard us say so. She has unbound us."

"Aye, but could be riding straight into trouble."

"I believe she may have a true skill for that. Weel, we shall gather a few men and see if we can find her."

"And then what?"

"And then I drag her back here and tie her to the bed."

Tatha winced and rubbed at the small of her back. After such a rigorous night, even a few hours of riding were proving to be more than she could bear. Riding north, so close to Sir Ranald's lands, was probably not the wisest route to take, but she had felt it was the one David would be least inclined to follow. Now, however, she wished to rest and did not dare to. She needed to get as far away from both men as she could as fast as she could.

As she prodded her little pony over the rocky trail, she frowned. It was very quiet, too quiet. She suddenly realized that none of the sounds one usually heard in the forest were there. It was as if someone had just thrown a smothering blanket over the area.

Her heart began to beat faster as fear crept over her. This was a warning, but of what? She touched her knotted cord, silently trying to pull forth the protection it promised, as she looked around. Just as she began to convince herself that she was succumbing to nerves, she saw a movement off to her right.

A man on a horse slowly became visible through the trees. Tatha turned her horse to the left, only to see another. Within moments she was surrounded.

"If ye mean to rob me," she said, struggling to remain at least outwardly calm, "ye will find some verra poor gain. I have little or naught that would be of profit for you."

"Nay, Lady Tatha, we dinnae mean to rob you," said a tall, thin man with a huge beak of a nose as he rode closer and tore her reins from her hands.

"How do ye ken who I am?" she demanded even as she frowned at the man, something about him striking her as faintly familiar.

"I oftimes visited your father's keep with your betrothed. I am Baird, one of Sir Ranald's men."

"How unfortunate for you."

Ice trickled through her veins, but she fought the urge to scream in terror. She had obviously ridden right into the midst of one of Sir Ranald's raiding

parties. She was right back where she had started from
when she had fled her father's keep. Her freedom had
been short, glorious, but short. The only hope she
had, and it was a very small one, was that she would
have a chance to speak to her father before the wedding. She might be able to make him listen to the
truth about Sir Ranald.

"Weel, I shallnae trouble ye," she said, trying and
failing to tug her reins free of Baird's grasp. "I was
just riding home to my father. Mayhap I will see ye
again at the wedding."

"Clever lass, but ye cannae fool me. Ye fled your
father's keep near to two months ago. Ye have no
intention of returning there. So we shall just take ye
to your betrothed and let him deal with you."

"Sir Ranald is nay my betrothed."

"He paid a handsome bride price for you."

"Then he can just get it back, for I havenae agreed
to wed the bastard."

She scowled at the man as he laughed and began
to lead her north toward Sir Ranald's keep. She knew
most people would consider her opinion that the
betrothal was void unless she agreed to it pure nonsense, but she did not appreciate being mocked. Then
she felt the weakening touch of defeat. What did
suffering a little mockery matter when she would
undoubtedly soon be dead?

David stood beside Leith staring down at the tracks
upon the ground and not wishing to believe what
they told him. Tatha had ridden right into the hands
of Sir Ranald's men. David felt sure she had not done
it on purpose, but that mattered little. She had been

taken out of his reach, and he did not think there
was any way he could take her back.

Without a word he mounted and headed back to
his keep. The tracks were old enough to tell him that
there was no point in trying to run her or her captors
down. She was gone, and he found that cold truth
too difficult to deal with, especially with all of his men
staring at him.

Once back at Cnocanduin, David went straight to
his bedchamber and poured himself a large tankard
of ale. By the time he had downed a second one he
felt a bit more in control, was even able to greet
Leith's entrance with some appearance of calm.
Inside he felt as if some animal were tearing him
apart. He wanted to rage, but knew that would gain
him nothing.

"He will hurt her," Leith said, helping himself to
some ale.

"I ken it," David whispered, shuddering a little as
his raging emotions tried to break free of the
restraints he had put upon them.

"Is there naught we can do?"

"I have already sent word to her father concerning
Sir Ranald's part in my mother's murder. Mayhap
he will bestir himself to change his mind about the
marriage."

It was not enough. David wanted to go to Sir
Ranald's keep and tear it apart stone by stone until
he found Tatha. He wanted to tear Sir Ranald apart as
well. Neither could be done, but the only alternatives
were meek, paltry ones that gave him little hope and
no ease.

Somehow she had burrowed herself into his heart, beneath his very skin, and he had not seen it. He had savored her passion and enjoyed her company, but had never allowed himself to look beyond that. In his mind all had been settled. He would marry the woman who so gloriously warmed his bed and made him smile, despite her lack of dowry, despite her red hair, despite the fact that she was left-handed, and even despite the beliefs she had that caused him such unease. Not once had he wondered why he would. Not once had he considered losing her. Now that he had, he felt a cold emptiness he feared could prove permanent.

He loved her. He saw that now. Now that it might be too late. David cursed himself and his blindness. He should have simply wed her and spit in the eye of all the possible consequences.

"Mayhap ye should send word to her father again," said Leith, watching his grey-faced cousin closely.

"Why? If claims that the mon he sold her to is a killer willnae move him, what else may?"

"Mayhap ye should tell him that she was here, tell him all she said about what Sir Ranald sought from her, about the maids. Is it nay worth the gamble? It may be all that is needed to make him recall his responsibilities as a father, and we could use his support. Aye, if we had it, we could go to Sir Ranald's keep and tear her out of his grasp."

"It will also tell him that Sir Ranald may weel have a righteous grievance against the Ruthvens."

"I ken it. I dinnae think ye will find anyone here who willnae be more than ready to take that chance. I would be willing. Donald would be, for his Sorcha is still carrying her bairn, grows rounder and heavier

with it every day, and 'tis a lively one. He tells us all
of its every kick. Robert's back is better, and he has
discovered a new way to enjoy his bonny wife. The
blacksmith near to kisses the ground your lady walks
on, for his son is alive and getting into trouble again
as all wee lads should.''

"So weel loved in such a short time?"

"Aye, by all of us, and I think mostly by you. She
saved your life as weel."

"Aye, she did. Ye had best be sure of this, Leith.
If that fool father of hers has no caring for her at all,
thinks naught of who she weds but only of the coin
weighting his purse, we could be setting ourselves in
the midst of a bloody feud with no hope of allies."

"I am sure. Send him word. If he proves to be such
a heartless bastard that he cannae e'en come to judge
the truth for himself, then once we are done with Sir
Ranald, we will go to his keep and steal all her sisters."

David laughed, surprised he could do so. Then he
realized that he had some hope now. Even if Tatha's
father did not join him, he had the support of his
people. Pulling them into the midst of a feud, something that could be long and bloody, for the sake of
a lass who was not a Ruthven, was something he had
been reluctant to do. He had feared that he would
be leading his people to their deaths simply to keep
a lass he wanted. It was clear that his clan wanted her
as well.

"Weel, find the lad who took the last message to
that fool Tatha must claim as her father," David
ordered. "I will try once more to rouse the mon's
conscience. We willnae wait long for him, however,
so we had best begin to plan our attack as weel."

"Dinnae worry, David." Leith briefly clasped his

cousin's shoulder in a gesture of sympathy. "We will get the lass back."

David prayed his cousin's confidence was trustworthy. He dared not think on all that could happen to Tatha while she was in Sir Ranald's hold, nor what the man might do to her when he discovered she was no longer a maiden. Or, if he had guessed correctly about what ailed the man, how he would treat her if she could not cure his problem. All he could do was plan, and pray she could keep herself safe until he could get to her.

"Where is my daughter?"

David stared at the huge scowling man standing in his bailey, only briefly glancing at the well-armed force he had brought with him. It had been four long days since he had sent the last message to Sir Malcolm Preston, and he had begun to lose hope. It was hard to believe this angry brute of a man was Tatha's father, but David was willing to accept any help he could get.

"As I wrote you, she is in Sir Ranald's hands," David answered. "I am preparing to go and take her back." His eyes widened slightly as a slender, dark-haired girl stepped up next to the man.

"One of my other daughters, Elspeth." Sir Malcolm scowled down at the girl. "She made me bring her."

David almost smiled. Perhaps, in his gruff way, Sir Malcolm was not as heartless as they had all thought. If such a tiny lass could not only defy the man but make him accede to her wishes, there might well be some softness beneath the scowl. He glanced at his cousin, thinking to silently share his humor, only to find himself fighting the urge to gape. Leith was star-ing at the slender girl as if some angel had just alighted and offered him the keys to God's kingdom. When he turned back to look at the girl, she was staring back at Leith and blushing.

"Pleased to meet ye, Lady Elspeth," he said as he took her hand in his and lightly kissed it, breaking her and Leith of the spell they seemed to be caught in. "Your concern for your sister can only be praised." He looked back at Sir Malcolm, who curtly introduced his son Douglas. "Let us go to the hall and have some ale and food whilst we discuss this matter. Not a long discussion, mind, for I am preparing to ride out after Tatha."

"Oh? And ye think ye have that right, do ye?" demanded Sir Malcolm as he, Douglas, and Elspeth followed David and Leith into the keep.

"I promised her my protection. Aye, and many here feel they owe her."

Sitting down and helping himself to a large tankard of wine, Malcolm grunted. "So she has been going about healing hurts, has she?"

As he too sat down and filled his tankard, David nodded. "She is truly skilled in the healing arts."

"Aye, her aunt taught her weel." Sir Malcolm's eyes narrowed. "Though some called the old crone a witch, and 'twas something whispered about Tatha from time to time."

"We are nay so foolish here."

"Nay? Wasnae that what got your mother killed?"

"Papa," Elspeth snapped. "I thought we came here to help Tatha. I dinnae think that will be easy if ye make the mon want to cut your throat."

"Ye are verra saucy for such a wee lass," he grumbled. "I but speak the truth."

"Aye, ye do, and 'tis best ye recall who decried my mother as a witch and whose men killed her," David said coldly. "That same mon now holds your daughter."

"A lass who is betrothed to him." Sir Malcolm held up his hand when both Elspeth and David started to speak. "A mistake. I see that now. The mon was old and ugly, but he was wealthy, powerful, and would have given the lass a household to lead, mayhap e'en a bairn or two. Or so I thought. Your last message has me thinking the old bastard was hiding the truth about himself. I talked with the maids and they confirmed your suspicions. Told the fool lasses they should have come to me. E'en a whore doesnae deserve to be beaten near senseless just because some old goat cannae get his rod to stand up." He grinned when Elspeth groaned, blushed, and hid her face behind her hands. "Ye wanted to come along." He blithely ignored the glare she gave him and looked hard at David. "Of course ye ne'er touched my lass yourself."

"I mean to get her back and marry her," David said, his look almost daring Sir Malcolm to argue with him.

"Weel, there could be a cost," Sir Malcolm began.

"Nay, Father," Douglas said. "No more. Ye have set that poor lass in the midst of deadly trouble with your fine plan. 'Tis clear it isnae the way to do things."

"Ye were ne'er fond of it from the start. Isabel and Bega didnae mind."

"Isabel and Bega would have wed with the Devil

himself and any one of his minions if it meant they wouldnae be spinsters any longer," snapped Elspeth.

"Aye, and the ones who bought them were nay old, useless men who may have blood on their hands," said Douglas. "I wonder now if all of his wives died of illness as he claimed or were set in their graves because he blamed them for his lack."

"Insolent lot," Sir Malcolm grumbled, but he nodded as he looked back at David. "All right. If ye want the fool lass ye may have her. Now, how do we get her back from that old bastard?"

Two hours later, as the combined forces of the Prestons and the Ruthvens rode out of Cnocanduin, David felt his hopes rise. He nudged Leith, pulling his cousin's gaze from the slender girl waving them farewell from the walls of the keep. David had caught Douglas grinning at both Leith and Elspeth, revealing that he too had noticed the bewitchment that had apparently seized the two. He was not sure it was something that ought to be revealed to Sir Malcolm just yet, however.

"What ails ye, cousin?" he demanded, biting back a grin when Leith blushed bright red.

"Tatha's sister is a bonny lass," Leith muttered.

"Aye, she is, and she smiles quite freely at you."

"I have no coin."

"Dinnae fret on that. It appears the father isnae as fierce in his ways as we thought, and the brother has clearly ne'er approved of the business. When we get Tatha back we will turn our attentions to getting ye the wee, bonny Elspeth."

"We will get the lass back," Leith said firmly.

David just smiled and prayed that his cousin was right to feel so confident. Tatha had been in Sir Ranald's grasp for four long days. She was a clever lass, resourceful and brave, but how long could she keep herself safe from the man? He had been tormented day and night with thoughts of all that could be happening to her, and he had to stop, for it was threatening to make him useless. David forced himself to fix his thoughts on the battle ahead and nothing else, a battle he must win.

Chapter Ten

Tatha winced as the light the guard carried stung her eyes. When Baird had delivered her to Sir Ranald, that man had glared at her for several minutes, then had her tossed in the dungeon. There she had been left, alone and in the dark. If she was right and the meager offering of sour ale and stale bread that arrived was really only sent once a day, she had been kept in the dungeons for four days. That also meant that Sir Ranald's silent, glaring visits also came but once a day, for she had endured those long moments of glaring four times. She was being punished.

She sighed as the silent guard changed her privy pot, left her a bowl of scummy water to wash in, and set down her meager meal. It was maddening to sit there alone, shrouded in silence and darkness, but she tried to be hopeful. At least Sir Ranald was not trying to assert his husbandry rights before the wedding. And if he was waiting to marry her it had to be because her father was coming. Her father had to frown on this treatment. The man had never even struck them when they were naughty, for all he roared and grumbled. Sir Malcolm could never be called a loving father, but he had never been cruel, and she prayed this would shock him into listening to her pleas.

She had barely choked down her unappetizing meal when another guard arrived with a large bucket of hot water, some of her clothes, and what looked to be soap and a drying cloth. He set them inside her cell, then turned his back. For a moment Tatha stared at the things he brought, then at his stiff back. Surely he did not expect her to bathe and change while he stood there? It quickly became clear that he expected exactly that. Praying that he had been ordered not to glance her way, she turned her back on him and began to wash. She even rinsed out her hair, then rubbed it dry with the cloth and combed her fingers through it. It was a tangled mess, but at least it was a little cleaner.

"Are ye done?" demanded the guard.

"Aye," she muttered as she tied off the last of her laces. "Now what?" she demanded when he grabbed her by the arm and started to drag her back up the stairs.

"Sir Ranald wishes to speak with you," the guard answered.

"I am overcome with joy."

"I dinnae ken why the old fool wants such a sharp-tongued lass."

"I am young?"

"Aye, that could be the way of it. Ye must have

made your father verra angry if he was willing to sell ye to this old goat.''

Tatha did not reply, for she had often thought the same thing. Unfortunately, she had been unable to think of one thing she had done that would make her father condemn her to marriage with Sir Ranald. She could only pray that her father simply did not know what the man was like and that he would listen when she tried to tell him, that she would at least be given the chance to speak to him.

When the guard did not lead her to the great hall as she had suspected he would, she tensed. If Sir Ranald's keep was much akin to the others she had been to then she was being dragged to the sleeping rooms. Feeling the first hint of panic she tried to pull free of the guard's hold, but he doggedly dragged her onward. When he reached a heavy, iron-studded door, he knocked once, opened it, and practically threw her inside. Before she could catch her balance he had shut it behind her.

"So, my wee bride, how do ye like your new bed-chamber?" asked Sir Ranald as he stepped up behind her and shoved her toward the bed.

"We arenae married yet," she said, straightening herself up and trying to meet his cold gaze with calm.

"We will be."

"Is my father coming to the wedding?"

She wondered why that simple question should make him scowl so darkly. Then she studied him more closely. He looked furious, but she sensed the anger was not all due to her blatant aversion to him. Something had gone wrong, and she began to suspect that that something was why he was about to try to claim his husbandly rights before they were actually married.

"Oh, aye, your father is on his way, but he will be too late."

"What do ye mean?"

"Your fine Sir David has been verra busy, verra busy indeed. He has been sending messengers all o'er the countryside, telling one and all that I killed his mother."

"And did you?"

"What does that matter?"

"It gives David a righteous grievance against you. 'Twill hobble what few allies ye have, for none will wish to put themselves in the midst of a weel-earned reckoning. And my father willnae make me marry a woman-killer." She edged away from the bed when he took a threatening step toward her. "Has my father learned the ugly truth about you, Sir Ranald? Is that why ye have brought me here? Ye mean to try to steal what is nay longer yours by right, dinnae you?"

He stalked her around the room. "Your father and I made a bargain. I gave him a hefty purse for your sweet hide. Ye are mine now."

"Nay, I am not and I ne'er will be."

When he lunged for her, she darted out of his reach. She raced for the door, but he grabbed her, dragged her to the bed, and tossed her on top of it. For a slim, aging man, he was surprisingly strong. Tatha also suspected that four days in the dungeons with little to eat or drink had severely depleted her strength. Despite the growing conviction that she could not win a fight against him, she struggled with all her might. It did not really surprise her when he got her firmly pinned down beneath him on the bed, but it was difficult not to weep over her defeat.

The too-wet kisses he pressed against her neck made her stomach roll. His bony fingers clawed at the laces of her gown, and she felt herself shrink away from even the promise of his touch. Her growing panic eased abruptly when she realized there was no hardness in his groin. He ground himself against her, but she felt only his hipbones and a faint soft shape that was probably his manhood. The man might maul her, might even beat her, but she began to think that he would never be able to rape her.

"Curse ye, ye are failing me too, just as they all do!" he screamed, and backhanded her across the mouth. "My wives, Lady Ruthven, all of them. Useless whores, the whole lot of you."

She cried out in pain when he shoved her off the bed and she hit the floor hard. " 'Tis nay the women who fail ye, ye great fool." She scrambled out of his way when he leaped off the bed and tried to kick her. "Ye have gone and damaged yourself somehow."

"Then cure it. Ye are a healer. Heal me." He grabbed her by the hair, yanked her back toward him, and slapped her again. "Heal me, ye twice-cursed bitch!"

"Is that what ye demanded of Lady Ruthven?"

"Aye, and she failed me. Then she forced me to make sure she couldnae tell anyone my secret. Aye, just like my useless wives, she needed to be silenced."

"Ye killed them all just because ye are impotent?"

"Nay!" He punched her in the face, releasing her hair when she fell backward from the force of the blow. " 'Tis their fault! They cursed me. Aye, that is what the bitches did, cursed me. And they didnae ken what I needed."

"Ye need a new pintle, ye old goat."

"Ye are no healer. Where are your potions and salves, eh? I cannae even get hard enough to seek the cure in your body. What good are ye, I ask ye? Eh? What cursed good are any of ye?"

"I dinnae think anyone can cure ye," she said, struggling to get to her feet so that she might evade his next attack. " 'Twas a wound or a fever, wasnae it? There is no cure, and ye are slaughtering women for naught."

"Nay, they all deserve what I deal out to them. And my secret is safe. And so will it remain safe."

Tatha tried to elude him when he advanced on her, but she was weak and unsteady. The blows he had already dealt her, her hunger and thirst, had all stolen away her chance to escape him. She cursed in frustration when he grabbed her and watched him draw his fist back with a sense of cold acceptance. He was going to kill her as he had killed the others, and there was little she could do to stop him.

A cry of alarm rang through the halls, and Tatha felt a surge of hope. It might not be anyone coming to her rescue, but any diversion at the moment could only be a blessing. If Sir Ranald was taken from her side for a while, she might be able to regain some of her strength.

She bit back a whimper of pain as he twisted his hand in her hair and dragged her over to the window. She could not see out, but whatever he looked down at caused him to go red with fury. He glared at her, then slammed her head against the cold stone wall. Tatha blinked once, then sank into darkness.

* * *

David was astonished at how easily they had gained the inner bailey of Sir Ranald's keep. His guard had been lax and slow to respond when they had seen his army riding hard toward their walls. They had been able to ride right through the gates, easily cutting down the men frantically trying to close them.

With Leith guarding his back, he fought his way into the keep itself. He ached to confront Sir Ranald, his fear for Tatha so strong it nearly had a life of its own. As he cut down the last man standing between him and entrance into the keep, he looked up to see Sir Ranald himself rushing down the stairs, sword in hand.

"Where is she?" he demanded, a little surprised that the man actually meant to face him.

"Ye mean the little whore of a healer?" Sir Ranald's smile was pure viciousness. "She wasnae as sweet a ride as I thought she would be."

David struggled to keep his rage harnessed, knowing the man tried to goad him into acting foolishly. "Her father stands at my side. Your keep is falling into our hands. The whole of Scotland will soon ken that ye are naught but a cowardly slayer of women."

"Aye, and my tally of dead whores has just increased by one."

" 'Ware, David," whispered Leith from behind him. "He tries to madden ye so that he may actually have some chance of killing ye."

"I ken it."

That knowledge did little to dull the sharp fear he felt, however. There was a good chance the man was lying, but he could also be telling the chilling truth.

He had held Tatha captive for long enough to do anything he pleased with her. David dared not think that he had come so close yet had failed to save her. That way lay madness.

"Ye killed my mother, didnae ye?" David said as he and Sir Ranald circled each other.

"Another whore."

"Is that how ye explain your own lack, Sir Ranald? Do ye blame your poor limp monhood on the lasses? Calling them whores makes ye feel like the mon ye can ne'er be, does it?"

As David had hoped, Sir Ranald was unable to endure even the slightest taunt. The man roared his fury and attacked. The strength the man showed was a little surprising, for he looked like an ailing, too-thin old man, but his skill was rough, his sword swings ill-timed and badly executed. It would not be a long battle.

"Where is she?" he demanded again. "Where have ye put Tatha Preston? Tell me, and if she is hale and unharmed, I may let ye live."

"Live? For what? To hang? To be laughed at? Nay, I think not. Your wee whore is dead, her soft, pale flesh cold. Ye rode her, didnae ye? Aye, ye did, and I made her pay for that."

It was clear that the man would never tell him what he wanted to know, would just continue to try to torment him with tales of the horrors he had made Tatha endure. Cursing the man, David strengthened his attack. Sir Ranald quickly weakened. Although it was tempting to make the man sweat and linger in the knowledge that he would soon be dead, David quickly delivered the death stroke.

Even as he stared down at the man's body, praying

that all Sir Ranald had said concerning Tatha's fate was no more than lies spat out by a vicious man, David heard Leith curse in surprise. A moment later one of Sir Ranald's men landed in a heap at his feet. David held his sword at the terrified man's throat and glanced over his shoulder. Sir Malcolm stood there glaring down at the man.

"I think this worm kens where the lass is," said Sir Malcolm.

"It would be wise to tell me," David said, his gaze fixed upon the trembling man-at-arms. "I have had a bellyful of lies and taunts and willnae tolerate another. If ye wish to keep your head on your shoulders ye had best speak the truth and do so quickly."

"Sir Ranald kept the lass in the dungeons for four days," the man replied, speaking so fast in a shaking voice that it was hard to understand him. "But moments before ye rode through the gates he had her taken to his bedchamber." He lifted one trembling hand and pointed up the stairs. "The door on the right at the head of the stairs."

David bounded up the stairs, faintly aware of the sound of a fist hitting a body. He guessed that Leith or Sir Malcolm had rendered the man unconcious rather than waste any time securing him. Even as he threw open the door the man had spoken of, he could hear the others pounding up the stairs.

A soft curse escaped him and his blood ran cold when he saw Tatha sprawled on the floor near the window. Sheathing his sword, he hurried to her side. As he knelt beside her, he saw her chest move and nearly wept with relief. She was alive. At the moment that was all that mattered.

Gently, he picked her up and carried her to the

bed. Leith and Sir Malcolm stood by the bed as David checked Tatha for any severe injuries. She had clearly been knocked around, and there was a sizable lump on the back of her head, but David could find no other wounds. He sat down on the bed and took her hand in his, lightly rubbing it warm between his two hands.

"The fool said Sir Ranald had only just brought the lass up here," Sir Malcolm grumbled, scowling down at his daughter. " 'Tis clear she managed to enrage him right quickly."

David stared at Sir Malcolm, torn between disbelief and anger. "I dinnae believe Tatha asked for this beating."

"That wasnae what I said. Dinnae tell me ye are one of them sensitive lads. I just said that the fool had been quick to beat her, and if ye try to tell me my lass didnae whet her tongue on his wrinkled hide then ye dinnae ken her as weel as I thought ye did."

"My father oftimes sounds as if he is saying something most unkind when 'tis nay the way of it at all," said Douglas as he entered the room and walked to the side of the bed.

"I hope ye arenae saying that I am kind," snapped Sir Malcolm, glaring at his son.

"I would ne'er insult ye so." Douglas frowned down at Tatha. " 'Tis a shame that the best healer we ken is the verra lass who needs tending."

"If she would wake, she would be quick to tell us what to do. I wouldnae be surprised to see her heal the dead one of these days."

David hid his surprise. Sir Malcolm's words were spoken in the same gruff, nearly angry tone he always used, but the pride he felt in Tatha's healing skills was evident. It was increasingly clear that he had wronged the man to think he cared nothing for his daughter.

"She will wake soon," David said. "Her breathing has already grown stronger and her eyes move beneath her lids."

"Are ye a healer too?" asked Sir Malcolm.

"Nay, but my mother was, and I learned a few things."

"The woman Sir Ranald called a whore and near confessed to murdering?"

"Aye, that woman."

"Why did ye let the mon live?"

"Why did ye betroth your daughter to him?"

"A lass needs a husband, a home, and bairns. I have eleven lasses with nay a dower between them. I took what I could get. Aye, the mon wasnae the best choice, but I didnae see the evil in him. Aye, and he was old." Malcolm shrugged. "I felt he would probably die soon and the lass wouldnae have to endure him long ere she was weel settled, a widow with lands and coin."

David stared at the man in bemusement for a moment. A quick glance at Douglas caught him hiding a grin. In his rough way Sir Malcolm had been trying to do what was best for his daughters, and if that best also filled his purse, so much the better. David did think that Tatha might have misjudged the man. If she had stayed to make her distaste clear, Malcolm might well have ended the bargain. Then again, he would never have met her. She had erred when she had run away in panic, but since that error had set her in his arms, David decided he would not chide her for it.

Tatha opened her eyes and David quickly grasped her by the shoulders, lightly pinning her to the bed. His touch seemed enough to swiftly still the panic that seized her a heartbeat after she woke. She stared up at him for a moment, then yanked on his arms, pulling him down into her hold. David cast a wary glance at her father, amazed to find him grinning.

"Ah, weel, my lass was ne'er a shy one," Sir Malcolm drawled.

David felt Tatha tense and met her wide gaze. "David," she whispered, "I didnae just hear my father, did I?"

"Aye," he replied. "He is standing by the bed."

Tatha squeaked in shock and gave David such a hard shove he slipped off the bed, barely stopping himself from sprawling on the floor. Douglas and Sir Malcolm both guffawed, and, as he straightened himself up, David caught Leith grinning at him. He turned his attention back to Tatha, who was staring at her father with a mixture of pleasure and wariness.

"Glad to see ye didnae take any harm, lass," Sir Malcolm said, awkwardly patting her on the shoulder. "Ye should be in fine fettle for your wedding."

"I willnae marry Sir Ranald," she snapped, then rubbed her forehead, just speaking having been enough to set it to aching.

"Of course ye willnae. The mon's dead."

"Oh." She frowned. "Then what wedding are ye talking about?"

"Ye are marrying Sir David."

Chapter Eleven

"It would be nice if, just once, someone would ask me if I wish to be married," Tatha grumbled to her sister Elspeth as the girl helped her dress in her finest dark blue gown.

All the way back to Cnocanduin, no more had been said of the marriage her father had so bluntly announced. David had made himself conspicuously unreachable and Tatha had ached too much to argue with her father. A part of her had not really wanted to argue anyway. She wanted David, loved him deeply. It simply troubled her that he might be being forced into a marriage he did not really want.

"This mon is a far better choice than Sir Ranald," said Elspeth as she pushed Tatha down into a chair and began to gently brush out her hair.

Although she had taken a potion to ease the ache in her head, Tatha still found having her hair brushed almost painful. "A far better choice. In truth, a mon who could do much better than a too-thin, left-handed redhead."

"He wants you."

"Are ye sure?" Tatha hated to reveal her uncertainty before anyone, but she needed someone to boost her courage, and Elspeth had always been one of the closest of her sisters, as well as highly practical.

"Oh, aye. He was readying himself and his men to go and try to rescue you when we arrived. Papa said he took a chance in sending for us because he confessed that ye had stayed with him. If no one believed his claims that Sir Ranald killed his mother then he was exposing himself to a great deal of trouble. After all, ye were another's betrothed wife."

"I ken all that. 'Tis why I left here. My presence so complicated matters that he could not fight Sir Ranald openly despite the raids upon his lands. Everything he tried to claim about Sir Ranald was put into question because I was here."

"He had clearly decided that that no longer mattered. He was going to war with Sir Ranald to get ye back."

"That does seem to indicate that he has some feeling for me."

"Aye, and he had already told Papa that he meant to wed with you as soon as he got ye out of that mon's grasp."

"Oh. I didnae ken that."

"Weel, there hasnae been much time for talking."

"I love the mon, Elspeth, and I just wish he felt the same."

Elspeth patted Tatha on the shoulder. "Trust me in this. He feels something for you. Leith said the mon was devastated to find ye gone and ken that ye were in Sir Ranald's grasp.''

"Leith says, does he?''

Tatha gave her sister a considering glance. Even though she had been groggy from pain when they had finally ridden through the gates of Cnocanduin, she had seen how Elspeth had run out to greet, not her family, but a blushing Leith. She had also seen the way the two of them could not stop looking at each other and smiling.

"Tatha? Did ye feel something for Sir David the verra moment ye set eyes on him?''

Tatha smiled at her blushing sister. "Aye, I did. Leith is a verra fine mon. Nay rich, but weelborn and holding a high place here.''

"Weel, aye, but he doesnae have a bride price.''

"Father still plays that game, does he?''

"I am nay sure.''

"Weel, if Leith wants ye, I think that, between him and David, they will talk our father 'round to liking the idea. Would ye be willing to marry a mon ye have but just met?''

"In a heartbeat.''

That was said with such conviction, Tatha did not even consider arguing with Elspeth. She decided it made her own qualms seem foolish. David had never spoken of love, but he did desire her. He was young, handsome, and she loved him. It was foolish to bemoan what she did not have when she was about to be given so much. She reached out and took Elspeth's hand, squeezing it gently in a silent gesture of support and comfort. She turned her thoughts to hoping Elspeth would also get what she wanted.

* * *

"Just go and speak with the mon," David urged, trying to hide his amusement over Leith's agitation.

In a way, David was grateful for the distraction Leith's problem caused him. It was preferable to wondering where his bride was and if, now that she was beginning to recover from the knock on her head, she would think to flee him as she had Sir Ranald. Turning his thoughts to helping Leith get the lass he had taken such a sudden fierce liking to kept him from racing up to Tatha's bedchamber and making sure she was actually getting ready to marry him.

"He wants a bride price." Leith dragged his hand through his hair. "I have naught. I am but your second-in-command. The lass could do better than me."

"Ye have a lineage as fine as hers and, although ye may ne'er be rich, I dinnae think she will suffer any hardship living here with us."

"She may wish her own household to lead."

"Mayhap that can be arranged. I plan to claim Sir Ranald's lands as a price for the murder of my mother. I may not get all of them, but I think something will be gained there. E'en if ye stay here, we may get ye a household of your own, a small one, aye, but one of your own." He frowned at Leith. "Are ye now wondering if ye want her?"

"Nay. I ken ye may think it madness, but I took one look at that lass and I was sure. Sure she was all I could e'er want." He straightened up and took a deep breath to steady himself. "Weel, there can be no harm in trying."

"I will go with ye. I dinnae think the mon is that set on getting money for his daughters. His thinking may be odd, but he seems to just want them to get what he believes all lasses need—a mon, a home, and bairns.''

"I ken what ye want, lad," said Sir Malcolm the moment Leith approached him. He sprawled a little more on the bench at the head table, sipped his ale, and studied Leith closely. "I dinnae suppose ye have any money.''

"Nay, not for a bride price, sir," Leith replied solemnly, "but I am nay a pauper. I have enough that your daughter Elspeth willnae be clothed in rags or starve.''

"It sounds fine to me, Father," Douglas said, smiling briefly at Leith, "if Elspeth agrees.''

Scowling at his son, who sat on his right, Sir Malcolm grumbled, "Aye, it would. 'Tis nay your purse that will go empty.''

"Your purse isnae that empty," David said. "Ye still have the bride price Sir Ranald gave ye for Tatha, and since he didnae deal honestly with ye, I believe ye get to keep it.''

"Aye, which means I need nay ask one of ye, but it wasnae meant to pay for two of my lasses," Sir Malcolm said.

"Ye still have seven." David reached out to grasp his tankard off the table and slowly filled it with ale. "I also ken a lot of men, unwed men. Aye, they may not fatten your purse, but they have titles and lands. Allies can be important. I dinnae even mind if, now and again, a few of your lasses stay here, and mayhap they could meet a few of these fine, landed, unwed gentlemen. Fine, honorable men who are sometimes left alone, for they dinnae have quite enough to please those with weel-dowered lasses."

"Ye have a clever tongue, lad. Aye"—he waved his hand at Leith—"if the lass wants ye, take her. I may not get any coin for her, but it does mean I dinnae have to pay for her keep any longer." He looked at Leith when the young man enthusiastically shook his hand. "She is a spirited lass. Take care of her."

"Oh, I will, sir," Leith said even as he hurried out of the great hall.

"He means to pull her afore the priest today, eh?" Sir Malcolm grinned, then winked as he lifted his tankard. "Two more of the wretched lasses gone. My burden lessens by the hour."

"I dinnae think it weighs as heavily upon your shoulders as ye wish the world to believe," David murmured, then squarely met Sir Malcolm's gaze. "He will cherish her."

"Aye, ye could practically smell their besotted-ness." He grinned when David and Douglas laughed, but then quickly returned to scowling. "And ye?"

"Tatha was mine the moment she set foot within my gates. It just took me a wee while to understand that." He glanced toward the door, saw Tatha entering the great hall, and immediately moved to her side. "How are ye feeling, love?"

Tatha looked up at him as he took her hands in his. His gaze was warm and filled with concern. That look eased her nervousness. He could not look at her that way if he were feeling at all trapped.

"I am fine," she replied. "I but ache some. I am glad I was ready to come down, for although I wasnae tossed from the room when Leith arrived, it was a near thing. Elspeth can somehow manage to shove

a person out of a room yet make it look so benign."
She smiled when he laughed and began to lead her
to a seat across the table from her father.

"The lad is eager to take advantage of the priest,"
Sir Malcolm said, scowling blackly as he studied her
bruises.

"Ye have agreed to his wedding her?" asked Tatha.

"Aye. They are besotted. I am glad I brought the
priest."

"Ah, I wondered where he had come from."

"Weel, 'twas clear from what your mon wrote me
that ye had been his guest since ye fled Prestonmoor.
Ye are both young and bonny. Felt a priest might be
needed." He cocked one dark brow but said nothing
more when Tatha blushed.

"And how fare Isabel and Bega?" she asked cautiously.

"They are wed and gone. Isabel was already packing
her things ere the words concerning her betrothal
had left my mouth. Bega will do better on her own,
nay longer under Isabel's thumb."

"They were nay unhappy, Tatha," Douglas added
quietly. "Truly."

"And your mon is going to help me wed off some
of the others," Sir Malcolm said.

Sitting in his chair at the head of the table, David
reached out to take Tatha's hand. "I will introduce
them to some fine unwed gentlemen. Ones who dinnae have one foot in the grave," he added with a sly
glance at her father. " 'Twill be up to them after
that."

For a while they talked of the battle with Sir Ranald.
Tatha told them all the man had confessed to her.
Then David and her father got into an amiable argu-

ment about which one of them had the most right
to try to lay claim to Sir Ranald's lands. She realized
that at some time during her rescue, David and her
father had become almost friends. It even appeared
that David had looked closely and understood that
the gruff, blunt exterior of her father hid, if not a
truly loving nature, at least kindness.

The arrival of Leith and Elspeth ended the discussion of lands. The couple held hands and blushed as
they reached the table. Their blushes deepened when
Sir Malcolm grunted and awkwardly patted both
young people on the shoulder.

"So there will be two weddings?" Sir Malcolm
asked.

"Aye, Papa," replied Elspeth.

"Good. Good. Now ye will be his problem."

"Aye, I will, and I intend to be a verra big one."

"That's my lass. Always do your best. Douglas, move
yourself and fetch the priest."

All of Tatha's doubts and concerns returned in full
strength as she and David knelt before the priest. She
tried to judge what David felt by the way he said his
vows, then by the way he kissed her after they were
made, but it only made her head hurt. Tatha was
relieved when he led her away from the increasingly
boisterous celebration early. She suspected the reti-
cence the guests showed, their comments tempered,
nearly polite, was because she had so obviously been
through an ordeal. She hoped Leith and Elspeth did
not have to suffer any extra tormenting because of
it.

Once in their room, David helped her undress and
slip on her night shift. They crawled into the bed and
he held her close. His kisses and the way he gently

stroked her told Tatha that he was not going to demand anything of her tonight.

" 'Tis our wedding night," she said, as she caressed his chest.

"Aye, but I can wait. Nay long," he said teasingly, "but at least until ye dinnae ache so badly."

"I think the time in the dungeon made me too weak to fight the fool off," she murmured, touching a kiss to his chest and feeling him tremble.

"Ye should ne'er have left, Tatha."

"I had to. My being here was tying your hands. Ye couldnae act as ye had to because all would question it as long as I was in your bed. How did ye get my father here?"

"I told him the truth. He isnae as hard as I thought."

"Nay, he isnae a bad mon. I may have erred in thinking I couldnae talk him out of the wedding he had arranged, but I fear I could think of naught but running when I heard Sir Ranald's name."

"Weel, it was foolish, as I think your father would have listened. I believe he simply doesnae ken how to show what he feels. Mayhap he was ne'er shown. He also seems to have a wee bit of difficulty understanding how others may feel about what he does or says. Howbeit, the moment he truly suspected ye were in danger he was here, armed and ready to fetch ye back. And he could see that Leith and Elspeth were besotted and gave little argument to a wedding."

"Aye, the truth is in how he acts, nay in what he says. Did he force ye to wed me, David?" she asked softly.

"Nay, lass." He tilted her face up to his and brushed a kiss over her mouth. "I wanted ye. In truth, I had long ago decided to wed ye, but there were a few matters that needed tending to first."

"Ye ne'er said."

"I ken it, and I should have. In truth, there was many a thing I should have said, and when I thought ye may be lost to me the words burned a hole in my gullet." He touched a kiss to her small, straight nose. "Ye are mine, lass. That has been the way of it since the day ye rode up to my gates, but I was fool enough nay to see it. The thought that I might ne'er be able to hold ye again left me cold and empty."

"Oh, David," she whispered, and then hugged him. "I do love ye." She frowned when he tensed.

"Ye love me?"

"Aye, but I willnae trouble ye about it—" she began, then found herself being heartily kissed.

"Idiot. I was about to tell ye that I love you." He smiled when her eyes filled with tears, then lightly kissed away the one that trickled down her cheek. "That wasnae supposed to make ye cry."

"Happiness can bring a woman to tears." She slipped her hand down to his taut stomach. "Do ye ken, I really dinnae ache that badly. Perhaps, if ye werenae too vigorous—"

David laughed and tugged off her night shift. "That could prove a verra great challenge."

Later, as she lay contentedly curled up in his arms, she decided he had more than adequately met that challenge. His lovemaking had been gentle, yet so filled with love that she had cried. Tatha smiled and wiped the last of the tears from her cheeks. She felt the warmth of his lips brush over her forehead and looked up at him.

"There is one thing I should like to do, David, if ye will allow it?"

He smiled down at her. "What?"

"I wish to go to the well," she said, watching him warily.

"Tonight?"

"Aye. I ken such things make ye uneasy, but I wish to bless our marriage at the well. 'Tis what pulled me here. 'Tis what brought us together. And although I am ne'er sure how much of the old ways are to be believed, I just feel, weel, compelled to go to the well tonight."

"Then we shall," he said, and got up, glancing her way as they both began to dress. "Just what are we going to do when we get there?"

After yanking on her shoes, Tatha went to the small chest that held her things. She pulled out a small, finely wrought silver wedding cup. "We will share a drink of the water."

"Dinnae look so wary, lass. Aye, I may ne'er believe there is anything special about the well, but it was important to all the women in my family and 'tis important to you." He held out his hand. "Come, let us go and do homage to it then. It will be, in a small way, as if I speak to my mother. 'Twould be verra fine if she could see how happy her son is."

They crept out of the tower house and, careful to avoid being seen by any of the guests or the servants, made their way to the well. David watched as Tatha smoothed her hands over the cool white stone, then filled the wedding cup with water from the well. He frowned slightly when she bent to touch the letters carved into the side of the well.

"The promise?" he murmured as he took the cup when she held it out to him.

"Aye. It promises protection, strength, and happiness." She smiled when he drank from the cup, and then she did the same. "In you, David Ruthven, I have found all three."

He pulled her into his arms and kissed her. "And I in you, my love." He smiled crookedly and glanced at the well, its white stone gleaming silver in the moonlight. "Mayhap the women of my family werenae so mad after all. There may indeed be magic in that well."

"I have no doubt about it. It gave me you."

BRIDE OF THE RED WOLF

Judith E. French

Prologue

Cnocanduin Castle,
Scotland
Winter, 1535

"No! I won't marry him! I don't want to marry
anybody!" the small, red-haired child shouted.

"Lass, lass," her nurse soothed. "Your grandfather,
the earl—"

"No!" Seven-year-old Fiona Fraser, heiress to the
land and titles and vast wealth of Cnocanduin, twisted
from the servant's arms and fled barefoot across the
icy floor to fling herself into a massive curtained bed.
"I won't!"

Burrowing under the heaped covers, she wrapped
her arms and legs tightly around her weeping mother.
"He can't make me!" she muttered angrily.

"Fiona." The heavy wooden door banged open,

and her grandfather's voice echoed through the chamber.

Fiona covered her ears with her hands. The earl was not a big man, but the tread of his boots rang louder than the howling of the wolves outside the castle walls.

"Fiona."

He didn't raise his voice. Grandfather never did, but when he spoke in that tone everyone leaped to obey him. Fiona clenched her eyes shut and tried to make herself very small.

Beside her, her beautiful mother sobbed louder, pleading with him in French. "Please, my lord. Have mercy, she is just a baby."

"I have given my word," Grandfather replied.

"But a barbarian Highlander?" her mother wailed. "A second son? With all that she will inherit, Fiona could wed a great nobleman."

"The Wolf of Glendruidh breeds strong cubs."

A wolf? Fiona's eyes snapped open and she peered out from under the blankets. "Grandfather? You want me to marry a wolf?"

His frown vanished and he laughed. Frigid air enveloped her as Grandfather's powerful hands yanked her from her warm nest and lifted her high. "Do you think I would betroth you to a beast?"

She grimaced. "Better a wolf cub than a boy!" she flung back. "I hate boys. They're loud and they smell."

"Trust me, lassie. You will not always feel that way." His faded gray eyes twinkled in the torchlight. "Come, they are waiting for us."

"My lord!" her mother protested. "She cannot go like this, in only her shift, her hair all atangle."

Grandfather's mouth firmed into a thin, hard line. "Enough. You should have readied her when I first sent word." Lowering Fiona to his shoulder, he snatched a fur throw from the bed and wrapped it around her as he strode toward the stair passageway.

Fiona clung to her grandfather's neck as they descended the twisting stone steps. Beyond the landing, the hall resounded with the swirl of bagpipes and the burr of deep Highland voices. Strange, hard-faced men, clad in shaggy furs and rough tartans, crowded the great room, pressing close around the roaring hearth amid the milling hounds and one shrieking goshawk.

The strong scents of whiskey and wet wool filled Fiona's head. She tensed in her grandfather's arms as a red-bearded giant caught sight of them and raised his cup in salute.

"The bride!" he shouted. "There, Duncan!" He dragged a sullen boy from the throng and shoved him forward. "Where's your manners, son? Can ye nay greet your lady wife wi' a kiss?"

Fiona's eyes widened. Was this the wolf's cub they had promised her to? He stood hardly a head taller than she, and he was as red and shaggy as a fox. His skinny knees were scabbed beneath his kilt, and his feathered Highland bonnet looked too big for his head.

She swore a French oath under her breath.

"Be brave," whispered her grandfather. "Remember, you are a Fraser. No Fraser was ever a coward."

Her mouth felt dry. Her heart was pounding. "Will you let these wolves take me away from Cnocanduin?"

"Not now, not ever. Cnocanduin is yours. This will always be your home."

"Then I am not afraid," she lied stoutly in her mother's tongue. "And if he tries to kiss me, I will knock him on his skinny arse."

Chapter One

"Fourteen years, Grandfather! It's been fourteen years since I've seen that fox-haired, snotty-nosed wolf's cub you pledged me to. Why should I marry him? How interested can he be if he's not come to pay his respects to his betrothed in all this time?"

"Since King James's death, there has been much unrest in the Highlands—in all of Scotland. Duncan has been fighting to defend his clan against invaders. You do not need me to tell you that our little Mary, our child queen, is far away in France, and our English enemies look north to see what they can steal. We cannot even trust our neighbors. Without a strong hand on the Scottish throne, greed has turned many good men to monsters."

"And this Duncan you would have me wed is no doubt among the greatest of these rascals. You expect me to believe that he has had no time in fourteen years to come to Cnocanduin to see if I am dead or alive?"

"It is true that Duncan has earned his nickname of the Red Wolf in battle. He is a fierce warrior, but he is an honorable man. And even though he's a second son, he is the best of Tearlach MacKenzie's get."

"A petty chieftain's son without a title to his name."

"That is your mother talking, lass. A title would not make Duncan a better man."

"I don't want to marry him."

"It matters not," the old earl thundered. "I have given my word. You and Duncan of Glendruidh are bound until death."

"A handfasting only." She rose abruptly and leaned over the table toward him. "I was a child, too young to know what I was agreeing to. I'll not be bullied into this match, not by you—not by anyone."

From the corner of her eye, Fiona saw the servants creep toward the door. Her grandfather's deerhounds whined and cowered at his feet, frightened by the harshness of his tone. *Let them tremble,* Fiona thought. She wasn't afraid of him, and she had a temper to match his own.

"I should have left you in France with your mother," the earl rasped. "I could have married again and raised up another son to be my heir."

"That old tale again?" Fiona turned her back on him and swept to a high-backed chair beside the fire. The hearth, high and wide enough to roast a full-grown bullock, blazed merrily, filling the air with the scent of apple wood. "I weary of this fighting between us, Grandfather," she said. "You know how I love you, but you ask too much of me. Perhaps you should have gotten another son to follow in your footsteps. I know I should have been happier if you did. I never asked to be your heiress."

He followed her to the fire, still a proud figure of a man, despite his shoulder-length, snow-white hair and his sixty-odd years. His legs were thin and gnarled beneath his kilt, and his once-sinewy arms had lost much of the muscle that had wielded a broadsword with the ease of a skean.

"You are a spoiled, ungrateful child. Since the day I brought you home to Cnocanduin, everything I've done has been for you. And this is the only thing I've ever asked of you in return."

Fiona's lapdog, a small, fluffy bundle of white fur, scampered from under a bench and flung himself into her lap. She patted Jouet fondly, using the distraction to summon her counterattack.

"If I am spoiled, my lord, who is it who has spoiled me? My mother married her comte and returned to her native land these five years past. I am what you've made me."

"She filled you with foolish notions of chivalry and romantic love," he scoffed. "Horse turds! What has love to do with a proper marriage? I never set eyes on your grandmother before we were wed at the church door. She needed a strong hand to protect this castle, and I needed a good woman to give me sons."

Fiona did not answer. Her grandmother, countess of Cnocanduin in her own right, had died long before Fiona's birth. Of her grandparents' four children, only Fiona's father had survived his childhood. And he had perished of fever in France when she was an infant. Fiona had often wished she had known him, but she hadn't. The old earl had been father, grandfather, and teacher to her, and she did love him dearly.

But not enough to throw away her life on a loveless marriage.

"Your grandmother and I learned to cherish each other," her grandfather continued. "We fit together like hand and glove, so that once she was laid to rest in the churchyard, I would never put another woman in her place."

"Maybe you should," Fiona murmured. "It isn't too late. You could find a young wife and—"

"Hush such nonsense," he commanded. "You are to be countess here, no other. And you will wed the Red Wolf when he comes to claim your hand. You will do your duty as those before you have done."

"I'd sooner join an order of enclosed nuns."

He laughed. "You? You, who reads poetry during Mass?" He shrugged. "My good hound Una is better suited to become a bride of Christ. Hardheaded you may be, but I do not think you such a fool that you would lock yourself inside a convent to rid yourself of an unwanted husband."

"If you wanted to choose a bridegroom for me, why not a nobleman? Edinburgh is full of titled men, men of manners, education, and good breeding that I would have much in common with. Why should you pick a Highland savage?"

His faded eyes filled with moisture. "Never forget that I came from the Highlands you scorn so much."

"That's different. No other man could compare with you. And your mother was a cousin to our own King James. I do not mean to insult you," she said.

"Doubtless this Duncan, this Red Wolf, cannot even write his name. He will come to our bridal bed smelling of cattle dung and ill-cured deerskins." She stood up again and cuddled her little dog against her breast.

"Duty to family, that is what matters, lass."

"Love matters to me, Grandfather. I will not take a husband without love. Better to be the beloved wife of a wandering gypsy without a copper to his name than lie beneath the thighs of some sweaty Highland laird who takes me only for the land and gold I bring."

"Enough!" Grandfather said. "This night I will send word to your betrothed. I am your guardian, and it is within my power to force you to wed Duncan of Glendruidh. This time you will not have your way."

Her spine stiffened. "Do as you must," she answered softly. "But I shall keep watch from my bower window. And the day I see the Red Wolf ride to Cnocanduin Castle, that day I shall throw myself from the parapets."

"I can lock you up, girl," he threatened.

"For how long? Your servants cannot watch me day and night."

"We shall see about that," the earl said, then turned and stormed from the hall.

Two weeks later, far to the north and west of the Scottish Borderlands, a young man pounded on the door of the widow Gillies's cottage in the dark hours of the night. "Duncan! Duncan! Father wants you." Fergus MacKenzie of Glendruidh took another deep breath and shouted, "I know you're in here, brother. Tormod saw you walking her home."

"Can't it wait until morning?" Duncan groaned

and sat up, carefully untangling his long legs from a pair of shapely feminine ones.

"Must ye go?" Jeannie murmured sleepily. "You've only just come back from the Isles. We've had no time together since."

"Duncan!" Fergus threw open the door, and the flare of torchlight illuminated the snug stone house.

"Sweet Jesu," Jeannie grumbled. "Is that you, Fergus? Are you daft to drag us from our bed on a cold, rainy night?"

"Is Glendruidh under attack?" Duncan growled. "Are the Munros reiving our cattle again? If you've summoned me on a fool's errand, little brother, I'll hang your ballocks from the—"

"Father wants you," Fergus repeated. "He wants you now! Word has come from Cnocanduin. Your fortune is in danger."

"What? Has the wee lassie come to harm?" Duncan rose from the bed and tugged on a long, homespun shirt before wrapping his battle-scarred, muscular body in the coarse folds of a woolen plaid.

"Duncan?" Jeannie sat up, pulling the blankets up to her waist. Fergus's eyes widened as he caught sight of her naked breasts, and she laughed and winked at him. "How is your wife, little Fergus? She'll nay be pleased to know you paid me a visit so late at night."

Duncan strapped on his sword belt, then leaned over and kissed her on the mouth. "Duty calls, sweetheart. I must see to this. I'll be sore angered if someone has made off with my child bride while I've been fighting Campbells in the Isles." He retrieved a leather cord from the floor and gathered his wild mane of hair into a queue at the back of his neck.

Jeannie frowned. "You be away to the Borders and leave me without a thought. And me without a man to look after me."

Duncan grinned as he pulled on his knee-high deerskin boots and laced them tightly. "You know you could have a fistful of husbands, lass, if you could be content to choose just one."

She sighed. "Maybe I will when you're gone south. Glendruidh won't be the same without you." She touched a fingertip to her plump chin. "About the milk cow . . ."

"You shall have your cow, Jeannie." He glanced at Fergus. "I've promised her the brown heifer with the jagged ear and white spot on her forehead. See that she gets it."

"Another cow? Best you do ride south, brother," Fergus replied. "You've already given her enough to start her own dairy."

"A lone woman must look after her own interests," Jeannie said.

Duncan laughed. "And no one can say ye have not."

She snuggled down in her bed as he followed Fergus out into the rainy night. Two shaggy Highland horses stood, heads down, rumps turned into the wind. Duncan gathered the trailing reins and swung up into the saddle of the nearest animal and tried to remember what his betrothed looked like.

What was her name? he mused. Felicia? No, it was Fiona. He was certain it must be Fiona. She'd been skinny and pale with great snapping brown eyes and mounds of orange-red hair. He hoped her hair had darkened to a proper brown. He'd never favored flame-haired women. It was his opinion that they were bad tempered and too free with their tongues.

Poor wee lass. God willing, she'd come to no harm. He had a soft spot for children, but even if he'd been as hardhearted as his eldest brother Tormod, he'd still go to Fiona's rescue. Cnocanduin was too great a prize for a landless man to forfeit.

"You'll get nay wife as rich as Fraser's lass again," his father was quick to remind him, once he'd reached the castle and climbed the winding stairs to the laird's chamber.

Tearlach was awake, fully dressed, and pacing the floor, despite the hour. Duncan's mother sat near the fire, wrapped in a blanket of wolf pelts and sipping a mug of hot soup. She smiled as he came in and offered her cheek to be kissed.

"Mother." He hugged her and planted a caress on her forehead. "You should be asleep."

"Where would I be but by your father's side when our favorite son is in trouble?"

"I'm in no trouble," he replied. "Besides, I thought Tormod was your favorite."

"You're all my favorites." She chuckled. "Some of the time. And this message from Jamie Fraser is nothing if not trouble for your future. Pay heed to your father. You cannot run off fighting again. 'Tis time you wed your lass, bedded her, and gave me grandchildren."

He smiled at her. It was impossible to be cross with his mother, no matter that she forgot that he was a man grown, and no child to be ordered here and there at her whims. "You look too young to be a grandmother," he said, and meant it.

The silver shadows streaking her midnight black hair lent an air of dignity to her slim figure. Few would guess that she had given birth to eight children, or that she had once held this castle against two score of raiders for twenty-seven days. And she had done it when she was six months gone with child and had only seven able-bodied men to aid her.

"Elspeth?" Duncan's father broke in impatiently. "Will you stop talking long enough for me to tell him why I summoned him?"

"From the looks of him, he wasn't sleeping," his mother answered. "Probably swiving some light-skirts."

"Has something happened to my child bride?" Duncan asked.

His mother chuckled again. "A child no more, Duncan," she chided lightly. "Fourteen years have passed since you took your vows. She must be twenty and one by now."

"Twenty and one?" He frowned. Could Fiona be that old? "Surely not," he muttered.

"What did I tell you, Tearlach?" she said.

"A letter has come from Jamie Fraser," his father grated. "He says that the lass refuses to have you, that she wishes to break the betrothal."

A wave of anger washed over Duncan. "Let me see it." He held out his hand. "She is well, Fraser's heiress. She has not been taken with the pox or stolen away?"

"Nay, lad," his mother assured him. "Fraser wants to keep the pledge he made between our houses, but he will not force the girl."

"He is too soft with her," Tearlach said as he handed over the roll of parchment. "But Fraser is eager for the match. He fears the English. He wants you to come at once to Cnocanduin."

"Just not as yourself," his lady mother explained. "It is quite a long letter. Come and sit by the fire where the light is better and I will read it to you. I believe you will be as intrigued by Jamie Fraser's strange invitation as I was."

"Intrigued or not, I will go to Cnocanduin," Duncan swore. "I'll nay be robbed of my bride or her fortune."

"Peace, my son," his mother soothed. "A countess is not assaulted like a castle. If you would have her and her lands, you will need more wit than sword arm."

"She is already mine, by the laws of church and Scotland. And no man or woman will take from me what I claim," he answered hotly.

His mother laughed. "So say you, my brave laddie. And I wish you well." She covered her mouth and suppressed another sound of amusement. "But you've had few women refuse you before today. And I think that the lady of Cnocanduin shall prove to be a lively opponent. I look forward to meeting her."

"And you shall," he said. "Once she is my wedded wife."

Chapter Two

March wind tore at Fiona's headdress and sent it tumbling across the meadow, but she didn't look back. Instead, she leaned low over her black mare's neck and urged the animal on. Slowly they drew ahead of her grandfather's clansmen and raced up the hill toward Cnocanduin Castle.

Fiona laughed as the mare leaped the low stone wall beside the kirkyard. Two more strides and they cut through the rutted lane between a flock of geese and onto the stony path that led up to the castle gate.

Narrowly avoiding a milkmaid leading a cow, Fiona clattered across the wooden drawbridge and into the small courtyard. Still laughing, she tossed her reins to a stable boy and prepared to dismount.

Suddenly, she noticed several brightly dressed gypsies standing on the outer steps leading to the castle kitchen. One man, in particular, caught her attention.

Tall and broad shouldered, he stood with his back turned to her. Night black hair cascaded down his red satin shirt, and a gold earring gleamed in one ear. Long, muscular legs were tightly clad in black velvet hose and soft leather shoes.

The gypsy bore no weapons but a single eating dagger thrust through the belt at his narrow waist, but still Fiona perceived an aura of danger about him. "Who is that?" she demanded of the stable lad.

"Gypsies, m'lady," the youth replied.

"I can see that for myself," she replied. "What are they doing here?"

The boy grinned. "Come to sing and dance for your birthday celebration, Lady Fiona."

That was odd, she thought. Her grandfather didn't usually give permission for gypsies to come inside the castle walls. He'd always complained that they were thieves and vagabonds. "Has the earl given leave for them to enter?" she asked.

"Aye, milady. 'Tis said that there will be music and feasting for all."

Fiona glanced back at the strangers. The tall man in the scarlet shirt looked more fighting man than ballad singer. It was obvious that she wasn't the only woman in Cnocanduin Castle curious about him.

Bessie, the cook's sluttish helper, leaned from the open kitchen doorway. Her pockmarked cheeks were scarlet, and her ample bosom overflowed the bodice of her gown. It was obvious from her shrieking giggles that Bessie found whatever the stranger was saying to be vastly amusing.

Fiona smiled at the stable lad and swung down from her mare's back. At that instant, her grandfather's huntsmen rode into the courtyard, and the gypsy turned around.

For an instant, his black devil eyes locked with Fiona's, and her breath caught in her throat. Then a slow, lazy grin spread across the tall gypsy's face, and he swept off his feathered Scot's bonnet and gave a deep, mocking bow.

"A good day to ye, lady," he called.

Fiona felt a rush of emotion. *By the cross!* Was ever a fallen angel so handsome? A powerful nose and high, craggy cheekbones dominated a warrior's face. Dark brows arched over eyes that seemed too wise for their years. And his sensual mouth . . . his mouth was both cruel and tantalizing at the same time. It was a face such as women dream of, a haunting image so brath and bonny that surely he could charm the birds from the trees.

Bessie seized the rascal's arm. "Careful, Davy," she hissed. "That's the laird's granddaughter."

For a heartbeat, the gypsy's composure wavered. Then what seemed to be genuine pleasure replaced the taunting courtesy. "Forgive my ignorance, m'lady. I dinna ken it was you. Ye be far more beautiful than any have told me."

Fiona dismissed his impudence with a cool smile, but still a tide of uneasiness washed over her. Her hair hung loose and tangled with twigs; her riding dress was streaked with mud. No wonder the gypsy had mistaken her position.

Recovering her dignity, she drew herself up to her full height, crossed the courtyard, and walked through the low stone doorway that led to the family quarters.

Both the thick wooden door and the yett, the heavy

iron gate that had hung here for time out of time, stood open, but the way was barred by a hard-faced guard.

"My lady," he said, bringing the point of his unsheathed sword to the floor. With a respectful nod, he stepped back to let her pass.

Fiona could not contain a smile. "Gruffydd." The Welshman took his duties seriously. He'd stood watch at the main entranceway since she'd been a small child, but he always stared at her suspiciously when she went in or out.

She sighed. Gruffydd was another sign of how much her grandfather lived in the past. English Border raiders might reive cattle and burn outlying villages, but no armed force had menaced the white stone of Cnocanduin since she was a child. Yet Grandfather's followers manned the walls day and night. His tenants kept iron baskets full of tar on every hill and tower ready to light the warning signal fires—the bale fires—as though attack on Cnocanduin were imminent.

Why couldn't he see the Scotland Borderlands were no longer wild and uncivilized? And why did he cling to the barbarous customs of another age, such as child betrothals?

If only Grandfather would be as reasonable as Lord Purves, the father of her dearest friend. Anne's parents had allowed her to choose her own husband. Now plump, merry Anne was the wife of an Irish lord and the mother of an infant son.

And Anne was three years younger than she was. The thought rose unbidden in Fiona's mind, and she tried to push it away. Of all Fiona's circle of friends, she remained the only one unwed. It wasn't that she hadn't dreamed of being properly wed and mistress of her own household, but in truth, she had seen no reason to trade the freedom she now possessed to be subservient to an unwashed Highlander.

I have too much of my French mother in me, she mused. *I enjoy romantic tales of knights and fair ladies, music, and the poetry of well-bred gentlemen. Let the Red Wolf of Glendruidh take some wild shepherd lass to his den. Will he, nill he, I will not have him.*

That evening, a late-spring storm swirled down out of the north to envelop Cnocanduin Castle and the surrounding countryside. In the courtyard, large, crystalline flakes tumbled in heaps and piled against the thick bull's-eye glass panes of the round window in the great hall.

A tree trunk burned merrily on the hearth, and the air was heavy with the scent of roasting beef and hot bread. The hall was crowded with retainers and castle folk, and Fiona had left her chambers to take supper with her grandfather and their guests.

She was still unhappy with the old earl for pressing her about her betrothal, but since he had not mentioned the subject today, she wouldn't either. Instead, she forced herself to smile winningly at their closest neighbors, John and Mary Hogg, who lived at Troughend. Sir John was bragging about the sixty head of fat cattle his son had stolen last Martinmas from the English below the Tweed. His third wife, a priest's daughter and forty years younger than her husband if she was a day, clapped and rolled her eyes and twittered as though he had not repeated the story a dozen times.

Fiona was bored. Two dogs were fighting over a bone below the salt, and the talk had turned to a battle fought at Piperden before her grandfather was born. It seemed to her that her wine had a sour taste, and there was a definite smell coming from the rushes underfoot.

Heaven spare me! Fiona thought. *Am I doomed to suffer one such evening meal after another until I am too old to care?*

Someone had brought a hawk into the hall, and it was hunting sparrows overhead. Fiona yawned behind her hand and covered her cup with a slice of bread. At Easter, Lady Christie had nearly fainted when another such prank had dropped a bloody pigeon into her lap. Perhaps the same would happen here. A dead sparrow in Mary Hogg's winecup might do much to improve the mood of this dreary supper.

Idly, Fiona toyed with the cooling mutton on her pewter plate, cutting it into smaller and smaller pieces with her ivory-handled eating knife.

Then from the shadows at the far end of the hall a violin's poignant strains drifted over the clamor. One by one, the castle folk grew still and leaned forward to listen as the big gypsy's rich voice resounded with the haunting ballad of "The Lonely Banks of Yarrow."

Fiona's throat constricted and tears clouded her eyes as the tall and devilishly handsome gypsy wandered from table to table relating the tragic fate of the lady known only as the Flower of Yarrow, and her star-crossed love for a serving lad. The beautiful lady's family believed her sweetheart Davy unworthy, and her brothers conspired to betray her trust and murder him.

As she rode down yon shadowed glen,
Dark sorrow rode beside her,
And she did spy her Davy slain,
Upon the banks of Yarrow. . . .

A gust of wind extinguished one of the torches over the high table, plunging the hall into semidarkness as the troubadour related the Flower of Yarrow's grief and her final fairwell to her father and brothers. Lastly, the gentle lady threw herself across her lover's grave and perished of a broken heart.

Silence gripped the crowd; then Jock Tait banged his wooden mug on the plank table and called for a man's song, full of fighting and heroes. Another took up his cry, and Fiona's grandfather tossed the gypsy a silver penny.

The vagabond caught Fiona's eye, grinned, and bowed low to the high table before sweeping into a spirited rendition of "Douglas at Otterburn." Another gypsy, still hidden in the shadows, played accompaniment for the bold singer on his violin.

Fiona straightened and stared back at the black-haired minstrel. Was he weary of his neck that he wished to dare the old earl's displeasure by making free with his granddaughter in full view of half the countryside? How dare a lowborn gypsy behave so? She would have found his arrogance amusing if it hadn't been so serious.

He followed "Otterburn" with a love song of the Western Isles, so moving that Fiona could almost hear the seabirds and the crash of the surf against the shore. Again, the moss-troopers demanded a song of clashing steel and daring raids, and the gypsy seemed eager to comply.

When he'd finished with a tale of Flodden Field, he moved close to Fiona and held out his hat. "Surely the lady has a song she'd like to hear," he said.

She felt her cheeks grow warm. Everyone was staring at her. "Sing 'The Gypsy Laddie,' if you please," she replied, more to put an end to his attention to her than because she wanted to hear it. "It's fitting for one of your kind," she added.

He swept the feathered bonnet across the rushes on the floor. "As you wish, m'lady," he replied. "But first you must cross my palm with silver."

This time she could not help but chuckle at his boldness. "Money I have none," she answered. "My grandfather has already paid you."

"A token, then," he teased. "A bangle or a hairpin to give my sweetheart."

"Give him something," Mary Hogg cried. "If you don't, I shall!"

This caused another round of raucous laughter from the diners. Her grandfather stood unsteadily and raised his cup in salute. "Can you not reward such a bard, Fiona?"

It was plain to Fiona that the earl had already downed many such cups this night. Doubtless his servants would have to carry him up to his tower bed again.

Impulsively, she yanked off her copper bracelet. "What is your name, gypsy?"

He grinned. "They call me Davy Fa."

"Well, Davy Fa," she said as she tossed her trinket to him. "You must make do with copper. Now sing for your supper."

"Your wish, fair lady of Cnocanduin, is my command."

Fiona tried to appear gracious as he leaped onto a tabletop and beckoned the audience to join him in the Scottish version of the tale of a faithless wife and a sweet-talking gypsy.

Last night you slept in a feather bed,
Beside your husband and baby.
Tonight you'll sleep on the cold, cold ground,
In the arms of your gypsy laddie.

The song went on for verse after verse with crofters, servants, fighting men, and gentlefolk on their feet and shouting the chorus. Cups and eating knives pounded against tabletops, and booted feet stamped the floor.

Fiona used the general confusion to slip out of the hall. When men and women took to strong drink, she preferred to retire for the evening.

With no fire to warm the stones, the narrow passageway was cold and damp, but Fiona paid it no heed. Cnocanduin was truly warm only in summer. She had trodden these twisting steps and prowled these rooms since she was old enough to walk.

She did not go up to her own quarters, but instead went down the steps to the holy well on the bottom level of the castle, a place she'd always considered peaceful.

Cnocanduin was very old, how old she wasn't sure. But Grandfather had told her that the original pele tower had been built in ancient times beside the holy well and a magic rowan tree. Over the years, the castle had grown around the old bailey until the well now lay far down beneath the main floors of the fortress.

The rowan tree had died once stone walls blocked

out the light, but a branched and barkless trunk remained. No one had dared to cut the tree for firewood and so it remained, so hard and blackened it seemed to have turned to stone. The well, a place where some said the blessed St. Joseph had paused to drink, still contained an abundance of sweet, pure water, doubtless one reason why Cnocanduin had never been captured by enemy forces.

When she was troubled, Fiona liked to go down to the well and run her fingertips over the words someone had carved into the stone long ago.

> *Any woman of pure heart who drinks from the well of Cnocanduin will find protection, strength, and happiness as long as it holds water.*

Somehow sitting there, staring into the holy well, made Fiona feel connected to the generations of women who had lived within these strong walls. Her old nurse had told her that the left-handed, red-haired women of the house possessed the second sight and could see images on the surface of the water if they looked hard enough.

Fiona was both left-handed and red-haired, but she had never seen anything but water, no matter how hard she looked. She decided that perhaps her mother's sensible French blood had blocked out the fey Scots' witching powers.

Tonight was no different. Fiona perched on the rim of the well, held her torch high, and stared down, but saw only her own reflection. The cellar was as silent as the grave. No sounds drifted down from the great hall above. Not even the squeak of a mouse or the rustle of a bat's wing disturbed the quiet of the rowan tree's vigilance.

"I wish I lived long ago," Fiona murmured. "I would like to know what it would be like to love a man so deeply that I would gladly die of a broken heart if I lost him."

"Was my singing so bad that my lady could not stay to hear what she had paid for?"

Startled by a man's deep voice, Fiona gave a gasp and fell forward. Her hand slipped, and she nearly tumbled into the open well.

The gypsy's strong fingers closed around her arm and snatched her back to the safety of solid stone. "Careful, my lady," he said. "If you were to fall in, none would hear you."

Fiona drew in a ragged breath. "Let go of my arm," she managed. Her heart raced; her mouth felt dry. "What are you doing here?"

"Lucky for you that I followed you." He released her and bowed.

Davy Fa's face was in shadow. She could not read the expression on his face. She swallowed the lump in her throat, trying not to show her uneasiness.

"Show me any disrespect and my grandfather will have you drawn and quartered," she warned him quietly. The torch was still clutched in her left hand. She did not think he would attempt to molest her, but if he did she would protect herself.

Davy stepped away and laughed merrily. "I would not harm a hair of your red head," he said. "I followed your ladyship only to be certain that you were safe. The earl, your grandfather, is a hard man, but not even he would put to death one who'd saved his heiress."

"You are very bold," she pronounced. Not wanting to seem a coward, she thrust the torch at him. "Since you are here, you may hold this for me."

He stepped back without taking it. "I am a free man and no one's servant. Call a footman to take your torch." He sat on the far side of the well and folded his arms over his broad chest. "I wonder why a lady would come to such a deserted place alone at night. Could it be you have come to meet a lover?"

She laughed. "I have no lover. How dare you say such a thing?"

"It seems I dare much, my lady," he teased her. "I only wondered. You are not wed and fair on to thirty."

"Thirty? Do you think me thirty?" Her good humor wavered at the insult. "I am scarce twenty and one, and none but you have ever guessed me older."

"Hmmm." He rubbed a clean-shaven chin and seemed to ponder her statement. "Twenty and one and not wed?" He shook his head. "Among my people a wench is considered long of tooth be she reach ten and six without a husband. But it may be that your left-handedness had deterred some would-be suitors."

"What makes you think I'm left-handed?"

"I saw you cutting your meat at table."

"You are observant."

"Some say a left-handed woman is bad luck."

"Some say," she replied tartly. "Superstitious nonsense."

He leaned over the well and dropped her copper bracelet in. It fell with a splash.

"My bangle! Why did you throw it away?"

He shrugged. "Perhaps it would carry your bad luck. I wouldn't wish to give it to—"

"That bracelet came from the land of the Danes. My grandfather gave it to me on my last birthday."

Davy put his hands over his ears and began to hum the tune to "The Lonely Banks of Yarrow."

"You are very rude," she said.

"You weary me with all this talk of dare this and dare that," he answered. "Have I not told you that I am of the free people? I eat your grandfather's beef and drink his ale by choice. Among my own kind, I am a prince. I'm not accustomed to being ordered about by women, not even one as lovely as yourself."

"First I am old and wrinkled, nearing middle age. Now I am lovely? You have a strange way of collecting patrons."

"Aye, perhaps, but I think you have too long had your own way in your grandfather's castle. A pity the earl could not find one to marry you."

"I am betrothed, for your information. And you will not sing such a shrill tune when the Red Wolf of Glendruidh cuts you down to size."

He stood and rested his fists on his hips. "Duncan? Tearlach MacKenzie's second son? You love him?"

"Love him?" She shook her head in exasperation. "Of course I don't love him," she explained patiently. "I don't even know him. We were handfasted as children. But I am told that he is a fierce and mighty warrior, one who would not blink an eye to whack off a gypsy's head."

"A whacker of heads, is he?"

"Yes. So I am told. He has killed hundreds, all better men than you."

"But doubtless he is scarred and ugly from all this fighting."

Fiona hesitated. Davy had hit upon one of her own concerns. "Perhaps," she admitted.

"And ill-tempered. All fierce warriors are ill-tempered with no sense whatsoever of humor."

"All the more reason you should be shaking in your boots." She edged toward the steps. This odd encounter was becoming even stranger, and she knew that a lady of the castle could not be alone with such a rogue without attracting malicious gossip. She would retreat up the stairs, leaving him here in the dark with whatever ghosts and fairy folk hovered here in the pitch black. "You threw my bracelet into the well, and I won't forget it."

"It was mine," Davy reminded her. "You gave it to me. It was mine to dispose of as I chose."

"You chose ill."

"You want it back?"

"You think me a fool? The well is bottomless. My bracelet is gone." She shook her head. "I should never have given it to you."

"If I give it back, may I claim a forfeit?"

"You can't. You threw it into the well. I saw you."

He took a step toward her, and his eyes met hers as they had in the great hall. "Then a forfeit would be no risk, would it, m'lady?"

"None whatsoever."

"Is it a bargain?"

She uttered a sound of derision. "What would you have of me? My maidenhead? You think me a slut. Why stop there? Why not demand my hand and title?"

"Nothing so great. I ask naught but a kiss, sweetheart."

"I am not your sweetheart."

"Is it a bargain?" he asked.

"Agreed. But if you jump into the well and drown, I'll feel no pity for one so stupid."

He spread his hands, palms up. "Can I trust you to keep your agreement? You'll not try to wiggle out of your agreement like a shoat in a drain hole?"

"Hardly." She laughed at him in spite of herself. "Produce my bracelet, and you'll have your forfeit."

He bowed, swept off his feathered bonnet, and plucked her copper circlet from the folds of his hat. "Your grandfather's gift, m'lady," he declared. "And now, you owe me my kiss."

Chapter Three

Fiona circled around the gypsy and fled up the steep stone steps. Where did the man get such arrogance? How could he imagine that she, an earl's granddaughter, would be so free with her favors?

It would serve him right if she reported him to the captain of the guard. A few days in the dungeon would clear Davy's head and teach him his place. She had only to run down this passageway to the yett and tell the sentry stationed there. Better still, she could return to the great hall and inform her grandfather. He'd have the rascal whipped behind a horse's tail.

But she knew she was too softhearted to do any of these things. Perhaps she had invited his bad behavior by her own boldness. Instead, she turned through a door, across a landing, and started up another twisting flight of stairs. At each floor, a candle burned on the window ledge, but Fiona didn't need the light.

She knew each worn step by heart, including the eleventh, the dead man's step, carved two inches higher than the others to trip an enemy.

The third level was one that made Fiona's heart beat a little faster. The landing here was always cold, no matter the time of year. None of the younger servants would go alone to the rooms in that section of the tower, said to be haunted by the ghost of a piper and his black sheepdog.

She kept her eyes on the rough, whitewashed wall. It wasn't that she was afraid to peer into the hall leading off the staircase; she just didn't care to.

At one spot, between the fourth and fifth floors, a block of stone projected from the wall at the height of a man's head. Household members knew to duck or suffer the consequences. An armed intruder would be at a disadvantage when he reached that turn. One misplaced foot, and he would tumble back to the bottom of the stairs.

Another hidden protection for the castle was the hole drilled in the step a half flight above. It was said that Mary Fraser had poured oil through the opening when pursued by an overardent suitor, causing an Englishman to slip and crack his head.

Fiona would not hesitate to do the same if the gypsy Davy dared to follow her up to her chambers. At least she thought she would. Now that strong stone and the privacy of the family quarters separated them, she remembered how good-looking he was and how the timbre of his rich voice had raised goose bumps on her arms.

Her anxiety eased, and she could smile at her own fears. Why was she running from a man such as Davy inside the walls of Cnocanduin? No harm could come to her here. Even a gypsy must realize that it was a crime even to speak to her with disrespect. Every fighting man, crofter, and servant within miles would give his life for her without hesitation.

This Davy was a clever one, she admitted. She had been certain that he'd thrown her bangle into the well. Barring real magic, which she doubted he possessed, he must have played a trick on her and hidden the bracelet in his hat. Wandering gypsies made their living by fooling honest folk. He'd deceived her with sleight of hand, and was probably a pickpocket to boot. Still, he'd made her laugh, and that was a plus in his favor.

Fiona's maids leaped up as she entered her outer chamber. Young Agnes's cheeks flamed at the shame of being caught napping. Her straw-colored hair stuck out from under her wrinkled cap, and the plump little face screwed up as though she would burst into tears.

"Yer bed's turned down, m'lady," she stammered. "Logs is burning on the hearth."

Nadette made no excuses. The aging lady-in-waiting had come from France with Mother and had served the mistresses of Cnocanduin ever since. Nadette had ruled the nursery and the other maids with an iron hand. She had supervised Fiona's lessons and seen that the sewing women provided clothing fit for a future countess.

"You come late to your bower," Nadette said in French. "Your eyes will be puffy and your face lined at morning Mass."

"It is not that late, 'Dette," Fiona soothed.

Sturdy Winifred came from the next room with her arms full of blankets and dipped a curtsy. "M'lady.

It is cold tonight. I thought you might need extra warmth."

The tall, broad-shouldered serving woman was a widow and the most capable of Fiona's servants. She didn't speak a word of French. She pretended not to understand it either, a constant bone of contention between her and the older Nadette. Her English was heavily accented with the burr of the Highlands, but her smile was wide, her hands clean, and her breath sweet. Winifred was Fiona's favorite, and the woman she asked if she wanted something done right.

Fiona had long wanted to put Winifred in Nadette's position, but her grandfather had forbidden it.

"It would be cruel to strip your Frenchwoman of her authority," he'd said. "Nadette is old and failing. Time will settle affairs in your bower."

Tonight Fiona wanted none of them near her. She desired to be alone to remember exactly what Davy had said to her and to bring to mind the enchanting refrain of his ballads. She allowed the maids to undress her, drape her in a night robe, and brush out her hair.

Then Fiona clapped her hands impatiently, soothed all three with kind words, and retreated to her inner chamber with its wide hearth and curtained bed. There she could dream of far-off times and places where true love was greater than death and no one forced an heiress into an unwanted marriage.

Her merlin screeched a welcome from the large cage near the window, and Fiona spoke softly to the bird. "Shhh, shhh, go to sleep now, Silk. Poor thing, you want to go hunting, don't you? Eat your mouse, and perhaps tomorrow the weather will be better."

The little hawk's black eyes watched her as she draped a homespun throw over the pen.

Restless, Fiona went to the window, opened the precious iron-bound glass shutters and then the larger wooden ones. Strains of a gypsy violin drifted up from the snowy courtyard below, but when she looked down, she couldn't see the musician. White crystalline flakes continued to fall, muffling the sounds of the stables and the soldiers' quarters.

The wind was cold. It tore at the bed linens and threatened the candle flames. Shivering, Fiona forced the shutters closed and locked both pairs.

She was tired. A decent night's sleep would make her feel much better in the morning. She blew out the candles, threw off her robe, and ran across the icy floor to leap into bed.

Another story above, on the top of the tower, Davy Fa knotted a rope around the parapets and tied the other end around his waist.

"This seems a wee bit unnecessary to me," Niall said. "If I want to give a lass a present, I usually hand it to her."

"Shut up and hold the rope," Davy said. "Let it out a little at a time."

"Your father will have my hide pinned to his stable door if you tumble off this tower," Niall grumbled. " 'Tis foolhardy, I say. Carry the wench off, bed her, and get her with bairn, I say. With a babe in her belly, there'll be no fuss over a wedding. She'll be wailing for one."

Slowly, hand over hand, Davy lowered himself down the rope over the edge of the wall. He braced his feet against the rough-cut stones and inched down toward the solar window a kitchen wench had pointed out as Fiona's.

The snow blew into Davy's eyes, blurring his vision, and the cold wind turned his hands and feet numb. Once, Niall let the rope out too fast, and Davy dropped nearly a yard, swinging out and back to knock his head against the tower.

"Easy!" he yelled up to his companion.

"Save your breath for the trip back up," Niall called.

Ten minutes later, Davy was forced to admit that Niall was right. Going up was definitely harder than coming down.

The sun had been up for two hours when Fiona rose from her bed. The air in the room was chilly after the warmth of her bed, and she pulled the fur-lined wrap around her bare shoulders.

One of the women had come and built up the fire and left warm water for washing on the table. At least Fiona supposed it had been warm. Now it was the same temperature as the chamber.

Fiona hurriedly bathed and pulled a clean linen shift over her head. She supposed that it was quite odd to prefer privacy to being washed by her maids, but her mother had been the same way.

Sunshine seeped through the cracks of the shutters, spilling over the white stone floor. *Sunshine!* Smiling, Fiona went to the window and opened it.

Most of the snow had already melted, and the temperature was rising. The white fairyland of the day before had changed to a green spring morning.

"See," Fiona said, pulling the cover off her merlin's cage. "I told you that today would be better." She turned back to the window for another look and noticed something on her windowsill.

"Whatever . . ." Puzzled, she picked up a silver filigree box no bigger than the palm of her hand. "How did this get there?"

She opened the tiny catch. Inside the box, nestled in a bed of lamb's wool, lay a silver chain and a heart-shaped bauble of amber. "Oh," she exclaimed. "How lovely."

Surely the box hadn't been on her sill the night before. She wondered if any of her ladies was playing a trick on her. She couldn't resist slipping the lovely object over her head, then decided to say nothing and see who would ask about her necklace.

The amber felt warm against Fiona's throat as she hurried down to the chapel for morning Mass a half hour later. None of her waiting women had said a word about the beautiful heart, so she was no closer to solving the mystery of who had left it on her window.

Fiona was still curious when she joined her grandfather and his guests for breakfast at the high table in the great hall.

The old earl greeted Fiona with a peck on the cheek. "You look lovely this morning, my dear," he said gruffly.

"Thank you, Grandfather." She curtsied and made her pleasantries to John and Mary Hogg, Father Michael, and the others. There was no sign of the gypsies, and Fiona couldn't help feeling somewhat relieved. If Davy Fa had left the castle, there was no sense in getting herself in trouble by relating last evening's conversation with the rash bard.

"We thought to go out hawking," her grandfather said. "The day promises to be mild, and there are no reports of any English brigands about. You may join us if you'd like."

"I'd love to come," Fiona replied, then leaned close to him. "Do you like my necklace, Grandfather?"

"Hmmm, yes, I do. Becomes you, m'deary."

The priest offered a short blessing. Fiona mumbled an "Amen" and reached for a piece of hot bread.

If the earl had instructed one of her ladies to leave a gift for her this morning, he didn't seem very interested in seeing it on her. Her grandfather was always generous, but this didn't seem like his normal behavior when he was pleased with himself. If the surprise was his, he wouldn't be able to keep the joke to himself for long. Shortly, he'd have been laughing and telling her where he'd bought the necklace.

An hour later, when Fiona joined the hunting party in the outer bailey, she was still waiting for the earl to reveal his joke. A serving lad followed her with Silk, her merlin, on his arm as she wound between the horses to her gray palfrey.

Hugh, a groom Fiona had known since she was a child, was holding her mare's head. Fiona stepped up on the mounting block and motioned for Hugh to lift her onto the sidesaddle.

"Be careful, m'lady," Hugh said. "She's full of ginger today."

He didn't let go of the mare's head, and Fiona frowned. But before she could order him to assist her, strong hands tightened around her waist.

"A bonny day for sport, my lady."

Surprised, Fiona looked into the gypsy's dark eyes. "You can't lay hands on—" she began.

Ignoring her, Davy set her on the saddle and tucked her foot into the stirrup. "It pleases me to see you looking so fine," he said. "The sunlight on your hair is a sight to make a man's heart leap for joy."

Butterflies tumbled in Fiona's belly, and she glanced at Hugh to see if he was as startled as she to hear the gypsy speak so to her. The groom's back was turned, and he didn't seem to have heard a word. Fiona gathered the reins in one hand and reached for Silk with the other.

"Lord Fraser has ordered me to carry the bird for you, m'lady," Davy said. "The footing may be slippery due to the melting snow."

She started to protest, but Davy looked at the boy and he passed the hooded hawk to the gypsy. He settled Silk on a leather cuff on his forearm and mounted a horse.

The earl and his guests were already clattering through the gatehouse and across the drawbridge. Fiona urged her mare after them. Davy swung onto a bay gelding and followed her.

Trying not to show her confusion, Fiona forced a smile, waved at the steward's young daughter, and urged Ivory, her mare, into a trot.

The water in the moat was low and muddy, and the snow had already melted off the outer bank. A shepherd doffed his hat as she rode by, and Fiona noticed several young lambs among his flock.

It was hard to remain subdued on such a beautiful spring day. The air smelled of growing things, and birds sang in the trees. Ivory tossed her head and mouthed the bit, anxious to break free and run.

Fiona kicked the horse and let her go. Ivory's gait was smooth as she sped over the ground. Davy kept pace with her on the tall, rangy bay. He didn't seem to feel the weight of the hawk on his arm as they galloped up hills and down, dashing through the trees in pursuit of the earl's hunting party.

Then suddenly Davy reined in his horse, pulled off Silk's hood, and slipped her jesses. The merlin leaped into the air and flew high.

Fiona guided Ivory into a circle and brought her back to where Davy sat. "Why did you loose her?" she demanded.

"Look there!" he said.

The hawk had spied a pigeon and was climbing to make her killing dive. Caught up in the excitement of the hunt, Fiona reined her mare around and urged her after the merlin.

For a moment it looked as though the pigeon was doomed, but the wily bird dodged the hawk's attack, fluttered into a thicket, and Silk returned to Davy's wrist without making her kill.

Instead of being angry, the gypsy looked at the hawk's ruffled feathers and laughed. Fiona, sorry for Silk but glad for the pigeon, laughed with him.

"Not good for our first attempt," Davy said.

"No." Fiona chuckled. "You're a poor falconer."

"Why me? 'Twas the merlin that missed, nay me."

"I suppose that's true," she admitted. "But as the hawk is mine, a gentleman would accept the fault."

"Aye, m'lady," he replied with a mischievous gleam in his eyes, "but a gypsy is no gentleman, is he?"

"No, he's a scoundrel." She couldn't help noticing how well he rode or how gentle his big hands were on her merlin.

"I'm pleased ye like my gift. 'Tis very old. Older than Cnocanduin."

"Your gift?" Her fingers went to the amber heart, and her eyes widened in surprise. "But how did you get it onto my windowsill? Only a bird could . . ."

He rode close beside her and reached under the edge of her velvet riding cap. "The same way I do this," he said. "Magic." Sunlight glinted off a silver coin that had seemed to come from her ear.

"Or witchery," she replied, only half-afraid. Her heart began to beat a little faster. "You are very good with sleight of hand," she pronounced. "I should have guessed that it was you who left the necklace." She put her hands to the clasp to undo it. "Of course, I cannot accept—"

"But you can," he said. "Who else would wear it so well?"

"It is very expensive," she replied. "I cannot—"

"I lied," he answered with a devilish grin. "I don't know who could have given it to you."

She could not help but be amused at his boldness. He had given her the present, but in truth, she didn't want to give it back. It was very lovely, and it felt good around her neck.

"Why do you sound like a Highlander, gypsy?" she demanded, suddenly changing a discussion she could not hope to win.

"Do I? And do I now?" He began to speak in the Romany tongue, saying words she could not begin to understand.

Fiona shook her head. "Not now, but—"

"My people have long roamed the wild Highlands. 'Tis natural we have picked up their way of talking."

She pursed her lips. "I have never known a Highland gypsy."

He put his fingers to his lips and made a courtly bow from the waist. "And has m'lady known many gypsies?"

"You are the first," she admitted.

"Good, then you begin with the best. Now." He reined his gelding around. "Let us hurry, or we won't catch up with the others and your grandfather will throw me into his deepest oubliette."

Fiona looked around. "Which way did they go?"

"That way, m'lady." He pointed north toward the low wooded hills.

"Are you certain?" she asked suspiciously. "I thought they went west."

"If it please you, we shall ride west," he replied.

"West," she said firmly. He might make her laugh, but she would cause him to remember who she was. A gypsy musician was little more than a servant, perhaps even less.

"West we ride," he agreed, "but if we cannot find them, the fault is yours."

Chapter Four

Fiona and Davy rode for the greater part of an hour without sighting her grandfather or his guests. Once, they stopped to fly Silk again. This time she brought down a blackbird, and Davy let the hawk devour it.

Fiona began to feel more at ease with the gypsy, but annoyed with herself when it became obvious that she'd chosen the wrong direction. Grandfather would be furious that she hadn't remained with the group. Cnocanduin Castle might be safe, but even seasoned warriors preferred to ride in company on the Borders. Here, any grove of trees could conceal an ambush by cattle reivers, English soldiers, or outlaws bent on robbery and murder.

Despite her uneasiness, Fiona was beginning to enjoy her adventure. Although a gypsy could never be considered a suitable companion, she'd spent far too little of her life alone with a rugged, virile man.

"Where exactly in the Highlands are you from?" she asked him, as they waded the horses through a low spot between two fields.

Davy shrugged. "Here, there, wherever the wind takes me. A gypsy's roof is the sky. His floor is the green earth, and his walls the mountains."

"You are well-spoken for a vagabond," she observed tartly. The water was deeper than she'd expected. Cold mud splashed up to her mare's belly and wet Fiona's boot. She wanted to turn back toward Cnocanduin Castle but she didn't want to admit defeat.

"A man lives as he can," he said. "A troubadour by his songs, a warrior by his sword, and a gypsy by his wits. A slow tongue would bring me few hot meals and fewer warm beds on a snowy night."

She glanced back at him. Davy was hatless today, and the breeze ruffled his thick, dark hair, making him even more handsome. The rough terrain bothered him not in the least, and he rode as though he were part of the animal. "For a man who makes his way entertaining, I am surprised that you wear a warrior's sword."

"Aye, I do. A man without a sword in Scotland is like a bird without wings."

"And you can use your sword? Without cutting off your own foot?" she teased.

He made a solemn face. "Pray God it be so."

They rode in silence for a while longer before she spoke again. "In your extensive travels, tell me, what have you heard of one Duncan MacKenzie?"

Davy's snapping black eyes narrowed. "Duncan of Glendruidh? Tearlach MacKenzie's cub? Not only have I heard of the devil"—the gypsy crossed him-self—"I have seen this one they call the Red Wolf."

"And . . . ?"

He shook his head. "Why would you ask about such a man?"

She felt a hollow ache beneath her heart. "Duncan of Glendruidh is such a brute?"

"Auld clootie's get."

Lucifer. Fiona shivered as a chill ran down her spine. "Mind your tongue, sirrah," she chided, more to calm herself than to admonish him. "I am betrothed to Duncan MacKenzie."

"Mary, Joseph, and St. John protect you, lady." Davy brought his bay up beside her and sighed heav-ily. "Is there no way of avoiding such a match?"

She nibbled at her lower lip. "My grandfather says I must keep the bargain, but I think I would rather die than wed a man I do not love."

He laid a sinewy hand on her arm and looked at her with compassion. " 'Tis evil you speak, m'lady. Death will call us all to his dance one day. Do not hasten his coming by such talk."

Fiona swallowed the lump in her throat. "What does he look like, this Glendruidh wolf?"

"Ask me not. Can a man judge another's counte-nance?"

"Is he ugly?"

"Red as a Highland bull and scarred like an old warhorse, the size and image of his father, Tearlach. He is strong, I'll give ye that. I've heard tell that he once ran ten miles with a wounded friend on his back."

She stiffened, and her palfrey sensed her ner-vousness and shied sideways. Fiona brought her under control with a tightening of the reins and a stern word. "My grandfather believes that I must marry a strong man who can protect my inheritance. I have heard it said that this Duncan MacKenzie has been in many battles and has never been defeated."

Davy scoffed. "The man who has never run from a fight is a fool or a liar. Heroes die young."

"I suppose his voice is harsh and burred. I doubt I would be able to understand a word he said."

"Aye, there's something in that. His speech has much of the barnyard in it. Some say he shouts like a trumpeting stag." He grimaced. "Others claim he bays at the moon like a wolf."

"You're making fun of me!" she protested. "I don't think that's a bit amusing."

"Nay, m'lady," Davy assured her. "I'd not frighten you without reason. It would make my heart sore to see a gentle lady like yourself bred to such a barbarian. He is as fierce as a wolf in battle. They say he has killed two hundred men in hand-to-hand combat."

Fiona covered her face with her hands. "I feared as much," she confided. "Doubtless the Red Wolf can neither read nor write his own name."

Davy's expression grew grim. "Neither can I, m'lady. Not in French or English."

"Nonsense," she replied. "One signs one's name the same in any language. But any gentlemen of the south . . ." She hesitated. "Most gentlemen . . ." She corrected herself. "Some learned gentlemen can read both French and Latin."

"The cursed English tongue as well?"

"Yes. Some can, but English is a rough language."

"You seem to speak it well enough," he remarked.

"Yes, by my grandfather's command. My mother

could not, but Grandfather has insisted that I be
properly educated. How could I be Countess of Cnocanduin if I could not speak to my own crofters?"

"And what of those folk who speak only Gaelic, the
true Scots tongue?"

"I understand a little. My grandfather knows it, of
course, but"—she wrinkled her nose—"Gaelic is the
speech of sheepherders and wild Highland savages.
What need does a countess have of it?"

"What indeed?"

Ivory trotted on up the next rise, but she favored
her right foreleg. Fiona signaled her to halt. "I believe
my mare has pulled a muscle. Help me down so that
I can walk for a bit."

"As you wish, m'lady." He dismounted, held the
hawk on one arm, and helped her out of the saddle
with the other as chastely as Father Michael might
do. Then they walked on side by side.

"I fear we are farther from my castle than is wise,"
she said finally. "We must turn back."

He looked down at her, and she realized how big
he was. His chest was deep and muscled, his legs
corded with sinew in his tight leggings. "You aren't
familiar with this terrain? I thought you told me that
you'd lived here all your life."

"I have," she answered. "But Grandfather is very
protective. I usually ride much closer to home."

"Do you know which way Cnocanduin is?"

She stopped short. "Of course I do. It is behind
us." Tremors of doubt plagued her. She had done
something very foolish in coming so far with this
stranger. What if he meant to lure her away to ravish
her or hold her for ransom?

Davy laughed. "I think not, m'lady." He tightened

the hood on her merlin and put the bird on the jutting branch of a dead tree.

"Are you arguing with me?" she demanded.

He took hold of her arms, and the touch of his warm fingers sent odd sensations running through her. Her mouth felt suddenly dry, and the lump had returned to constrict her throat.

"Let me go!" she cried. "If you—"

"Heed, hinny, dinna go all frightened on me," he said, slipping into a rough Highland brogue. "See there!" He turned her to the left, then released her and pointed. "There, above the treetops. Is that not the tower of Cnocanduin?"

"Yes, yes, it is," she stammered. "But how did you know?" She looked at him with wide-eyed wonder. "Is this more of your magic?"

Davy laughed. "Nay, m'lady, 'tis not. I was so certain that you were leading us in the wrong direction, I eased to the left, then left again until we came full circle. Your castle is not more than two miles away."

"You may not lay hands upon me," she protested. "Are you daft that you do not know how much danger you put yourself in? You could be hung for abusing a lady of high birth! My grandfather has the power of pit and gallows. He may be aging, but his mind is sharp. He is a great earl, a man to be feared by the likes of you."

Davy stepped back. "I have offended you?"

"Y-yes, you have," she stammered. Her heart was racing, but whether it was fear or the sudden shock of his hands holding her she could not tell. Butterflies tumbled in the pit of her stomach, and she felt light-headed. "You may not handle me like one of your

Highland lassies. I am a highborn lady. I will be Countess of Cnocanduin.''

He sighed heavily and looked crestfallen. "I did not mean to overstep my boundaries, lady. I wanted only for ye to see that I'd brought you safely home, not carried you off like a stolen cow." He turned and walked a few yards away, then returned with a handful of sweet violets. "I am not a man who often says he is sorry," Davy murmured. "Let the scent of these flowers speak for me."

Fiona stared at the bouquet of pale purple violets nestled in a cluster of bright green leaves. She tried to speak, but no words would come. Instead, moisture clouded her vision as she reached out and took them.

"Have I offended you further?" The lilt had gone from his voice. She could hear the barely controlled anger beneath the surface.

"No," she managed. She could smell the fragrance of the delicate blooms. "How did they survive under yesterday's snow?"

"They are as tough as they are beautiful." Davy's taut jaw relaxed, and he flashed an endearing grin. "As I think you may be beneath your fine feathers."

"You dare much for a man who owns nothing but the clothes on his back," she challenged.

"As a Roman once said, 'Painters and poets alike have always had license to dare anything.' "

"What Roman? What are you talking about?"

"His name was Horace, and he lived in the holy city of Rome just before the time of Lord Jesus."

"I have never heard of this Horace," she replied haughtily. "I believe you're making it up. How would a gypsy know anything of a long-dead Roman?"

Davy shrugged. "My sword master taught me, first

Horace and Cicero, then how to swing a blade without cutting off my own body parts."

"You are an outrageous liar. What gypsy ever had a sword master? Likely you picked up whatever you do know about fighting in some dockside brawl."

"Likely," he agreed. "But I hope I don't have occasion to use what skill I have. Horses are coming, from that direction. Fast." He took her by the waist again and set her back into the sidesaddle, then mounted his own horse.

"My hawk!" she cried.

"Let us see who comes first," Davy replied. "If I must fight to protect you, I can't be hindered by a bird."

"I won't leave her," she argued. Reining the gray mare close to the branch, she took the heavy bird onto her arm and prepared to ride.

Eight men on horseback appeared at the crest of the hill. "There!" one shouted. The group wheeled their mounts and rode toward her and Davy at a gallop.

"It's all right," Fiona said when Davy's hand went to his sword hilt. "It is Gruffydd and a patrol from Cnocanduin."

They sat and waited as the Welshman and the earl's men-at-arms thundered down on them.

"Lady!" Gruffydd called. "Are you unhurt?"

Four guards with unsheathed weapons surrounded Davy. Rob Geddes tried to put a sword to the gypsy's throat, but Davy whipped out his own blade and blocked Rob's blow. Steel clashed against steel, and the soldier's sword flew through the air and landed in the grass.

"Say the word and he dies!" Gruffydd shouted, joining three others in closing in on Davy.

"No!" Fiona yelled. "Let him be. We were lost, nothing more. The gypsy did nothing to harm me."

"Well for him he did not," the Welsh guard replied, waving back his men. "Lest we would take his head and swing it from the walls of Cnocanduin Castle."

"He would have done it too," Winifred assured Fiona once she was safely back in her tower bedchamber. "What were you thinking to fall behind Lord Jamie and become lost? You could have been murdered."

"Or worse," Nadette scolded in French.

For once the Frenchwoman and the Scot were in agreement. Even young, red-cheeked Agnes was shocked by what had happened to her mistress.

"A woman has but one maidenhead to lose," the maid murmured. "Joan Bell was took by the English last year. She come back home wi' a babe swellin' under her apron, and Gordon Wilkie, the miller, what was to wed her took the widow Tait to kirk instead. Joan borned her bastard in a cow barn and run off to Glasgow wi' it. No decent man would have her without her maidenhead, lady."

"I assure you all, my maidenhead is intact," Fiona said heatedly. "Stop fussing over me. I'm fine."

"But it does your reputation no good to be seen alone with such a fair broth of a man," Winifred reminded her. "It's not my place to speak of such, but—"

"Yes, yes, Winifred, I know," Fiona said. "What was

I to do? Davy Fa was most gentlemanly toward me. He even drew his sword to protect me when—"

"A gypsy with a sword," Nadette grumbled in her own tongue. "That is as odd as a lapdog with two heads. It is not natural."

"And him so dark and handsome." Agnes gathered up Fiona's soiled riding cloak. "Cook do say that Lord Jamie will have the skin off the gypsy's back for this."

"Oh, bother!" Fiona cried. "Enough of your chattering! You're worse than crows." Snatching a cap from Nadette's hands, Fiona pinned it in place and hurried out of the room and down the stairs.

She dreaded seeing her grandfather. The captain of the guard had told her that the earl was furious with her. Knowing Grandfather, the sooner she went to him and made her apologies, the sooner he would forgive her. But she simply couldn't face him yet.

She slipped a hand into her pocket and fingered the crushed violets she had hidden there. She needed to be alone, away from prying eyes and scolding tongues. From force of habit, she found herself continuing on down the stairs, past the great hall landing, down to the lowest depths of the castle, to the brink of the holy well.

In the daytime, small rays of light spilled through narrow shafts above, keeping the cellar from utter darkness. Fiona did not bother with a candle. She made her way to the rim of the well and sat there, hoping that the magic of the spot would ease her troubled thoughts.

She could not get Davy Fa out of her head.

He was a lowly gypsy, a man utterly forbidden to one of her birth. Yet she could not help the rush of emotion she felt when his image formed in her mind's eye.

Davy was worldly and witty, handsome and brave. He told her she was beautiful, not as other men had done, but in a manner that made her believe his words. Davy had given her a precious necklace of amber, enchanting it to her windowsill.

She remembered his hands when he'd offered her the violets. They were hard and rough for one who made his living as a minstrel. His nails were cut straight across and clean, a rarity in any man, let alone a commoner.

Davy Fa was wicked in his unabashed pursuit of her, and romantic, and oh, so very daring. And she was a noblewoman of high degree betrothed to a kilt-wearing, red-maned savage.

It was the stuff of old ballads. The words to Davy's song, "Gypsy Laddie," fell like silver raindrops into her thoughts.

> Come away with me, my hinny and my heart,
> Come away with me, my dearie,
> And I'll make for you a bed of heather green,
> And your lord shall not come near thee. . . .

Fiona shivered. Why were the women of old so brave? Where did they find the courage to throw off husband and duty to follow their hearts?

And for the briefest instant, she imagined herself running barefoot over the heather, bathing in some icy Highland stream, and sleeping in Davy Fa's strong arms.

"My lady! My lady! Are ye down there?"

Winifred's voice cut through Fiona's reverie.

"The earl calls for you, m'lady! You must come at once! They mean to throw the gypsies into the dungeon, and Hugh says Lord Jamie says he will hang them before sunset."

"No!" Fiona cried. "He cannot!" Heart pounding, she ran up the stairs toward the great hall to confront her grandfather's anger.

Chapter Five

When Fiona reached the carved screen just inside the entrance to the great hall, she stopped, arranged her hair, and fixed a smile on her face. "My lord," she said as she stepped through the archway into the vast room and made a curtsy. "What is wrong?"

Everything was wrong. She knew that by one glance. Servants had taken away the high table and left the earl's high-backed chair on the raised platform. Her grandfather sat there in his second-best robes with his earl's belt around his waist and a scowl on his lined countenance. On one side of him stood his steward, on the other, the captain of his guard.

Fiona's knees went weak. The last time she had seen the old earl like this, he'd pronounced a death sentence on two murderers and had their bodies hung in an iron crow cage at the crossroads.

Fiona's gaze swept the room. There, not ten feet

from the earl, stood two men-at-arms with Davy chained between them. The other gypsy, the man who'd played the violin so sweetly, was also in irons, but Fiona paid little heed to him.

"My lord," she repeated loudly as she drew close to her grandfather. "What is this? What have these gypsies done wrong that you pass judgment on them?"

For an instant, Fiona's gaze met Davy's. She'd expected to read fear in his eyes. Instead she felt a blaze of defiance.

What kind of gypsy are you, she wondered, *who can face down a belted earl in his own hall and not be afraid?*

Knowing tears would not move her grandfather an inch from his purpose, she smiled gaily at him. "My ladies said you wished to see me, my lord."

The earl pointed at Davy. "This man put you in great danger today when he lured you away from the hunting party! And one of Gruffydd's men swears he saw him lay hands on you."

"Oh, no, Grandfather. That's not true. It was my own fault. Davy begged me to ride on, but I saw a pigeon and wished my hawk to make the first kill. The man stayed with me and protected me. If he wished to do me ill, he had every chance. Surely his heart is pure and good."

Her grandfather leaned forward in his chair, brow wrinkled, eyes narrowed. She swallowed. Grandfather could be very hard when he wanted to.

"Please, m'lord," she continued. "Consider that the fault was mine. Punish me, but do not punish a good servant who wished only to bring me home to these walls."

The earl looked from her to Davy and grunted.

"Throw them in the dungeon," he ordered. "I will think on this and make a decision tomorrow."

"But Grandfather—" Fiona protested.

"You've heard my decision, girl," he roared. "Get you to the women's quarters before I throw you in the dungeon as well!"

Fiona made a hasty curtsy and fled the hall. She knew he was bluffing. He'd never lock her down in the dark with the damp and the rats. He'd never even laid a hand on her in anger, not if one didn't count swats across the bottom when she was very small. No, Grandfather was a kind and just parent, but she knew better than to argue with him when he was in such a mood.

But she didn't climb the steps to her quarters. Instead she went to the chapel and spent the next half hour in reflection on the day's events. If someone told her grandfather that she'd not obeyed him, she could argue that she'd been on her knees in front of the altar. To that the earl could have no rebuttal.

She did not go to supper. Rather, she waited until she knew that Grandfather would be at his evening meal, then took a light and went down to the dungeons below the keep.

A guard opened the inner barred door when she knocked. If he was suspicious of her reasons for visiting the prisoners, he didn't dare ask. The steps to the cells were steeper than those leading to the holy well. Both stood on the same level on solid rock at the heart of Cnocanduin, but no passageway led from one cellar to the next.

There were cobwebs and the squeak of scurrying rodents at the bottom of the stairway, but no additional guards. The cells here were carved in rock

Davy whispered something she couldn't hear to his comrade, and Niall retreated to the recesses of the cell. Then Davy pressed close to the rusting bars, covering her hand with his. "I'd not have you risk your own safety by coming here," he whispered.

"I do not. My grandfather would never harm me."

"You say not, but you also claim he has betrothed you to this butcher, the Red Wolf of Glendruidh. He will use you harshly, and make of you a breeding mare. He has many women, they say."

"He will not if he becomes my husband!"

"Ah, but you said you would not wed him. What of that, lady?"

She felt a rush of strength run through her veins. "I will not. I cannot. I only meant that if I did, which will not happen, I could not permit such behavior."

"But you will marry him," Davy murmured sadly. "You will go to Duncan MacKenzie, and good Niall and I to the crow cage. I will hang tomorrow, lady."

"No!" she protested. "You won't. I won't let you."

"I have seen it," he said. "Gypsies have the sight. I have witnessed my own hanging."

Tears sprang to her eyes. "No, don't say that, Davy. I could not bear for you—"

"Not bear it? How not bear it? It's my neck that will feel the prick of the hemp. I am nothing to you. As you have told me, you will be countess here, and I am a wandering gypsy. My bones will be picked clean by the crows and then tossed into some cow pen until sun and wind turn them to dust."

He raised her hand and turned it to kiss the palm. Sweet sensations ran up her arm, and she tried to pull back but he held her fast.

"No, you must not!" she hissed. "Please."

"Why not? I am a dead man. Would you not give a dead man a single kiss?"

"Nonsense," she cried. "I would not kiss a dead man at all."

He kissed the pulse at her wrist.

"Stop that," she said again, but she did not pull away even when he relaxed his grip on her hand. "Stop saying you're going to die. This is all a misunderstanding. My grandfather is not a monster. He rewards his good servants. He doesn't hang them."

"Tell that to the executioner."

She couldn't help thinking how well her hand fit in his, how natural it felt to have him hold it. "You must trust me," she urged. "I will undo the mischief I have caused."

From the back of the cell came the poignant notes of Niall's violin. Softly, Davy began to sing.

> Gi' me one kiss, my bonny lass,
> One kiss to last the morrow.
> For I must die on Martinmas,
> And ye shall weep in sorrow. . . .

Tears began to spill down Fiona's cheeks. Leaving the candle behind, she ran to the stairs and made her way up them, finding her way by the feel of the stones. The guard jerked upright, as she reached the barred gate and began to pound on it.

"M'lady—" he began.

She didn't stop to hear the rest. She rushed into the hall again, found her grandfather absent, and asked the nearest servant where he had gone.

"To the stables, lady," the cook's assistant replied. "You did not come to table. Will you want—"

"No! I am not hungry."

Heedless of the curious stares of retainers and Father Michael, she hurried outside to the stables. There she found the earl appraising the hindquarters of a mare he was considering buying from a neighbor.

"Where is your cloak, girl?" her grandfather asked when she appeared at his side. "There's a chill in the air. It smells like rain. Would you catch your death of ague and leave Cnocanduin without an heiress?"

"Can you think of nothing but this castle, Grandfather?" she demanded. "Please, you must listen to me."

He waved away the grooms and continued to stroke the black horse. "What do you think of her, girl? Will she drop fine colts? Notice the width of her chest and the length of her legs."

"I didn't come to talk about horses," she said. "It's the gypsies. It's not fair—"

He shook his head. "Do not bother yourself with them, Fiona. I've decided to hang them tomorrow. I should never have allowed them into Cnocanduin."

"But why? I told you that Davy—the taller man, the one who rode with me—did nothing wrong. And his friend wasn't even—"

"You are too excitable, Fiona. You remind me of your mother. They are just gypsies. What matter if there are two less? They are thieves and rascals all."

"You don't hang a man without reason," she protested.

"Oh, I have reason. Hogg said he is missing cattle. He found one butchered a few days ago. Likely the gypsies stole it. They are ever free with other men's beef."

"But Davy protected me. He stayed with me all day and—"

"Exactly. And what will your betrothed think? You had no women with you, no trusted servants. If he had his way with you, you'd not dare say so for fear of never finding a husband. This gypsy has smeared your name. From his own lips, he admitted he may have spoken too boldly to you and that he touched you. It is enough to warrant a death sentence."

She clutched her grandfather's sleeve. "Please," she begged. "You must listen to reason. I don't want—"

"What you want does not always matter, Fiona. You forget that I am lord of Cnocanduin. Go to your room and pray for his soul if you wish to do something of use. Tomorrow he hangs. At sunrise."

It was close to midnight when a cloaked figure crept down the hall to the guard's station beside the dungeon stairs. A torch illuminated the gate, but no man-at-arms stood at his post.

Fiona breathed a sigh of relief as she pulled the heavy iron key from a peg. She hadn't known how she would distract the sentry. She'd been afraid she might have to knock him unconscious.

Quietly, she made her way down the twisting steps. Only when she reached the bottom did she dare uncover the lantern she carried in her left hand.

"Davy," she whispered. "It's me."

She heard a slight movement in his cell as she crossed the stone passageway and turned the key in the lock. Instantly Davy pushed open the door, and both he and Niall came out.

"I've come to help you," Fiona murmured. "Don't speak. Follow me." She led them back up the steps and past the guard station.

Without saying a word, the two men followed her through the castle, climbing stairs, cutting through rooms, and finally ending in the great hall.

She went to a spot behind the high table and pushed aside a tapestry. Then she handed the lantern to Davy and ran her hands along the stone blocks. One section, nearly chest-high on Fiona, tilted and slid on an oiled hinge. She glanced back at Davy.

He cupped his hand for her to use as a step. With his help, she scrambled up and crawled into a tunnel too low to stand in. "Close the stone behind you," she whispered.

Soon all three were inching their way along the dusty passage. The confined crawlway led downhill and toward the outer castle walls by a tortuous path that twisted and turned until Fiona lost all sense of direction.

The air was so stale that the lantern soon flickered and went out. Spiderwebs tangled in Fiona's hair and stuck to her face. It was all she could do to keep from coughing, but she dared not make a sound.

Fear gripped her. Images of demons and dead things rose in her mind. What if they reached the other end and found the entrance plastered shut? She hadn't been in this tunnel since she was seven. What if the roof had collapsed or the walls pressed in too tightly for a man as big as Davy to get through? What if the three of them were trapped here until they died?

"How far?" Davy asked when it seemed to Fiona that they had been crawling for hours.

"I don't know," she answered.

"What do ye mean, ye dinna ken?" Niall demanded.

"It's been years since I came through here," she murmured. "But I could never get you through the main gate. I—" Her head struck something solid. "Ouch!" she cried.

For a moment she froze. Then she pushed against the wooden panel. To her relief, the hatch opened and fresh air poured in.

"Are you all right?" Davy put his hand on her leg.

"Yes," she said. "This is it. Shhh." She squeezed past a statue of Mary into the nave of the village church. Davy and Niall climbed out behind her, and Davy slid the panel back into place. "We're outside the walls," she said. "But we're in the village. I have horses waiting in the woods."

"Why are you doing this for us?" Davy asked her.

She shook her head. Even she wasn't sure. The escape hole that she'd just revealed to the two gypsies had been a family secret for hundreds of years. Meant as a last resort in times of siege, the passageway could bring death to all inside Cnocanduin. "You must swear never to tell what I've just shown you," she said urgently. "Swear in the Holy Mother's name."

Davy nodded. "On my immortal soul, I so swear."

"And I," agreed Niall. " 'Twas a bold thing ye did fer us, lass."

"I just couldn't see you die," she murmured.

"Will ye go back the same way?" Niall asked her.

"No, I couldn't stand to do that again. I'll see you to the horses; then I'll wait in the trees until morning. Later, when the crofters go into the castle to bring supplies, I'll go in with them. The guard changes just before morning Mass. The night men-at-arms will believe I went through in daylight, and the day—"

"I see," Davy said. "But these horses you spoke of? If we take them, we will be horse thieves, will we not?"

"I suppose," she replied. "But better live horse thieves than dead musicians."

Davy chuckled. "Spoken like a true Highlander."

It took them only a few minutes to thread their way through the houses, across a common grazing area, and into the forest. As she'd promised, the horses were waiting.

"I was afraid whoever you'd bidden to bring them here would fail you," Davy said.

"Me too," she agreed. "But I have a few loyal friends. One is a groom. He came to Scotland from France with my mother, and stayed to serve me. I see Gautier has chosen well. These are good animals. They will carry you safely beyond the reach of my grandfather's anger."

"How can I thank you?" Davy said.

"By getting away," she answered softly. "I would like to think of you singing your songs and not lying in a crow cage."

"Hurry," Niall hissed. He mounted the nearest horse, a big bay Fiona recognized as one of her grandfather's fastest animals.

"Good-bye," Fiona whispered.

Davy was standing so close that she could feel his breath on her forehead. He wanted to kiss her; she knew it. And she knew she would let him. She closed her eyes and tilted her face.

She felt his warm hands on her shoulders, skimming the surface of her cloak. She held her breath.

Surely he was not so stupid that he would miss his only chance.

And then she gave a muffled cry of alarm as Davy flung her cloak over her head and tossed her over his shoulder. "What? What are you doing?" She tried to scream.

She kicked and struck out with her fists, but the folds of the heavy woolen cape trapped her and made it difficult to breathe, let alone cry for help.

She felt him leap into the saddle with her crushed hard against his chest, heard the thuds of the horse's hooves against the mossy ground, and his deep mocking laughter. And then they were galloping madly through the trees, away from Cnocanduin Castle and everything she held dear in the world.

Chapter Six

After a few minutes, Fiona's struggling became frantic as she uttered muted cries of distress. "Quiet, lady," he warned her.

She shuddered and went limp.

"By the Mass," Niall called. "You'll suffocate her."

Davy slowed his horse to a trot and shifted the woman's weight from his shoulder to the front of his saddle. "Listen to me," he said sternly to his prisoner. "I'll unwrap you if you'll promise not to scream."

She lay against him, seemingly unconscious.

Concerned, he yanked the big animal up short and slid down with his precious burden. He laid Fiona on the damp, mossy grass and pulled the thick cloak off her head. She didn't move.

Her eyes were closed. She looked like a wilted flower washed up on a Highland beach. Worried, he placed his fingertips over her lips to see if she was breathing.

Niall reined up and circled back to halt his horse beside them. "Have you killed her, then?" he demanded.

Davy's gut twisted and he went all hollow inside. "Lady," he repeated. "Fiona?" Leaning close, he grasped her shoulders and shook her. "Wake up!"

A hard left fist connected with his cheekbone. In a heartbeat, the wench went from helpless beauty to shrieking kelpie, the ghostly water sprite who sought to murder travelers.

Niall's roars of laughter rang in his ears as Davy clapped one hand over her mouth and tried to subdue her with the other. She got in another stinging jab to his eye and a glancing blow to his nose before he pinned her wrists over her head.

"Stop! Stop! I don't want to hurt you, lass!" he said as he wrestled her to a standstill.

She bit his hand.

Davy swore a foul oath, but he kept his fingers clamped tightly over her mouth. "Hist!" he said. "Enough!"

She muttered something against his hand.

"I'll let go of your mouth if you promise not to scream."

She nodded.

Cautiously, he did. This time she made no sound, but her eyes were like daggers. "Don't make me tie and gag you," he said to her. "I can if I must, but you won't like it. Truce?"

"A truce? With you? God rot your bowels, you—"

He muffled her curse with his hand. "What talk is that to the man who loves you?" he demanded.

She tried to bite him again.

"She loves you!" Niall cried, bent double with his laughter. "She desires ye . . . above all men."

"Lady." Davy leaned down to her and whispered in her ear. "I'd sooner cut off my right arm than harm a hair on your head. I love you, and I want you for my wife."

Her eyes widened and she gasped for breath.

"Aye," he said. "I do love ye. If you'd but listen to what I have to say." Cautiously, he removed his hand again.

"Villain!" she accused.

The sweet woman scent of her was unnerving. She was all tangled hair and warm, soft skin. Her chest heaved from exertion, and the vein at her throat throbbed.

He'd lied to her. What he felt was not love, but something more primeval. He desired her. He wanted her for himself. This was a lass fit to ride beside him, to grace his table and bear his bairns. And one he would welcome into his bed, one he would never tire of as he had all the others. Passion for life ran deep in this flame-haired Border woman, and he recognized a bold, lusty spirit to match his own.

Slowly, he let go of her wrists. "Enough? Can there be peace between us, dearie?"

She nodded and sat up.

He took her right hand to help her rise, and she slapped him so hard with the other that stars exploded in his head.

By the faith! I must remember she's left-handed, Davy thought.

Niall toppled off his mount and rolled over the rocky ground in unrestrained glee.

Fiona snatched a skean from a hidden sheath at her ankle and held the little knife in front of her as she backed away.

" 'Ware!" Niall shouted amid his bursts of glee. "She's got a blade! She'll skin ye, crown to heel."

"Get away, you lying scum!" Fiona warned. "I'll kill you if you try to touch me again. I swear I will. Take the horses and go back to the gates of hell where you were spawned. You shall not have me."

Davy's good humor began to evaporate. "Lady," he reasoned, "you will get us all killed. You are nay within your grandfather's castle walls. All manner of evil men roam the Borderlands by night."

"I see that," she answered.

There was none of the wilted flower in her now. She was all nerve and steel, her back as straight as a lance, her knife held low in a proper fighting stance. He didn't doubt for a moment that she'd gut him without blinking an eye.

"Damn me, but you are a lass for bards to make songs about," he said. "But any warrior with a brain knows when he is outnumbered. There is no shame in surrendering to fight another day."

"I'll carve out your liver and hang it from Cnocanduin's tower," she threatened.

Niall pounded the grass with his fists while tears of delight spilled from his eyes. "She will too, ye great ox," he gasped. "She'll spit and roast you over a Beltane fire."

"A fine start this is to our honeymoon," Davy said sharply.

Off to the north, a wolf howled. Curtains of fog were beginning to blanket the meadow, and clouds slid across the moon's silver disk.

Hair rose on the back of Davy's neck. *Danger!* He could smell it. He couldn't hear hoofbeats, but he knew in his bones that armed men were riding toward them.

Some called his mother a witch, but he'd never known her to voice an evil thought. Although she was a devout Christian, her blood was pure Pict, the ancient ones of Scotia who possessed the sight. And whatever her powers were, he alone of his brothers had inherited them.

"Come, lady," he said, his voice dropping to a whisper. "Death comes riding. We must away or shed our life's blood on this spot of earth."

"You're lying again," she flung back. "Do you think me a fool to—"

Niall leaped up and caught her from behind, pinning her arms to her side. This time she did not cry out. She stood, stiff and proud, waiting for him.

"Do your worst," she murmured. "You may ravish my body but I will curse your root and seed to the seventh generation."

Davy twisted the knife from her hand, brushed his lips to hers, and vaulted into the saddle. Niall let go of her and mounted his own horse.

His animal tossed its head and whinnied, and the call was answered by a nicker from the forest below them. "They're coming," Niall warned.

Davy rode close to Fiona and held out his hand. "Trust me, hinny. I'd die before I'd dishonor ye."

"Why should I? That may be my grandfather's men come to rescue me and hang the both of you from the nearest tree."

"Aye," he agreed. "It could be, but the uneasiness

in my gut tells me that they are English soldiers or worse.''

"What could be worse?" she answered, but she grabbed his hand, and he yanked her up, belly-down across his saddle.

Niall was already moving away, not galloping, but walking his bay. Davy pulled her upright in front of him, a formidable task with the tangle of her skirts and the folds of her cloak.

Now they could hear the jingle of saddle harness and the creak of armor. Niall guided his animal into a gully, and Davy followed.

A stranger's voice pierced the fog. "I tell you, I heard a horse whinny." The thick accent was pure Yorkshire.

"Ghosts."

"Edgar would rather fight ghosts than Scots."

"Aye'ah, and swive 'm too," another man observed.

"English," Davy whispered into Fiona's ear as he covered her mouth with his hand once more. "Shhh."

She sat as still as a statue. He couldn't even hear her breathing.

Niall's horse snorted, and sweat trickled down the back of Davy's shirt. His mouth tasted of fear, not for himself, but for the woman in front of him, the lass he'd sworn a blood oath to protect and cherish.

English raiders this far north into Scots territory must be desperate men. They'd commit murder for Fiona's slippers, let alone her cloak and fine clothing, his weapons, and the valuable horses.

He tried to estimate their numbers by the sounds of the horses, but without seeing them, it was difficult at best. A score, perhaps thirty men bent on robbery and destruction. He doubted that this was an official raid. The English boy king's generals sent hundreds to burn and loot, not dozens.

Outlaws would take no pity on a gently born lady such as Fiona of Cnocanduin. They would share her white body among themselves, then leave her dead and trampled in her own blood.

And if the worst happened, he was to blame. He'd lured her from her grandfather's strong walls. She was his now. No one would take her from him save over his cooling corpse.

Seconds, then minutes passed. The reivers slowly filed past, and Davy's dry mouth was beginning to grow moist again when the bay whinnied at the departing horses.

An Englishman shouted, and Niall put heels to his mount. Davy lashed the black with the ends of his reins and prayed that Fiona's groom had chosen the fastest animals from the earl's stables.

Davy tightened his arms around Fiona's waist as the big horse leaped forward.

"That way!" a bandit cried. "To the left!"

Davy took his reins in one hand and raised the other to his mouth. Then he howled a wolf's challenge so near to the real thing that his horse trembled in fear.

He whipped the black downhill and away from the raiders, driving the animal through a rock-strewn burn and up the far bank. The stones clattered under the horse's iron-shod hooves, but he never missed a stride.

Behind them, Davy heard the scream of men and animals as some rode over the brink of the gully and tumbled down to have others crash atop them. But enough survived that first obstacle to give hot chase.

Away to the north, he and Fiona and Niall rode with the devil's hounds behind them. And all the while the mist clamped tight so they could not see beyond their horses' heads, and distorted the sounds of their pursuit.

Uphill and down, through glens and fields they galloped until the horses began to falter. Even though the black was carrying double, he kept pace with Niall's bay, but when the animal's breathing became ragged, Davy looked for a den to hide in.

Salvation came in the form of a light burning on a rise. Davy turned the black horse toward the signal fire, and as he did, he heard the sound of a hunting horn and Scottish voices.

"Beware!" Davy yelled at the top of his lungs. "English! The English are coming!"

A torch waved and then another. Davy urged his tired horse along a hard-packed path, and they dashed into a village.

"Fire! Fire!" Fiona screamed.

"We're Scots!" Niall bellowed. " 'Ware the English raiders!"

Men and women spilled from the houses. Babies wailed and dogs barked. Davy caught sight of gleaming steel as a giant crofter burst from his doorway with a broadsword in hand.

"Kill the English bastards!" Niall shouted.

Davy reined his black left to avoid the naked giant running from a smithy with a sledgehammer in his fists. "That way!" Davy said, pointing in the direction they'd just come from. "The English murdered Father John!" Then he dug his heels into the horse's sides and galloped out the far side of the village.

Niall laughed. "That should hold the English for

a while. And who is this poor, dead Father John they murdered?"

"I'm not certain," Davy said. "But the English must have murdered at least one Scottish priest by the name of John. And the villagers seemed out of sorts. If the outlaws wanted a fight, I think they found one."

"You've got the horses and you're far enough away from Cnocanduin; can't you let me go now?" Fiona asked.

"Let you go? What are you saying?" Davy replied. "I told you, lass, I mean to make you my bride."

"I cannot wed a gypsy."

"A question, lady," Niall put in. "What made you cry fire back there? There was nay fire. The English hadn't set any houses aflame yet."

"You fools," she retorted. "Call out 'English,' and some cowards may hide under their beds. Yell 'Fire,' and each man will fear it is his bed on fire. That's how you get villagers out of their homes."

"Clever as a vixen," Niall replied.

Davy nodded reluctantly. "Reason, I suppose."

"Yes, sensible reason," she said. "As sensible as the decision that I cannot wed one of your low station. I will be a countess."

Davy slowed his horse to a walk. "But I love you. Does that count for nothing?"

"I don't love you."

"You will when you come to ken me better. I'm lovable, am I not, Niall?"

"Will I have to kiss ye if I answer aye?" the brawny gypsy replied.

"A gentleman does not show his love by stealing a lady from her home and family," Fiona said. "Take me back."

"I can't," Davy answered. "I've chosen you."

"Nonsense." She twisted in the saddle to look him in the face. "Release me, and I promise no harm will come to either of you."

"He cannot," Niall echoed. "If he does, he loses his honor. It is gypsy tradition to steal the woman you love. How else are marriages made?"

"How else indeed?" Fiona said sharply. "You've carried me off, nearly smothered me, and treated me roughly. I'd not wed you if you were the last man on earth."

"Ye make a fuss about the small things," Davy said. "What am I to do? You've stolen my heart. I looked into your beautiful face, and I was forever lost."

"Liar." She thumped him on the chest once more. "You've stolen me for ransom, I know you have. You think my grandfather will pay—"

"Not a silver penny will I take from him," Davy protested. "Nay, you are wrong, lass. It is you and you alone I want. You I must have, though it bring my early death."

"There's a stable just ahead," Niall said. "I remember it from when we passed this way before, on our way south. The house is deserted and the roof gone, but the stable is sound. We could sleep there a few hours and let these horses rest."

"Good thinking," Davy replied. "They'll carry us farther if we don't push them beyond flesh and blood."

"I will not spend the night with the two of you in some barn," Fiona protested. "It is not decent."

"You're right," Davy agreed. "Niall will keep watch for the English, in case they get past the village. You and I are handfast. It will break no rules of—"

"We are not handfasted," she said. "I am betrothed to another. You know that. I am promised to Duncan MacKenzie of Glendruidh. If you don't release me, you'll have not only the Earl of Fraser's troops after you, you'll have this Highland brigand and all his bare-kneed clansmen."

"She has a point," Niall said. "Better for you to stand watch and me spend the night in the hay wi' the lady. As your blood brother, I would not want to see ye place your life in the Red Wolf's jaws for the sake of a lass. I'll take that risk for ye."

"Bastards!" Fiona cried. "You both have souls as black as tar. Let me go, or I swear—"

"A lady should not swear," Davy said. "And a gypsy wife is gentle of speech."

"She does her husband's bidding," Niall agreed.

"I am not, and I never will be, your wife!"

"It will nay do," Niall said.

"It will nay do at all," Davy echoed. "A gypsy woman is chaste. My mother would not approve of us living together without the benefit of book and marriage lines."

"Your mother wouldn't approve?"

Davy fought to keep from laughing. "Nay, she would not. And she is a most formidable woman. Is she not, Niall?"

"She is, my friend. I'd not dare oppose her. Here, here is the stable, as I said." Niall stopped his horse and slid down. Then he lifted Fiona from the saddle and set her lightly on the ground.

"Hang on to her until I get off," Davy grumbled. "I'd not wish to chase her in this mist."

"Aye, and you mind to hold her tight. For she looks more kelpie than woman to me. Let her run into the mist, and she may change back into the water sprite she is," Niall said.

Davy dismounted and handed the black's reins to his friend. Then he lifted Fiona in his arms.

"Please don't do this," Fiona murmured.

The note of fear in her voice shook him to the core. "I told you, lass. I'd die before I'd dishonor you. You are as safe with me as if you be on the church altar." He kissed the crown of her head. "Until we take our vows, that is. After that, I will be the best husband I can, but I'm only a man, and I've heard tell that a wife is a hard master to serve. Never being married before, I wouldn't ken, but if you—"

"Stop it," she said. "Stop making fun of me."

He pretended to drop her, and she responded by flinging her arms around his neck and hanging on tightly.

"That's better," he said. And when she opened her mouth to argue, he kissed her tenderly.

Her lips trembled under his and tasted of honey. That pleased him so much that he kissed her again, and this time she was definitely kissing him back.

Chapter Seven

Davy carried Fiona into the stable. He'd sworn not to do anything to harm her honor, but having her in his arms was enough to tempt a saint to sin. More than anything, he wanted to lay her back on the hay and make slow, sweet love to her. He wanted to touch her and caress her. He wanted to kiss her breasts and stroke her belly and thighs until she cried out and writhed with desire.

Suddenly aware of the tightness in his groin, he swallowed the knot in his throat and tried to remember that this woman would soon be his wife. He must do nothing to betray her, no matter how difficult it was for him to restrain himself from taking her here and now.

Almost as though she could read his thoughts, Fiona broke the kiss. He could hear her panting breaths in the stillness of the dark barn.

"Please put me down," she murmured.

"Fiona, lady, ye must love me," he said as he obeyed her wish. "Love me as I love you, or I will die from wanting you." His lips tingled from their caress. He wanted to keep kissing her. He wanted to do far more.

"You don't understand," she pleaded. "My grandfather will come after you with fire and sword. He will destroy your home, your family. He will kill you, Davy."

Steeling himself to keep from tumbling her in the hay, he caught a lock of her hair between his fingers and raised it to his lips. The scent was clean with a hint of green apple. This was a wench who bathed, and not just at her moon time. He smiled. Fiona Fraser would suit him very well indeed.

"Hist, hinny. I take more killin' than most folks realize. A gypsy is like a fox. Now you see him, now you don't. If need to, I can lead the hounds through the bushes and briars, and over stony ground."

"Do you swear you mean me no harm? On your mother's soul, do you swear?" she whispered.

"Aye, lass, on my good mother's hope of eternal life. I mean you honorable wedlock. And you have my word that I will not take you as a man takes a woman until we have made our vows in front of a holy priest."

She uttered a small, strangled sound. "How do you suppose you can carry me off, nearly get me killed, then expect me to forget all that and make a marriage with a landless gypsy?"

"For love, lass. For love." He sighed dramatically. "Can ye tell me that you have never wished to choose a man for yourself? Can you look me in the eye and tell me you would rather lie with Duncan MacKenzie than a man who has risked everything to have you by his side?''

"Words, just words," she said. "And you are free and easy with them."

He took her hand and pressed it against his chest. "Can ye not feel the beat of my heart, fair Fiona? It throbs for you. And if you spurn me, it will beat no more. I will die for love of you."

"Where are you taking me?" Her voice was small and weary. He felt a flicker of compassion for her. The ride had been long, and she'd been brave.

"To my mother, lass. 'Tis the gypsy way." He kissed her knuckles one by one. "I promised her that—"

Fiona snatched back her hand. "What do you mean?" she demanded suspiciously. "You couldn't have promised her that you'd bring me to her. You didn't know me until a few days ago."

"Nay, you misjudge me," he soothed. "Among our people, it is often the man's mother who says when it is time to choose a wife and start a family. Who, I ask ye, would know him better? 'Dun—' " He bit back his words. " 'Davy,' she says. ' 'Tis time. Follow your heart and find one to walk beside you all the days of your life, and bring her to me that I may bless your union.' Those were her very words."

"Done what? What were you about to say? I think you are a very good liar, Davy Fa."

"*Done,* aye," he agreed. "She told me that 'It is time ye are done with kissing the wenches and leaving them. It is time to think of choosing just one woman and forsaking all others.' That's what she said."

"I-I don't know what to think," Fiona stammered. "I don't trust you, but—"

"But you love me," he supplied.

"No! I don't love you. Not exactly. But neither do I want to see you hanged."

Warmth filled his chest as he remembered what she'd done to break him and Niall out of Cnocanduin. He had begun this task out of love for the Fraser lands and cattle, but now . . . Now he thought his father had made a far better bargain for him. "Give me your cloak," he said gently.

"Why?"

"Do as I say, woman."

He took the garment and spread it on the hay. "Sleep, Fiona. I will keep watch with Niall. In the morning we will talk again. But you will need your strength. We have far to ride to reach my mother's house."

"She lives in a house? But what of 'the sky is a gypsy's roof and the mountains—' "

"Aye, that's true. But my mother has a house of her own in the Highlands, a place of stout walls with chickens scratching round the door and fat sheep in the byre."

"I am not a gypsy, Davy. I'm the granddaughter of an earl. I have responsibilities to the people of Cnocanduin. I cannot abandon them or my grandfather . . . even if . . ."

"If ye wished to?" he finished. "Sleep, hinny. Tomorrow will be time enough to worry. Close your eyes and sleep. I will protect you."

"We ran from those English today, Davy. But Grandfather said that running isn't always the way. A farmer can't gather his fields of grain and flee with them. A woman can't hide her house from raiders. There are times when it takes a strong warrior to hold land and protect the people. My grandfather is such a man. He does not have the gift of a honeyed tongue or song, as you do, but he is wise and filled with courage.''

"I hear you, lass. Now sleep."

Leaving her, he went outside and found Niall unsaddling the two horses. "This is not so easy as I thought," he confided.

"Lies never are," Niall answered.

"There's a lot of childish innocence in her, for all her age," Davy said. "She believes this stuff of romance.''

"Why shouldn't she?" Niall answered. "You've had enough practice in telling lassies what they want to hear.''

"You like her too, don't you?"

"Aye, but ye needn't scowl. Not in that way. I'm not fool enough to lose my heart to my best friend's woman.''

Davy stroked the black horse's neck. "I begin to think that my mother did me no favors by suggesting this.''

Niall dropped the bay's saddle on the ground. "You know what my way would be. Quick and honest. You'll make a fair husband, Davy Fa. The sooner the matter is settled, the sooner you can return to your duties. There might be less time than you think.''

"Why do you say that?"

"Jamie Fraser is an old man. His hand shakes when he lifts a cup of whiskey. Cnocanduin is too rich a prize to stand unguarded. Many would dare much to take it.''

"How could any take the castle and the title when I have the little countess?''

"How many people know her face? One red-haired

lass is much like another. If the right man kills the earl and captures Cnocanduin, he could put another wench in her place. Then your game will be lost.''

"I have no intentions of losing this game or this woman." Davy took the horses' bridles. "I'll find water for them, and I'll take the watch. You get some sleep. I want you to go on ahead. Find my cousin Calum and three or four trustworthy clansmen. Arrange an attack on my camp at the pass north of Kinrara's stone cross.''

"In the folds of the Glen Feshie Mountains?"

"Aye. There's a small spring not far from the cross. We'll be camped there in a week. Tell them to come at us the following morning as we enter the pass."

"A week? Be ye certain? That's hard riding for a horse carrying two. And hard on a lass to go through such country so fast.''

"Are ye deaf, my friend? We'll be there in a week. And I wish to prove my courage to my new bride. Let Calum and his followers pretend to abduct her, and I will fight them off one by one with my trusty sword. Warn them to make me look a hero, but not so real they take off my head in the process."

Niall sighed. "More lies, Davy?"

"And warn Murdo Rennie that I'll be taking a few of my cattle. Tell his sons not to watch the herds so carefully this week."

"You mean to steal your own cattle?"

Davy shrugged. "You'd nay wish me to steal another man's, would you?"

Fiona opened her eyes and blinked. For a moment she couldn't remember where she was. Then she tried to sit up and found herself pinned to the straw by Davy's strong arm.

She took a deep breath and stared up. Rays of light poured through the holes in the thatched roof overhead. The stable smelled of musty hay and mouse droppings, and sparrows pecked the ground beside her.

"Davy," she whispered. "Davy?"

"Aye, sweet?" He stretched.

She felt a moment of panic as she tried to remember what had happened the night before. "We didn't—"

"No, my lady. I did as I promised. I watched over you while you slept."

"Let me up." Excitement and fear raced through her, but she had never felt more alive . . . or more a woman.

When he took away his arm, she rose and brushed the hay out of her skirts. Her hair was partially undone, and her stockings prickly. She needed to use the water closet and to wash the sleep from her face.

"There is a well outside," he said, seemingly reading her mind. "I will see to the horse. Do whatever needs be and meet me back here shortly. Don't think to run off. The village is too far for you to run, and I don't mean for you to escape me."

What have I done? she thought. She'd not meant for Davy to steal her, but she had made it easy for him by breaking him out of the dungeon, getting him out of Cnocanduin, and providing him with horses. In saving him, she'd willfully abandoned her home and responsibilities. Guilt played heavily on her mind.

But along with guilt rode the tantalizing attraction to a man like none she had ever known before. Each time he touched her, each time she bounced against him in the saddle, she'd felt a charge of energy jolt her. His wooing words were not to be believed, but oh, so sweet and welcome in her ears.

Marrying him was impossible. Staying with him was impossible . . . but imagining what it might be like to ride forever through the flower-strewn hills with such a man beside her was a wicked temptation.

When she returned, she found Davy sitting cross-legged on the ground eating a loaf of bread spread with butter from a stone crock. He offered her a chunk and she took it.

"Where did you get this?" she asked. "It's still warm from the oven."

He grinned mischievously. "Never ask a gypsy where he gets his meal. I have eggs as well, but they are not cooked and—"

"No, thank you," she replied. "I am not hungry enough to eat raw eggs." She glanced around. "Where is your friend?" The bread tasted heavenly. She was so hungry she could have eaten the entire loaf by herself. She devoured the piece he had given her, licked her fingers, and washed it down with cold water from the well.

She wanted more and said so.

Davy shrugged. "Gone. It is the gypsy way. At least Niall left us the black horse."

"I hope you don't plan to eat him."

He seemed to consider, then shook his head. "No, he's worth too much. We can always sell him or trade him for a dancing bear."

"A bear?"

"Bears draw customers. They are great moneymakers. I can teach you to read palms. If you get good enough, we'll make a fortune. We can leave the High-lands and travel to London or even Ireland.''

"Lord forbid," she answered. "I want nothing of palm reading or bears. I don't even care for sleeping on the ground in the rain or having an empty belly." She rested her hands on her hips. "I must ask you again, beg you," she said fervently. "Please take me home.''

"I am, my heart. I'm taking you to my home, to the Highlands, to my mother."

"Not willingly, never willingly."

"Aye, so you say. But in time you will think differ-ently. I could tie you, but I think it will be a more pleasant journey if I don't.''

Since the bread was gone, she began to undo her hair and comb out the tangles with her fingers. "I should not have kissed you last night," she mur-mured. "It was wrong of me."

"Not wrong, Fiona. Right."

"My grandfather will pay a great ransom if you return me with my maidenhead intact."

He shook his head, and one lock of dark hair fell over his forehead. She noticed that he had shaved his face since evening and wondered how he had managed. "No silver can buy you from me," he said. "You are mine, now and forever. I live only to protect and cherish you.''

"But you won't let me go."

"Nay," he replied. "I cannot."

"I shall never see Cnocanduin or my grandfather again?''

"Do you think I am so cruel?" he replied. "Of course you will see them. Once we are wed and have a child on the way—''

"A child? You expect me to bear your children?"

"Naturally. Is that not what the Church teaches us marriage is for?"

Tears welled up in her eyes. "This is wrong. Very wrong, and I will never forgive you."

"In time you will," he answered. "In time all will be made right, and you will be glad it happened this way."

"Never."

"Never is a long time, Fiona. Would you rather you had been married against your will to the Red Wolf?"

"Maybe. I don't know," she cried. "Right now I see little difference between you."

All that day, she and Davy rode north. They avoided villages and outlying farms, and kept to the lonely tracks. Often Fiona would look over her shoulder to see if they were being followed, but she never saw any riders.

At noon they stopped beside a fast-rushing burn, and Davy caught two trout using hairs from the black horse's tail to make a snare. He built a fire and cooked the fish. She ate an entire one, and it was delicious, even without salt or bread.

After Davy had extinguished the fire, he set her up on the horse and mounted behind her. They rode until it was too dark to see. She slept supperless that night, curled beside him in her woolen wrap, and awoke with a cluster of delicate, creamy-white pansies with butter yellow centers scattered around her.

Each day became a treasure of wild vistas and shared laughter. Davy showed her green valleys and rushing burns crowned with veils of fairy mist. The hours on horseback slipped away, one by one, as he told her stories and sang merry songs. He pointed out the tracks of roe and other wild creatures, and he knew the sight and song of every bird.

Now that they were away from the settled south, Davy no longer avoided other people. He was a wonderful companion once she realized that no pleas or arguments would change his mind about taking her home. Often he recited poetry or teased her with riddles.

They talked about everything from the proper way to cook porridge to the reported ill health of the English boy king. Surprisingly, Davy listened thoughtfully to her opinions, even when her ideas differed from his.

They ate fish from the streams, bread, milk, and eggs bartered from lonely crofter's dwellings, and greens gathered along the streams. Twice, to her horror, Davy rounded up a cow and drove it ahead of him until he found a buyer.

"Thief!" she accused after she'd watched him sell an abducted cow to a village butcher. "I'll have no part of your dishonest cattle dealings!"

He'd replied with an outrageous tale that the beasts were his, animals that had simply wandered away from his home.

"And you recognize these cows?" she demanded. "They've come miles and miles from the Highlands, and you're telling me that you just happened to stumble on them?"

"Aye," he agreed, "although I know it does seem a little strange."

"More than a little strange," she answered. "I'll tell on you, I vow I will. I cannot abide dishonesty."

He'd shrugged. "A gypsy's life is hard, sweeting. Sometimes a man must live as he can, and what's a few beef among friends?"

"Stealing cattle is a hanging offense."

"Aye, I suppose it would be. If the cows weren't mine to begin with."

Davy did not attempt to kiss her again, and she wondered why. Not that she would have permitted such liberties, she told herself. But it was odd that he wouldn't at least try to have his way with her.

And stranger still that she cherished the memory of those stolen kisses and secretly yearned to taste them again.

The fair weather changed to foul, but they kept riding north and west. They passed shepherds with their flocks and grazing cattle, but fewer homes. Fiona's bottom and legs were sore, and she was often hungry, but she had to admit this was an adventure such as she had dreamed about.

"Where are these Highlands?" she demanded on the fifth day. "Must we keep riding forever?"

"It seems so, doesn't it?" he answered. "There!" He pointed straight ahead. "Watch there. When the clouds break you will see mountains. Can't you smell the change in the air? We'll be entering my homeland soon."

That night they shared a shepherd's hut. Davy told the man that she was his wife, but when she tried to say otherwise, Davy laughed and touched his forehead.

"She sees things, my lady wife," he murmured. "She forgets the names of our three boys and wanders away from home so that I have to go and fetch her."

"Ye should take the poor lassie to St. John's Kirk," the shepherd replied. "The priest there has the finger bone of St. Joseph. If you give a silver penny, your wife can touch it. I've heard of many healings through this relic. The finger bones are powerful.''

Davy had given the shepherd bread and cheese, and the lad had shared a mutton roast with them. The shed was heaped with hay, and Fiona slept soundly.

When they awakened in the morning, the sun was out and the shepherd had already driven his sheep to another pasture.

After breakfast, they continued north, up a deep glen and through a pass with high hills on either side. Fiona gave a little shiver as the high country closed in around them.

What must my grandfather think? she wondered. *Does he believe I'm dead or that I've simply vanished?*

Two days later, in midafternoon, they camped beside an ancient stone cross. ''We will rest here a day or two,'' Davy said. ''The horse is growing thin and needs time to graze.''

''Am I to eat grass as well?'' Fiona demanded.

''No. I've some coin left from the sale of that cow. I will leave you here and go over that rise. There's a farm there. I'll see about finding us some porridge, bread, and cheese.''

''And vegetables,'' she grumbled. ''I'm tired of meat all alone. I'd give my earrings for some juicy turnips.''

''Turnips?'' He shook his head. ''My mother loves turnips. She will like you very well, I think.'' He motioned to a tiny stream. ''You can wash while I'm gone, and do whatever it is that lassies do.''

''I can? Thank you, m'lord. How kind of you,'' she

replied tartly. He looked hurt, and it was all she could do to remind herself that he was a villain, that he'd snatched her away from her home to force her into an unwanted marriage.

"You wound me," he said dramatically. He'd put a hand on the saddle and was about to mount when suddenly Fiona heard an unearthly screeching.

She glanced up to see eight savage Highlanders charging down the hill toward them. The warriors' barbaric faces were painted for war, and the blades of their deadly broadswords flashed in the sun. "Davy!" she cried. "Look!"

"MacKenzies!" He drew his own weapon. "Get behind me, Fiona! I'll not let them take you!"

Fear numbed her, but she could count. The fierce clansmen outnumbered Davy. He'd be cut down trying to save her. "Can't we reason with them? They can't know I'm the Red Wolf's betrothed."

"All the more reason we must fight," he answered. "These savages will carry ye off to the Red Wolf's den!"

"Run and save yourself," she begged him. "Let them take me. I won't have your blood shed for me."

"Nay, lass," he shouted boldly as he raised his sword to block the first man's slashing attack. "For your love, I would gladly die!"

Chapter Eight

The first Highlander, a shaggy, barefooted, black-bearded brute in a saffron tunic and Viking helmet, pounded down on Davy two full lengths ahead of his companions. Roaring like a lion, the attacker swung his two-handed broadsword in a whistling arc.

"No!" Fiona screamed as the huge blade sliced down to cleave off Davy's head.

The gypsy's counterstroke was too swift for her to see. One second the Highlander was rushing forward, and the next he groaned and sprawled on the reddened earth.

"Get to the horse!" Davy shouted, but her feet seemed rooted to the ground. "Do as I say, woman!" he urged. "You'll get me killed for certain if ye stand here gathering dew."

The next howling clansman was not so tall as Davy, but broad, with arms like young tree trunks. His midsection was protected by a shirt of chain mail. His teeth were filed to points, and his shaven head was painted with a red crusader's cross, leaving only a long fringe of blond hair trailing over his shoulders.

"Munroe! Munroe!" he shouted.

Davy turned and tossed her small skean to her. "We're deep in shit now!" he cried. "To horse! Before 'tis too late!" Then he leaped to meet the swordsman.

Fiona caught the knife and tucked it into her bodice. She heard the clash of steel as she darted toward the black horse. Then suddenly her way was barred by a pimply youth in a purple and gray kilt.

"Nay!" he shouted. He swung his targe at her, and it struck her shoulder and knocked her to her knees. Laughing, he dropped the round shield and seized her right arm, but her left had already retrieved the knife.

"Put that down!" he commanded. "You've nay the nerve to—"

She jabbed his hand with the point. He yelped and let go, and she dodged around him and ran for the horse. As she thrust her foot in the stirrup and tried to scramble up onto the gelding's back, she caught sight of Davy.

The bald man was down, and her gypsy was holding off two more Highlanders while a third and fourth circled behind him. She was no expert on hand-to-hand fighting, but she knew a master at work when she saw one.

Davy wielded his weapon like some mighty warrior from a song. Stroke by stroke, he drove his adversaries back, slicing and jabbing, dancing free of their return blows and blocking counterattacks. Four men against one, but not only was he holding his own, he had the lot of them on the defensive, fighting for their lives.

Two men down and probably dead, one howling like an injured puppy, and four more surrounding Davy. That made seven, but she'd counted eight when they'd swarmed down the slope. Where was the last man?

Her unspoken question was answered as another leering warrior loomed up at the horse's head and grabbed her foot. She kicked out with her free leg and felt her heel slam into his head.

The black horse whinnied and reared. Fiona clung to the mane and pulled herself into the saddle. She was past fear now. Everything seemed to be happening in slow motion. She could feel the sun on her face, smell the crushed heather under the gelding's hooves, hear the ring of steel against steel.

The straps were too long for her to reach the stirrups, but she clung to the horse with her knees. "Davy! Davy!" she shouted, as she lashed the animal between him and the man at his back. "Jump up!"

The warrior on her left slashed at the horse's belly with his sword. Neighing in pain, the black wheeled and kicked at him. Davy parried an attack, ducked a blow, and whirled to slap the horse's rump with the flat of his sword.

The gelding exploded under her. He broke into a gallop, and nothing Fiona could do could stop him. She knotted her fingers in the animal's mane and crouched low over his neck as he bolted away down the valley.

She couldn't look back. The odds against Davy were now five to one, and she knew how the uneven contest must end. Salt tears clouded her vision and streaked down her cheeks.

Then, without warning, a column of heavily armed horsemen poured down from the ridge waving their weapons and screaming, "A MacKenzie! A Mac-Kenzie!"

The war cry echoed from scores of throats as the wild Highlanders led by a red-bearded giant swept past her to thunder down on Davy's futile battle.

She tried to rein the black to the left to avoid the ferocious riders, but several hard-faced clansmen veered from the main party and closed in on her. She whipped the black faster, and for a time it seemed she would outrun them, but then the glen ended in a high wall of tumbled rock.

Trapped, she wiped away her tears and straightened her shoulders. She would meet them as a Fraser, and if the red-bearded barbarian was her betrothed, Duncan MacKenzie, she would not show fear before him either.

It did not matter now what happened to her. Davy was dead, and she'd lost him before she'd ever been able to tell him that her heart had welcomed his wooing. Without Davy's laughing voice and snapping dark eyes, the joy would go out of her life.

A tall, young, auburn-haired man took hold of the black's bridle. "Are you Fiona Fraser, granddaughter to Jamie, Earl of Cnocanduin?"

She nodded. She could not speak. She wondered if she would ever be able to speak again.

"Your grandfather sent word to Glendruidh that you had been stolen by gypsies. We have been looking for you." His dirt-streaked face crinkled as he grinned, exposing even, white teeth.

He couldn't be her betrothed, Fiona thought. He wasn't old enough, and he didn't look like a man who had spent the last years at war.

"Come, do not be afraid of me," her captor said. "I am your brother, Fergus." His tanned cheeks flushed redder still. "I mean I am Duncan's brother and will soon be yours," he explained. "Are you hurt, lady?"

She remained motionless. Hurt? Was she hurt? How could her heart be shattered and not show?

"Are you too frightened to say anything?" he demanded.

"I am not frightened of you or any other knobby-kneed Highlander," she answered.

An older, rusty-bearded warrior galloped up on a chestnut stallion and reined his spirited animal in hard.

"Duncan?" the first man demanded.

The newcomer nodded. "We nay come a scrap too early, I'll tell ye that. The Munroe women will have cause to weep tonight."

"How many of them?" Fergus asked.

"Eight."

Fergus grinned. "That's eight less cattle thieves for us to deal with."

"But . . ." Fiona looked from one man to the other. "I thought they were MacKenzies that attacked us. Davy said—"

"Nay," Fergus replied. "That sorry bunch? They are Munroes."

"Were Munroes," the veteran corrected. "They're wolf bait now."

"Why did they want to kill us?" Fiona asked. "We'd done nothing—"

"You had a horse a crofter could not buy with five

years' labor. In these times, a thief needs little reason
to kill.'' Tall and sinewy, the older Highlander's lean
face was scarred, and his Roman nose bore the telltale
evidence of old battles. Hooded gray eyes shadowed
by fierce, shaggy brows inspected her. "This be Jamie
Fraser's heiress?"

"Aye," the younger man said. " 'Tis her."

*Please God, don't let this one be my husband. I'll never
sleep through Mass again,* Fiona prayed. Swallowing the
dust in her throat, she managed to ask, "Duncan
MacKenzie?"

The haughty Highlander shook his head. "Nay, I
be Tormod, heir to Glendruidh."

"Our oldest brother," Fergus supplied.

"Davy Fa," Fiona said. "The gypsy? Is he . . ." The
words shriveled in her throat. "Did they . . ."

The flat gray eyes studied her again. "You show
mickle care for a gypsy who stole you away from your
home and family," Tormod said.

"He was the bravest man I've ever seen," she said.
"If . . . if he is dead, he gave his life for me."

Tormod shrugged. "All men die, but not all die
bravely. He is gone. You will never see Davy Fa again."

Fiona swayed as blackness threatened her. *I will not
weep,* she told herself. *I won't.*

He bade me give ye a message," Glendruidh's heir
said.

She fought the tide of weeping. "What were his
last words?"

Tormod grinned wolfishly. "He wants ye to ken
that he is sorry. He hopes you will forgive him."

"That's all?" she asked.

"One more thing."

Fiona bit her lower lip.

"The gypsy deceived you. I am to say that he was really Duncan MacKenzie, your betrothed."

"What?" She shook her head, unable to accept what she'd just heard.

Tormod's horse nipped at the black gelding. Fiona's mount shied, and she struggled to hold her balance on the saddle.

The russet-haired fighter shrugged. "So he said. He told me to tell you that he tricked you, but that he was sorry. And . . ." Tormod chuckled. "He said he wanted you to know he was my brother, Duncan MacKenzie."

"Another lie," she murmured softly. "Nothing but more lies."

Tormod rested a callused hand on his sword hilt. "What more can ye expect from a gypsy?"

Davy's outrageous claim—that he was Duncan MacKenzie—rode uneasily with Fiona for the long days and nights it took to travel back to her home on the Borders. Why waste his last words with another lie? Why hadn't he said that he loved her? Why had he chosen to tell her yet another untruth, one so outrageous that it would trouble her dreams and bring her pain whenever she thought of it? For if he would fabricate such a tale when he was dying, what hope was there of his entering heaven? Not only did she doubt all that he had told her, but she had great fears for his immortal soul.

Fiona was escorted on her return journey by the dour Tormod MacKenzie, two maids, a young priest, a sensible older cousin of Duncan's named Seonag, and a troop of two hundred Highlanders. Her betrothed did not join them. He did not even come to welcome her to his homeland.

"He was injured in the fighting," Tormod explained. "He is feverish and has no wish to see you this morning. Later, when you make your wedding vows, will be time enough."

In truth, she was glad he had not wished to meet with her. She was certain that the red-bearded giant riding at the head of the MacKenzie charge was indeed Duncan. But she had not seen him again. No doubt he suspected that she was no longer a virgin and blamed her for running away with Davy Fa.

Apparently her bridegroom's anger kept him from making himself known to her, but wasn't sufficient for him to break their engagement. What Tormod had said was true. Her wedding day would be soon enough to meet this Red Wolf of Glendruidh.

How she wished that Duncan MacKenzie would call off the alliance. If she could not be with Davy, she wanted to remain unwed, to live out her life single.

Somehow the trip, which had passed easily when she'd ridden north, wearied Fiona. The wildflowers seemed to have lost their vivid color, and the scents had faded. The sky remained dull gray, and the rocky stones beneath her horse's feet echoed her inner emotions.

She had not chosen to run away from Cnocanduin with her bold gypsy, but his charm had overcome her resistance, and she had come to love him as he'd claimed to love her. Now the romantic adventure had come to a sad end, and she must pick up the pieces of her shattered life and try to start anew.

She began by falling to her knees in front of her

grandfather and begging his forgiveness when she was ushered into the great hall of Cnocanduin.

For a long moment, the faded eyes stared into hers, and then he lifted her by the hand and enfolded her in his arms. That was her undoing, and she couldn't stop the flood of tears.

"I am so sorry," she sobbed. "I didn't mean—"

"Shhh, shhh, lass," he'd replied gruffly. "What is done is done. You are here now, safe within these stone walls. That is what is important."

"I was foolish and ungrateful," she murmured.

Her grandfather had patted her back and wiped her nose with a bit of linen that a servant offered. "There, there. I've been foolish and ungrateful a time or two myself."

Then he'd dismissed her with a smile and turned to make Tormod MacKenzie and his rough followers welcome at Cnocanduin.

Fiona's ladies had welcomed her with open arms. Young Agnes had burst into tears at the sight of her, Winifred had squeezed her hands, and even stern Nadette had softened enough to whisper a few endearments in French.

Nothing would do but that Fiona be tucked into bed and stuffed with roast chicken, bread and honey, and strawberries. Nadette brushed out Fiona's hair and redid it to suit herself while Agnes piled wood in the fireplace until Fiona's chamber was overly hot.

"You poor wee lamb," Winifred fussed. "We have worn our knees thin with prayers for your safe return. You have the blessed Virgin to thank for your salvation."

"*Oui,*" Nadette agreed.

"Please," Fiona said. "Leave me. I am very tired. Let me sleep."

Clucking her tongue, Winifred shooed the others out, then smiled one last time before leaving the room. "Truly, m'lady, Cnocanduin was not the same without you. Even the earl, God keep him, was not himself. Hearing that you were safe and coming home added years to his life."

"Thank you," Fiona replied. "It is good to be home." She closed her eyes and did not open them until she heard the door click shut.

And then she began to weep softly again.

I'm home and safe, she thought bitterly. *But what right do I have to be unharmed when Davy lies in a cold grave, when I will never see him again this side of heaven?*

She stayed in her chambers for two days, and when she came down to the great hall at her grandfather's request, she found that Tormod and his MacKenzie horde had departed.

"They will return after the harvest," the earl said. "I hope that you have learned some valuable lessons from all that has happened, and I hope that you will not shame me on your wedding day."

"No, sir," she murmured, curtsying deeply. "I will not. If Duncan MacKenzie will have me to wife, I will marry him." *But I will never love this wild Duncan,* she vowed silently. *My heart will forever lie beneath the green heather with Davy Fa.*

"Good." Her grandfather kissed the crown of her head. "You are a good lass. I knew that in time you would see the wisdom of doing your duty to Cnocanduin."

"And to you, Grandfather," she whispered.

He took her hand and led her back to the high table. "Bring food and drink," he called to the servants. Then he motioned to a musician with a lute. "Sing and play. Let us make merry, for the Lady of Cnocanduin has returned, never to leave us again."

"Never," she promised. "So long as my husband does not order me otherwise."

"He will not," the old earl said. "Not for long. These walls are too strong, and the world is too dangerous for such a prize as you are, child. Here you will be cared for and protected, and here you will raise up another lord or lady for Cnocanduin to follow after you."

"Yes, Grandfather," she had agreed. "For you and for Cnocanduin."

"And for you," he promised. "You will find happiness in your marriage. You may not think it now, but in time you will."

The summer days spilled away all too quickly. Leaves turned and dropped from the trees, and the first hints of autumn winds blew down from the north.

The weather turned cloudy, and the crofters hurried to bring in their crops. Often the earl rode among them, and a subdued Fiona accompanied him. She listened to all that he said, paying heed to his instructions for harvest and his order that a tenth be set aside for the poor.

September arrived all too quickly, and Fiona was often busy from before dawn until dusk settled over the castle tower. Stores must be filled, cattle, sheep, and swine fattened for butchering, poultry driven into the fields to gather the last of the fallen grain.

Fish and eels must be smoked, honey must be gathered. Herbs and healing plants had to be dried, and milk made into butter and cheese. Wool must be carded and spun, and feather ticks cleaned and restuffed.

Winter would bring bitter, wet weather, and what Cnocanduin Castle folk had not put up, they must do without. And now the inhabitants prepared to clean the fortress from top to bottom. Fiona directed the servants as they emptied the middens, forked out the stables, scrubbed kitchen, hall, and upper chambers, and finally laid fresh rushes on the floors in preparation for her wedding.

As October and her marriage day approached, Fiona's days were crowded with dress fittings and arguments with castle cooks. She had to sit in judgment in the local court beside her grandfather to settle disputes among the crofters and village folk, and she had to oversee the new wall hangings that the sewing women were preparing for the chapel. Yet each day, she found a few minutes to slip away and go down to the quiet peace of the well where Davy had worked his first magic for her.

Her tears were dried up; at least she thought they were. But her love for him had not faded with summer's flowers; instead it had grown stronger.

Often she would lean on the rim of the well and stare down at the still surface of the water and whisper her heart's wish aloud.

"One last look," she said as she dipped up a cool cupful and drank deeply. "If I could have anything, it would be to see his face one last time."

But the power of the well did not work for her. The water remained calm, and no image of her lost love appeared.

"I should have told you," she murmured. "I wish I had told you. I love you, Davy Fa."

"Lady! Lady!" Agnes's squeaky voice echoed down the stone stairwell. "They come, lady! Make haste!"

"Who comes?" Fiona answered, although she already knew who the maid was hollering about.

"The MacKenzie, lady! We saw him from the tower window. He comes with hundreds, nay, thousands of wild Highlanders! Your bridegroom comes!"

Fiona sighed, straightened her spine, and slowly climbed the steps to meet her destiny.

Chapter Nine

Sunlight reflected off kilt brooches and the swords and targes of the MacKenzies as the wedding party neared the entrance to Cnocanduin's gate. Highland pipes swirled her grandfather's greetings from the walls.

As Fiona leaned on the stone windowsill of her tower chamber, she could see men and women, livestock, and dogs, a virtual army moving down the valley toward the castle. Banners proclaimed the clans, not only MacKenzies, but their friends and neighbors, the McDonalds, the McLeods, the Grants, and Sutherlands. All had dressed in their finest regalia to bear witness to this great match between the Fraser and MacKenzie families.

Fiona had not expected so many. Even Cnocanduin would be hard-pressed to provide shelter, meals, and entertainment for hundreds. That must be the reason for the herds of cows and flocks of sheep. The High-landers were not lacking in courtesy to bring their own meat on the hoof. The wedding would be held on the first day of October, but the feasting and merrymaking would go on for at least a week.

And not all the guests would come from the north. Her grandfather had sent invitations to the mighty of the south of Scotland as well: the Armstrongs, the Douglas brothers, the Hoggs, the Maxwells, the Turnbulls, the Raes, the Richmonds, and the Grahams, to name but a few.

Alliance between two powerful families was cause for rejoicing, and Fiona, stripped of her girlish notions of romantic love, could see the reasons for it.

A strong hand on Cnocanduin would help to keep the peace, not only in the Borderlands but in all of Scotland. Even the English would think carefully about launching an assault against an earl who could call an army of fighting men from the Highlands to stand at his side.

Fiona promised herself that despite her reluctance, she would honor her wedding vows. She would be a good wife and a good mother to the children, pray God, that came from the union. She would bear up under the indignities marriage to a Highland barbarian would bring, and she would strive to keep peace in her household as well.

Duncan MacKenzie might still be angry with her for what had happened with Davy Fa. But after their wedding night, when he realized that she'd come to his bed a maiden, she hoped that he would forget and forgive.

"Come, dress me." Fiona forced a pleasant expression as she called to her ladies. "I must be ready to go down and welcome my new husband and his family and friends."

An hour later, her wayward curls neatly arranged and covered with a stylish cap, wearing her gayest gown of blue velvet trimmed in silver ribbons, Fiona made ready to go down to the great hall. She had reached the outer door when a little page came running up the stairs.

"Lady," he called breathlessly. "You are nay to come down." She recognized the nine-year-old as Arlie Maxwell, a freckle-faced hellion come to learn the art of war and statesmanship from her grandfather.

"What nonsense is that?" Winifred demanded. "Of course my lady is wanted to—"

"Nay, the Highlander— Beggin' your pardon, lady," Arlie said. "Your bridegroom, Duncan MacKenzie, has asked that you remain above stairs until you meet at the altar."

"And my grandfather permitted such a thing?" Fiona asked. She had not missed the saucy look in Arlie's eyes. He was enjoying this, the rascal. She'd made him wash behind his ears and brush his teeth more times this summer than he'd cared for, and he was probably happy to see her brought down a peg or two.

"It is my lord earl's command, lady."

Winifred covered her mouth with her hand, and Agnes looked as though she would burst into tears. Nadette hissed a French oath under her breath.

"Thank you, Arlie," Fiona said, taking care to hide

her distress from this young distributor of castle gossip. "Tell my grandfather that I will not intrude upon the festivities in the great hall, if that is his wish."

He grinned, and a lock of his thick brown hair fell over his forehead. He knuckled the offending strands aside and glanced hopefully at a dish of sweets on the sewing table.

"And take care that you do not serve my grandfather's guests with dirty hands," she added tartly. Then she sweetened the rebuke with a sugared walnut. "Off with you," she ordered, "but see that you are in bed at a decent hour."

Much later, upset and angry, still wearing her finery, Fiona crept down the winding stone stairs. How was she to make a marriage with a man who would not even be in the same room with her? How could she forgive such an insult in front of so many guests?

If she had Duncan MacKenzie in front of her, she would not answer for the welcome she would give him! "He deserves to be throttled with his own kilt," she muttered peevishly.

Her first impulse had been to go down to the hall and face him, but she couldn't shame her grandfather so. She must remember who she was and act the lady, no matter how ungentlemanly Duncan MacKenzie might be. Instead, she was retreating to her special place, where she could bid good-bye to the man she loved and search for the fortitude to go through with the wedding.

She need not have taken care to move softly. The guests in the great hall spilled out into the passageways and crowded the doorways. Most were strangers, and most had enjoyed the wine and stronger spirits that the earl had provided. It was easy for Fiona to slip unnoticed through the entranceway leading down to the well.

To her surprise, torches burned along the walls. Someone had been here before her; perhaps her grandfather had brought guests to view St. Joseph's well and the ancient rowan tree. She hesitated, listening, but the noises from above were muffled, and all was silent and peaceful here.

She sighed and went to the rim of the well. The chamber seemed magical tonight. She could easily imagine the women of Cnocanduin who had sat here and stared into the water. Thoughtfully, Fiona traced the words of the ancient blessing.

> *Any woman of pure heart who drinks from the well of Cnocanduin will find protection, strength, and happiness as long as it holds water.*

Why didn't the charm work for me? she wondered. *There is still water in the well.* Her throat constricted as she undid the silver chain at her throat and nestled the amber heart in the palm of her hand.

"Just one last time," she whispered as she dropped the necklace into the well. "Please show me Davy's face one last time."

Her precious token vanished beneath the dark surface, followed by a single tear. "Good-bye, Davy," Fiona murmured. "Good-bye, my forever love."

And then gooseflesh rose on her arms and a shiver ran through her. There, in the widening circles, a familiar image formed.

"Davy?" she cried in disbelief.

"Aye, hinny, 'tis me," a deep voice said.

Strong arms closed around her, and she twisted to stare up into the face of a red-haired ghost with Davy's voice and features.

"How?" Her strength failed her, and she would have fallen if he hadn't caught her.

"Nay, nay, sweeting," he murmured. "Do not fright me so."

She closed her eyes, then opened them again. It was Davy. It had to be. What other man had such laughing eyes, such a smile? Yet his hair was different, and surely her Davy had not had a scar across his forehead.

"What cruel sorcery is this?" she whispered. "Are you real or spirit?"

His dark eyes welled up with tears. " 'Tis your gypsy laddie, lass, and Duncan MacKenzie as well. I am one and the same. Did not my brother—"

"That was the truth?" she demanded. "You were telling the truth when you said that you were MacKenzie?"

"Aye. I expected ye to be angry, but after so long—"

She pulled loose and smacked him hard across his cheek, then dissolved into tears. "I'm sorry," she said. "I'm sorry. I didn't mean—"

He rubbed at the rising imprint on his cheek. "You pack a mighty wallop, lass. You'll make a fine MacKenzie, all right."

She backed away. "Your hair. It's red." And it was, not fire red, or orange, but the rich reddish brown of autumn leaves. "Davy . . . the gypsy's hair was black as night."

He gave a mighty sigh. "Dyed, lass, the better to convince you."

She shook her head. "It was you all along." Shame flooded through her. "You must think me the greatest fool in Christendom."

"Nay, Fiona. I am the greatest fool. I stayed away for years, thinking I was wedding a title. I wasted time we could have had together." He took hold of her hand, lifted it to his lips, and kissed it gently. "I love you, Lady of Cnocanduin. Your castle is strong and your lands are fair, but I would gladly take you to wife were you a barefoot gypsy wench without a penny to your name."

"You tricked me," she accused.

"I did, and I have suffered for it."

"You let me believe that you were dead."

"Nay, that was Tormod. He has a cruel sense of humor. He probably thought it a good joke to tell the truth, but make it seem another lie."

She sat down hard on the edge of the well, her knees too weak to hold her up. This was all too sudden, and her head felt giddy and her stomach churned. "Why didn't you come to me after your MacKenzies saved you? Why did you let me come home thinking that you were—"

"I was wounded." He touched his forehead. "Here, and . . ." He motioned to his thigh. "And here. My father's men carried me from the field unconscious. I lost a lot of blood, and by the time I was well enough to ride, you were home again."

"But you didn't write to me."

He shrugged. "I canna write, lass. I suppose you'll have to teach me if you think it's important."

"You couldn't send a messenger?"

He frowned. "My father fell off his horse. You met my father at Kinrara Cross, didn't you?"

She shook her head. "I met two brothers, but not your father."

"He's hard to miss. He's over six feet tall, with a head like a lion and shoulders like a horse. He looks like me, but he's not so handsome."

"Red-haired?" she asked.

"Aye, that's him, although his hair is more gray than red now. But his beard is as red as Fergus's head."

"I think I saw him, but I thought he was Duncan. You, I mean. I assumed he was my betrothed." Fiona knotted her hands in the folds of her skirt. "Surely my grandfather didn't approve of your deceit in coming here in disguise and—"

"Your grandfather is the one who warned me that I was in danger of losing you. He knew who I was when I came here playing the part of a gypsy bard. He wanted you to fall in love with me."

"He wanted me kidnapped?" This was beyond belief. They had all conspired against her. It would serve them right if she never forgave any of them.

Davy—Duncan—shook his head. "Not that. That happened. He had me locked up to win your sympathy. He never meant to hang me. But then you broke Niall and me out of prison—"

"And you stole me away."

"Aye. But that was before I fell in love with you."

"You do not know the meaning of love."

"Teach me," he murmured. Then he pulled her into his arms and kissed her, tenderly at first and then with passion. "I do love ye, lass," he whispered. "More than my own life, I love you. And if you will forgive me, I will spend the rest of my life proving it to you."

"How can I trust you?" she demanded between kisses. "How do I know you will not make our marriage a tangled web of lies?"

"On my mother's soul, I swear it," he promised. "No more lies, not ever again."

"I don't believe you even have a mother," she replied.

"Aye, I do, lass," he said. "And you and she will get on like two peas in a pod. The gypsy disguise was her idea."

"Your mother's idea?"

He kissed her again, and she tightened her arms around his neck. Butterflies were tumbling in her belly, and she could think of nothing but his touch, his lips on hers.

How could she let Duncan get away with such a rotten trick? On the other hand, she had come to the well looking for a miracle. And now that she'd been granted one, was she fool enough to refuse it?

"Why didn't you want me to come down to the hall?" she murmured. "Were you ashamed of me?"

"Nay, my hinny and my heart. I wanted to meet you alone, and I knew you would come here tonight."

"How did you know?"

"I have a gypsy's sight," he teased.

She could not help but laugh. "And a gypsy's silver tongue." She took a deep breath. "I was hurt, Duncan. I thought I'd lost the man I loved, and it tore me apart."

"I should never have tried to deceive you, Fiona," he admitted. "I should have courted you honorably and asked you to become my wife. Can ye forgive me?"

"I might," she said, "if I get a proper proposal of marriage."

He took both her hands and raised her up. "You deserve that, my lady, my love." His deep voice grew huskier still. "Will ye do me the honor of becoming my wife, Fiona?"

"Aye, I will," she replied with as good an imitation of a Highland accent as she could give. "For I love you with all my heart and soul, rogue and rascal that you be."

Then he seized her around the waist and, laughing, swung her high. "You will never be sorry, Fiona Fraser. I promise you that much."

And she never was.

IF WISHES CAME TRUE

Colleen Faulkner

Chapter One

Cnocanduin Castle
Border Country, Scotland
1725

Six-year-old Mary Catherine MacDonal crept along the cold, stone floor of Cnocanduin's great hall. She could hear the laird of the castle speaking, but she couldn't quite make out her father's words. Something important was about to happen, though; she could tell by the tone of his voice and by the arrival of the unexpected visitors so late in the evening in such poor weather.

Mary Catherine sneaked closer to her father, keeping her back to the wall, crawling on her hands and skinned knees. Behind her, her cousin Magnus, five years her senior, followed clumsily. He was always

following her, always imitating her. Cook said it was
because he didn't have any ideas of his own.

Keeping one eye on her father, Mary Catherine slid
beneath a big side chair that smelled of tobacco and
her father's favorite spotted hound. From this vantage
point, she knew that she could hear, but not be seen.

"Scooch over," Magnus whispered with a shove.
"Else I'll tell you're listening in on private conversations again, and it will be tablecloths you'll be hem-
ming."

Mary Catherine stuck her tongue out at her cousin,
but reluctantly slid over. She hated needlework so
much that it was her father's favorite form of punishment. "You'll never fit," she warned. "Too much
pudding."

"You know him?" Magnus nodded toward the
unexpected visitors as he tried to squeeze under the
chair.

She stared at the two strangers. One was an old
man with white hair that fell across the tartan plaid
he wore thrown around his shoulders. She could tell
he was important by the large gold brooch that
pinned his Highland tartan at his shoulder. Was he
her father's family? Sean MacDonal had come out of
the Highlands a long time ago to marry her mother
and become laird of Cnocanduin.

But it wasn't the man with the white hair who
intrigued Mary Catherine. It was the young boy with
him—older than she, but not as old as Magnus. He
wore his hair cut short and squared off just below his
ears. His cloak was threadbare and moth-eaten. Rain
soaked his hair and puddled at his feet, but he wore
no tartan or brooch. He didn't even wear the wool

of her native Borderlands. He looked English to Mary
Kate. And he had a sad look in his big blue eyes.

"Are you daft? I said, do you know him?" Magnus
squeezed her against the chair legs, practically crush-
ing her with his weight as he attempted to fit his
entire plump body beneath the seat.

"The boy?" She was unable to take her eyes off
him.

"Nae. The man, goose! Is he one of your father's
family? The MacDonals come to cut off his head to
settle an old dispute?"

She elbowed him sharply. "Nae. The old man
hasn't come for his head. I don't know him. He's not
come to Cnocanduin before, I'll vow that."

"Mary Catherine!" Sean MacDonal's voice boomed,
startling her. "Is that any way for the lady of the
house to behave, creeping in the shadows and hiding
beneath chairs?" He waved a broad, rough hand.
"Come, come, do not leave our guests waiting."

Mary Catherine's cheeks grew warm with embarrassment as she crawled out from under the chair
and bounced to her feet. As she hurried across the
room, she licked her hands and tried to smooth the
wild array of red hair that she knew stuck out like a
witch's mane.

"Good even', sir." She caught a handful of the
green woolen skirt of her arisaid and bobbed a curtsy.

"My daughter," Sean MacDonal said proudly.
"Mary Catherine MacDonal."

"She looks like her mother," the old man mused.

Her father smiled that smile Mary Catherine knew
well, the one that took him far from her to a different
time in the past, a different place.

The old man gazed down at Mary Catherine and

smiled as if he knew her, as if he knew everything about her—everything that had happened in the past, everything that would happen in the future. She felt the hair rise on the nape of her neck.

"And this, Mary Catherine, is Robert Drum." Her father indicated the wet boy.

She didn't know if he had forgotten to introduce the man, or if he didn't want her to know who it was. She guessed the latter.

"The boy is an orphan and I have been asked to foster him," her father continued. "It would be our duty to see him schooled, fed, and sheltered. Would that be acceptable, lass?"

Mary Catherine couldn't help but squirm as her father spoke to her as if the decision were hers. It was his way, and she loved him fiercely for it. As the only child of Sean MacDonal and Mary Campbell, she would someday be mistress of Cnocanduin, and all the land and responsibilities that came with it would also be hers. He had told her for as long as she could remember that she must play an active part in the life of Cnocanduin.

"Aye, Papa." She spoke softly, staring at the boy. "We would certainly take him in."

The boy stared back with his sad blue eyes.

"So ye see, Rob," the old man said, giving the boy a gentle shove forward. He had a Highland brogue like her father's. "All will be fine, just as I promised. You'll be kept warm and safe at Cnocanduin."

"Daughter," Sean MacDonal continued, "take young Robert up to the boys' sleeping quarters. Find him some dry clothes and a bit of bread and cheese in the kitchen. I'm certain he be hungry, as well as cold."

"Aye." She bobbed a curtsy again.

The old man reached out and squeezed Robert Drum's thin shoulder. "Good health, child. Safe-keeping."

The boy said nothing, but followed Mary Catherine across the great hall past the stone fireplace, where her father's clansmen lounged with the hounds. They had come from the Highlands with Sean MacDonal, and Cnocanduin had become their home as well.

"You might as well go too, Magnus," her father called, his voice echoing off the ancient timbers, smoke-colored overhead. "But mind your manners."

Mary Catherine heard Magnus knock over her father's chair in his mad scramble to climb out from under it. A moment later he trailed her and the boy down the shadowy stone corridor lit by candle sconces.

As soon as they were out of earshot of the great hall, Magnus began to torment the new fosterling. "English," he taunted, skipping behind them. "Stinking English pup!"

"Shut up, Magnus." Mary Catherine whipped around. "Shut up else I'll tell!"

" 'Shut up else I'll tell,' " her cousin mimicked. Then he gave the boy a hard shove. Magnus liked shoving. Cook said it made him feel big because he had such a wee mind.

Robert hit the stone wall hard, but caught himself before he fell. He never made a sound.

Mary Catherine leaped between them. Magnus was bigger than Rob and had an unfair advantage. She hated unfairness in anything. "Keep your hands to yourself, Magnus MacDonal," she said angrily. "Papa said—"

" 'Papa said—' " Magnus repeated. This time he shoved *her*.

Pale, thin, wet, Robert Drum balled one hand into a fist and struck Magnus hard in the nose.

Magnus screamed and pitched to the floor, clasping his face. Blood streamed from between his fat fingers.

"Never hit a woman," Rob told Magnus softly as he massaged his fist.

Mary Catherine broke into a grin and rested her hands on her hips. "You'd best run and clean up that nose before Papa sees it and gives you another."

Magnus stood, still nursing his wound, and ran past them, blubbering. "I'm gonna tell my mama. I'm gonna tell!"

Alone with the boy, Mary Catherine suddenly felt strange. She glanced up at him shyly. "That was a brave thing you did, Rob Drum. Dumb, but brave." She smiled. "Now he'll really beat the tar out of ye, first chance he gets."

"Never hit a woman," Rob repeated, pushing back a wet lock of brown hair. "That's what my mama said."

"Where is she now? Her and your father?" she asked gently, guessing the answer, but needing to know. Her father said he was an orphan; that could mean only one thing.

"Dead."

Mary Catherine shivered. She was old enough to understand *dead*. "Brothers or sisters?"

"No."

Mary Catherine's lower lip trembled. Her mother was dead too, and she had no brothers or sisters either. But she had a father who loved her. Rob Drum had no one.

Mary Catherine wanted to reach out to him. She wanted to take him in her arms and cuddle him as she cuddled the kittens in the barn. She wanted to make him stop hurting, as she knew he must hurt.

But she didn't try to touch him. Instead she said simply, "I'm sorry." And she meant it. "I could be your sister. I could love you."

Rob Drum didn't say anything, but the timid smile on his face told her she had made a friend.

Five years later

Eleven-year-old Mary Catherine heard Maisie's infernal giggling again, and gazed up at the barn's roof. "That's it," she said to herself. "You think you can outsmart me, Magnus MacDonal? I think not!"

She slid the lid firmly onto the rain barrel at the front corner of the two-story barn and climbed on top of it. She tucked the blue wool of her arisaid between her legs, and shimmied up the crudely cut wooden drainpipe.

Mary Catherine didn't like high places. She could crawl under the floorboards of a room to listen in on a conversation, she could handle any type of rodent that creeped or crawled, she could even dive off the rocks into the stream, but she didn't like heights. She didn't climb trees and she didn't hang out of the windows of the tower like her cousins. Mary Catherine liked to keep both feet on the ground.

But Maisie's annoying giggle was just too much. She had to see what the scullery maid was laughing about. Why had they locked themselves in the hayloft? She had to know why Maisie thought sixteen-year-old Magnus was so funny. Mary Catherine had known

Magnus since she was born, and she had never thought him funny. Dull-witted, slow, lumbering, aye, but never funny.

First Mary Catherine had tried to climb up the ladder inside, into the loft, but Magnus had slammed the trapdoor down and told her to go play with her dollies, and Maisie had giggled some more. Mary Catherine didn't even have any dollies. Magnus practically knocked her off the ladder in his haste to block her view, and she didn't like it. Not one bit.

So if she couldn't get in through the hatch in the loft floor, she'd get in another way. There was a door on the second story on the far end of the barn that the men in the fields used to load haystacks into the loft. If Mary Catherine could just get to that open door from the roof above, she could swing inside.

Wouldn't Magnus be surprised then?

Gritting her teeth, Mary Catherine shimmied the rest of the way up the rain gutter and grasped the edge of the roof. Without looking down, she threw one leg up and then the other and pulled hard until she lay belly-down on the slick, mossy roof.

Mary Catherine felt dizzy and her stomach did a flip-flop. Maybe this wasn't such a grand idea. . . .

But she wasn't a quitter. Besides, Rob had climbed onto the barn roof just last week, and if Rob could climb the roof, Mary Catherine could certainly do it.

Maisie giggled again, the sound followed by Magnus's low voice. Mary Catherine couldn't make out what he was saying. She wondered if she would think it was funny, if she'd heard. Probably not. She didn't like Magnus much. Partly because of the way he was, but mostly because he treated Rob as if he were his servant.

Mary Catherine liked Rob Drum—no, she loved him. He was her best friend and her constant companion. Only lately they hadn't had as much time to play. Her father kept him too busy. When he wasn't studying Latin or reading books, he was practicing loading a musket, or taking target practice with the fine Highland blade her father had given him for his thirteenth birthday.

Mary Catherine swallowed the lump in her throat and reached up with one hand. If she didn't look down, she would never know she was high off the ground. She hoped. But as she crawled up, her stomach got sicker and her head spun faster.

Halfway up the side of the pitched roof she wondered if she really cared why Maisie was laughing.

"Mary Kate, by God, what are ye doing?"

The sound of Rob's voice both startled her and flooded her with relief. Rob was here now. Everything would be all right. Rob could always make anything all right.

"Mary Kate?"

"R-Rob?"

"What are ye doing on the barn roof?"

She wanted to look down, but she was afraid to. "Magnus is in the loft," she said shakily. "He and Maisie. I wanted to see why she was laughing."

She heard Rob grunt with disapproval, or something else she didn't recognize. "Mary Kate, ye don't belong on the barn roof. Ye'll fall and break your neck, and break your father's heart at the same time."

She thrust out her chin with determination, but still didn't look down. "You climbed the roof last week, Rob Drum, and I dinna see a broke neck on you!"

"Stay right there," he called. "I'm coming up."

She gave a little laugh. Stay here? Where did he think she was going? "Aye," was all she could manage in reply.

Below, Mary Catherine heard Rob clamber onto the rain barrel, his feet scraping on the old gutter. It seemed as if it took a fortnight for him to reach her after he climbed up onto the roof.

He covered her left hand with his. "Ye all right?"

She nodded, staring at the mossy slate. "Aye."

"Now listen, it's only a wee bit farther to the top—"

She shook her head. "Not to the top. It's too far."

"It's not." His tone was light and playful. "Mary Kate, it's only a wee bit farther. You're almost there."

"And . . . and then what?" She turned her head to look at him. Rob had grown in the last year. His thin, boyish face had turned to manly angles, and he'd grown more than a foot. For years he and Mary Catherine had been nearly the same height, but now he towered over her, all legs and long, gangly arms.

"And then ye'll see," he said as if he had a surprise for her. He tightened his grip on her hand. "We can do it together. Now come on with ye." He inched up a few slate tiles, holding on to her hand.

Having little choice, Mary Catherine followed him.

"That's right," he encouraged in a calm, soothing voice. "We're almost there." Another two feet and he released her hand and shimmied onto the roof's peak, straddling it with both legs.

Mary Catherine kept her gaze focused on a lump of moss beneath her nose.

"Mary Catherine, I won't let you fall," he said softly. "Now give me your hand. If your papa finds us up here, we'll both be in hot wax."

Mary Catherine didn't know if it was the threat of punishment or the sound of Rob's voice, but something made her reach for Rob's hand.

"Got ye," he said, clasping her hand tightly. "Now up just a little farther. That's it. Aye, that's it. Ye've almost got it now."

Mary Catherine climbed higher, following his voice, clutching his hand.

"Now throw one foot over."

She did as he said because she didn't know what else to do.

"There." He grasped both of her hands in his, making her look directly into his blue eyes. "Wasn't that easy?"

"Now what?" she asked shakily.

"Now ye slide back just a wee bit." He released her hands and began to move toward her, leaving her no choice but to shimmy backward. "Don't look down," he said as they slid along the roof's peak. "Just look at me, Mary Kate. Nothing, no one, but me."

Mary Catherine thought she heard Maisie laughing, but she was too busy concentrating to be sure.

"Good, good. Here we are, lass." Rob threw one leg over the roof so that he was facing the opposite side from where they'd climbed up. "This is the best part."

"The best part?" Her voice trembled.

"Put your leg over." He clasped her hand again and his hand was warm and firm. "There you go."

Mary Kate squeezed her eyes shut as she balanced her bottom on the roof, still holding tightly to his hand. "Now what?"

"Open your eyes and look down."

"But you said don't—"

"Open them."

She opened her eyes to see a tall stack of hay below them. "That's how ye got down last week?" she questioned doubtfully.

"The best part of the climb. Worth the climb."

Mary Catherine looked down. The haystack was high, but it still seemed far away . . . far down.

"Don't ye trust me, Mary Kate?"

Of course she trusted him. She trusted Rob Drum as much as she trusted her father. "Aye, I suppose."

"Come on with ye then, before we're caught."

She eyed him. "Will ye tell me what Magnus and Maisie were doing, if I go?"

He scowled. "Nae." Then he winked. "But I will share the dried-apple tart I've got in my bag." Without warning, he grabbed her around the waist and pushed off, pulling her with him.

Mary Kate flew down the roof, the blue sky stretching out before her. She was dying; she knew she was dying. Then the roof fell out from under her. But even before she could scream in earnest, she dropped into the sweet-smelling hay below.

Limbs tangled, Mary Kate and Rob floundered, laughing and throwing hay.

"I told ye it was fun," he said as he lay back in the hay and plucked a bit of straw from her hair.

She grinned, panting as she sat up. "Ye saved my life, Rob Drum."

He laughed, fishing an apple tart from the little cloth bag he wore around his waist. "Hardly." He split the pastry in half and offered the part with the most apple bits to her.

"Ye did." She gobbled the sweet, sticky tart. "Ye saved my life and now, now I'll have to marry ye, sir."

Just last night her father had been telling a tall tale of Scottish Highland adventure where the woman had said just that after the man had slayed the sea monster in the loch. It sounded very romantic to her.

Rob threw back his head and laughed, and she noticed that his voice was deeper than it had been.

"What?" She punched him in the arm. "You don't want to marry me?"

He reached out and brushed a crumb from the corner of her mouth, and she licked it off his finger.

"Of course I want to marry ye," he said. "But I can't marry ye. You're the lady of the manor and I'm just a servant. You should marry Magnus, like your aunt says."

"You're not a servant, and I'll marry whom I want." She wiped her mouth with the back of her hand. "And I'd sooner marry a swine than Magnus MacDonal, cousin or no! Papa can't make me marry him and neither can you!" She gave him another hard punch in the arm for good measure.

He laughed. "All right, all right." He threw up his hands to block her next assault. "I'll marry ye. Only I think we'd better wait a wee bit longer to wed, at least until I'm fourteen."

Her frown turned to a smile. "All right, Rob Drum." She stood up and began to brush the hay from her clothing. "I'll wait on ye a wee bit longer, but, mind ye, I won't wait on ye forever."

Six years later

The lively country dance tune came to its final note and all the dancers slapped their hands together in applause. Mary Catherine's handsome dance partner,

Charles Fraser—or was it Charles Campbell?—tried to catch her by the arm, but she darted out of his reach and into the safe haven of brightly colored gowns, waistcoats, and tartans.

"Mary Catherine, dance with me." Magnus appeared before her out of nowhere, his face beet red and his pig nostrils flaring.

"Saints in heaven, Magnus." She waved her hand in front of her face. "You smell like a brewery. If Father finds out you've been overindulging again—"

" 'If Father finds out,' " he mimicked, wiping at a greasy stain on his new coat. "Just hush your pretty mouth, Mary Catherine," Magnus continued, "and dance with me." He attempted to take her hand but she pulled it away. "Mama's looking at us," he said. "She expects me to dance with you. Everyone expects us to dance."

The years passed, but to Mary Catherine little seemed to change at Cnocanduin. Her gaze strayed as her mind wandered from Magnus's whining. She hadn't seen Rob in hours. Where was he? It was her father's seventieth birthday. He should be here.

"No one expects anything, Magnus," she said tartly. "It's all in your pudding, laced-with-whiskey head."

"Mama says that if we're to be wed—"

She walked away, unperturbed. If they'd had this conversation once in the last year, they'd had it a hundred times. Ever since she'd finally grown breasts, their wedding was all her aunt Agnes talked about. "We're not to be wed. I'm not marrying you."

She stopped one of Magnus's friends. The music began again and the dancers circled around her. "Ruddy, have you seen Rob?"

"Nae." He caught his dance partner's hand and danced away.

"Mary Catherine, come back," Magnus called as she dodged the dancers, making her way across the great hall.

But she was faster and more clever than Magnus, and she slipped away.

Mary Catherine stopped at the head table and brushed her hand across her father's shoulders, which did not seem as broad as they had once been. "Happy birthday, Papa," she whispered in his ear.

He smiled up at her. His face was creased with wrinkles and his hair had long gone silver-gray, but his eyes were still the same heavenly green. And they still sparkled with the fire of earlier years. Cook said it was those eyes that had made Mary Catherine's mother fall for the Highland rogue so many years ago.

Mary Catherine passed her father's table and slipped out of the great hall, away from the music and confusion. She had enjoyed the dancing for a while. And she enjoyed seeing her father have such a fine time, but she missed Rob. She missed being with him, talking with him. And she was certain she knew just where to find him.

Since they'd been children, they'd had a secret place to meet. Cnocanduin Castle was old, and once upon a time, before so many towers and rooms had been added, there had been a single pele tower built beside a well and a rowan tree. Over the years the castle had been built around the old bailey until finally the stone walls blocked the sunlight and the tree died. No one had ever cut the tree down, and Cook said that some believed that St. Joseph had once drunk from the well. She said that some believed the well to have magical powers; some believed visions could be seen on the well's surface or wishes could be granted to the true of heart. Cook said that Mary Catherine's mother had believed.

But Mary Catherine didn't believe in magic. She believed in faith, in justice, in honor and duty to those she loved. Still, she liked to sit by the well and the blackened stonelike tree that was now in the bowels of the castle. It was quiet and cool there, a place to think without being disturbed. But best of all, it was her and Rob's secret meeting place. They had been coming here since they were children.

Mary Catherine lifted her emerald gown of watered silk and descended the curving stone steps into the darkness, using the rope that ran down the wall to steady herself. Sure enough, she was soon rewarded by the soft glow of lamplight, and she knew whose lamp it was.

"Don't feel like dancing?" she asked Rob, who sat on the well's low stone wall.

He smiled, but did not glance up. He had grown into a handsome man with angled features, sun-bronzed skin, and silky chestnut hair that brushed his shoulders.

He took his time before answering her. "You were well occupied. A thousand suitors."

She rolled her eyes. "You could dance with another, Rob Drum."

He stared down into the dark well. "I suppose. But it wouldn't be the same, would it?"

With their childhood behind them, both were feeling the width and breadth of the chasm that separated their social statuses. Mary Catherine was the laird's daughter and the mistress of Cnocanduin. Rob was an orphan, worse, an Englishman. He was without lands, title, or monies. Without a past.

Over the years, Mary Kate and Rob had questioned Sean MacDonal of the particulars of who Rob was and how he'd come to Cnocanduin that rainy night. Who had his family been? Why had an English boy been brought to the Borderlands by an old man in a tartan? But Sean had always been reluctant to discuss the matter. He insisted he knew nothing. He had simply taken the boy as a favor to an old friend he had known in his youth. His friend had requested that he not ask questions, and Sean had complied.

So Rob was not a servant, but he wasn't a MacDonal either. And Mary Catherine suspected that it was for this reason that he sat here alone while everyone else danced in merry celebration.

She sat on the edge of the wall beside him. "Magnus tried to corner me and get me to dance with him. He was drunk." She ran her finger along the stones of the well, rounded by time and others' hands. Perhaps even her mother's. "He started that nonsense again about Auntie Agnes wanting him and me to marry."

Rob smiled distantly. Still he stared into the well. He didn't look at her, and it made her feel sad.

"I told him I wasn't marrying him," she said, tossing back her mane of red hair that she had surrendered to unruliness years ago. "Because, of course, you and I are already betrothed." She laughed. "Remember?"

He laughed with her, but his voice was melancholy. "The haystack after the barn roof incident. You wanted to find out what Magnus and the maid were doing in the loft."

She chuckled, feeling her cheeks grow warm. But

she wasn't embarrassed. She could never be embarrassed with Rob. It was he who had eventually explained to her what Magnus and the girl were doing, what men and women did. It was Rob who had held her in his arms the first time she had bled her woman's blood. He had held her tightly, soothed her fears, and then taken her to Cook so she could explain to Mary Kate the wonders of a woman's body. One more reason to love him . . .

As she watched the shadows play across his broad back, she wondered if he knew that, secretly, she still held that girlhood desire to marry him.

Of course she knew realistically that she couldn't marry him. Not an Englishman without a past. He could never be the laird of Cnocanduin. Her father's clansmen would never accept him. What Scot would follow such a man into battle, should the need arise? Mary Kate was old enough to realize that when it came time to wed, she must marry out of duty to Cnocanduin. Her mother had married for the well-being of the castle and its land, and she would do the same.

Rob smiled, his eyes glimmering with memories of their childhood. "You know . . ." He brushed the backs of his fingertips against her cheek in a gentle caress.

Mary Kate's breath caught in her throat. For a moment she thought he might kiss her.

"Sometimes . . ." He withdrew his hand as if he didn't believe he had the right to touch her. "I wish we were still those children, sliding into the haystack," he said sadly. "Making wishes . . . promises we didn't know we couldn't keep."

Mary Kate's gaze met Rob's, and in her heart she

knew he meant the promise to marry her. He did know she loved him; he loved her too. Suddenly a sense of desperation swept through her. Of course they couldn't wed, but perhaps . . . "Rob—"

He shook his head. "Don't, sweet. Don't say anything you'll later wish you'd not said. We both have our places here at Cnocanduin, and we both know that. It's best we forget our childhood foolishness."

There was a lump in her throat that she could not swallow. Truth in his words she couldn't swallow. "And what of our feelings?" Her voice trembled. "For each other? We forget them too?"

He rose from the wall of the well. "Aye, Mary Kate. It's best for all."

Then he turned his back to her and walked away and never saw her tears.

Chapter Two

Cnocanduin Castle
Six years later
1742

"Are you comfortable, sir?" Rob asked as he eased Sean MacDonal into his bed.

"Aye. Yes, yes!" He waved a wrinkled hand. "Out of my way, lad. Ye treat me as if I'm a wee babe in need of coddling." He frowned, the wrinkles in his forehead deepening. "Where's Mary? Have you seen my Mary?"

Rob stepped back to make room at Sean's bedside for his daughter.

"Papa, Rob's only trying to help. Don't be so cross." Mary Catherine pulled the wool blanket up to her father's gray-bearded chin, ignoring his comment about her mother. Since his stroke in the spring he'd recovered greatly, but his memory was still muddled and his mind not as sharp as it had been.

"Damned leg," Sean grumbled. "Body's falling apart. Damned old age."

She sat on the edge of the rope bed. Rob moved quietly about the chamber, lighting candles and stoking the fire on the hearth.

"It's just a little touch of the gout." She smoothed the wool coverlet her mother had woven many years ago. "You'll be up and about, good as new in a few days."

"I'm nae immortal, ye ken. I'm getting old. Getting sick. Someday I'm going to die—"

"You're not going to die," she argued, refusing to meet his gaze.

He grabbed her wrist. "Mary Kate, sweet love, we all die."

He rarely called her Mary Kate. His endearment brought tears to her eyes that she had to blink away. "I know that," she answered, her tone light. "Of course we all die. But not now, Papa. You're not dying tonight. Tonight you're having ham and potatoes with leeks for supper, and then you're going to smoke your pipe and share a dram of scotch with Rob here before you go to sleep."

"I'm not saying I'm dying now, this week, or even this month, daughter. But don't you ken?" He slipped deeper into the accent of his youth, as he always did when he became emotional. "I will die someday, sooner than later, and I doon want to go to my grave worried fer ye and your safety."

Because she was still unwed. She knew that was what he meant; he just didn't say it. At twenty and three she was well past the age of marriage, especially for a woman with so great an inheritance. "I'll be fine. Cnocanduin will remain strong."

"I hope." He closed his eyes, patting her hand. "I pray, dear daughter, for ye."

She kissed his forehead and rose from the bed. At the bedchamber's arched doorway her gaze swept over her father. No matter how she wanted to deny it, he *was* aging. At nearly seventy-six, his skin was wrinkled and thin and his body was shrinking. Since his stroke he was often confused; he could remember his schoolmaster's name from when he was a lad, but not the names of his favorite hounds. He recognized Mary Catherine and knew she was his daughter, yet he kept forgetting that his wife had died giving Mary Kate life twenty-three years before. As of late, Sean MacDonal spent more time by the fire in the great hall telling tales of the past rather than living in the present.

"You pray for me?" she asked from the doorway. "For a man, a husband?"

He turned in the bed so that his gaze met hers. His green eyes seemed clear, his mind once again sharp. "For your safety and happiness," he corrected. "I told ye, daughter, and I'll tell ye again. I'll not rush ye. A Highland lord will come into your life, capture your heart, and take his place beside you at Cnocanduin. It happened to your mother. It will happen to ye."

A Highland lord, indeed, she thought. But she smiled at him with tenderness. A man had already captured her heart long ago. She had no need, no desire for Highland lords. "Thank you," she said softly.

Her father's brow furrowed. "For what, lass?"

"For being my daddy."

He smiled and closed his eyes. "Send your mother up directly, daughter."

"Yes, Papa."

Rob waited outside the chamber for her. When she had waylaid him in the great hall, in need of his strong arm to get her father up the flights of steps, Rob had just come in from riding. He still wore tight-fitting woolen trews, a wool and linen *leine-chroich*, and a tattered Highland bonnet of her father's, his MacDonal white cockade still attached.

Rob was as much Sean MacDonal's son as the old Highlander would ever have. It seemed that over the years Rob had drawn comfort and some sense of belonging from her father's Highland clan. Despite his English birth, he seemed more a Scot than Magnus or many of the men her age. Many of the young men in the Borderlands were losing their accents, casting aside their Scottish traditions as well as their native clothing, but Rob seemed to cling to the old ways.

Rob smelled of horses, and leather, and his own masculine scent she instantly found comforting. He'd been gone for days to Edinburgh to sell cattle, and she'd missed him. It was only when he was gone on her father's business that she realized how much she relied on him now that a good deal of Cnocanduin's responsibilities rested on her shoulders.

He folded his arms over his broad chest and leaned against the stone wall. Only then did she realize he'd been lying in wait for her, not merely waiting for her.

"It's time, you know," he said quietly. There was tension in the way he stood.

She closed the door behind her, stalling for time. She knew what he was going to say; she just didn't want to hear it. "Time for what?"

"You need a husband. It's your duty to wed before your father passes on. Give him peace of mind."

She took a candle from the sconce on the wall and started down the corridor, the woolen skirt of her arisaid swishing as she walked.

His words smarted.

Rob had once promised *he* would marry her. Of course she knew he couldn't. She understood that with her head, just not with her heart. "I swear, everyone in this household—you, Magnus, Cook, Aunt Agnes—you're all like magpies." She touched her thumb and forefinger together again and again like a bird's beak. "Peck, peck, peck. Telling others what they should do, how they should lead their lives."

He hurried to catch up with her. "You're being defensive because you know I'm right."

She set her jaw, disguising her hurt with agitation. It was Rob's fault she'd not yet married. His fault because no man she met could hold a candle to him. "I am *not* being defensive."

How did he always know her so well? For months she'd been considering her unwed state. Her father said he wouldn't rush her. He said he wanted her to be happy. But she also knew that he worried about her and her safety. The Scots to the north were growing restless, again talking of freedom from the English Crown. This was not a time for Cnocanduin to go unguarded. Not with the English so close in proximity. If they chose to set out north to the Highlands to settle the unrest, they could march right through Cnocanduin.

"Why is everyone so concerned with my marriage bed?" She turned the corner sharply and started down the stone steps that would take her from the family quarters on the fifth floor. "I don't see Magnus married."

"His mother won't let him. Dear Auntie Agnes is still hoping you'll take leave of your senses and marry her little boy," Rob teased, trying to lighten the conversation.

It was common knowledge in the castle that Agnes, Sean's sister-in-law and a widow, had been petitioning for a betrothal between Mary Catherine and Magnus since they were children. Worried about securing her own place at Cnocanduin, and those of her sons, Mary Kate understood her aunt's motives and took them as well-intentioned. Without property or finances of her own, her elderly aunt wanted to be certain she would always have a home, and the best way to see to it was to have her son marry directly into the family. What Agnes didn't understand was that no matter who Mary Kate married, she would never put her aunt out or see her want for anything.

"Me marry Cousin Magnus? Frosty day in hell," Mary Kate muttered.

Rob darted around her and halted directly in front of her, blocking her way in the narrow stairwell. He took a deep breath as if he knew what he wanted to say, but had to prepare himself. "Mary Kate, I'm serious. Talk in Edinburgh is not good. The Campbells and the MacDonalds up north are getting rowdy. There's talk of bringing Bonny Prince Charles home."

A sputtering candle on the tiny windowsill cast little light. The dark, cylindrical stairwell smelled of melted tallow, smoke, and damp stone.

"There's been talk for years. All talk, no show. Charlie is nae coming home." She lifted the candle higher so that she could see his face. "What about you? You're older than I. Practically graying." She touched his temple.

"Am not." He pushed aside her hand.

"You're not married," she said with a sweep of her hand, drawing the candle dangerously near him. She thought of their childish betrothal agreement so many years ago and wondered if he even remembered now. Maybe he was suddenly anxious to see her married because he had thoughts of marriage of his own. Had some lass in the village caught his eye? The thought hurt too.

"We're not talking about me." He took the candle from her hand. "We're concerned about you because you're the mistress of Cnocanduin. You are the only heir. Sooner or later Cnocanduin will have to declare herself Jacobean or Hanoverian, and then she must be able to defend herself and her choice."

She rested her hands on her hips. "Get out of my way. My father waits for his supper."

"Choose a husband before your father chooses one for you," Rob urged. "Before he makes his brother's eldest son his heir by marrying you off to him."

She grimaced. "Magnus? My father wouldn't. He says I may choose my own mate. He says he's a patient man. You know our Sean MacDonal, always a romantic. He thinks a man will come to me one day and fall at my feet in utter devotion. He waits for true love for me." She gave a humorless laugh. "A Highland lord, of course. Nothing but the best for his only child."

"But who knows what a desperate old Scotsman might do in his last days to save his daughter, as well as his beloved wife's legacy?"

"He wouldn't make me marry Magnus. He knows what Magnus is," she said stubbornly.

"Aye," he conceded. "You're right. He wouldn't make you wed Magnus, but who will he make you marry? Wouldn't you rather control your own fate?"

Mary Catherine's shoulders slumped. She ran her fingers through her vibrant red hair, which fell over her shoulders. Rob was right. A woman in her position did need a husband. One with lands, monies, a man befitting her status, but most important, a man of family honor. She needed a husband her father's clansmen would follow in battle, should the need arise. In his dotage, Sean MacDonal seemed to recall only the romance of his union with his wife. Lost was the fact that Mary Campbell had married him because she was forced to. She married him not out of love, but to protect Cnocanduin. The love had come later.

"I don't want to wed," she said softly, surprisingly close to tears for the second time that evening. *Not if it can't be you,* she thought. "I don't want Papa to get old and die. I want things to stay as they are here at Cnocanduin." She ran her hand over the collar of his plaid outer garment that she'd patched with her own needle. "I want to sup with you, walk the hounds with you . . . ." It was on the tip of her tongue to say "Sleep with you," but she was thankful she couldn't.

At the moment Rob wasn't certain he could go through with this. How could he encourage her to marry another man when he loved her so deeply? The thought ripped his heart in two.

But in his torn heart, Rob knew he was doing what was right. What was noble. He, an orphan without land, monies, or even certainty of his name or heritage, could not have Mary Kate MacDonal of Cnocan-duin. And if he could not have her, his duty to the love he felt for her was to find the best possible man for her. He owed it to the man who had lovingly raised him as his own son. He owed it to Mary Kate. He owed it to the love he knew they would never consummate.

Rob swallowed his pride, his own intense desire for her, and said what he knew he needed to say. Mary Kate would listen to him; she always did. Maybe that was what hurt most. He knew she would follow his advice.

"Choose a husband, Mary Kate." He grasped her wrist and gently removed her hand from his chest because it hurt too much to feel her touch. He had no right to her touch, no right to her love.

"Choose now," Rob insisted, wondering if she heard the strain in his voice. "Whilst you still have a choice."

She groaned and threw up her hands. "Let's say I did decide to wed. How would I find a husband? I don't even know who the eligible men are in the shire. I don't have time for teas, dancing, and calling. I have a home to run here; crofters to nurse, working men to feed, cattle to buy and sell—"

"Does that mean yes?" Even as he spoke the words his heart tore further, and he wondered how that was possible. How much pain could one man suffer and still survive? He cursed his English birth and the mother and father he could not recall save for flashes of memory of their scent and hushed voices.

Rob dug in and pressed on. "You'll consider wed-ding?"

"I'm thinking about it," she snapped, darting under his arm.

"I could help," he heard himself call down the stairwell as she descended into darkness. Was he mad? It was bad enough he was encouraging her, but to offer to aid her? What was he thinking?

He was thinking who better to help her choose a husband than the one person who loved her most?

"You could help?" She grabbed the thick guide rope and took the steps faster.

He chased her down the twisting narrow stone steps, unconcerned for her safety. For a stranger, descending the crude stone steps in the darkness could have been fatal, but Mary Kate knew every step by heart. She knew where the eleventh step, built two inches higher, lay in wait to trip strangers in the darkness. She could climb to and from the tower with her eyes closed.

"Does that mean yes?" he asked again.

"Aye," she said softly.

"Aye?"

"Aye, Rob Drum," she conceded.

Was that sadness he heard in her voice? Regret? Could it be possible she still loved him? Even after all these years of them pretending it wasn't so? The thought that she loved him should have consoled him, but somehow it made his situation more tragic.

"Find me a husband," Mary Kate said with resignation now in her voice. She reached the second story, whipped around the corner and out of his sight. "Just find me one that doesn't snore, will you?"

Rob had to laugh. His Mary Kate had always had such a rich sense of humor. He had to laugh because if he didn't, he would cry.

* * *

"Mary Kate, wait. Will you listen to me?"

Ignoring Rob's protests, Mary Catherine urged her gelding over the low stone fence beside the kirkyard, keeping her head down to prevent losing her cap in the branches of the old elm tree.

"Duck!" she shouted just before she heard him groan and branches scrape.

Chuckling to herself, she cut across the lane and onto the stone path that led to Cnocanduin's gate. Her mount's hooves sounded on the wooden drawbridge as she pulled back on the reins and rode into the courtyard.

"Mary Kate, damn it! I've been following you for a week with this cursed thing and I won't be put off any longer."

Rob galloped up beside her and jumped off his mount. He grabbed her horse's reins. "I've the list, but you must sit down and look at it with me."

"The list, have you?" She kept her tone businesslike. It was the only way she could deal with this. The only way she could keep her heart from breaking again and again. She wouldn't think about what she really wanted. She wouldn't wonder how Rob really felt about her plans to wed. She just wouldn't.

Mary Kate dismounted with the aid of his broad shoulder. A stable boy came running to take both the horses.

Rob adjusted her riding hat. "Yes, I've got the blasted list." His voice was businesslike as well. "I've had it for days and you well know it."

She plucked off her leather riding gloves, crossing the courtyard. Rob followed her through the stone doorway that led to the family quarters. At the yett, one of her father's clansmen swung open the iron gate and allowed them both entrance. Though the castle had not been threatened in years, her father still insisted that the guards keep their posts.

"Is it a long list?" She stepped into the entry and made her way up the stone stairs to the great hall. One wainscoted wall was lined floor to ceiling with portraits, nearly half of red-haired women. Cnocanduin women. Through the decades the family name changed, Fraser, Campbell, Ruthven, Cummings, MacDonal now, but the eerie fact remained that it was the red-haired women of the household who inherited the castle and lands. Mary Catherine's own mother's portrait held a prized position just to the left of the great mantel over the fireplace.

Rob remained on her heels. "Long enough to find a suitable husband on it."

Halfway to the stone hearth she was greeted by one of her father's panting, licking hounds. She reached down and stroked the mutt's head, scratching her behind the ears. Her father's bitch rolled on the floor with delight, her pink teats sagging with milk. "And how are those pups today, Molly? Good, are they?"

She walked to the hearth, past her father's empty chair. Two spotted pups slept soundly, curled up on the woolen throw in the seat. "Hm," she mused. "Papa must have gone for a walk."

"Are you going to tell him?"

"Tell him what?" She dropped into a chair in the semicircle of chairs pulled close to the fire. Here was where her father spent most of his time now, so she had tried to make it as comfortable as possible for him. She had surrounded him with his favorite pieces of furniture, books to read, his beloved hounds.

Rob took the wooden stool at her feet. "That you're actively seeking a suitable husband."

Her forehead creased. "Are you mad? Of course I'm not going to tell him. He's still waiting for a Highland lord to ride in on a great white steed and sweep me off my feet, remember?" She picked up an apple from a bronze bowl and took a bite.

"What now?" she asked. She offered him the apple and he took a bite. Juice ran from the corner of his mouth and she wiped it with her finger and took back the apple. There was nothing out of the ordinary in sharing an apple with Rob, but she couldn't help thinking how strange it would be to bite from the same apple as another man. A husband.

He crunched the crisp fruit. "You look at the list and see who might interest you."

"I don't have to look. None of them interest me."

Rob slipped a piece of parchment from inside his *leine-chroich.* "I've also added a few men you may not know, from the south and—"

"I'll not have a Lowlander," she announced, taking another bite. "You get too far south and they call themselves Scots, but they might as well be the king's men."

He lifted one eyebrow.

She couldn't tell if he was amused or irritated. Today she couldn't tell how he felt about her plan at all.

"I can assure you that they are all good Scotsmen," he said patiently. "I also chose a few from farther north."

"This is a ridiculous idea." She shook her head. "This is never going to work. How am I going to choose?"

"Why not interview them? See who you like."

"You mean who I could tolerate." Her gaze met Rob's. "And just how do I go about this interview?"

A flash of emotion crossed his face, and she sensed he was not being entirely honest with her. Maybe not with himself either. His calm behavior was all an act. He was upset. He wished he could marry her. He wished it as much as she did.

"I don't know how you should conduct the interviews." Rob snapped the paper impatiently. His smooth demeanor was cracking just a little. "I'm just trying to help you, Mary Kate. Decide what qualities you want in a husband. Make a list. You love lists. Check them off, scratch them out."

Mary Kate stared at the paper. This was a bad idea; she knew it was a bad idea. But she had to try to think with her head and not her heart. She wanted to do what was right, for her father, for Cnocanduin. She *had* to do what was right.

"Those men wouldn't be interested in me." She indicated the list doubtfully.

"Certainly they would. You're beautiful, clever—"

"Wealthy," she added.

"Wealthy, and the mistress of the great Cnocanduin. If word gets out that you're finally in search of a husband, there'll be a line through the bailey in a week's time."

She glanced up. "Word had better not get out."

"Word of what? Who got out?" Sean MacDonal hobbled into the hall, leaning heavily on a gnarled fruitwood cane. "Are those damned dogs out again?"

Rob rose to help him to his favorite chair before the hearth. "Word of our St. Michael's festival, sir," he lied smoothly.

Her elderly father peered into Rob's face. "We're celebrating St. Michael's? A festival at Cnocanduin?"

"By your leave, sir."

Sean brightened. "Aye, I do love a horse race. We've not had a festival at Cnocanduin in years. My Mary always did love a festival."

Rob scooped both pups from the chair, planted them on the floor, and helped Sean ease down. "It was Mary Kate's idea." He gently lifted Sean's bad leg and propped it on a padded stool.

She grimaced. "It was?"

"If you're in agreement, sir, we'll make the arrangements. Send out the invitations."

Invitations. The minute Rob said the word, she caught his meaning. Invitations would be sent out to invite neighbors, friends, and family to the festival, but the invitations would include the men on Rob's list. His list of suitable suitors.

"I do love a festival," Sean repeated. "A fine idea, lad."

Rob flashed her a smug grin.

Finished with her apple, Mary Catherine tossed the core into the hearth and it sizzled. "Fine idea," she muttered miserably. "Fine day for a festival. Fine day for a blessed hanging."

"Hanging? There's to be a hanging?" Sean leaned over the chair toward Mary Catherine. "Have we caught those reivers? Are we going to hang them? I do love a good hanging, nearly as much as a good festival."

"No, Papa." Mary Catherine rose and kissed his fuzzy white cheek. "We've not caught the cattle thieves, but we've posted more guards."

A puppy gnawed on the heel of Rob's boot. He moved his foot, toying with the hound. "The Maxwells had two dozen head stolen this week, sir, and a fire set in their granary by the thieves."

"Bastards." Sean thumped his cane. "If I didna have this bum leg, I'd catch them, I would, and see them hang. In my day we hanged first, asked questions later, aye."

Mary Catherine eyed Rob. She hadn't told her father how serious the cattle thievery had become because she didn't want to worry him. Cattle stealing had been going on in the Borderlands for centuries. The English crossed into Scotland and stole cattle. The Scots crossed into England, took back their cattle, and a few extra just to make their trip worthwhile. It was the way of the land.

"Don't worry, sir, we'll find the reivers."

"We?" Magnus came swaggering into the great hall, wearing an English riding coat, paid for with Sean MacDonal's coin, no doubt. His mother trailed behind him, fussing with the tail of his frock. "No *we* about it. *I'll* find the thieves and see them hanged from their scrawny necks." He postured, attempting to suck in his sagging stomach. "I already have Cnocanduin men on the task."

At his mother's urging, Magnus was always trying to impress her father with great boasting and words of intention. His talk was rarely followed by deed.

"My Magnus will see to the matter, I warrant you," Aunt Agnes reiterated.

"You can always count on me, Uncle. We're blood. MacDonals." He cut a sideward glance at Rob. "Such tasks should be left to *family* members, not servants and the like."

"Rob is nae—"

Rob caught her arm and silenced her. It had been the same since he had arrived at Cnocanduin a wet orphan. Magnus taunted, she defended, and Rob tolerated. Magnus had not, however, ever raised a hand against Mary Catherine, not since Rob had flattened him in the hall the night of his arrival.

Rob gently extricated himself from the playful puppy. "I've duties to attend. By your leave, sir."

Sean nodded, granting Rob's dismissal.

Mary Catherine moved to follow him.

"Where are you going, cousin?" Magnus had taken the chair beside Sean and was picking through a tin of sweets Rob had brought her father back from Edinburgh.

"I've duties to attend, Magnus." She smiled sweetly, but her tone was rich with sarcasm. "Not all of us here at Cnocanduin lead such a life of leisure as you."

As if rallying to her side, one of the spotted pups took her words as a signal to cock its leg and piddle on Magnus's calf.

"Christ's bones!" Magnus shouted, leaping up. "Look what the little creature's done! He's ruined my new stockings."

Aunt Agnes bounced out of her chair, waving her hands frantically. "Oh, my! Oh, my. Hold still, let Mummy see." She leaned over, dabbing at the leg of his long breeches with her handkerchief.

Sean let out a hearty laugh and reached down to

retrieve the guilty pup before Magnus took out his anger on the wee thing.

Mary Catherine and Rob took the moment of confusion to make their escape and hurried from the great hall.

Chapter Three

"I do wish you'd put on one of your more comely gowns," Aunt Agnes fussed as she brushed Mary Kate's damp hair. "A woman of your station should look it on a day like today."

Mary Kate slipped one foot into the soft leather of her riding boot. She felt as if she were dressing for her own funeral. She didn't want to interview men for the position of husband. She wanted Rob Drum, and if she couldn't have Rob she wanted no one. But duty was duty.

Mary Kate glanced at her aunt. "They can take me as I am or not at all," she said irritably.

She immediately regretted her tone. She wasn't angry with her aunt, only fearful now that the day of the festival was upon them. Somewhere, milling about in the courtyard at this very moment, was the man she would marry.

"They?" Her aunt pulled the brush through her hair, tugging hard. "They who, dear?"

"The men." Mary Kate winced as the brush caught on a tangle in her hair, and she waved a hand absently in the direction of the courtyard, stories below.

"The men?" Her aunt reached for a green velvet hair ribbon. "You mean the eligible men, dear?"

Of course eligible men were on her aunt's mind. They were on everyone's mind in the castle. With her father's failing health, Mary Kate's lack of a husband had become a primary concern of every man, woman, and child at Cnocanduin. With politics what they were, a strong husband for their mistress could mean the difference between life and death to those who lived inside and near the castle walls.

Mary Kate had not intended to tell her aunt of her plan to find a husband. She hadn't intended to tell anyone, but before she could stop herself, it all came tumbling out.

"Oh, my, oh, my," her aunt repeated as she began to pace the room and wring her hands. "What an ... *original* manner to choose a husband," she said carefully. "Only you, niece, would concoct such a design."

Mary Kate rose from the stool. She hadn't told her aunt that Rob supported her in the plan or that he was actually aiding her in making her selection. Aunt Agnes, like Magnus, had always dwelled on the fact that Rob was a fosterling, and had never seen him as an equal to Mary Kate or her own sons.

"Please don't tell Papa, Auntie Agnes. He won't understand; it will only confuse him." She glanced up anxiously. Growing up, Mary Kate and her aunt had had their differences, but Mary Kate knew

Agnes's heart was in the right place. "And once I choose a husband, I'll seek his approval, of course."

"Of course," Aunt Agnes echoed.

Mary Kate met her aunt in the center of the chamber floor and offered her hands. "I'm sorry. I shouldn't have burdened you with this."

"Nonsense." She squeezed Mary Kate's hands in her small, dry ones. "You're an unusual woman, Mary Catherine. So modern. So much like your mother before you, God rest her soul." She took a quavering breath. "So perhaps this is not such an unusual way to seek a suitable husband as some might think."

Mary Kate looked into her aunt's gray eyes, amazed that such a simple, old-fashioned woman could accept such a contemporary idea as a woman choosing her own husband, especially by such eccentric means. "Thank you for understanding. For listening."

Her aunt released her hands. "Tell me, what method have you chosen to . . . narrow the field?"

Mary Kate hitched up her woolen skirt to adjust her woolen stockings. She had dressed in a simple green-and-blue tartan plaid arisaid with her mother's elegant silver brooch the size of her hand fastened securely at her breast. She had tied her hair back in a green ribbon, and donned a green cap with her father's MacDonal cockade attached.

"I thought the St. Michael's festival games would be the perfect venue. The horse race, the target contests. I've need of an accomplished husband; I should well know their skills."

"Aye, aye." Aunt Agnes bobbed her head. "Ye were always so practical, Mary Catherine. Even as a wee child."

"And—" She eyed her aunt. She'd not even told

Rob of this idea yet; it had just come to her last night. "And I thought I might give the contenders a riddle."

"A riddle?" The elderly woman's eyes widened and she patted her mobcap nervously. "Whatever do you mean?"

Mary Kate shrugged. "I need a clever husband, as well as a skilled one. I'll give the men riddles and see who is best at solving them."

"You'll choose a husband on the basis of a riddle?" the elderly woman asked incredulously.

"Makes as much sense to me as being betrothed to someone before he's off his nursemaid's lead lines or being forced to wed at daggerpoint, as was my mother."

"Now, now." Agnes waggled her finger. "Your father was good to your mother, God rest her soul." She crossed herself. "He loved her fiercely."

"Aye. I know." Mary Kate softened. "But I'd prefer to choose my own husband. I need one quickly, and with as little fuss as possible. I've an ailing father to tend to and a castle to run here."

Agnes made a clicking sound between her teeth as she paced. "So . . . any bachelor could . . . compete," she said slowly. "Any *appropriate* bachelor."

Mary Kate didn't quite understand. "Well, aye, I suppose."

Her aunt looked up, brightening. "Then my Magnus, he would be eligible. He's in contention." She reached out to take Mary Kate's arm. "He would make a fine husband, I'm certain. He rides well." She went on faster than before. "The men respect him. He's an excellent horseman, and he's very clever, you know, my Magnus. Some don't think so, but he is. Aye, very clever."

Mary Kate didn't know what to say. Magnus was none of those things. Magnus was the laughingstock of the castle. She wouldn't marry Magnus if he were the last Scot on God's green earth, but she didn't have the heart to tell her aunt that. She wouldn't hurt her for the world, especially not when she was being so understanding. And what harm would there be in letting her aunt think Magnus had a chance, at least for a short time? "I . . . I suppose Magnus would be . . . a consideration, Auntie."

Agnes clasped her hands together in glee and then fluttered them like a bird's wings. "Oh, my, oh, my. I must tell him at once. He must ride his best. Shoot his best."

Mary Kate threw up one hand. "Auntie, please. I didn't want anyone to know. I didn't want it to be so obvious. These men, they're not livestock to have me treat them so disrespectfully."

She backed toward the outer door of the chamber. "I won't say a thing." She put her thin finger to her lips. "Not a word."

Before Mary Kate could speak again, her aunt was out the door and nearly sprinting for her own quarters.

With a groan, Mary Kate closed the door. "I should just leap off the tower now," she muttered.

"Who's leaping off the tower?" asked a masculine voice from the far side of the door.

She yanked it open. *Rob.* She hadn't expected him. Not here. "Are you eavesdropping?"

He walked in. "Nay. Certainly not. That was always you." He touched her playfully under her chin. "Now what's Auntie about? Still trying to sell her darling?"

He seemed so lighthearted this morning. Too lighthearted to suit. Once again she wondered if it were real, or if he, as was she, was simply disguising his real feelings. Did he dread today as much as she did? She rolled her eyes. "It's worse than you think. She knows what I'm doing. About the men."

"She knows? How?"

She groaned in confession. "I told her."

"You told her?"

"Not on purpose." She flopped onto an upholstered chair, feeling more uncertain of her ridiculous plan by the moment.

"Perfect. Word should reach Edinburgh by noonday tomorrow. Better prospects." He perched on the arm of her chair.

"That's not funny."

He looked down at her, his mouth turning down disapprovingly. "Are ye wearing that?"

"What?" She bounced out of the chair. "What's wrong with this?" She adjusted the silver brooch, a representation of her status. "It's a festival," she protested. "Not a coronation."

He frowned. "You're looking for a husband, Mary Kate. You should appear the mistress of the castle, not the milkmaid."

She crossed her arms stubbornly. "They don't know I'm looking for a husband. Besides, this is what I like. It's what I'm comfortable in. It's what the lady of a manor really wears."

He removed the infamous list from inside his *leine-chroich* and opened it. "No, they don't know your quest yet, but they will soon enough. Now listen. I intend to see you introduced. You must circulate among your guests." He gestured. "Get to know some of the gentlemen a little better. You should ride on the hunt this morning as well. You can tell a great deal about a man by the way he hunts—how he treats his dogs, his servants, his respect for the animals."

It peeved her that he was being so gallant about the whole damned thing. Maybe she'd read him wrong. Maybe he didn't care. "Should I take notes?" she asked tartly.

He glanced up from the list. "Mary Kate, this isn't going to work if you don't give it a decent effort."

She perched on the arm of the chair opposite Rob. "I know," she conceded with a sigh. "I just hate this feeling, as if I'm to go up on an auction block."

"Nae, Mary Kate." He winked. "It's *they* who are about to cross the block." He rose and indicated the door. "Shall we go?"

Mary Kate rose slowly from her chair, mentally preparing herself. "All right. I'm ready." She passed him and glanced over her shoulder. "I'll be charming, witty, gracious—just *swear* you won't leave my side. I can't do this alone."

"Fair enough. Now smile, Mary Kate." He brushed her cheek with his fingertips. "This isn't your hanging, love."

"Nae?" She lifted her hand across the base of her throat as they left her chamber. "Then why does it feel like it?"

Mary Kate mingled among her guests in the garden off the courtyard, smiling, greeting, offering her hand in neighborly friendship. Tables had been set up with food and drink, and despite the early hour, musicians played lively Scottish ballads from a dais set up against the north wall. It seemed that everyone within miles of the castle had accepted her father's invitation to their St. Michael's festival, and she was quite sure that there were a few families here who had not been invited.

The longer the morning went on, the more she wished she and Rob could slip away to their secret place at the well. Then again, as anxious as he appeared to marry her off, perhaps she would rather not be alone with him. Every word of encouragement he uttered felt like a knife wound in her chest. "I've had enough visiting. Let's mount up," Mary Kate said to Rob, feeling uncomfortable in the social atmosphere. She headed for the side of the courtyard where riders were already astride their horses.

"Let's be hosts for a few moments longer," he countered, steering her toward a young man, obviously waiting for an introduction, that or his turn in the privy.

Mary Kate wanted to protest, but short of making a spectacle of herself, there was no way to stop Rob.

"Charles, let me introduce you to the mistress of Cnocanduin," Rob said as he grasped Mary Kate's arm tightly and propelled her forward toward a gentleman in green-and-white plaid.

"Mary Catherine MacDonal, Charles Moffatt. Charles, Mary Catherine MacDonal."

Mary Kate took one look at Charles's balding head, which he was attempting to cover with long wisps of hair creatively plastered to his bare pate, and mentally checked him off the list. "Pleased to meet you, sir."

"You know Charles's sister, Anne," Rob said, obviously trying to help her into a conversation with the grinning fellow.

Aye, the slut is probably tumbling in yonder barn with

Magnus right now, Mary Kate thought as she nodded politely to Charles and made some inane comment about the weather.

As quickly as possible, Rob tactfully guided her toward the next possible suitor. "Mary Kate, you can't do that."

"Do what?" she asked innocently.

"Disqualify a man before he opens his mouth. Charles Moffatt not only owns Waverly to the east, but has holdings in a shipping company in the Indies. He may not be fair of face, but he's a wealthy man, and his father has spoken to your father on more than one occasion on the subject of a union between Waverly and Cnocanduin."

She took a mug of ale and a small meat pie from a nearby refreshment table. She'd not yet broken her fast and she was starved. "The man is balding."

"So?"

"I have nothing against a bald pate, but did you see the way he had taken that long strand and twisted it on his head to make it look as if he had hair?" She wrinkled her nose and took a sip of the cold ale. "How do you think he got it to stick on his bare head? Glue made from ground hooves?"

Rob frowned and nudged her forward. "So you do not want Charles seated near you at the banquet tonight?"

"We shall see how poor my other prospects are."

He sighed, making a mark on his list with a bit of burnt stick. "Next, Alex Kerr. I think I just saw him."

"Next, we mount for the hunt. Look, everyone's waiting for us." Finishing the ale, she passed her cup to a serving girl, and, licking the last of the tart from her fingers, she wove her way through the horses in search of her own.

They would be hunting a wild boar that had been troubling the crofters in the district for months. At first the boar had been blamed only for the death of a few late calves, but a fortnight ago, it had attacked a small child and would have killed it if a neighbor had not come to the child's rescue with his scythe.

As Mary Kate approached her horse, held by one of her stable boys, she saw a man approximately her own age making a beeline for her. She was certain she recognized him, though she couldn't remember his name. At least he had a full head of hair.

"Good morn to ye."

At first glance Mary Kate saw a handsome young man with shaggy dark hair and a fair complexion.

He lifted his bonnet in greeting.

A face I suppose I could look at every morning for the rest of my life, she thought.

Then he grinned and bared two rows of blackened, crumbling teeth. For a moment Mary Kate feared she'd gag. Was that smell his *teeth,* for sweet heaven's sake?

"Of Berwickshire, second son, large herd of cattle, good family," Rob whispered in her ear. "Smile."

Mary Kate forced a smile, but she couldn't stop staring at his rotting teeth. "Good morn to you . . ." She couldn't recall his name again; she'd been too intent upon his teeth.

"John Bell," Rob whispered impatiently in her ear.

"John," she interjected.

The grinning young man offered her a hand to lift her into the saddle. "It was indeed kind of you and your father to invite us for the festivities. I extend an invitation to our own home, Lochlar." His hand lingered over hers.

Mary Kate pulled away, taking up her reins and mentally checking John Bell and his cattle off her list. She could never sleep with a man with such poor teeth. It would give her nightmares.

"Thank you so much, sir," Mary Kate said, reining her mount in the opposite direction. "Enjoy the hunt."

Rob mounted and rode up beside her. "You have to give them a chance."

Mary Kate rode over the drawbridge, beyond the walls of the castle to where the hunting party was gathering. Hunting dogs barked and paced nervously as several boys attempted to keep their charges from tangling their lines.

"Did you see his teeth?" she hissed, slipping her riding gloves on. "Atrocious."

"No, I wasn't looking at his teeth. He's a handsome man and his cattle stock is superior."

She sank her heels and urged her mount forward. "So you marry him, Rob Drum."

The hunting party set off in the direction of the bog to the north, where the boar had been sighted the night before. The serving boys ran ahead with the barking dogs still on their leashes. The riders fell in behind.

"Good morning, Mary Kate."

She glanced up to see who boldly called her by her first name without being introduced. It was Ian Ferguson. She knew him because she had sold cattle to him on several occasions in the last few years. He was the only son of Mac Ferguson, who had died on Candlemas Eve. His lands touched Cnocanduin's lands on the western border. Mary Kate didn't often hear female gossip, but she guessed that Ian was spoken of as an excellent catch for a husband.

"Morning, Ian." She nodded, trying to keep in mind her goal. Rob was right. She did have to give this a fair effort. "Looks to be a good day for the festival."

The air was still chilly, but the sun rising in the east was bright and bold and its warmth was already burning off the mists of dawn.

"A fine day, indeed." He pushed his horse forward between her and Rob, and Rob dropped back.

Mary Kate glanced at Rob, wanting him to ride with them, but he shook his head, urging her with one gloved hand. He wanted her to talk to Ian Ferguson. He was on the list.

"How is your father?" Ian asked. "I understand he's slowed down a wee bit."

She turned her attention to the man at her side, studying him carefully as she spoke. Decent teeth. Silky, dark hair that appeared to have been washed recently. Comely enough face. He had a crook in the bridge of his nose, but it added character to his attractively rugged face. She couldn't find fault with Ian Ferguson's appearance.

"Father is well, though moving a little slower as of late." She chuckled. "Thank you for inquiring. His leg has been giving him a fit again—gout, so he thought he ought not ride this morning. He'll be joining us for the games and racing and supper tonight, though."

Ian's leg brushed hers as they rode, and she had

to fight the impulse to pull away. She had never ridden so close to another man save for her father or Rob. She was so near to Ian she could feel the heat of his thigh, smell his skin. His scent was not unpleasant, only different from what she was used to. Different from Rob's.

"I have always admired Sean MacDonal," Ian said. "Any man who comes out of those barbaric hills and makes a life for himself here in the Borders is a fine man by me. A fine man."

Mary Kate nodded because she didn't know what to say. Rob had instructed her to converse with the men, but she wasn't really sure how. She rarely indulged in social discourse with anyone. It was always related to the daily working of Cnocanduin. With cattle, or fieldwork, or house repairs she was comfortable, but conversation just for the sake of passing time seemed silly to her.

If Ian was aware of her lack of confidence, he gave no indication. He seemed to be content to carry most of the conversation. "A fine man you have there," he said. "Good cattle man."

Mary Kate glanced at Ian. "My man?"

He hooked a thumb behind him. "The Englishman —Rob Drum. Your father has sent him on matters of cattle on several occasions. I have to confess he's a far sight more knowledgeable than your cousin."

Ian chuckled and Mary Kate chuckled with him. But at the same time she couldn't help but feel offended. Rob was more knowledgeable of cattle and Cnocanduin's herds because he worked hard and learned from the older men, whilst Magnus spent his time avoiding work, tumbling maids, and allowing his mother to coddle him. "Rob's not a servant," Mary Kate said defensively.

Ian dismissed Rob with the wave of one gloved hand. "Aye, I ken. I've heard the story. Your father took him in and fostered him. An orphan. Your father is a fine man to take an English boy."

No, he didn't ken at all. Mary Kate stared at the pommel of her saddle. Ian's words only reiterated what she knew. Everyone in the shire considered Rob a servant. No one would accept him as the lord of Cnocanduin.

"Say, there's my cousin. I suppose I'd better go and speak to him." He urged his mount faster, pulling away from her. "Save me a dance tonight, will you, Mary Kate?" He flashed her a handsome smile that she knew any woman in the county between the ages of ten and sixty would pine for, and rode off.

Rob trotted into Ian's place beside Mary Kate. He nodded thoughtfully. "Possibility?" He lifted one brow.

She wanted to say no. She wanted to cross Ian Ferguson off the list. She just couldn't think of a good reason why. And this was so hard to discuss with Rob. "A possibility," she conceded with a groan.

"Excellent."

As they entered the wooded edge of the bog, hoofbeats pounded behind her, and Magnus rode up beside her. "Good morning, dear cousin," he panted, out of breath.

"Good morning, Magnus."

He was wearing his English coat, but a proper Scottish bonnet.

"And how are you this fine morning? You're looking quite bonny, I might say." He spoke in a stilted manner, as if repeating what someone else had said.

His mother, perhaps? Had Aunt Agnes told him what Mary Kate was about? She must have.

Rob winked at Mary Kate. He knew what she was thinking. He always knew.

"I'm quite fine this morning, Magnus." She slowed her horse, taking care that he found his footing on the wet ground. Thin-branched, stunted trees stretched over her head, and the air was thick with the smell of stagnant water and mud.

"I intend to bring down that boar this morning, you know."

"Do you?"

"Aye. And when I do, I shall present its head to you."

"How lovely."

Just then the pitch of the hounds' barking changed.

"Aha," Magnus cried. "It sounds as if the hounds are on to the beastie now."

"Appears so."

"Excuse me." Magnus tipped his head and raced forward toward the head of the hunting party, his ample belly quivering as he rode.

"Shall I add him to the list?" Rob waved the slip of parchment.

He'd been teasing her about Magnus's desire to marry her for years. He didn't really think the match was suitable. It was just a joke between them.

"There's still time," he teased.

Glaring at him, she snatched the paper from him. She was not in the mood for his jesting this morning. "I'd sooner sleep with the boar."

He smiled, a sadness coming over his face. "Aye,

Mary Kate," he said slowly. "What am I going to do with you?"

It was on the tip of her tongue to say "Marry me." But she didn't, because, of course, that would have been a ridiculously silly thing to say. Even hurtful. Yet the more she observed the "likely candidates," the more aware she became of the differences between them and Rob. How could she marry one man while wanting another? Worse, how could she be content as wife to one man while continually seeing the one she truly wanted?

"Listen to the dogs," she said in a desperate attempt to curb her thoughts and ignore her misery. "Sounds as if they're tracking the boar. You'd better hurry. You've probably the best chance of bringing him down of all of them. If the kill is yours, you earn a place of honor at the head of the table with Papa and me tonight. I need you to be there."

"If they have found him, I just want to be certain they kill him." He lifted his reins, breaking eye contact with her. "I don't belong at the head table." As he broke into a trot he called over his shoulder, "You coming?"

"Nae." She slowed her horse to a walk. "Not in the mood for hunting. You go and bring me that boar's head."

Rob's rich laughter echoed in her head as he rode into the bog, leaving her with her list of prospective bridegrooms and a sense of gloom she couldn't shake.

Chapter Four

Rob hurried to catch up with the lead group of hunters. The servants had set the hounds free and they were barking and baying wildly, close on the heels of the wild boar.

"Ahead!" Charles Moffatt pointed into the dense undergrowth of the bog. The riders were bunching up, struggling to make their way into the thick foliage where the path fell away.

"Aside! Aside," Magnus puffed, attempting to ride his horse between two riders.

Rob's shoulders tensed at the primal squealing sound of the wild boar as the hounds ran it down. A wild boar could be deadly, and he knew better than to ride into the thicket without his full concentration. But how could he concentrate on the hunt?

How could he concentrate when he was losing his Mary Kate to another man? Of course he wasn't really

losing her because she'd never really been his. He
knew that. He knew in his head, at least, but he didn't
feel it in his heart. For as long as Rob could remember,
he had loved Mary Catherine MacDonal. From that
rainy night when he had first stood in the great hall
of Cnocanduin, he had loved her as he would love
no other.

And now he was helping her find a husband. . . .
Just the thought made Rob's stomach churn. Not only
was he handing Mary Kate over to another man out
of some strange sense of what was right, but he was
aiding her in finding that man. He had to be insane.

Still, he knew this was best. When he thought with
his head and not his heart, he knew he had to help
Mary Kate find a husband. She was certain her father
would never make her marry Magnus, but what if he
somehow won her by default? Magnus was slow-witted,
crude, and weak. He always had been. Surely Ian
Ferguson or Charles Moffatt or even Alex Kerr would
be a better choice.

At this point he had to cling to that thought.
Remain steadfast and determined. He had to think
with his head and not feel with his aching heart. It
was the only way he could get through this.

"I say, aside!" Magnus shouted angrily, forcing his
way past Rob on the narrow path.

Magnus cried out as his horse lost its footing in the
slick, dark mud, going down on one foreleg. The
horse managed to right itself before falling, but came
up with one lame front leg.

"Christ almighty!" Magnus swore angrily, jerking
on the reins. "Idiot horse!" He attempted to bully
the horse forward. "I have to bring down that boar.
Mother expects me to—"

"Magnus, he's hurt." Rob reined in behind Mary Kate's cousin. "You can't ride him like that."

Magnus sawed on his reins. "I have to shoot that boar. Mother expects me at the head table tonight," he whined.

Knowing he would be wasting his breath to argue, Rob dismounted. He caught the reins of Magnus's horse, preventing him from pushing the injured horse any further. He wanted to be there when the boar was brought down, but not at the expense of one of Cnocanduin's best steeds. "Here, take my mount."

Rob doubted Mary Kate would appreciate his helping Magnus; his was the last face she wanted to see at the head table. But at this point what chance would Magnus have of making the kill? The other riders were already ahead of him. And left up to Mary Kate, he knew she would have easily chosen the horse's safety over her own preference for dining partners.

Magnus stared at him, taken aback by Rob's generosity. "Take yours?"

"Hurry. It sounds as if the hounds have the boar. The riders won't be far behind." He held the horse as Magnus dismounted. "I'll walk your horse back." He tossed Magnus the reins of his own mount and then crouched to get a better look at the injured animal's foreleg.

Magnus rode off without so much as a thank-you . . . not that Rob had expected one, or ever did.

Speaking softly to the injured gelding, Rob turned him around and started back for Cnocanduin. Behind him he could hear the baying dogs, the shouting of men, and the squeal of the wild boar as they cornered him for the kill. Secretly, Rob had wanted to be the one to kill the boar because he knew it was important to Mary Kate to see the crofters safe. He wanted to do it for her. Foolish . . .

As he had told her, he didn't belong at the head table anyway. And he was still doing something for her, wasn't he? Caring for her animals as she would care for them.

Within half a mile, Rob met up with Mary Kate. "Rob? What's the matter? Are you all right?"

He grinned despite the heaviness he felt in his chest because her beautiful face always made him smile. "I'm fine. Magnus's horse stumbled, 'tis all."

She jumped down easily from her own saddle. "Is he all right?" She knelt on one knee in the deep grass and ran her experienced hand over the swelling foreleg.

"Mary Kate, he's fine. Just needs a day or two to mend." He caught her hand. "Get up off the ground. You'll soil your clothing."

Satisfied the horse wasn't severely injured, she rose, her nose wrinkled. "Soil my clothing? Oh, please, Rob. I don't care about my clothes."

The sunshine fell across her shoulders, casting flaming red hues in her long hair hanging down her back. Her sun-kissed face with its sprinkling of freckles across the bridge of her nose radiated a natural beauty that Rob knew came as much from within as without.

Sweet heaven, he loved her.

"You ought to know me better than that by now," Mary Kate continued.

She appeared unaware of his observations, or his devotion. It was better that way. Easier for them both.

"When have I ever given a lick about what I look

like?" She fell into step beside him, leading her own mount back in the direction of the castle.

"They have the boar cornered." He pointed over his shoulder. "You might still have time to be there to see Magnus make the kill. He's probably bullied his way to the front by now."

She rolled her eyes. "No, thank you. It's bad enough, should he make the shot, that I should have to tolerate his company at the supper table tonight."

"His and the boar's head," Rob teased. She laughed, poking him in the side with her elbow.

Rob loved being with Mary Kate like this, as friends, as workmates. And as he walked back toward Cnocanduin with Mary Kate by his side and the sun dancing merrily over their shoulders, he wondered how he would be able to endure seeing her in another man's arms.

"Once around yonder tree," Sean MacDonal directed his guests loudly, pointing down the lane. "And back, and the winner shall receive a seat at the head table and this handsome purse." He jingled a cloth purse filled with silver coins. It was a hefty sum her father offered as the prize for the winner of the St. Michael's Day race, proof of his generous spirit.

"Riders, on your mark."

Mary Kate offered her arm to help her father up from the chair the servants had brought out into the grass beyond the drawbridge, but he would have no part of her assistance. Even at seventy-six and with his mind failing, he still held the pride he carried with him from the Highlands to Cnocanduin all those years ago. Sean MacDonal stood tall, with only the aid of his cane, and raised a red scarf.

Standing beside her father, Mary Kate searched the crowd of riders for Rob. He was an excellent horseman, and the mount he had chosen was her father's own stallion. Astride Graybeard, Rob would surely win. The sum of money her father held in his purse would mean a lot to Rob. He received a small stipend each month from Cnocanduin's coffers for the services he provided, but this was real money. Money with which he could begin his own herd of cattle.

"Set!" Sean cried. "Go!" He brought one withered arm down, fluttering the red kerchief, and the riders were off.

The crowd of friends and neighbors, mostly women, children, and elderly men, cheered, calling the names of their favorite riders. Mary Kate couldn't help but notice that several unmarried women called Ian Ferguson's name and waved their white handkerchiefs for him.

Great clouds of dust billowed as the riders raced the stretch between the castle and the tree with the red rag tied around it some half a mile in the distance. In a matter of seconds, Rob pulled ahead of the other riders.

Mary Kate couldn't contain herself. She leaped up and down, waving her arms wildly. "Go, Rob! Go!"

"Oh, my, oh, my," Aunt Agnes worried, fluttering her hands. "It's so dusty. Dear Magnus will have a fit with his breathing. So dusty."

Mary Kate craned her neck to see Rob turn the tree and start back, the other riders close on his heels.

"Rob! Rob Drum!" Mary Kate cried excitedly. "Come on! You've got them! You've got them all!"

Out of the corner of her eye, Mary Kate spotted movement alongside the road just ahead of the riders. With the dust and the bobbing heads all around her it was difficult for her to make out what it was she saw. Something. Someone. Surely not someone . . .

A child. The moment Mary Kate realized it was a small child starting across the road, she darted forward.

She didn't know who the child was, or where he belonged, but she knew it wasn't in the middle of the road. Not in the path of at least three dozen galloping horses.

"No! Get back!" Mary Kate screamed. But the child was too far from her. Didn't anyone but her see what was happening? Dear God, did the riders see the toddler? A little boy. She could see now that it was a little boy still in nappies.

Mary Kate would never make it to the child before the horses did. Still, she ran as hard as she could, her heart pounding. She screamed, her lungs burning, her skirts gathered in both hands so that she could run faster.

The riders didn't see the little boy. She was certain of it. What man would notice a wee peasant child? Not with the dust and the excitement of the race . . .

"No!" Mary Kate screamed as the riders descended upon the baby.

Then, just when she was certain she would witness a disaster, she saw Rob lean over, one arm stretched downward. In a nearly Herculean movement, he swept the child into one strong arm and lifted him off the ground, then reined in his horse. An instant later the pack of riders thundered by.

Mary Kate threw up her hands with a cry of relief. She stepped off the roadway just in time to allow the riders to pass. She heard Ian Ferguson's name being called. He had taken the lead when Rob had fallen back. He had taken the race.

By the time she reached Rob, a young crofter's wife—the child's mother, no doubt—appeared at his side.

Thick tears ran down the woman's sunburned cheeks. "My babe. My wee babe," she blubbered. "Oh, thank ye, thank ye, sir. He was with me one minute, I swear to ye. Gone the next."

"It's all right. He's all right," Rob said, handing down the runny-nosed little boy to his mother.

The woman held the little boy tightly to her bosom and started back across the field to her cottage. The little boy peered over his mother's shoulders with big brown eyes and gave a little wave as she carried him off.

"Rob, you saved him. You saved that little boy's life," Mary Kate whispered, in awe of the man she had known her whole life.

He shrugged, seeming embarrassed. "Nae." He slid off his horse and walked him back toward the crowd. "They would have pulled up. I just didn't want to see the lad frightened."

Mary Kate knew the other riders would never have seen the little boy in time, never been able to think as quickly as Rob had. And even if they had, not one of those men would have been able to snatch a child so cleanly off the ground. She didn't care what Rob

Drum said; he had saved the little boy from injury, perhaps even death.

"But you lost the race," she said softly. "You lost the purse." She met his gaze. "I'm sorry. You'd have won if you'd not pulled up for the boy. You'd have had enough money for the cattle you want."

"Wasn't meant to be." He smiled down at her, and his smile made her weak in the knees.

"So." He nodded toward her father. "I see it's Master Ferguson who won the race. Handsome, polite, wealthy, and an excellent rider. Definitely a possibility, nae?"

Mary Kate couldn't bear to answer him at that moment. She didn't care who had won the bloody race. Only one man had given up the purse and the honor of the win for the sake of a snotty-nosed peasant's son. In her heart, only one man was the winner. In her heart only one man was worthy of Cnocanduin.

The one man who couldn't be her husband.

Rob patted her father's stallion's withers. "I'm going to the barn to rub down old Graybeard; why don't you join your father and Ian?"

She glanced at the crowd around her father and his winner. Everyone was calling Ian's name, slapping his back and offering congratulations.

"I'll walk you to the barn first," she said.

He opened his mouth to argue, then nodded. Rob always knew when to push her and when not to. "But then it's back to the festival with you. It'll soon be time to prepare for the banquet. You'll want to change into the new gown your father had me bring from Edinburgh."

"Just to the barn," she conceded.

"Want a ride?"

When they were younger, he had always offered her a ride to the barn after he'd been out with the men. It had always been his way of reconciling the fact that she was often left behind with the women.

"Sure."

He offered his hand and gave her a boost into the saddle. Graybeard was a tall gray stallion, so tall that though she was an accomplished rider, Mary Kate felt awkward and unbalanced so far from the ground.

Rob led the horse into the rear of the barn. Inside, it was quiet save for the sounds of other horses munching their oats and the swallows twittering as they flew between beams high above her head. With the doors closed, the barn was dimly lit by pinpricks of afternoon sunlight. It was a warm, peaceful place that always made Mary Kate feel safe and loved.

"Down with ye. Graybeard needs his rubdown." Rob held his hand up to help her dismount.

Mary Kate didn't know what happened next. She'd been mounting and dismounting horses since she was three. Either her blasted skirt caught on the edge of the saddle or she shifted her weight too quickly, because suddenly she pitched off the horse.

Rob threw up both strong arms to steady her, but it was too late. She fell off the horse, somehow on top of Rob, knocking them both to the ground.

Mary Kate lay dazed and flat atop Rob—atop his broad chest—her mouth only inches from his.

Her eyelashes fluttered as she breathed deeply. He smelled of horse and hay, and muscle and maleness.

He was looking intently into her eyes. She was gazing into his. They were so blue.

Mary Kate didn't know who moved first. There was no thought involved. Only instinct.

Rob lifted his head. She lowered hers.

Their mouths met and her lips half parted in a sigh. The moment flesh met flesh a spark of energy leaped between them. Her sigh became a groan of pleasure. Suddenly she realized she had waited her whole life for this feeling, this one kiss. Perhaps she had waited for all of eternity.

Rob lifted his arms from the barn floor to tighten them around her waist. Mary Kate moaned softly, her fingers finding the blades of his shoulders as she parted her lips to taste his tongue.

She had to taste him. She just had to, or surely she would die right here and now.

"Mary Kate." Rob groaned. She gave no protest as he rolled her over in the fragrant, crackling straw. She wanted him to kiss her like this. She wanted to feel his body pressed against hers, his hips molded to hers. She wanted his kiss to last forever.

When Rob finally lifted his mouth from hers, they were both panting heavily. She was dizzy from lack of air and the realization of what she'd just done. What *they'd* just done.

"Oh, Mary Kate, I'm sorry," he whispered. "I shouldn't have. . . ." As he spoke, he brushed back the hair from her eyes, plucking away a bit of straw.

Tears stung the backs of her eyelids. She was so happy, yet . . . so sad. "It takes two," she said softly, gazing into the blue eyes she loved.

He moved off her and she immediately felt loss,

emptiness. Offering his hand, he helped her to her feet. She began to brush the straw from her clothes.

She didn't know what to say.

He didn't know what to say.

"I should go." Her clothes free of the telltale evidence, she ran her hand through her hair.

"Aye, before you're missed."

She studied the straw at his boots for a moment, then lifted her gaze. Against her will, tears gathered in the corners of her eyes. She wanted Rob Drum so badly. She wanted him, not just now, but forever. She wanted what she knew she could never have. "Rob, I wish—"

He reached out with one finger and pressed it to her lips. "I know," he said softly, tears in his own eyes. "I know, Mary Kate."

And then she left him, left him for her father's great hall and her duty to Cnocanduin.

"Cook?" Rob leaned on the wooden worktable where the old woman was busily rolling out biscuits for the evening's feast. Cook was a gypsy woman with rich olive skin and raven-wing black hair peppered with gray. He didn't know her name; she'd always been simply "Cook." He didn't know how old she was either, but she had to be old. She'd been here since he'd arrived, since Mary Kate had been born, maybe since Sean MacDonal had come out of the hills to marry Mary Campbell.

"Aye, what is it, lad? Hand me the flour." She pointed. "You, wench," she shouted to a maid hurrying by with a steaming trencher of meat. "Hurry.

To the table with that loin before it grows cold and I skin you."

Cook took the flour tin Rob offered and sprinkled a handful on the table to make a dry surface for her biscuits.

"Cook, tell me about the well below the castle."

"What about the well?"

"You said it was magic. When Mary Kate and I were little, you told us it was magic."

She lifted one black brow, staring so hard into his eyes that it was difficult for him not to look away under her scrutiny. "Ye believe in magic, Rob Drum?"

"I . . . I don't know. I think I want to." He could still taste Mary Kate's mouth on his. He was a desperate man. He wanted her. He needed her. In his heart he knew she felt the same way.

"What do you want to know about the well?" With strong arms she rolled out the biscuit dough.

"I want to know about the magic. You said it was magic, but you didn't say how."

"They say there was once a stone marker below with words inscribed," the woman said. "Something about a promise as long as the water ran." She shook her head. "But that was before my time."

"There's no marker now," Rob said. "If there was, I would know about it."

She cut biscuits carefully with a circle of tin and set them on a cooking sheet. "So perhaps the magic of the well, it is gone. Magic doesn't last forever, lad."

"But what was that magic? What did the well offer? For whom did it offer its magic?"

She halted her work, gazing into his eyes again. When she spoke, it was softly, her words for him and him alone. "They say the magic was only for the mistresses of Cnocanduin, or those who would become the mistress.''

"How did it work? Could you just make a wish?'' He brushed the cook's arm with his hand. Time was running out. At this moment Mary Kate was seated between Ian Ferguson and Magnus at the head table in the great hall. Both men had been rewarded places at Sean's table because of their accomplishments of the day. Magnus had somehow managed to make the kill in the boar hunt, and Ian had won the race.

Rob knew he had nothing to fear in competition from Magnus. He had always been a joke between Rob and Mary Kate. Rob knew that no matter how Agnes pushed her, Mary Kate would not marry him. But Ian . . . Rob had seen Mary Kate laughing with him. He had seen the way Ian looked at her. If Rob was going to act, he would have to act fast or he would lose her forever. "Cook, I have to know," he said.

"I tell you, I don't know. Try it. Have the mistress try it. But only the mistress can make the wish." She shook a bony, floured finger. "That much I know. And you must hurry. The walls of Cnocanduin speak to me. Ye ken?''

Rob sensed that Cook understood the relationship he and Mary Kate shared. He sensed she knew they wished it could be more.

"Just make a wish? That's all she has to do?''

She shrugged her broad shoulders. "I would drink from the well, just to be certain. To bind the wish.''

"That's it?''

"Perhaps it will work, perhaps not." She lifted her tray of biscuits and started for the fireplace. "But let me know if it works, eh, lad?''

She winked, and for the first time in years, Rob felt

a sense of hope. He knew it didn't make any sense. Magic well, indeed. But if the kind of magic he and Mary Kate had shared during that single kiss existed, surely other types of magic existed as well.

Chapter Five

Mary Kate sat between Ian Ferguson and her cousin Magnus at the head table in the great hall. Servants conveyed trays of hearty Scottish food: beef, mutton, potatoes, turnips, beans from the garden, meat pies and puddings, crusty breads, and rich gravies. Steam rose off the trenchers filling the hall with the tantalizing aromas of Cnocanduin's famous kitchen.

As the diners were served, Mary Kate made conversation with Ian and Magnus, the guests of honor, as well as with Charles Moffatt to Ian's right. All three men were in a jolly mood, aided by the free-flowing ale from her father's cellar. For their benefit and that of her objective, she tried to appear as jovial as they were. As the evening wore on, she began to realize that the three men were competing for her attention. As each prospective bridegroom served her the choice tidbits of meat and vegetables from the serving trays, they attempted to outdo each other with tall tales of amusement and bravery.

Everyone's eyes were on Mary Kate as she talked with the men. She could hear her guests' voices buzzing in her head. They were all talking about her. Who would be her husband? Who would she choose?

Obviously Agnes MacDonal had had a busy afternoon. Despite her reassurance that she would not speak of Mary Kate's search for a husband, she had wasted no time in telling every man, woman, and servant within a two-mile radius of the castle—under strict confidence, no doubt. The titillating secret was apparently the most exciting news that had hit the shire since Mary Kerr had run off to Edinburgh with Jesse MacDonald's husband last May Day.

And while the St. Michael's Day festival guests gossiped, Ian and Charles endeavored to surpass each other with stories of their own conquests. Magnus, unable to keep up, for he had no tales of conquest he could speak of in female company, slowly withdrew from the conversation. Ignoring his mother's eye batting, hissing behind her hand, and blatant pointing, he gradually drank himself into a quiet stupor. Soon his head drooped, and Mary Kate slid his soup aside to prevent him from drowning in his bowl. Leaving Magnus to sleep, Mary Kate laughed at Ian's and Charles's silly stories. She oohed and aahed at the tales of capturing cattle reivers and hunting wild game in treacherous mountains.

When Ian stood and called for a toast, she drank to her father's health as well as to her own. She accepted small gifts of thanks from neighbors, many no doubt hoping to put in a good word for themselves or their sons. She tried hard to give the evening her best effort. After all, this had been her idea.

But her heart was neither in the conversations nor in the cheerful toasts. She didn't want the trinkets her neighbors presented her. Rob's absence from the festivities was painfully evident to her. As she sipped her ale sparingly, and pushed her food around her plate in circles to appear as if she'd eaten, she thought of him and of the kiss they had shared in the barn.

They had never kissed before. They hadn't dared, not because they hadn't wanted to, but because both knew it could lead nowhere. Nowhere but heartache. And now Mary Kate realized how right they had been.

Remembering what had passed between them, Mary Kate ached to feel Rob's mouth on hers again. Her arms throbbed for want of the heat and the comfort of holding him tight. Yet here she sat, entertaining two men she was considering marrying, and yet she was thinking of another. How could she choose Ian or Charles to be her husband, to kiss, to bed, to share her life with until death parted them? How could she choose between these men when she wanted no one but Rob?

Mary Kate caught sight of her father. He smiled at her, grinning proudly—no doubt at the idea of his daughter surrounded by eligible men. He winked and nodded in the direction of Ian and Charles, who were in a heated conversation on the pros and cons of a certain musket powder.

Mary Kate couldn't resist a smile. She wanted to make her father happy. She wanted to do what was right. She owed it to him, to her dearly departed mother, to the red-haired women of Cnocanduin who gazed down at her from their portraits on the walls

of the great hall. If marrying Ian Ferguson or Charles
Moffatt, balding head and all, would protect Cnocanduin, how could she not marry? How could she not
sacrifice her own desires for the good of those who
depended on her for their livelihoods, their very lives?

Ian spoke to Mary Kate, boldly brushing her arm
with his hand, and she forced herself to turn and
speak kindly. Determined, she lowered her lashes as
she had seen other young women do, and played the
demure Scottish lass with the great inheritance.

All the while Magnus, his head resting on the table
beside her, softly snored on.

Rob stared at her as if she'd just sprouted another
head. "You're going to what?"

Mary Kate, down on her hands and knees in her
herb garden, yanked another weed. "I'm going to
give them a series of riddles."

"Riddles?" He threw back his head and laughed
merrily, his voice echoing off the stone wall of the
courtyard. The sound frightened a flock of doves
nesting in the eaves of the garden house and they
took flight into the early morning sky, their wings
beating rhythmically.

"Riddles," he scoffed. "This whole scheme grows
more ludicrous by the day."

"Ludicrous?" she snapped. " 'Twas your idea in
the first place. You said I needed a husband." She
was angry with him. Angry because he wanted her to
wed to protect herself and the castle. Angry because
he wasn't a Highland lord on a white steed. "This
whole bloody idea was yours, Robert Drum!"

"Now, now." He covered his head with his arms

as if to protect himself from a blow. "I'm sorry. You're right." He lowered his hands. "I'm sorry, Mary Kate. Tell me about the riddles."

"Move." She tapped his boot with a gloved hand. He took a step back and she scooted along the herb bed, pulling weeds furiously. "I'm going to give them riddles to solve. For each riddle, the first to solve it is the winner. The man who solves the most will be my husband."

"Mary Kate." He rubbed his temples with his thumb and forefinger. "You can't give a man riddles and tell him that if he solves them he can marry you."

"Why not?" She gently pushed aside her newly transplanted foxglove and pulled a weed hiding beneath the leaves.

"Because . . . because," he stammered. "It's absurd! That's why."

"No more absurd than my vetting men for the position without them knowing it."

He hooked his thumbs in the waistband of his woolen breeches and chuckled wryly. "I fear they know it now, don't they?"

That was one of the things she had always loved about him. He could always make the best of a bad situation. He could always make her see the humor. Would Charles or Ian ever affect her that way? Somehow she doubted it.

"Aye, and everyone in the Borderlands, thanks to dear Auntie Agnes."

"Actually I'm surprised she told."

"Why?" Mary Kate asked. "She's always been a gossip. She has little else to do with her time."

"I know, but I would have thought she'd have

wanted to keep the playing field narrow. To give her son a better chance."

Mary Kate groaned.

"You did tell his mother ye'd give him a fair chance. And he did kill the boar and present you with the head at the banquet," he reminded her.

Her groan turned into a giggle. "Then he proceeded to get himself drunker than Davy's sow. Poor sot, he's still abed."

Rob laughed with her, and she laughed perhaps a little harder than she felt like because she didn't know what else to do or say. But what could be said? She was certain that he no more wanted to see her marry someone else than she did. No words were necessary. They understood each other perfectly at this moment.

"Well, perhaps you ought tell Aunt Agnes her son is still in the running. Give him the riddles as you do the others. We both know he'll not be able to solve them."

She nodded. "Aye, good thinking. You're always so diplomatic, Rob. For an Englishman," she teased.

He smiled at her jest. "Ah, Mary Kate," Rob said quietly, staring down at her as her laughter subsided. "I didn't mean to criticize your idea. It's a fine one actually, befitting of you. If riddles are what you want, have your riddles. I want only to see you happy."

She took a deep breath, feeling the moment of intimacy pass. It really was better this way. "I suppose we ought to tell them—Ian and Charles."

"I understand why Ian. He's handsome, gallant, and nearly as wealthy as you are, but why Charles? What of his glued pate?"

"I don't mind the baldness, but that whip of hair would have to go." She lifted one shoulder in a shrug.

"Lack of hair aside, he's attractive enough. Friendly. He'd make a solid husband."

"He'd let you boss him around."

She eyed him. "And your point is?"

He picked at his sleeve. "Your husband should be strong of character. Strong enough to stand up to you." His gaze met hers. "And I can attest to the battles that will be waged."

This time she didn't allow herself a smile. There was that intimacy between them again. She wouldn't be able to feel like this with Rob once she married. It would be wrong. Practically adultery. Adultery of the heart.

She returned her attention to her weeding. "You'll speak with them?"

"Aye. If you want, I can. I've business with Charles today anyway. I can ride over to Waverly when I'm done there." He kicked at a weed she had pulled from the bed. "What should I say?"

"I don't know. You'll think of something."

"As you wish, mistress."

Mary Kate sat back on her heels as Rob walked away. *Mistress.* He had never used that term before. It had always been *Mary Kate.* Now it was *mistress.* The chasm between them was widening. She could feel it. She could hear it in his voice. Soon he would be the servant and she the married mistress of the castle. It was inevitable. Wasn't it?

"Mary Catherine! Mary Catherine!" Agnes called as she sprinted across the wet grass. Her aunt was looking mighty lively these days for a woman of fifty.

"Here, Auntie. In the garden."

Agnes rushed up behind her and Mary Kate felt obliged to rise and greet her aunt. She dusted the dirt off her cotton garden gloves. "Good morning, Auntie."

"Good morning, dear. Goodness, you're about early this morning, and looking so fresh."

"How's Magnus this morning?"

Aunt Agnes fluttered her thin hands. "Oh, my, oh, my. I don't know what got into him last night. He intends to come down and apologize himself . . . as soon as he rises."

Mary Kate lowered herself to the ground again. She had too many things to do this morning to spend time chatting. If Aunt Agnes wanted to talk, Mary Kate could well talk while she weeded. "Mayhap Cook has a tincture to settle his stomach."

"Oh, my, aye, yes, I should ask."

Her aunt fell silent as Mary Kate pulled several weeds and glanced up again. "Was there something else, Auntie? Have you need of more thread or cloth? I had Maisie take it to your chambers this morning."

"Oh, no." She fluttered her hands. "The cloth is fine, dear. I just . . ." She took a quavering breath. "I wanted to speak with you . . . on behalf of my son."

Oh, no, Mary Kate thought. *Here it comes.* "Aye? What of Magnus?"

"The riddles." Agnes clasped her hands with resignation. "Magnus killed the boar and I think he should have a right to attempt the riddles. Even with his besotted behavior last night, I think he deserves a chance."

Mary Kate tossed a weed. What could she say? Magnus barely had enough sense to get in from the rain. He wouldn't be able to solve any riddles. It was foolish to pretend he would. But she felt trapped, and again, she didn't want to hurt her aunt's feelings. Rob was right; she should just allow Magnus to continue in the competition and disqualify himself. "If . . . if you wish, Auntie," she heard herself respond.

"Oh, my! Thank you. Thank you. You're such a sweet dear."

Mary Kate watched her aunt retreat across the damp morning grass. *God help me!* she thought wryly. *I'd best make those riddles difficult or I'm liable to end up the wife of Magnus MacDonal yet.*

She chuckled at the thought.

And then I should have to get myself to a nunnery.

"Riddles?" Ian Ferguson stood in the hall of his father's castle staring at Rob in disbelief.

"Aye," Rob answered.

Charles Moffatt had made the same response. He had declared the idea ridiculous. But when he learned that this was the only way Mary Kate MacDonal would consider him as a prospective husband, he was quick to agree to the terms of the challenge.

"That's preposterous." He paced before the great stone fireplace. "I find it difficult to believe that Sean MacDonal would condone such an idea."

"He doesn't know about it, and should anyone speak of the matter with him, my mistress says he would immediately be disqualified." Rob took a wide stance, patiently tucking his hands behind his back. This was so damned hard to do.

But even as he stood there, passing Mary Kate's message to one of her prospects, his mind lingered on the well. Was it really magic? If it was, how could he get Mary Kate to make a wish? He knew her well enough to know she was too practical to even consider such a possibility. And what would he have her wish for? If they made up their minds to run away and marry, where would that leave Mary Kate and her beloved Cnocanduin? A union wasn't good enough.

Rob's wish would be that he had never been born an Englishman. Never been born a nobody. His wish would be that he was actually a Highland lord. That was what he would have Mary Kate wish, if she was willing.

Rob nearly laughed out loud at the absurdity of the idea. He couldn't believe he was even considering the possibility that the well could grant him—them— such a wish.

Ian was speaking, and Rob knew he had to concentrate on the task at hand. The magic well was too far-fetched an idea. Maybe he could get Mary Kate to the well and convince her to make a wish, but in the meantime, he had to follow through with his promise to find her a husband. Even if it killed him.

"The union of our lands would be greatly profitable to Cnocanduin." Ian postured, throwing back his shoulders and thrusting out his chest. "My reputation is without tarnish. I am respected by my men for being honest and fair." His gaze met Rob's. "I must speak frankly in saying that surely Mary Kate realizes I would make an excellent husband for her. An excellent father to her sons, if I should be so bold as to say so."

Rob stiffened at the mention of children. He did not want Ian to be so bold. Rob knew the marriage would be consummated. Of course, God willing, Mary Kate and her husband would have children. But at Ian's mention of such intimacies, Rob's hackles went up. She belonged in his arms and his alone.

"If she didn't believe you an excellent prospect," Rob said shortly, "you would not be in the running now, sir."

"I must confess that I have always dreamed of living in the great Cnocanduin," Ian said, stroking his strong chin. "Since I was a boy. And Mary Kate . . . with that fiery hair. She's lovely. Our temperaments would suit." He glanced up. "Who else is in contention?"

"Charles Moffatt."

"Charles Moffatt!" Ian scoffed. "He's not man enough to be lord over Cnocanduin or Mary Kate MacDonal! Who else?"

"She hasn't said for certain, but I would guess her cousin. If her aunt has her way, at least."

Ian burst into hearty laughter. "I must confess I don't know Mary Kate well, but well enough to know that she'd not wed that swine."

Rob waggled a finger. Of course she would never consent to marry her cousin. But if Ian truly wanted Mary Kate, Rob wanted him to fight for her. That way, if he won, she would be all the more precious to him. "But he is her cousin," Rob reminded. "The MacDonals always marry cousins. And he already knows the workings of Cnocanduin."

Ian strode back and forth, deep in thought. On his third turn, he glanced at Rob, man to man this time. "Tell me the truth. Have I a chance?" he asked quietly.

It was Rob's opinion that Ian would be Mary Kate's best choice for a husband. With Ian Ferguson, she would have the best likelihood of finding some happiness, or at least contentment. "You have an equal chance as the other two."

"I would make her a good husband," he said. "I would love her."

Ian's sincerity cut Rob to the quick. *Press on,* Rob thought. *Press on. Duty.* "So may I tell the mistress that you are in agreement to her terms?"

"I'm not much with games of the mind, but aye, I'm in."

Rob turned to go. "Come to Cnocanduin tomorrow night. After the laird has gone to bed, the riddles will be presented."

Chapter Six

"Mary Kate," Rob said hesitantly as they sat before a blazing fire in the great hall. The laird was abed and they were awaiting the arrival of Charles Moffatt and Ian Ferguson. Tonight Mary Kate would provide the men with her riddles.

"Aye?" She turned to him. She wore her hair down this evening in waves of rich auburn that framed her lovely face.

She was so beautiful in the firelight that it hurt Rob to look at her. "If I asked you to do something that made no sense to you," he said hesitantly, "would you do it?"

She turned in her father's chair until her knees almost touched his.

She seemed calm tonight. Resigned to her fate. Too resigned to suit Rob. He had to try to win her.

He knew the only possibility was impossibility, but he would never forgive himself if he didn't at least try.

"Aye, I suppose I would do something that made no sense. I jumped off that barn roof, didn't I?" She smoothed her blue-and-green plaid woolen arisaid. "I would do it if it wouldn't harm anyone." Her brow furrowed. "Whatever are you talking about?"

She looked tired, and he wondered if she was lying awake at night as he was. "I would never ask you to harm another or yourself. You know that."

Her gaze narrowed. "Out with it, Rob." She gestured. "What is it you want me to do?"

He heard the hounds barking in the front hall and he stood. One of Sean's clansmen had allowed a visitor to pass through the yett. It was Ian or Charles or both.

Rob had to ask her before he lost his nerve. "Would you meet me at the well tonight? After the men have gone?"

Again her brow furrowed, this time suspiciously. "What for?"

"It's not what you might think," he said quickly, before she had a chance to speak the obvious concern and think him a rogue. He looked away and then back at her, knowing his cheeks colored. "It's not that I wouldn't want another kiss . . . that I'm not dying for one—"

She made a sound in her throat, and he had to glance away. She wanted his mouth on hers as badly as he did.

"I want you to—" He cut himself off. "It will sound too ridiculous here. Will you just come? Come and trust me?"

She never hesitated. "All right. I trust you. I'll come."

Her words left him nearly giddy. She trusted him. She would make the wish for him. He knew she would. And maybe, just maybe—

Sean's pack of hunting hounds came bursting into the great hall, barking in announcement of the callers.

Mary Kate rose as both Ian and Charles appeared in the arch of the doorway.

"Here we go," she whispered.

Mary Kate smiled and extended her arms in welcome. "Charles, Ian, how good of you to come so late." She slipped into the role of hostess and mistress of Cnocanduin. If she concentrated on that role and not why the men were here, it would be easier.

She tried to push aside thoughts of Rob and why he wanted her to meet him at the well. He said he had a ridiculous request. He couldn't be planning to kidnap her, could he? The question, of course, was that if he did, how hard would she fight him?

But kidnapping didn't seem likely; he said his request wouldn't harm anyone. But she couldn't imagine what he wanted. She would have to give these men their riddles and get them out of the castle if she were to find out.

"I won't pretend the circumstances are not unusual," Ian said, taking her hand and kissing her palm. "But thank you for the kind welcome. I've always felt welcome within the walls of Cnocanduin."

A kiss, Mary Kate thought. *Very bold of him . . . and very dashing.*

"Good evening," Charles said. "I brought you

some flowers. I picked them in my courtyard." He offered her a bundle of the last of the season's blooms.

Some were more weeds than flowers, but that made them all the more endearing. And to her surprise, he had cut the offending locks of hair he had used to conceal his baldness. His bare pate could no longer go unnoticed, but was far more attractive than his previous hairstyle.

Mary Kate wondered if Rob had said something to him about his hair. But why would he? He had already said he thought Ian would make a better husband. Her only conclusion could be that he had mentioned Charles's hair out of a sense of fairness. After all, it was unfair that she judge a man solely on hair. Rob had always been a fair man.

"Thank you, Charles," Mary Kate said, accepting the bouquet. "That's very sweet of you."

Rob took the flowers from her and went to bring wine to the table.

"Well, come, gentlemen. I'll nae waste your time." Mary Kate indicated the end of the scarred oak dining table where Rob was setting out goblets. "Please, sit."

"Am I late?" Magnus walked into the hall, hastily tucking his white shirt into his woolen breeches. "Mother said I would be late."

"Ian and Charles have just arrived," Mary Kate said. "Join us."

He sat beside Charles. "I hate riddles; you know that, Mary Kate. I told Mother I hate riddles."

Mary Kate ignored Magnus's whining. "I understand Rob Drum has already gone over the rules with you." She took her father's chair and the men sat. "I have two riddles. Should it be necessary, as in the case of a tie, I'll provide another." She passed out three sheets of paper. On each sheet she had carefully written out the same riddles.

"I hate riddles," Magnus muttered. "Riddles are stupid."

"Now remember," Mary Kate proceeded. "There is to be only one winner for each riddle. The man who brings me the correct object first, scores. There are no points for second, even if the guess is correct."

"These are objects?" Charles asked, scanning the sheet by the flickering light of the candles on the table.

"Aye. All objects. Common objects."

Rob moved quietly around the table, pouring wine, acting so much like a servant that she wished he weren't here. She didn't want the other men to see him like this, her lackey.

"Of course it goes without saying: no one may give you aid in solving the riddles." She took a deep breath. She couldn't believe she was actually going through with this. "Any questions?"

Charles folded the sheet of riddles carefully. "Has . . . have you an idea when you wish to wed?"

"As soon as possible. But the details will be discussed later with my father, once we announce the betrothal." She turned to the handsome man on her left. "Questions, Ian?"

"Nae." He smiled at her as if he already knew he would solve the riddles . . . and win her.

Did he already have an answer?

She didn't know how she felt about that. On one hand she wanted to get this over with as soon as possible. On the other, she didn't want any of them to be able to solve the riddles. Then she could declare them all unfit and give up on this whole ludicrous scheme.

"Mary Kate," Magnus said, glancing up from the page of riddles. "Will there be just one wedding feast or a series of days of feasting?"

Charles covered his hand with his mouth to keep from laughing aloud. Ian coughed to cover a snigger.

Mary Kate smiled. The riddles had been an excellent idea. Magnus was too dull-witted to solve even one. "We can discuss that later," she said gently, almost feeling sorry for him, or at least for her aunt. Magnus was no match for these men.

Her gaze swept over the three men. "Very well, then if you have no further questions . . ." She rose and lifted her goblet.

The men rose.

"May the best man . . ." She hesitated. "Win," she finished.

An hour later Mary Kate crept down the steps to the old bailey, carrying a candle to light her way. It was always dark down here, even at midday, but for some reason it seemed darker tonight.

She could see no candlelight flickering from below. Rob must not have arrived yet.

She reached the bottom step and halted. Tonight the room was damper, cooler than usual. The shadows cast from her candle danced eerily on the plastered walls. Tonight the old bailey seemed removed from the castle built above and around it. It seemed to be a place apart from time and the realities of the world.

Mary Kate heard a sound and she instantly lifted her candlestick high in the air. "Rob?"

"Here," he answered.

She exhaled. "Why are ye sitting in the dark?" She walked toward the well, where he sat perched on its low wall. "You nearly gave me a fright."

He chuckled. "You're not afraid of the darkness or of anything in this castle. She's yours, Mary Kate MacDonal. She's you," he said thoughtfully.

Mary Kate set the candlestick on the wall and tightened the woolen wrap she wore around her shoulders. She was chilled. "Aren't you the pensive one tonight?" She stood near him, yet not too near. She didn't want to get into a situation where an opportunity might lend itself to another kiss. Not tonight. Not the way she was feeling. Tonight she feared she might not be able to stop at just kissing.

"Tell me what you want me to do," she said quietly. "It's late. I'm tired. We both ought to be in bed."

He ran his hand over the plastered wall of the well he perched on. "Do you remember when we were children what Cook told us about this well?"

She shrugged. "Vaguely. Something of magic. More of Cook's gypsy nonsense."

"Do you remember what she said about your mother?"

Suddenly Mary Kate felt odd. Her skin prickled. She became more aware of the feel of Cnocanduin wool against her skin. She could smell the cold stone of the walls around her and the freshness of the spring-fed water below. "What about my mother?"

Rob rose. "Mary Kate, Cook said your mother believed in the magic of the well. She believed wishes could be made—granted."

"It was just a tale Cook told to amuse two children," she defended quickly. Her response was perfectly

rational, but somehow it came out sounding irratio-
nal. "Papa never said anything about the well."

"Magic is usually left to women—just as Cnocan-
duin is left to her women." Rob studied her carefully.
"Perhaps he didn't know. Maybe she never told him.
Ever think of that?"

Mary Kate felt uneasy. What was she doing down
here in the middle of the night alone with Rob? It
wasn't seemly. Not with her about to announce her
betrothal—to someone.

She knew she should turn around and go back up
the steps. Back to the safety of her chambers, where
Rob's presence wouldn't raise questions, comments
. . . desires. There was no reason for her to be here.
She didn't believe in magic, or wishes.

She didn't believe because she couldn't afford to.

"Mary Kate, will you do something for me?"

She took a step back, knowing what he was going
to say before he said it. "This is silly," she argued,
wondering what she was afraid of. "Ridiculous, Rob."

"Would you make a wish?" he pleaded gently.

"Make a wish? Why? This well can't give us what
we want, Rob." Her voice broke. "We have to accept
our fate. Our duty to those we love."

He reached out to take her hand, and she let him.
"What harm can it do?" he whispered. "What is there
to lose by a moment of whimsy?"

His warm hand felt so good around hers.

"Please, Mary Kate, for me?"

Her gaze met his. Shadows played across his angular
face, and she wished she'd never been born the
daughter of Sean and Mary MacDonal. She wished
she had been born poor, without lands or money.

She wished she had been born an English nobody, free to do what she pleased.

He sensed her hesitation. "It can do no harm."

She shook her head, tears welling in her eyes. "It's not going to come true. Making such wishes. Hoping. It will just break our hearts."

His face was so close to hers that she could feel his breath on her lips. She could almost taste him.

"Already broken," he whispered.

Her resolve wavered. "Rob, it will only make you feel worse."

"It will make me feel better," he countered. "Give me hope. We all need hope, Mary Kate."

She glanced over his shoulder at the well. "This is foolishness." But even as she spoke, she moved toward the well, her hand still in his.

"So it will be one last foolish act between friends. Like the barn roof."

He was too convincing. Mary Kate knew this was preposterous. She'd be embarrassed ever to tell anyone she'd done such a thing as make a wish to a well. But how could she tell Rob no? How could she not do this one thing for him?

"I'll do it," she said, fighting the sudden hope rising in her heart. "Just tell me what to do and let's get it over with."

He squeezed her hand and let go, walking to the well. "You just have to drink. Make the wish and drink." He leaned over the wall and pulled on a string.

She heard water splash and watched him pull up an old bucket from the depths of the ancient cavern. She had not been entirely honest when she had said she didn't really recall what Cook had said about the well. She remembered that she said the castle had been built around the well and the rowan tree. That the very place where Cnocanduin stood had been considered blessed.

"Wish what?" she asked. She just wanted to get this over now. Do what he wanted her to, say what he wanted, and then run and hide beneath her bed linens. "What do you want me to wish?"

"What do you want?"

"What do I want?"

"What you want, Mary Kate. What you truly want."

She knew what he meant. It was hard now to say the words right to his face. "I want you," she said softly.

"Just me? If you wanted just me we could have run off and married, gone against your father's wishes and said to hell with Cnocanduin."

He had a point. Bless him, he knew her so well, understood her so well. "I want you to be my husband, but I want it to be right." She spread her hands. "That's what's so ridiculous about all this. I want you and Cnocanduin."

"So wish for it."

"Just like that? But how? We can't change who you are or what's expected of me."

"It's magic," he said, holding the bucket in both hands. Water sloshed over the side and down his hands. "You don't have to know how it should come about. Just ask. Make your wish." His voice was filled with excitement, with hope.

She studied his face for a moment. "All right," she murmured. "Then I'll wish for you. To have you and Cnocanduin. To make it right."

"That's my lass."

Mary Kate closed her eyes and cleared her mind of all the turmoil of the last weeks. She pushed aside her fears, her sadness, her intense desire to comply with her duty. She consciously relaxed every muscle in her body, and slowly felt her mind clear.

I wish . . . I wish . . .

Her lips moved, but she did not speak aloud. And when she was finished, she cupped the fresh well water in her hands and drank.

The water was icy cold and sharp on her tongue. Clean, fresh. It was the best water she had ever drunk in her life. She swallowed and opened her eyes.

"There," she said, wiping her mouth with the back of her hand. "I made the wish."

"Now you have to believe." He set the bucket on the wall. "Do you believe in the magic of the well, Mary Kate? In the magic of Cnocanduin?"

She reached out and brushed her hand beneath his beard-stubbled chin. She wanted to believe. Sweet Father, she did. But how could she? Did she dare?

She looked at him through the veil of her lashes, feeling his sense of hope and excitement wash over her. "I think I believe," she answered honestly. "Will that be enough?"

He kissed her gently on the cheek. A kiss not of lovers, but of love. Of optimism. "It will have to be, won't it?"

"We should step outside the castle walls and settle this here and now," Ian declared hotly.

"Where is your sense of integrity?" Charles raised his voice. "You heard her yourself, Ian Ferguson.

Mary Kate MacDonal will have no dishonesty. She won't marry a dishonest man."

"Gentlemen! Gentlemen!" Mary Kate threw up both her hands, slipping between the two men before fists flew. "Calm down."

"I arrived first. I passed over the bridge first, and I have brought the answers to the riddles," Charles declared triumphantly.

"He cut me off on the path to the gate," Ian countered. "And I have the answer to two of the riddles, as well!" He pointed an accusing finger. "He should be disqualified for cutting me off."

"Disqualified?" Charles thrust his face in Ian's. "If anyone's to be disqualified—"

"Charles! Ian! I will not have this in my home. Enough! Enough or you will both be disqualified for disturbing the peace!"

Ian backed down.

Charles turned away to collect himself.

Mary Kate took a deep breath. She stood in the courtyard between the two men, her hands on her hips. She had known this was a poor idea. What had possessed her to challenge the men with riddles?

The men's loud voices had attracted the attention of one of her father's clansmen, guarding the front yett. He watched from his post with obvious amusement. A housemaid beating rush mats in the courtyard tried hard to pretend she was busy at work, all the while listening intently. And Mary Kate could have sworn she saw her aunt's head poke out a window overlooking the courtyard, then duck back in before Mary Kate caught her.

Mary Kate eyed Ian and Charles. "This was not how I had envisioned this competition, gentlemen."

"What now?" Charles questioned. "How do we settle this matter?"

Mary Kate's first impulse was to send both men packing. They were behaving in a petty way. But whose fault was that? This had all been her idea in the first place.

"Charles, you have the answer to both riddles?"

"Aye," he declared, smirking. "Here in my pack." He patted a leather bag he wore on his shoulder.

"And you say you reached Cnocanduin first?"

"Cnocanduin proper," he amended.

"Now wait a minute," Ian interrupted.

Mary Kate placed a hand on Ian's broad chest to keep him back. "And you have the answer to both riddles as well, Ian?"

"Aye."

"Well then, why don't we see what you both have. If both are wrong, this is all a moot point, isn't it?"

"And if we're right?" Charles asked. "He says he has the two answers, but I was here first. Only one winner, you said."

Charles was beginning to sound like Magnus to Mary Kate.

"I said let me see what you have," she said, her patience waning. "And then I will see what's to be done next."

Both men slung the bags from their shoulders and dug into them.

" 'The beginning of eternity, the end of time and space,' " Charles recited from memory. " 'The beginning of every end, and the end of every place.' "

"An 'E,' " Ian declared, pulling a sheet of parchment from his bag. On the sheet he had written the letter *E* in a strong, masculine scrawl.

"An 'E.' " Charles snapped. He had drawn an *E* and then cut it out.

" 'Runs over fields and wood all day,' " Ian began to recite. " 'Under the bed at night. Sits not alone. With a long tongue hanging out, awaiting a bone.' " He snatched a leather boot from his bag. "A shoe."

Charles pulled a lady's slipper from his bag. "A shoe. It should really be a shoe," he argued. "That's a boot."

Mary Kate just wanted to walk away. She held up both her hands again.

Her suitors must have realized she had reached her limit of patience because they both fell silent.

"One last riddle," she said quietly, "will decide." As she spoke, she prayed that her wish would come true now, at this moment, or at least soon, so that no riddle had to decide anything.

"What if Magnus brings the object first?" Charles grumbled. "It will be a tie again then."

"I think Magnus has declared himself out of the competition. I've not seen him since last night. Now, gentlemen, I have work to do. Here is the last riddle." She didn't give them a chance to respond because she wanted to rid herself of both of them.

" 'I look at you, you look at me,' " she said, recalling an old riddle her father had told her as a child. " 'I raise my right, you raise your left. What am I?' "

She picked up a crate of dried beef she had been carrying from the smokehouse. "Good day, gentlemen, and good luck."

Though with any luck at all, she thought as she walked away, *this will all be a moot point.*

Please let the wish come true, she begged silently. *I believe. I believe.*

From behind a stone wall, Magnus watched Ian and Charles stand for a moment staring at each other like two bantering cocks, then head out of the courtyard. As luck would have it, Charles bolted first. No doubt he was in a hurry to get home and contemplate the last riddle.

Magnus debated for only a moment before making his move. Mary Kate knew him too well. He wasn't smart enough to figure out the riddles she had given them last night. He wasn't going to win the contest. But that was all right. He didn't want to marry his cousin anyway. He loved Maisie. It had all been his mother's idea that he and Mary Kate wed. It always had been.

But that didn't mean that Magnus didn't care what happened to Mary Kate. He loved his cousin, even if they didn't get along. Even if he didn't know how to show it. Ian Ferguson would make a good husband to Mary Kate and a good laird to the castle. He was strong-willed like she was. He was fair, too. He wouldn't put Magnus out, or his mother.

Magnus whispered Ian's name, and when Ian turned to see where the voice came from, Magnus signaled his neighbor to join him behind the wall.

Magnus wasn't smart enough to solve riddles on his own, but he had a good memory. And the last riddle Mary Kate had repeated was one her father had recited to them as children.

Chapter Seven

"Mary Kate, what do you want me to do about Ian Ferguson?" Rob said quietly.

Mary Kate sat before the blazing fire in her private sitting room in an effort to escape her duties as mistress of the castle. Mainly she'd come here to hide from Ian or Charles, and the fate that she feared awaited her.

But destiny was hurling her forward whether she hid or not. Ian was downstairs waiting for her. He told Rob that he had the solution to the last riddle. He wanted to see her now; he wanted to make the betrothal tonight.

"It's late," she argued, drawing her feet up beneath her in the chair. "Tell him to come back tomorrow." She was on the verge of tears.

She was stalling, of course. She didn't want to see Ian because she didn't want to have to agree to marry him as she promised. She wanted to wait here in the quiet of her chambers and wait for the wish to come true. She wavered. If it was going to come true . . .

"That's not fair, Mary Kate. Ye've had those two men race all over the countryside for you. You said you would see them day or night, should they solve one of your riddles."

She didn't glance at Rob for fear of crying. He was damned calm. Didn't he care that if Ian held the solution to the riddle, she was going to have to marry him? Didn't he care about her anymore? About them? "You're certainly accepting this rather easily," she snapped.

"Mary Kate," he said quietly, "it's going to be all right."

She watched the flames leap and lick the firewood she'd just tossed onto the hearth. "How can it be?" she whispered. "I didn't get my—" Her voice caught in her throat. She felt as if she were shriveling up and dying. She wanted to die. ". . . wish," she managed.

Rob covered her hand on her lap with his. "You don't know that you didn't get your wish, not yet," he said as if telling a secret, a hesitant thrill in his voice. "I think it's going to happen. I think our wish is going to come true. We just have to give it time."

She gazed up at him, his smile seeming to convey confidence from him to her. Rob honestly still believed that her wish, *their* wish, was really going to come true. So why shouldn't she?

She gave a little laugh. "This is making me crazy. Waiting. Hoping, praying things will change."

"I know. It will come true. But in the meantime, you should let me send Ian up." Rob squeezed her hand reassuringly.

"Why?" She frowned. "If you believe in the well, why shouldn't you want me to delay seeing Ian? Give the wish time to come true?"

He squatted in front of her chair, still holding her hand. "Because it's only right that you go on as intended. What if you altered the wish by not following through with your intentions to marry Ian?"

The way he explained himself made perfect sense. And that made Mary Kate all the crazier. She glanced over his head at the fireplace, feeling herself tremble inside. She concentrated on the flames of the fire and took a deep breath. "You're certain this is the right thing to do?"

"Aye."

She returned her gaze to his calm face. "And you're certain it's going to happen? The wish is going to come true? I'm not going to be stuck with a man I can never love?"

"It's going to happen," he said passionately. "I can feel it in my bones."

It was on the tip of her tongue to ask what would happen if the wish didn't come true, but as she gazed into his eyes, she felt his sense of hope washing over her. She smiled. There was no need to ask "what if" because she believed. She believed because he believed. Because she had to.

Then she thought about Ian and the unfairness of using him this way. "But what about Ian?" she asked. "Is this fair to him, making him think I intend to wed him when I don't?"

Rob shrugged, still clasping her hand. "Who's to say that we should alter his fate? Who knows what could happen to him because you break the engagement at the last moment? Something wonderful, perhaps."

She hesitated for only a moment. "All right," she said confidently. She could feel her spirits lifting, even as the words came out of her mouth. "Send him up. I made the wish, and the wish is going to come true. We just have to play along in the meanwhile."

He squeezed her hand once more and released it. "I'll escort Ian up and give the two of you a minute alone." He winked from the door. "Just not too much time."

She turned in her chair so that she could watch Rob go. "I want you to know I love you. I'll always—"

"Shhhh." He lifted his finger to his lips. "Don't say it now. Later. When there's more time."

The door closed quietly behind him, and she turned back to the warmth of the flames. As she watched the red and yellow flames dance on the hearth, a giggle bubbled up from deep inside her. "It truly is going to come true," she whispered. "I'm going to marry Rob."

The following days and weeks flew by at a speed that made Mary Kate dizzy when she thought about it. The day after Ian Ferguson solved her last riddle and brought her a silver mirror, he asked Sean MacDonal for her hand in marriage. At first Sean protested, but it was easy for Mary Kate to convince him she truly wanted to marry Ian. She even hinted that she loved him.

Mary Kate knew it was deceitful to tell her father such tales. She knew she was probably going straight to hell for lying to him, but she felt as if she had no choice. As the days passed she became so certain that the wish was going to come true that she was convinced that this was all part of the fate of Cnocanduin.

Ian was anxious to wed, so Mary Kate made a leap of faith and allowed him to set the date for Christmas Eve. Ordinarily a betrothal period would have been longer, but with Mary Kate so old and her father in poor health, family and neighbors were thrilled to see her finally marrying. If anyone had anything unkind to say, it was behind closed doors. Even her aunt Agnes, after recovering from the idea that Mary Kate would not wed her Magnus, became enthusiastic about the wedding. It had been a long time since there had been a wedding at Cnocanduin—not since Sean and Mary's marriage.

Between wedding plans, plans for Ian to move to Cnocanduin, and the busy day-to-day running of the castle as winter approached, Mary Kate barely had time to think about the turn of events. And it was just as well. As long as she didn't contemplate too much, she didn't have time to dwell on what would happen if the well wasn't magic.

She was thankful, Rob was busy too. In the following weeks, they saw little of each other, and when they did, they kept their conversations focused on Cnocanduin and their duties. They kept their exchanges friendly but removed, and neither spoke of the wish. They didn't dare, almost as if for fear that it wouldn't come true if they dwelled on it.

A week before the wedding, Mary Kate stood in the middle of the bedchamber her father and mother had once shared. Sean had long ago moved to a smaller chamber and insisted Ian and Mary Kate should have it now. Although it was difficult for her to imagine sleeping in her parents' bed, she knew it made sense, and accepted her father's advice. She kept telling herself that she and Rob would share this bed; it was what kept her from going mad as the rest of the household prepared for her wedding to Ian.

Because it had been a long time since the chambers had been occupied, there was a great deal of work to be done before the wedding. While the walls were being repainted, the furniture polished, and the floor resanded, Mary Kate directed the hanging of new bed curtains and window draperies. They were a gift from her father, but Rob had brought them back on his last trip to Edinburgh. He had chosen the bed curtains that would keep them warm beneath the covers on blustery nights.

"Here, mistress?" Maisie asked. The maid perched on a stool, both arms high in the air as she stretched a panel over one of the bedchamber windows. As she stood, arms outstretched, her progressing pregnancy was evident.

The unwed Maisie had not yet confessed who the father was, but Mary Kate, along with everyone else at Cnocanduin, had a good idea. Mary Kate knew that as mistress of the castle she would eventually have to deal with the matter. A man had to own up to his responsibilities, but she was still hoping that Magnus would be a man and speak up on his own.

"Aye, Maisie. Those drapes go on that window. The larger sets on the larger windows."

The maid struggled to hold up the heavy fabric while she fumbled with the rod that swung out on a hinge. She took one step and nearly tumbled off the stool.

"Whoa, easy there, Maisie." Mary Kate caught her hand and steadied her. "You'll fall and break your neck. Here, let me hold up the fabric whilst you slip it over the rod."

"Thank you, mistress," Maisie said with relief, dropping the bundle into Mary Kate's arms.

As Mary Kate held the fabric in her arms, she stared out the window. From the fifth floor she could see a wide panorama of the breathtaking lands that surrounded Cnocanduin. *Her* lands.

Movement far below and to the south caught Mary Kate's eye. It was a group of riders on horseback. *How odd*, she thought. It was early morning, too early for visitors, and Rob had taken a good number of her father's men east to Ian's property to move some cattle.

The approaching men made Mary Kate uneasy. "Maisie, do you see those riders?"

The girl glanced out the open window. "Nae, I don't see no riders."

"There, south." Mary Kate pointed. "Beyond the copse of trees."

Maisie squinted, climbing down off the stool. "My eyes ain't never been much, mistress." She stared harder. "Aye. I think I see them."

"Take these." Mary Kate thrust the draperies into the maid's arms and spun on her heels.

She swept into the sitting room beyond the bedchamber. "Aunt Agnes, where's Papa?"

Her aunt was busy polishing the mantel over the fireplace. "In the courtyard getting some sun, I believe."

"What about Magnus?"

"About somewhere." She turned. "What's wrong, dear?"

"Auntie, will you please fetch Papa and take him into the great hall? Then have the servants close and secure all the doors and windows on the bottom two floors."

Mary Kate hurried out of the room. She didn't want to frighten anyone, but there should not be any riders approaching the castle at the speed those men were moving.

"Mary Kate, is something wrong?" Agnes called, trailing behind her.

Mary Kate took the winding stone steps two at a time. She wasn't afraid; she had too much to do to waste time being afraid. This was her land, her property, and she would defend it should the need arise. "I hope not," she said as much to comfort herself as her aunt. "I certainly hope not."

Downstairs, Mary Kate raced into the great hall. Not a single man was to be seen. She grabbed two old blunderbusses from a rack on one wall and snatched up a bag of shot and powder left for emergencies such as these. If the men approaching were cattle thieves, she had to be concerned not only with the cattle in the pasture, but her barns as well. In the last four months two barns on neighboring lands had been burned by the thieves as diversions. While property owners rushed to save their barns, the thieves rounded up cattle and drove them south.

Her barns were filled to the seams with the hay and grain it would take to feed the cattle through the long winter. If she lost the fodder now, the results would be devastating. By Christmas, feed would be an outrageous price, if it could be found at all. It could take Cnocanduin years to recover from such a loss.

"Magnus?" Mary Kate shouted as she hurried out of the great hall and into the front entranceway. "Magnus, are you here?" Her voice echoed vacantly off the plastered ceiling overhead as if proof that she was all alone.

Outside she met with the yett's guard. It was Angus, a man nearly her father's age who moved as slowly. "Angus, fasten the gates. Send a boy out to draw up the bridge at my word."

"What be it, mistress?" The old Scotsman laid his hand on his dirk.

"I'm not sure; perhaps nothing." She swept past him, the heavy guns cradled in her arms. "But secure the castle just the same. Have you seen Magnus?"

"Headed for the horse barns, mistress. Is there trouble?"

"Riders approaching from the south. Fast," she added, growing more anxious by the moment. They had known for months that thieves were out and about. Why wasn't the castle more prepared? Where were the watches they had discussed? Magnus had said he had taken care of the matter. If she hadn't been so damned concerned about her wedding to Ian, and mooning over Rob, she would have checked up on him.

"I want all women and children inside," Mary Kate ordered, her thoughts going in a thousand different directions at once. "Any men you can locate should take up arms. I'm going to the barn."

"Mistress, wait," Angus hollered after her. "If it's

thieves, ye belong inside Cnocanduin's walls." He thrust out his sunken, aged chest. "I can protect ye inside."

"Rob took a dozen men with him," she called over her shoulder. "If I don't protect the barns, who will?"

"Mistress—"

"Your post, Angus," she ordered.

Just over the bridge, Mary Kate spotted her cousin. "Magnus! Thank God," she shouted. "Take a weapon. I think the cattle reivers are approaching."

Magnus turned to face her, his squat face going pasty white. "What? What's that you say? Reivers, here?"

"Magnus, I don't have time for this. They're going to be here any second." Her voice rose in pitch. "Could be cattle reivers. It's uninvited guests, I'm sure of that. Now take this and come with me." She shook one of the blunderbusses. "If we can get into the hayloft and shoot down on them, we might be able to discourage an attack."

He was trembling from head to foot. "Perhaps I should run to Ferguson's for help."

"There isn't time." She attempted to shove the weapon into his trembling hands. "Come on, Magnus. We haven't time to dally."

But still he didn't take the blunderbuss. He seemed frozen with fright.

"Magnus!"

"Magnus," came a woman's voice from behind. It was Maisie. She stood on the castle side of the drawbridge, her hands pressed to her growing belly. She was crying.

"She won't go back, mistress," Angus grumbled.

"Women here at Cnocanduin, they never do as their men tell them. In my day—"

"Maisie, go inside and see to the children."

The maid's gaze moved from Mary Kate to Magnus.

Magnus took one long look at Maisie and wrapped his fingers around one of Mary Kate's muskets. "I know I'm going to regret this," he mumbled. "Maisie, do as you're told," he hollered to the maid. "Inside where you'll be safe."

"Take care, Magnus, love," the girl cried passionately.

Mary Kate took off at a run, Magnus panting behind her.

They didn't make it all the way to the barn before the first riders appeared. The moment Mary Kate saw them, she knew they were the thieves that had been menacing the Borderlands these last months.

The riders were a rough group of more than a dozen Englishmen with scraggly hair and hard faces. They were heavily armed and dressed for swift travel. They had to have grown bold after their last successful trips into the Borderlands. They looked like men who could kill.

Mary Kate wasn't just afraid for her cattle; she was afraid for the people of Cnocanduin. Her people. With a cry of fear threaded with anger, she rounded the barn to get out of their path. "Magnus," she hollered as she turned the corner and spun back around.

He had stayed behind.

"Magnus, take cover!" she shouted, fearful for his life.

She gazed around the corner, blunderbuss drawn,

just in time to see Magnus raise the gun she had forced into his hands.

Oh, God, Mary Kate thought. *I should have let them take the cattle and burn the barns. This isn't worth Magnus's life.*

"H-halt," Magnus shouted, obviously petrified.

One of the thieves burst into crude laughter. He rode down on top of Magnus, but instead of shooting him, he hit him in the head with the butt of his weapon.

Magnus collapsed in a heap. Mary Kate took aim on the nearest rider. If he tried to shoot her, she'd shoot back.

Her heart hammered in her chest as she attempted to hold the heavy gun steady.

Where the hell were the men of Cnocanduin? Rob had taken many, but there still should have been men to raise arms.

The thief who had struck Magnus wheeled his mount around and started back the way he came. Mary Kate didn't understand what was happening. The thieves were shouting to each other, riding in a circle around the barnyard.

Then someone struck flint to a torch and Mary Kate realized they were going to set the barn on fire. Her barn, the one she and Rob had jumped from, hand in hand. "No!" She lifted her blunderbuss to shoot the fire-starter.

Without warning, all hell broke loose in the barnyard. One moment there were just the thieves; then suddenly the area was filled with her father's clansmen, and Rob. It was Rob! He rode her father's horse, shouting orders to the MacDonals.

Mary Kate was relieved and frightened at the same

time at the sight of him. Rob wouldn't let the cattle thieves burn her barns, but what if he was injured protecting the castle and its property? She'd give a hundred barns in exchange for his safekeeping.

"Prisoners! We want prisoners!" With a clean shot, Rob hit the fire-starter in the leg, and the man fell from his horse, screaming in agony.

A dozen more shots sounded rapidly. The thieves were so surprised by the attack from behind that they barely had a chance to fire back. When they did, they missed their targets. Thieves fell from their horses. Englishmen screamed in pain, and riderless horses bolted as the battle cries of Sean MacDonal's Highlanders filled every corner of the yard and echoed off the castle walls. Rob brought one thief after another down off his horse, and yet still managed to stay astride.

The fight in the barnyard was over as quickly as it had begun. One minute the Highlanders were firing on the thieves; the next they were leaping off the moving mounts and wrestling Englishmen to the ground.

"I want them alive," Rob ordered, his mount prancing excitedly between her father's men and the fallen thieves. "Tie them up. Their wounds can be attended to after they're secure."

Mary Kate stood at the corner of the barn, the blunderbuss resting in her arm. She was stunned. Her sweet, gentle, dear Rob had become a fierce warrior and leader before her eyes. Without a flicker of indecision or a hint of uncertainty, he had ridden into the pack of thieves, leading her father's men, and he had beaten them.

"Is that Magnus MacDonal?" Rob leaped from his

mount to go to her cousin, who was still lying face-down in the dirt.

"Aye," one of her father's men responded.

Mary Kate bolted forward. "Is he all right?"

Spotting her for the first time, Rob paled. "Mary Kate, what are you doing out here?" He grabbed her shoulder roughly. "You should be inside with the women!" His voice shook. "Didn't Magnus—"

She dropped her weapon and went down on one knee beside Magnus. Without asking or waiting for help, she gave her cousin a hard shove and rolled him onto his back, quickly assessing his injuries while Rob towered angrily over her.

Magnus had a bloody gash on his forehead, but he was breathing.

"He was knocked down trying to defend me and the castle," she said, using the hem of her arisaid to wipe the blood from his forehead. "Magnus? Cousin, can you hear me?"

Someone must have given the "all safe" cry, because the barnyard was filling with people. Clansmen dragged the thieves to the barn to be tied up until the proper authorities could arrive. Servants and crofters were everywhere. Everyone was talking at once with excitement. The MacDonal clansmen had gone to battle with the cattle reivers and won. It was the first time they had fought in years, and everyone was horrified and exhilarated at the same time.

"Magnus. Oh, my, oh, my!" Aunt Agnes appeared at Mary Kate's side, fluttered her hands in front of her face, and promptly fainted at Magnus's feet.

Two serving women squealed and threw out their arms to cushion her fall.

"Someone help her," Mary Kate hollered to one of the maids. "Get my aunt some water."

Maisie ran across the yard and knelt beside Mary Kate, her face bright red with tears. "Is he . . . is he dead?"

Mary Kate never cared much for Magnus, but she had come to respect him in the last weeks. He had bowed out gracefully from the competition to win her hand, and eased his mother's worry over the matter. Something told her that after his brush with death he would take up his responsibility to Maisie and their child.

"No." Mary Kate gave a little laugh, surprised by the tears that caught in the corners of her eyes. "He's all right. He's going to be fine. Just a bump on the head."

Magnus was coming around, groaning in pain.

Maisie slipped Magnus's head into her lap and brushed his blood-matted hair from his face.

"I'll have someone fetch some water for you to clean up that gash," Mary Kate said, rising. "I can stitch him in the great hall, should he need it."

Agnes came to and sat upright with the aid of the house servant.

"Did we get them all?" Mary Kate asked Rob, surprised by how woozy she felt now that the whole incident was all over.

Rob was instantly at her side. "Not all, but no more than three or four escaped. I'll send some men after them once I know the castle is secure. You all right?"

She pushed aside the hand he extended to steady her. "Fine, I'm fine. Just scared half out of my skirts. Any men killed?"

"None."

Her heart was still pounding in her chest, but she felt in control again. "Injuries to our men?"

"Robby-Red is checking for me, but I don't think so."

She walked toward the drawbridge. He followed.

"I should find Papa," she said. "He might be worried."

Rob touched her arm and she felt his heat through her sleeve. "Mary Kate, are you certain you're all right? Ye should never have left the courtyard."

"Never left the courtyard? Ye think I was going to sit and spin wool whilst Englishmen stole my cattle?" She gave a little laugh, covering her emotional turmoil with indignation.

Now that the danger was over and the thieves thwarted, she was unsteady on her feet. Seeing Rob face the thieves, risk his life for her, for Cnocanduin, only strengthened her love for him.

All she could think of was what if the wish didn't come true? What would she do then?

Rob must have sensed what she was thinking because he rested his hand gently on her shoulder. To any bystander watching, it would have seemed an innocent enough gesture, but to the two of them, it was intimate. "Stay strong," he said softly. "Stay true. It's going to happen. We're going to be together forever. Ye just have to have faith."

She patted his hand and walked away, once again filled with reassurance. In her heart, Mary Kate knew that Rob's faith was strong enough to carry her to the very altar at Ian's side, if it had to.

Chapter Eight

A week later Mary Kate stood alone in the bedchamber that had been her parents'. Here her mother had come to terms with her marriage to the Highlander, Sean MacDonal. Here they had fallen in love and, after many years of desperately wanting a child, Mary Kate had been conceived. When Mary Kate was born, it was here that her mother had died. The room had such a past, and she wondered with a strange sense of excitement what its future would bring.

Tonight the bedchamber would be hers and Rob's. Never mind that Ian was downstairs waiting to marry her. Every day since the attack on Cnocanduin, she had felt a stronger sense that something wonderful was about to happen. Something magical.

Laughing to herself, she turned slowly around in a circle in the center of the room. The crackling fire on the hearth cast shimmering light over the bed and bed curtains. It filled the room with heat and the subtle scent of dried heather that someone had thoughtfully tossed onto the coals. The bed linens had been drawn back invitingly. This was it. Her marriage bed. She stared at it, but she could hardly believe it. She was going to be married. Tonight. To Rob.

Mary Kate didn't know how it was going to happen. How it could possibly happen. She just knew it would.

The case clock beside the bed chimed, startling Mary Kate. She glanced at the clock. There was only half an hour until the ceremony, and she was standing barefoot in a linen shift. She'd have to hurry if she was going to make it to her own wedding on time.

Rob stood on the drawbridge and stared at the walls of Cnocanduin castle that stretched into the darkness. The cold wind whipped through his hair and sliced through his woolen cloak. Snowflakes fell lightly, settling on his uncovered head and on the tip of his nose.

He was supposed to be inside, helping Sean dress for the wedding. So far he'd been unable to force himself beyond the impressive stone walls.

His faith was wavering. He had told Mary Kate the wish would come true. He had believed and he had made her believe. Now they were less than an hour from the wedding ceremony between Mary Kate and Ian Ferguson.

What if Rob was wrong? What if the well wasn't magic?

He clenched his fists at his sides, fighting the lump that rose in his throat. He couldn't think this way. He had to believe.

He had to believe.

"I believe," he said aloud. His voice bounced off the cold stone and reverberated in his ears.

"We believe!" he shouted, filling himself with confidence again.

Then Rob crossed the drawbridge and entered through the castle yett. He had a wedding to get to. His own.

Mary Kate stood between her father and Ian Ferguson beneath her mother's portrait, in Cnocanduin's great hall. Detached, she watched the priest's bobbing Adam's apple as he spoke. The room was lit with a thousand glimmering candles and smelled of fresh rushes and pine boughs. Her father and her aunt were here, a beaming Magnus and his new wife Maisie, splendid in a fine new gown that pulled tightly over her pregnancy. Her closest friends and family had gathered together to wish her well.

All right, she thought, surprised by how calm she was, considering the fact that the man standing beside her was not the man she intended to bed tonight. *We've been tested to the limit.*

We believe. We believe.

She knew Rob was standing somewhere behind her. She could feel his gaze boring into her back. She could smell the woodsy scent of his skin. She could almost taste his mouth on hers.

We believe. We believe, she repeated. And in her head she could hear Rob chanting the same.

"We believe," she dared murmur under her breath.

Ian glanced sideways at her and frowned.

"We believe," she repeated, ignoring him. "So make it quick."

Suddenly a shout from one of her father's clansmen sounded off the walls of the great hall, startling Mary Kate and cutting the priest off in midsentence.

The wedding guests turned toward Angus in shock.

"Sir!" Angus cried, directing his attention to Sean. "Beggin' yer pardon to interrupt, but looks like we got company." He hesitated, as if hating to be the bearer of bad news. "Uninvited guests. The thieves, I fear."

"What? What?" Sean demanded of Mary Kate. "All the guests aren't here?"

Mary Kate turned, the petticoats of her emerald green satin wedding gown billowing at her ankles. Was this it? Was this interruption somehow related to her wish?

This had to be it!

But how? She was as confused as her father, just for different reasons. *How could the thieves have anything to do with our wish coming true?*

She looked for Rob as she called out to Angus. "The thieves, are you certain? Do they approach from the south?"

The three or four cattle reivers that escaped last week had not been caught, but she found it hard to believe they would attack Cnocanduin again so soon. Had they returned to avenge the arrest of their accomplices?

Everyone was talking at once—the guests, her father, Ian, even the priest.

"Aye, thieves, I suspect, but not from the south. They've come around the castle," Angus hollered over the din of the room. "They ride out of the north."

Mary Kate opened her mouth to shout orders to her father's men, but Rob, bless him, beat her to it.

"Take arms," he commanded. He had no authority over Sean MacDonal's clansmen, yet they moved to obey without question.

"Take arms, men," Rob repeated calmly, but insistently. "Women, to the doors and windows!" He ran for the cases along the wall that housed the castle's munitions and began to pass them out to every able-bodied man in the great hall.

"We have more guests?" Her father turned in a circle, bewildered and tapping his cane.

"Stay here with your father," Ian told Mary Kate as he ran to join the other men.

Mary Kate grabbed her father's arm. She had no idea what was going on; all she knew was that her wedding to Ian had just been interrupted. She knew the magic was working; she just didn't know how. "Papa, no, not wedding guests. The cattle reivers." She patted his arm to soothe him. "Angus thinks they're back."

Sean hobbled toward one of the northern windows. "Cattle thieves? I say we hang the bloody buggers by their own ropes." He reached the window and caught the shutter a woman was attempting to swing shut. "That's what we did in my day, by Mary, mother of God."

Mary Kate laid her hands on her father's thin shoulders. "Papa, let Elsa batten down the shutters. We must protect the women and children."

But Sean clung to the windowsill, staring out into

the darkness. "Cattle reivers, hell," he muttered, pointing. "Don't ye see the banner they carry?"

"Banner?" Mary Kate attempted to guide her father away from the window. "Papa, thieves don't carry banners."

"Course not," he grumbled, pushing her away with surprising ease. "But the MacKenzies of Culloden sure as hell do."

"The MacKenzies?" Mary Kate never knew when her father was babbling nonsense or when his mind was utterly clear. Who were the MacKenzies? Would they fulfill her wish and bring her and Rob together?

"You know these men, Papa?"

Her father turned away from the window and started for the door on the far side, his cane tapping on the polished plank floor as he strode through the crowd, laird of the castle once more, if only for a few moments. "Aye, lass—old friends come from the Highlands to call."

Mary Kate hurried after her father. "Rob, come here," she said, motioning frantically to him. "Papa says it's not thieves," she told Rob. "They fly a Mac-Kenzie banner. He says they're friends out of the Highlands."

Rob was instantly at Mary Kate and Sean's side. "Ye know the visitors, sir?" He carried a blunderbuss in his hand.

"Aye, aye, didn't I say so, lad?" he asked impatiently.

Mary Kate's and Rob's gazes met for an instant. They were both thinking the same thing: This was it. The wish had worked; they had only to wait and see how. Yet both were afraid to speak of it for fear of breaking the magic spell that was surely at work. The look they exchanged said they would have to be patient, wait, and see what would unfold.

At the landing, Sean started down the steps, giving Mary Kate and Rob no choice but to offer their assistance.

"Send men out to welcome the MacKenzies." Sean elbowed Rob. "You, lad, go out to meet them, bring them in. Welcome them to Cnocanduin's hearth," he said, obviously pleased by their arrival.

The three of them walked to the door. Though her father certainly seemed to know what he was talking about, she still hesitated. She had to keep Cnocanduin's safety foremost, even in the light of the magic. "Were you expecting the MacKenzies, Papa?"

"Aye." He halted, concentrating. "Nae, nae, I don't think so." He glanced at her with a smile. "But what do I know? I can't remember what I ate this morning to break my fast." He gave a laugh and started for the yett.

Angus stood guard at his post inside the yett.

"Did ye see them?" Rob asked the clansman.

"Aye."

"Do they indeed carry a banner?"

"Aye," Angus said gruffly. "Didn't spot it first off. A MacKenzie banner, 'tis."

Mary Kate looked to Rob for counsel. "Do you think it's safe?" she asked.

"I think so," he said quietly. "The MacKenzies are well known and friends to the MacDonals, but I can be sure."

She nodded in agreement. Her pulse was racing, her heart pounding. She could see the same excited anticipation in Rob's eyes.

Rob laid his hand gently on her father's. "Wait

here, sir, and I'll fetch the MacKenzies for ye. No need you should go out into the snow to greet them.''

Sean grinned. "Good thought, lad. Make old Wills wait on me." He cackled. "Can't believe he's still alive. Holy bones, the man's older than I am!''

Mary Kate stood beside her father and waited for Rob to return. Behind her, she heard Ian calling her name, searching for her, but she didn't respond.

A moment later Rob returned, escorting several snow-covered men. There was such an odd look on Rob's face that she stared at the men.

To Mary Kate's shock she recognized one of the visitors. Or at least she thought she did as an old memory flickered and came to life in her mind. A memory of a rainy night and a rain-soaked old man in tartan plaid. The boy he'd brought to her father for fostering . . .

It wasn't possible, was it?

But by the look on Rob's face, she knew he recognized the old man too. He was thinking the same thing.

A strange sense of wonder washed over her as she stared at the stranger who wasn't really a stranger. Somehow Mary Kate knew that Wills MacKenzie knew Rob. He knew where Rob had come from before the night he arrived in Cnocanduin a wet, eight-year-old orphan. Wills MacKenzie knew because he had been with Rob.

This was all part of the wish. It had to be.

"Wills MacKenzie, ye old ram!" Sean MacDonal exclaimed, throwing his arms around the white-haired visitor. Wills MacKenzie hugged him back. "Good to see ye, Sean.''

"You mean you're shocked as hell to find me still alive!"

"And this has to be *him*," Wills said proudly, turning to Rob.

"Aye, our Rob," Sean answered, grinning.

"Well," MacKenzie said, "do you ask us into your hall, Sean, or must we drip here at the gate?"

"Come in, come in." Sean headed back up the stairs, without aid. "Come and warm yourself. Join our celebration. My daughter was just about to wed Rob."

Mary Kate's eyes widened in surprise. What did he mean, she was marrying Rob?

Rob caught up to her.

"Do you realize who that is?" she whispered excitedly to him as they followed her father and the MacKenzies up the stone staircase and into the great hall. She held up the skirts of her wedding gown to keep the hem from getting wet from the melting snow the visitors dripped on the floor.

"It's him, isn't it?" His tone was hushed, but equally filled with wonder. "All part of the wish, I guess," he whispered.

"But how? Why—"

He turned to grin at her and winked. "I suppose we'll just have to wait and see."

At the entrance to the hall Ian grasped Mary Kate's arm. "What's going on here?" he demanded. "Have thieves set upon Cnocanduin or not?"

"Nae," she said. "Not thieves."

"Then who are these men? How dare they interrupt my wedding!"

"Calm yourself," she said. "They're Papa's old

friends come out of the Highlands to pay their respects.''

"Old Highlanders?" Ian scoffed. "We've halted my wedding in midvow for a herd of decrepit Highland sheep?''

His comment irritated her, but she held her tongue. How could she explain what she didn't yet understand? "As soon as I know what's happening, I'll tell you," she answered honestly.

At the hearth Sean passed out drafts of Cnocanduin scotch to his visitors. The men were laughing and joking, talking as if they'd been expected all along. But never in all the years Mary Kate could remember had Sean once said he expected the man, Wills Mac-Kenzie, to return. She had never heard his name mentioned.

Rob caught her hand, squeezed it as he ignored Ian's cold stare, and then entered the circle of men.

The sounds of the wedding guests faded in Mary Kate's head. She forgot Ian Ferguson at her side. Every bit of her attention was focused on Rob and her father and Wills MacKenzie.

"I know you, sir," Rob said, walking straight up to old MacKenzie.

The man with long white hair met Rob's gaze squarely. "Do ye now?" He grinned, obviously pleased.

"You brought me here when I was a boy," Rob said. "That night. I remember. I remember the rain and you saying you would take me somewhere where I would be safe. You brought me here to Cnocanduin."

"What else do you remember, my lord? Of your past. What came before."

His address as *my lord* did not escape Mary Kate or

anyone else in Sean MacDonal's great hall. A burst of wild, exhilarating hope threatened to bring her to her knees. If he were truly a Scot and a lord, no one could argue his right to marry her.

Rob did not flinch. "Nothing. I have never understood why but, I remember nothing before that night."

"It's just as well, my lord." MacKenzie reached out and touched his arm to comfort him. "The death of your parents was very hard on you, as were the days that followed. The mind has a way of protecting children."

"Sir," Rob said, his deep voice echoing off the smoke-colored timbers high in the ceilings. "I am not Rob Drum, am I?"

MacKenzie glanced at Sean. His gaze searched the crowd of wedding guests whose attention was completely upon them, and then he met Rob's intense gaze again. "Nae." He took a deep breath, and it seemed that all of the room held their breath with him. "Ye are not Rob Drum, but Rob MacKenzie, the Earl of Dunn."

Everyone exhaled at once. Everyone but Mary Kate and Rob. Neither of them could breathe.

Rob MacKenzie? An earl? Mary Kate's legs felt weak.

Rob stared hard at the man. *"Who,* sir?"

"Rob MacKenzie, son of Charles MacKenzie, my good cousin, God rest his soul."

"God rest his soul," the other MacKenzies echoed.

"Then I am not English?"

"Nae." MacKenzie's tone was too serious not to be taken seriously. "Not a lick of English blood in your bones."

"Then why did you tell Sean I was English? Why the name Drum?"

"I must apologize, sir. But it was the only way I could think to keep you unharmed. I brought you here to Cnocanduin to keep you safe," Wills said apologetically.

"From what? Whom?" Rob was obviously trying to take all the information in.

"Damned Chalmerses. They've been feuding with the MacKenzies for two centuries, only one took the fighting too seriously. When your father married his sister Lizbeth, Albert Chalmers went crazy. Your mother and father went into hiding for some time, but eventually Albert found them. He killed your father, eventually your mother, to get to you."

"His own sister?" Rob asked numbly.

"Aye. Cold bastard, Albert was. Tried to kill you, too, but I was too smart for 'im." Wills tapped his temple. "I brought you here, far from Culloden and safe from the Chalmerses."

"So why now?" Rob flexed his fingers. "Why do you come now and tell me this?"

The old man threw back his head in laughter. "Because, lad, the old bastard is dead! We beat him, you and I, thanks to Sean MacDonal and his hospitality."

Rob stood, his hands at his sides. "Rob MacKenzie," he said as if trying the name on his tongue. "A MacKenzie."

"Yer father had to sell his land to keep him and your mother fed and clothed all those years, so ye have no land coming to ye and only a little money. But the title still stands, your lordship." The old man bowed his head, and the other MacKenzies nodded to pay their respects.

To Mary Kate's amazement the entire room of wedding guests nodded in reverence. Rob MacKenzie was the only titled Scotsman among them.

Coming out of her fugue, Mary Kate stepped forward, leaving Ian behind. She wasn't certain if she understood everything that had just taken place, but what she did understand was that her Highlander had come down out of the mountains for her. He'd been here all along. Filled with a sense of awe, she slipped her hand in Rob's.

Slowly Rob turned to her. His gaze met hers, and his eyes were as blue as she had remembered them that first night.

"It came true," he said under his breath. "Your wish came true."

She wanted to say it was impossible, and yet here were the facts. Rob was not Rob Drum the Englishman, but Rob MacKenzie, the Highlander, and titled too. He could no longer be considered an orphan, no longer be considered an English pup. He was a Scot, the same as any man in this room. Every MacKenzie in this hall could verify the truth. Rob was a man worthy of Cnocanduin.

Rob turned to her father. His voice was hushed and respectful. "Sean, Ian, may Mary Kate and I speak with you privately?"

"What about the wedding?" Sean questioned loudly. "Are you going to marry my daughter, or aren't you?"

Mary Kate turned to Ian, and she could see in his eyes that he didn't know exactly what had just happened, but he knew he would not be a bride-groom this day.

"Please, Sean, it will only take a moment." Rob worked Mary Kate's hand in his. "And then we shall give you that wedding you've been waiting for."

As Mary Kate walked at Rob's side behind her father and Ian, she knew what she would have to say to Ian would not come easily. But still, she felt as if a leaden weight had been lifted from her shoulders. She felt so light that she thought she might lift off the floor. Her wish at the well had come true, and she was going to marry her Rob.

"Please tell me this isn't a dream," she whispered, running her palm over his bare chest as she and Rob lay naked in the bed that had once been her parents'. She rested her head in the crook of her husband's arm, her entire body still tingling from their love-making.

Firelight spilled across the rumpled bed linens, illu-minating Rob's strikingly handsome face. "Not a dream." He kissed her forehead.

"But how—"

"Your wish, silly goose. The well."

"But that's impossible." She sat up, feeling like her old self again. Always logical. Always sensible. "A wish can't change the past."

He sat up to face her, and her heart gave a patter as she gazed lovingly at his bare, muscular chest and broad shoulders. They had already made love twice tonight, but again she felt the heat of desire for him.

"Perhaps, perhaps not. But it can bring the past to light. Couldn't it?"

She struggled to make some sense of it all. To find solid footing in her mind. "Wouldn't Papa have said something, indicated at some point that you weren't English?"

"Wills said he didn't tell your father because he felt I would be safer that way. That we would all be safer that way."

"It's all so amazing, so hard to comprehend." She pressed her fingers to her temples. "It makes me crazy thinking about it."

He caught her chin with his finger, lifted it, and planted a kiss on her lips. "So don't think about it, Mary Kate MacKenzie."

Mary Kate let her eyes drift shut. She was so happy she thought she would burst. Rob was her husband, her husband until death parted them, and then beyond.

"I love you," she said softly.

"I love you." He kissed her again. "And I have something for you, wife."

Her eyes popped open. "Have you, what?"

"Nae, not so fast. Solve this riddle and ye shall have your wedding gift."

She laughed.

"I'm serious." He took her hands in his. "Listen closely. It has no top or bottom," he said. "But it can hold flesh, bones, and blood all at the same time. What is it?"

"Hold flesh, blood, and bones, but no top or bottom?" Mary Kate was always so good at riddles, but she couldn't think. She was too happy, too gloriously confused.

"Oh, I don't know. Let me see!" She rose on her

knees and threw her arms around him, pressing her bare breasts to his chest.

He leaned over the bed, taking her with him. He drew something from his clothing, tossed on the floor earlier in the heat of their passion, and then sat up again.

"What is it?" She covered his face with kisses.

Rob took her hand and slipped something cold and hard over her finger. "A ring," he whispered. "My mother's wedding ring. Wills MacKenzie gave it to me."

Mary Kate stared at the tiny gold circle around her finger and then met Rob's gaze. No words were necessary. She had lost her heart to his blue eyes seventeen years ago.

Put a Little Romance in Your Life With
Fern Michaels

__Dear Emily	0-8217-5676-1	$6.99US/$8.50CAN
__Sara's Song	0-8217-5856-X	$6.99US/$8.50CAN
__Wish List	0-8217-5228-6	$6.99US/$7.99CAN
__Vegas Rich	0-8217-5594-3	$6.99US/$8.50CAN
__Vegas Heat	0-8217-5758-X	$6.99US/$8.50CAN
__Vegas Sunrise	1-55817-5983-3	$6.99US/$8.50CAN
__Whitefire	0-8217-5638-9	$6.99US/$8.50CAN

Put a Little Romance in Your Life With
Hannah Howell